The Seventh Veil of Salome

THE SEVENTH VEIL OF SALOME

SILVIA MORENO-GARCIA

New York

Copyright © 2024 by Silvia Moreno-Garcia

Published in the United States by Del Rey, an imprint of Random House, a division of Penguin Random House LLC, New York.

DEL REY and the CIRCLE colophon are registered trademarks of Penguin Random House LLC.

Hardback ISBN 978-0-593-60026-9
Ebook ISBN 978-0-593-60027-6
International edition ISBN 978-0-593-87149-2

Printed in the United States of America on acid-free paper

randomhousebooks.com

1 3 5 7 9 8 6 4 2

First Edition

Book design by Fritz Metsch

For Lavie Tidhar and Crawford Kilian

But when Herod's birthday came, the daughter of Herodias danced before the company and pleased Herod, so that he promised with an oath to give her whatever she might ask. Prompted by her mother, she said, "Give me the head of John the Baptist here on a platter." And the king was sorry, but because of his oaths and his guests he commanded it to be given. He sent and had John beheaded in the prison, and his head was brought on a platter and given to the girl, and she brought it to her mother.

—GOSPEL OF MATTHEW

When I looked on thee I heard a strange music.

—OSCAR WILDE, *Salome: A Tragedy in One Act*

The Seventh Veil of Salome

Joe Kantor

I'D SPENT most of the day tucked away at the Musso & Frank Grill on Hollywood Boulevard, working through a pile of notes. Its high-backed, padded red leather booths were the perfect hiding spot for harried writers trying to clobber their way through script changes and, boy, did I have script changes.

Some folks called Max Niemann a bully and others called him a genius. I called him an obsessive workaholic. I was laboring on yet another draft of *The Seventh Veil of Salome,* and I was the third writer that Niemann had hired. His propensity for new notes was enough to send any scribe howling out the door, but I didn't mind him. Previously, I'd done work for other directors of note: Howard Hawks, who liked to mutter disparaging comments about Jews, and I'd had to stomach Michael Curtiz's creative barrage of hyphenated insults—*no-good-son-of-a-bitch*—ad nauseam. Niemann didn't think highly enough of writers to abuse them, reserving his barbs for his actors and assistants, so I was in a relatively serene state of mind.

After a couple of whiskey sours and a plate of grilled lamb kidneys, I tucked my portable Smith-Corona Sterling into its case and headed back to the studio to deliver the pages Niemann had been asking about. Pacific Pictures was a midsize player. The gorillas in the business were MGM, Paramount Pictures, 20th Century Fox, and Warner Bros. The crown jewels of Hollywood. Then you had

RKO, Universal, Columbia, and of course Pacific Pictures. We were not providers of Poverty Row fare, like Grand National, but we didn't have MGM's dazzling facilities, either. We made a heck of a lot of mindless comedies, our share of corny romances and dramas, and a couple of big-budget opuses each year. Just as you'd expect, like clockwork.

Things were changing, though, in more than one way, around town. The antitrust case against the majors dealt a blow to the mega studios, and TV was picking up speed and viewers. Charlie Chaplin sold his studio at La Brea after being declared persona non grata in the US, and a bunch of writers decamped to Mexico for fear of the House Committee on Un-American Activities. I'd stayed put. HUAC had lots of us spooked, but I needed the work, and work meant living in Hollywood.

So, nu, anyway, that's not what your documentary is about, I know. Salome, let's talk about her.

Among all this hustle and bustle, there was Niemann's elusive *Seventh Veil of Salome*. It was one of those sword-and-sandal flicks that were terribly popular back in the day. You were not a real studio if every couple of years you didn't have at least one picture with a camel, a palace, and a garbage plot thinly inspired by a Biblical story. Hedy Lamarr squeezed the biceps of Victor Mature in *Samson and Delilah*, Gregory Peck romanced Susan Hayward in *David and Bathsheba*, and now it was Niemann's—and my—turn to make more meat for the masses, like an employee stuffing sausages for the Hebrew National Kosher Sausage Factory, except when you worked there you got to eat a tasty sausage and you didn't have to worry about evading a code administrator eager to mark every other page as objectionable.

Niemann's project had been in the works forever, and Fred Dressler was breathing down his neck. They'd start shooting soon, no doubt about it, and if the studio was lucky Niemann wouldn't return with a three-hour monstrosity. Niemann was good, but he was stubborn, and we were already making bets on how far behind the production would fall once it began what was sure to be at minimum a ninety-day shoot.

At the lot I ran into Harry Merriam, who was a serviceable writer of women's pictures and a prodigious gossip. He pulled me aside and told me that Niemann had tested a girl and finally found his Salome.

"Absolutely, and I'm Burt Lancaster," I said.

Niemann had screen-tested every actress in town for more than a year and hadn't signed anyone. Word was the screen tests were a publicity stunt, and he was biding his time, desperately trying to get his hands on Jane Russell, but the sexy brunette wasn't biting. She was finishing a stint at RKO. She'd just done an adventure flick for them, *Underwater!*, which had sailed into rough seas after a model called Lyn Jones sued the company for using her as an uncredited body double in publicity pictures. Then, at the premiere for *Underwater!*, which took place in a swimming pool, Jayne Mansfield's bikini top had popped off, a neat trick that soon became a regular occurrence with Jayne.

Jane Russell was probably fed up with gimmicky flicks like that and likely suspected *The Seventh Veil of Salome* was another silly gimmick. Anyhow, no Russell and no Mansfield had been signed, but that wasn't my business.

"The girl's a nobody," Harry said.

"Now I know it's a lie," I replied. If Niemann couldn't snatch a bona fide star, surely he'd avail himself of a semi-famous starlet or a pretty pinup. There were heaps of girls itching to get a crack at films. "Max's not going to have a nobody anchor his flick, and even if he'd wanted to, Dressler won't let him. They'll grab a cheap, reliable contract player, mark my words."

"You haven't seen her. She's a real peach of a girl. They're giving her a tour of the studio."

"Fakakta," I said and took out a cigarette and then, just as we were beginning to talk about other business, Harry pointed excitedly to the building in front of us.

"There she is. That's the girl. That's Salome."

She was wearing a simple yellow sundress and sandals, and her hair hung loose down her back. She had a nice figure, but so did many budding stars, often with the help of strategic padding. She had a pretty face, but a good makeup artist can make a siren out of a dumpy librarian. A certain elegance in the walk elevated her a tad, perhaps, but that can be learned. The pouty, kissable mouth was a delightful touch, and yet I wasn't convinced I'd have chosen her picture from a stack of glossies.

And then the girl looked at us, as if sensing our gaze, her wide eyes locking with mine for one second before she looked away, a nervous, hesitant smile dancing on her lips. Shyness warring with delight, with pride; poise and caution in the turn of the head. Charming, but more than that it was the gesture, the look, of the character as I'd imagined her. Temptress and vestal maiden in one.

As you write a story you hope for the best when it comes to casting. Sometimes actors are close to the mark, and often they're far from what you pictured when building the part. This, however, was the first time I'd seen a character I'd been working on drift off the page and into a studio lot, breathing, walking, living. I immediately saw what the casting director must have glimpsed: the luscious, exciting possibilities that lay ahead. The girl, swaddled in silks and sequins, set against exotic vistas and sand dunes with dramatic music punctuating her entrance.

That minuscule tilt of the head, the long fingers brushing away a rogue strand of hair from her face: during a close-up the viewers would swoon.

But even as she stood there in a sundress with a flower print, with nothing but the California sun to light her face, the truth was plain to see. This, there was no denying it, was Salome in the flesh.

It's a tragedy what befell her. How do you tell a tragedy, anyway? For all the artistic tricks a writer can deploy, I suppose the only way to do it is you start by saying *there once was a girl* . . .

The Seventh Veil of Salome

PRESENTED IN VITACOLOR!

Cast

Herod Antipas, the Lord Tetrarch, ruler of Galilee and Perea

Herodias, wife of Herod

Salome, daughter of Herodias and Archelaus

Marcus Julius Agrippa, cousin to Salome

Josephus, advisor to Herod

Lucius Vitellius, Roman proconsul

Sextus Marcellus, Roman soldier

Jokanaan, the prophet

Title card: The palace of Herod Antipas

Salome

HOW STILL and stifling the day was, with no breeze to stir Salome's flowing dark locks of hair, dark like supple plums or purple grapes from Alurus. The sea looked as if it had been painted with a dainty brush, and the fishermen's boats lay motionless upon this expanse of azure. Sitting under a yellow awning that protected the balcony from the sun's rays, Salome was bored by this stillness, by the heat of the day, and by her mother's incessant prattling.

Herodias spoke of the proconsul's imminent visit, of King Aretas, whose skirmishes had drained the energy of the tetrarch's forces, of their cousin Marcus Julius Agrippa, who perhaps plotted against them or perhaps not, and of prefect Pontius Pilate, who perpetually antagonized her family.

"And my Lord does nothing to quench the vicious mutterings of that madman," Herodias added, referring to the preacher called Jokanaan. The man stirred dissent throughout the streets and of late troubled her mind.

"What might Herod do to him?" Salome asked.

Two servants fanned the women. The one standing next to Herodias carried an ostentatious flabellum made with the feathers of an ostrich, while the one closest to Salome held a smaller peacock fan with an ivory handle.

"Toss the wretch in a dungeon. Cut off his tongue . . . some action must ensue," her mother said, wringing her hands. "The Lord Tetrarch . . . perhaps you might speak to him."

Herod Antipas, the Lord Tetrarch, was not only her mother's husband but also Salome's half-uncle: Salome's father and her uncle had been born of different mothers.

Salome's father, Archelaus, had married Herodias when she'd been but eighteen and a great beauty. Ten years later, Herod Antipas had paid a goodwill visit to his little brother. Herod Antipas had known Herodias since they were children, for she was also a member of the Herodian family and a distant cousin of his from one of their minor branches. The tangled knots of Salome's kin had become even more tangled when Herodias had repudiated her husband and married Herod Antipas.

That Herod Antipas already had a wife, daughter of King Aretas of Nabatea, did not matter. That Herodias was a married woman and her husband would have much to say about this development was also of little importance to the tetrarch, who had been seized with a boundless passion.

Salome had never understood this; she could not fathom how such madness could take root in a person's heart, driving them to strife, battle, and doom, all in pursuit of the flimsy, gossamer-thin sentiment people called love. Salome had not loved yet, and such passions struck her as frivolous.

"Why would he listen to me, of all people?" Salome asked. "You would be better addressing Josephus about this matter."

"The Lord Tetrarch listens intently to you," her mother said, her gaze hard as she stared at the sea.

Salome had noticed her uncle's eyes on her for the past few months, as well as the acid tone that had crept into her mother's voice. She'd noticed this and disliked it, thus she shrugged and arranged her fringed yellow shawl upon her shoulders.

A servant went to her mother's side and whispered in her ear, and her mother smiled. "Tell him he may come in." Herodias turned to Salome and said, "Marcellus pays us a visit."

"Mother, not today," Salome muttered tiredly.

"Come now, you must be polite," Herodias replied, and the goodwill the woman held toward the young soldier made Salome conclude her mother had indeed noticed how Herod's eyes lingered on his stepdaughter and perhaps sought to rid herself of the girl.

Marcellus was a strong young man with a crooked nose he'd earned after falling from a wild horse in his childhood, and an easy smile that charmed many a lady. He was an ambitious eques who had been sent to man a garrison and to subdue the bandits that roamed the roads and disturbed the peace. For a month or two he'd enjoyed Salome's favor. That had passed, which was not unusual.

Salome was witty and learned. She knew how to play the harp, how to sing with a clear, fresh voice, and how to dance with exquisite ease. But she could also comb and spin wool, like a virtuous maiden ought to. She knew the works of Horace, Hyginus, and Ovid, but also Hipparchus. She was beautiful and relished this beauty. Men were a pastime to her; she collected them like other women collected strings of pearls. Marcellus, honest and a tad dull, could not have held her attention for long.

After greeting Herodias and Salome, Marcellus asked the ladies if they might accompany him to the textile market. A shipment of rare silk and fine linens from Berytos had arrived and he intended to purchase gifts for his sisters back in Rome, but did not know what to pick.

"I am dizzy with the preparations for the tetrarch's birthday celebration," her mother said, "but Salome has a fine eye for silks."

"It's too hot to go anywhere. But at least it might rid me of this silly talk of Jokanaan and the tetrarch," Salome replied, waspish.

Her mother looked irritated, but Salome took Marcellus by the arm, and they exited the chamber.

It was indeed hot outside despite the awning on their handsome litter, and Salome found the space too narrow: Marcellus's arm was but an inch from her own. Only a year before she had kissed him under the shadow of a palm tree and such closeness would not have concerned her, but her fickle mind had turned from him.

Still, she looked at the strong profile of the young man at her side and wondered if he might not make a decent marriage prospect. He was of a good family and ambitious enough that he was sure to rise through the ranks of the equites. Yet he was a Roman.

Salome was an Idumean. Her people had clashed with the Jews, and although the Jews had made them their vassals, later her grandfather Herod the Great had gained the friendship of Rome and crowned himself King of the Jews, ruling over the whole region. A fine revenge. But his children had not fared as well as he had, and now the land was divided into a tetrarchy, and Pontius Pilate governed over Samaria, Judaea, and Idumea, which had been the rightful lands of Salome's father before her uncle Herod helped depose him and stole his wife.

Josephus, Herod's most trusted advisor, had indicated that Salome ought to take a Nabatean husband and in this way heal the wounds of a conflict that had raged between King Aretas and Herod for more than a decade. There had also been suggestions that her cousin Agrippa, who had been raised at the imperial court in Rome, might make a good husband. But Agrippa's fortunes had turned as of late, and he was said to be in debt to many parties. There was also talk, though muted, that a prominent Jew from Jerusalem might be the best choice, for the Jews still bristled at Herod and his Roman friends, and here, too, alliances might be strengthened with a good marriage. A Greek nobleman from Smyrna was a more unlikely but not implausible candidate.

Each of these choices made Salome wince. Her cousin Agrippa was dangerously cunning. The Nabateans had hated her family for too long to be trusted, she thought the Jews from Jerusalem quarrelsome and silly, the Greeks from Smyrna were haughty and vain, and she loathed the Roman soldiers for their coarse strength. They gave themselves the airs of noble lords even if they had been born barbarians and peasants, and Marcellus, despite his pleasant smile, was too uneducated and simple for her.

And yet he might take her to Rome, which sometimes thrilled Salome with thoughts of its poets and scribes, its enormous temples and wide roads, and all the excitement that might be found at the imperial court. Nevertheless, she also despised Rome. Bloated, greedy Rome, which had made her grandfather king but had purloined her father's territory, condemning him to exile and suicide.

Even while Salome thought of all these options and discarded them, she remembered her uncle's eyes upon her and rubbed her arms, making the golden bracelets around her wrists tinkle.

The party. He'd want her to dance at his birthday party.

The street of the luxurious textile sellers where they were headed was too narrow for even a litter, and Marcellus helped her descend from her cushioned seat so that they might walk together.

"You are quiet today," Marcellus said.

"It is the heat that numbs my tongue. It is not my fault. We should not have gone out," Salome said.

"There is a tavern where we might have refreshments nearby, although I fear at this time of day Jokanaan might be preaching there. It is his haunt."

"That old man preaches at a tavern?"

"He is not old, and he preaches in the square in front of it, warning drunkards and dice players of their sins."

"You've met him, then?"

"I've seen him in passing."

"They say he's called my mother a whore." Salome smiled at Marcellus's shocked face.

"Your mother's marriage to the tetrarch offends him," Marcellus said politely.

It offended Salome, too. She thought of her cool, composed uncle and recalled her rambunctious father. Archelaus had been a jovial man who laughed often and carried his daughter upon his shoulders. But Herodias had laughed little. She'd called him a dunce, a drunkard, a shame.

"We should listen to him preach," Salome said, adjusting her orange veil, which covered the lower half of her face and identified her as a noblewoman, though the gold on her ears and fingers would have served as a badge all the same. "It might be amusing. They say his hair is tangled and filthy with mire and dust, and he dresses in sackcloth. Come, let's hear him speak."

"I'm not convinced we should. The rabble tends to follow the preacher."

"You can protect me," Salome said, clinging to his arm and looking up at Marcellus with her kohl-lined eyes.

Marcellus, blushing like a virginal youth, acquiesced and guided the girl to the spot where the preacher was usually to be found. This was a small square with a fountain surrounded by various and sundry businesses, from the tavern that sold wine brought from Samothrace and Sicily to the men peddling onions and dried fish.

A crowd had already gathered around the preacher, and there were so many people assembled that Salome could not get a look at the man, although she could hear him talking.

"You burst with too much pride and adorn yourself with gold, yet remember: there is no other king than the Eternal God!" the preacher said, and there were mutterings and whispers among the crowd.

"They say he eats only locusts and honey," Salome whispered, "but he yells with the strength of a man who swallowed a whole ox for breakfast."

Salome saw a small overturned cart and urged Marcellus to help her climb upon it so she could have a look at the preacher. She giggled as she balanced herself on her tiptoes like a dancer and gazed at Jokanaan.

The preacher wore a garment of coarse cloth and a leather girdle, and his long hair flew past his shoulders. But he was not the wizened madman Salome had pictured, and the mirth dried upon her lips.

He was young, Jokanaan. His face had no wrinkles, his eyes were bright. His body was slim and straight like the stem of a lily, and his hair was luxuriant and carefully combed. It was not dark like a cluster of grapes, like Salome's hair, but a dark reddish-brown like the trunk of a cedar. He had a perfect mouth, kissable and sweet, and an aristocratic face that ought to have been crowned with silver and gemstones. He wore shabby sandals and cheap clothes that chafed his soft skin.

He was the most beautiful man Salome had ever seen.

By chance perhaps, or perhaps stirred by the intensity of the girl's gaze, the young man lifted his head and looked in her direction. Their eyes were locked together for a moment.

It was a knife, his gaze; it rent her. Her chest was cut from chin to navel and her heart was plucked from her body with that look. It was a flaming arrow, his gaze. It made the blood in her veins boil, and she feared it would evaporate. It was a mace that struck her head, his gaze. It made her stumble and feel faint.

Jokanaan glanced away. She continued looking at him, looked

until the crowd dispersed and Marcellus helped her down from her perch—she did not notice that his fingers lingered perhaps a tad too long around her waist. She did not comprehend the words he said about the stall with silks that they ought to visit. Her eyes were fixed upon Jokanaan, who was walking out of the square and away from her.

She followed Marcellus like a somnambulist, deaf and blind to the sights and smells of the businesses down the streets, ignorant of the people she bumped into, thinking only of the man she had just seen.

Salome, who had loved no one, not the young Syrian who had gifted her a black mare, nor the Moabite merchant who had placed a superlative emerald around her neck, nor the laughing Babylonian twins who'd come to court and charmed her with their songs, not even the Roman soldier who now took her by the hand . . . Salome, the haughty and capricious girl who was twice a princess and might be expected to one day wed an equally exalted prince . . . Salome was pierced by the sword of love that day and gave her heart to a beggar preacher.

Cathy Shaughnessy

NANCY HARTLEY and I met because we were both living at the Decateur, which was an apartment building near the corner of Sunset Boulevard and Fairfax Avenue, filled with mostly movie types. Extras, script girls, the occasional negative cutter, that sort of crowd. Nancy had tried to get into the Hollywood Studio Club but didn't make the cut. That was a women's-only hotel that provided room and board. Kim Novak and Rita Moreno stayed there. Real actresses, you know? Girls who were going places. Not bit players, like us. Well, the Decateur wasn't quite as nice, and Nancy wasn't quite *in* the movies.

Not for lack of trying, though. She was pretty, and she'd had good training. Her old man was in vaudeville when that was still a thing. After bookings became slim, he moved to Hollywood to get his girl into pictures. I guess he was trying to raise himself a child star, like Shirley Temple. They lurked around town for a while, meeting producers and casting directors, but nothing came of it even though Nancy was a wonderful dancer.

That's one of the things people don't get when they talk about her. That she had talent.

I guess Nancy got tired, maybe she wanted a normal childhood, and when she was about thirteen or so she moved back with her mother. Then when she was, I dunno, I guess twenty-odd years old, she decided to give Hollywood another try.

By the time *The Seventh Veil of Salome* started shooting in '55 she was twenty-six and she'd worked various jobs, mostly as a model or a restaurant hostess. I know what people say about her, but there's no truth to that story that she was a prostitute and Jay Rutland was one of her customers. Or that Benny was her pimp. At worst, she accepted "pickups," but what girl didn't? In LA if you were a good-looking woman, you walked two blocks and a guy would try to pick you up, and it was a free meal or a ticket to a show you couldn't afford.

People make all kinds of things up. She was a nice girl, determined and capable. She was perfect for the role of Salome. What happened to Nancy was thievery, an outrage. There was no girl in Los Angeles who could have outdanced Nancy.

Nancy

PIERCE LIT a cigarette the second they were done fucking. He took his chain-smoking seriously and claimed the only person who smoked more than he did was Tallulah Bankhead, whose brand was English Gold Flakes. He also claimed he'd fucked Tallulah once, although Nancy didn't think that was a great accomplishment: dishwashers and cab drivers could assert that same honor, if you trusted the rumors bubbling around town. But right then a different rumor was bothering her.

"Is it true Lili St. Cyr tested for Salome?" she asked.

"Her?" Pierce said with a chuckle, watching Nancy as she strutted around the room and tried to find her underwear. "She's not a real actress."

"Hughes thinks she could be one," she said.

"Baloney. If you read her name anywhere, it's because Hughes's publicity people are cooking up a stunt for her, but she has no chance of anything more than walk-on roles."

Nancy regarded Pierce skeptically. Word was that Howard Hughes was an odd duck, controlling and paranoid, but he had enough money to promote his many lovers and would-be girlfriends. If he wanted, Nancy was convinced he could make Lili St. Cyr into a star.

"Besides, she's a blonde. They're not looking for a blonde," he added.

"What about redheads?" Nancy asked as she lifted her arms and fiddled with her bra. "You said you'd get me an audition and it's been weeks, and all I hear is this and that girl tested for the part."

At only thirty-three Pierce Pratt was already going bald, and his gut was growing bigger, courtesy of too many martinis and not enough exercise. His main attraction for her lay in his connections.

Pierce let the ash from his cigarette fall into a small copper ashtray. "I am getting you an audition. I talked to Stuart Holden, and it's practically a done deal."

"When?"

"Next week. Or the week after that."

"Pierce," she said, irritated.

"I swear. The problem is that Isadora Christie is on vacation somewhere in Mexico, and when she's not around the director seems unable to take calls. That assistant they have helping out in her place is an idiot. In any case, I got Holden to promise me he'd meet with you."

She sat on the bed and scooted close to him. "Really?"

Tessa had read the cards for her earlier in the week. Nancy had picked the Wheel of Fortune, which meant a great change was upon her. A "dual transformation," Tessa said. "Fateful meetings." Maybe this was the portent she'd read.

"You have amazing legs, honey, and you'd look terrific in a harem outfit."

"It would be wonderful," she said, but when he attempted to pull her in for a kiss Nancy stood up and gave him a playful smile. "I'll be late."

She didn't have anywhere to be, but Nancy didn't want Pierce thinking he could monopolize her day. If he procured her that audition, then she might be more generous with her time, but for now an hour was all he could expect. She finished getting ready and headed back to her place.

Nancy's apartment, rented by the week, came cheaply furnished. It consisted of a Murphy bed, a table and two chairs, a hot plate instead of a kitchen, and a rickety fan. The one window was hard to pry open and the décor was limited to a bad reproduction of Botticelli's "Venus."

She'd lived here for a year. The building had been cool and sophisticated when it opened in the twenties, with its Jazz Age geometric mosaic patterns inlaid into the facade, but it was now in a state of neglect, and most of the mosaic decoration had crumbled away. She'd had better lodgings once on account of a married man who had put her up in an apartment with a large aquarium filled with tropical fish. Then his wife discovered this arrangement, and Nancy had been ordered to decamp. Nancy had smashed the man's aquarium with a hammer, letting the water soak the plush carpet beneath. When the fish stopped gasping for breath she wrapped them in old pages from a newspaper, placed that in a box, and mailed it to the man's home as a parting gift.

No matter. Nancy was used to moving around, used to the little ups and downs of life. Things were finally looking up lately. At one point she had been reduced to posing for Wallace's disgusting nudie pics, but she'd picked up real modeling work, and there was her budding friendship with Pierce Pratt, who worked at Pacific Pictures' casting office. There was the possibility of landing the part of Salome.

Nancy knew it was a long shot. Many actresses were vying for Salome, and she was an unknown, but Marilyn Monroe had started the same as her, working for the Blue Book Modeling Agency. Granted, Nancy was not with the Blue Book Modeling Agency but with a smaller agency that barely phoned her for any decent gigs. But she had paid for makeup, beauty, fashion, and charm lessons. She could dance, courtesy of her father. She took a good picture. She knew she could nail this role and nab a contract. Not a six-month option, which is what she'd managed to obtain before, a few months after she'd moved back to Los Angeles. Back then she hadn't known what was what; she hadn't realized the girls the studio executives wanted to fuck only got six-month options and were discarded. You had to aim for five, seven years. That meant they were serious.

Back when she'd gotten that six-month option she'd been over the moon. She even invited her old man out for dinner, told him she was going to be in films as he stared at her with a raised eyebrow. But she didn't secure a single role, and the option lapsed. Sometimes she had to borrow money from her father, and it stung, but she hadn't seen him lately. He was a fuck-up who worked as a bookie. He'd been a tap dancer, once. He'd had a face, once.

Nancy was unbuttoning her dress when the phone rang. The one good piece of furniture she'd bought for the apartment was a vanity with a large mirror where she piled her perfumes, lipstick, costume jewelry. The phone sat between two pictures of her: one modeling shot in a bikini, the other a picture of her as a kid when she'd danced as Little Nan Hartley. She was one year younger than Shirley Temple, although she often put down her birthday as 1932. It was a habit, from when her father tried to make her appear younger than she really was. Everyone loved a prodigy.

She let the phone ring thrice before picking up and looked in the mirror, checking her lipstick. "Hello."

"Hiya, baby doll."

"Hi, Benny," Nancy said, suppressing a sigh.

Benny Alden was both fun and annoying. He was too pushy, too needy, always wanting to know what she was up to or who she was going out with. He resented his position of not-quite-a-boyfriend in her life, but she couldn't see herself becoming serious with him.

First of all, there was the problem of Benny's employment. She'd never been able to pinpoint exactly what Benny did. Odd goods filtered through his apartment. The first time she'd gone over to his place he'd had ten toasters sitting on the bed, which was good for a laugh. She knew he dealt dope, and he was proud of the fact that he sold heroin to musicians, who were the type that gravitated toward that stuff. All the jazz greats were dope-heads, that's what he said—Charlie Parker, Miles Davis, Billie Holiday, Dexter Gordon. He boasted that he even provided several actors with heroin. Bela Lugosi, who'd once been a big horror film star, was a customer. And Carlo Fiore, a failed actor who'd turned to screenwriting, was apparently a close friend.

At first Nancy had been impressed with Benny's credentials, with the knowledge that he rubbed elbows with music and artsy types, but she quickly realized that the fact that Benny might have once sold heroin in both New York and LA wasn't a badge of honor, nor did it offer any useful connections.

Second of all, Benny's shady, amorphous, and variable line of employment meant he was surrounded by a disreputable crowd. He was good friends with a sleazy doctor who made croakers, counted several fast-living pimps among his drinking buddies, and had introduced her to people like Wallace Olrof, purveyor of por-nographic reels and pictures. Nancy's crowd was as dubious as Benny's, but she was trying to push her way up, and she couldn't see how Benny and his buddies could fit into her world if she obtained that part in *Salome*. The studio would balk at such associates.

No, Benny was not boyfriend material, yet she was also unwill-ing to cut him loose. He was sweet on her. Sometimes he'd lend her rent money, and he'd bought her a snappy suit and the silver bracelet with charms that she liked to wear on her left wrist. He was also an okay fuck and, if you didn't focus on the gap in his teeth, he wasn't bad looking. Maybe he drank too much, and maybe she tried to match him in his inebriation too often, and this wasn't a recipe to happiness, but she was not the type to bake cookies and stay at home practicing needlepoint.

Sometimes Benny scratched an itch, and so what? But she wasn't sure she wanted him that weekend. She felt exhausted after having to grin and make nice with Pierce.

"I hope you're not busy tonight. I've got plans for the evening," he said.

Nancy sat down on the bench in front of the vanity and took off a shoe, rubbing her foot. "I've had a long day. I don't want to go out."

"Oh, but you do. Listen, Kent Shaw has a friend who recently rolled into town, and the friend wants to head out for drinks and maybe dancing. So Kent asks me, 'Do you know any good-looking girls who might want to go on a date with us guys?' and I say, 'My sweetheart Nancy has many pretty friends.' So, what do you say? It would be a triple date."

Nancy remembered Kent Shaw vaguely. He played the trumpet and hung out with Benny from time to time, usually when Benny had female friends around. Benny wasn't a pimp, no, but he liked to call in favors, and sometimes this included phoning a girl or two so she would liven up a party.

"I dunno," she said, examining the nail polish on her toes. "I don't like those joints the music types like Kent visit. They're dirty."

"We'd be going to Romanoff's, doll face. I thought you'd like to eat there, that's why I called. Kent's friend is picking up the tab. Jay something-or-other is his name. Princeton man, momma's boy, and owner of a fat bank account."

Nancy perked up at that, twisting the telephone cord around a finger. She'd always fancied dining at Romanoff's, but she didn't want to be pawed by a desperate, ugly Princeton man. Benny said no worries, she'd sit next to Benny, and they could have one of the other girls keep the man company. After agreeing on a time to meet, Nancy said goodbye and began pondering who she could ask to join them on this date.

Benny said he wanted two pretty girls. Cathy Shaughnessy was pretty enough and lived only two floors down, but Nancy was hard-pressed to think of someone else on a Friday night. She phoned half a dozen friends and got nowhere. She was desperate enough that she even thought to knock on Tessa's door.

But Nancy discarded the idea. God knew Tessa could be counted upon to make her laugh, and she read the cards for the girls, but she was too cheap to join anyone having dinner at Romanoff's. After all, the girl turned tricks to make ends meet. Tessa was material for a hot pillow joint, not a decent restaurant.

Finally, Nancy was able to chat with Karen Perkins, a fellow model who jumped at the chance of a free meal, and all was settled.

Nancy, never one to look dowdy, took special care with her appearance that night. She wanted to impress Benny and outshine the other girls. She didn't much care what the Princeton man thought of her. She pictured him as a slightly shabbier version of Pierce Pratt, balding at the temples and with a gut that was contained by a girdle. But he'd get what he asked for: three pretty girls at his table, and she would be the prettiest one.

Nancy was not a natural redhead, but she thought she wore the color well. She liked to dress in blue to bring out her eyes, and her hourglass figure was best served by tight outfits. Her clothes were of a nice quality. They had to be. Making connections, scoring modeling gigs, obtaining the odd bit part required her to look good. When people asked her what she did she said, "Actress," and aimed to resemble a starlet. That Nancy was a professional party girl more than she was an actress didn't matter.

By the time Benny rolled around in his car and they jumped in, joking and laughing, Nancy thought she looked flawless, and she could see by his expression that her on-again-off-again lover agreed with her opinion. Kent and his friend were already waiting for them at Romanoff's, so Nancy and Benny and the others asked to be taken to their table.

Nancy had been thinking about the stars she might see or the food she might eat at the restaurant, and hadn't much considered the company she'd keep. The restaurant was famous for its chocolate soufflé and strawberries Romanoff, and that was what she was most interested in as she walked through the large ballroom wallpapered in orange, green, and yellow, trying to spy one of the regulars. They said Bogart was a fixture there, normally sitting at one of the seven reserved booths that were meant for stars and bigwigs.

She was so distracted by the contemplation of her surroundings, by the sight of silk and diamonds and the clinking of glasses, that she did not immediately greet their host for the evening, even as he introduced himself.

"I'm Jay Rutland," he said as he stood up and politely stretched out a hand in greeting.

It took her a few seconds to react. She'd expected a pudgy, unappealing fellow who was desperate enough for a date he had to ask a friend to find him a girl. But Jay was a slim young man of about her age in a dark gray suit with a subdued pinstripe, white shirt, and navy blue silk tie. He had a fine jawline and was handsome in a relaxed, unstudied way.

"Nancy Hartley," she said, ignoring Benny, who was pulling a chair so she could sit next to him, and instead picked a spot at Jay's right.

The evening went smoothly, with Kent and Cathy doing most of the talking and Jay shooting her appreciative glances now and then, while Benny gave her furious looks across the table, unable to speak more than the occasional sentence to them, stuck as he was with Cathy by his side.

"Kent said something about you and Princeton," Nancy told Jay while the waiter brought them a fresh round of drinks and Benny was busy listening to Kent go on about a clarinet player.

"I'm all done with Princeton," he said. "I graduated last year: classics."

"You want to be a teacher or something?"

"No. I couldn't figure what to study, so I signed up for the first thing I could find. I tossed a coin and landed on the letter 'c.' The truth is I want to make music."

"You play the trumpet like Kent?" she asked, a little disappointed that she might be talking to a simple musician.

"I play the piano."

"You have an engagement at a club or something?"

"I don't really have a job. I think I'm good enough to play clubs, though."

"You're an unemployed musician and you wear that nice suit?" she replied and shook her head. "I don't believe it. Those cuff links of yours look like real gold."

"They *are* real gold," he said. "My dad's Randolph Rutland, of the Rutland Navigation Company. I'm his useless youngest boy, James."

"My, my. A rich pretty boy. You're practically an endangered species," she said, glad he hadn't gone to an Ivy League university on a scholarship. That would have been a drag.

He laughed; she threw him a dazzling smile. "How long are you staying in town?"

"No idea. I hardly know a soul. Except for Kent, of course. We met in New York last winter. To tell you the truth, I was going to spend today listening to records and fix myself a Scotch and soda."

"What hotel are you staying at?" she asked, her voice low.

"I'm renting a house on Beverly Drive."

"Where exactly? Maybe I can say hi sometime."

He twirled a fork, gave her a big grin, and whispered back the address. Then he made a silly joke that had her honestly laughing. They touched glasses. They were close enough it wasn't exactly just friendly, but not too chummy that it would really mean anything if she didn't care to steer it that way. Benny, across from them, had stopped talking completely and stared at her.

They wrapped it up not long afterward, the girls piling into Benny's car. He was tight-lipped on the ride back, but as soon as she stepped out of the car he jumped out, came around, and grabbed her by the arm while the other girls made their way inside the building.

"What do you think you're doing, Nancy?" he asked. His voice was almost a growl. Normally she liked Benny when he was jealous, but right then she wanted to get rid of him quick, so she threw her head back and replied in a biting tone that meant she wasn't willing to engage in a drawn-out argument.

"I'm going to bed. It's late. Night, Ben."

"I don't mean now. Back there, at the restaurant. You were practically sprawled over that guy's lap."

"You said we were supposed to be friendly, that he wanted to have a nice night out."

"I didn't mean a nice night with my girl."

"Don't be stupid," she said, brushing his hand off. "The guy wanted to chat, what was I gonna do, tell him to shut it? It was a decent dinner, that's what it was. He spent half the night talking about jazz. What the hell do I care what music Kent's buddies listen to?"

"Yeah, okay," Benny said, looking relieved. He knew she didn't give a fig about jazz.

"Okay what, you filthy ape? You probably bruised me with those giant mitts of yours," she said, rubbing her arm for dramatic effect. "I have a shoot next week. What am I gonna tell the photographer? I should cut you loose, that's what I should do."

"Nancy, don't be like that."

She continued rubbing her arm, then ran a hand through her henna-tinted hair.

"Sorry for getting mad, doll face."

"You can make it up to me next week," she said, which immediately had Benny looking giddy.

She kissed Benny quickly, assured him she was terribly tired, and went up to her apartment. Back in her room, Nancy carefully reapplied her lipstick and waited for a half hour, leafing through a magazine, before she made her way downstairs and found herself a cab.

Jay Rutland's house on Beverly Drive was a lovely two-story ranch-style home set on a steep cliff. She climbed its steps and rang the bell, and he answered the door himself seeming honestly surprised. She walked into his living room with a confident strut, looking around and taking in the plush carpet and the expensive teak and mahogany furniture. What a difference from her cramped room at the Decateur. It was grander than Pierce Pratt's apartment, because not only was this a whole house, probably with a pool in the back, but it was clearly the domain of someone with taste. Aside from the lovely furniture she spied a piano, fresh white flowers, and fancy paintings that looked like the real deal and not cheap reproductions.

Jay, in a plush red robe and black slippers, looked as upscale as his surroundings. A flawless object to covet.

"I didn't really think you'd come," he said as he helped her slide out of her coat.

"Well, you said you hardly knew a soul in LA, and it's a pity to drink alone. Can you make a martini?"

"Not a good one. Want to listen to a record while I try to remember the recipe?"

"Baby boy, don't tell me I'm going to have to teach you everything," she said, practically purring with delight.

He laughed good-naturedly, and she was pretty sure that despite the gleam in his eye Jay Rutland wouldn't insist on sex the first time she came over, so she simply shoved him in the direction of the nearest couch and crawled atop him. She'd wanted to fuck the guy the whole night. Benny's glares had only made it more fun.

She was tired of Benny's pitiful excuses for dates and the cheap diners he took her for lunch, or the clunker he drove. She'd seen Benny's one good suit too many times, and he wasn't half as attractive as Jay Rutland.

Nancy quickly kissed him, rubbed her hands all over him, cooed sweet nothings. She was ravenous, eager for someone nicer, better than the bunch of wannabes who usually sang her praises, than the worthless lovers she'd taken, than that husband she'd married and divorced years before. Nobodies and losers.

She thought it was a sign from the heavens that she'd met Jay. There he was, that pretty rich boy, and there was her audition on the horizon, and she couldn't figure a single thing that would ruin her perfect future. Because it had to work this time. It couldn't be like the others. This time, Nancy promised herself, this time she had a winning ticket and the cards had spelled the future, hadn't they? Wheel of Fortune. Fate, dual transformation.

Isadora Christie

MY TITLE? The full title? Principal research aide. What a funny title—it means nothing when you look at it. Officially, I was Max Niemann's assistant, and my main task was to read books he might be interested in adapting. Unofficially, I did a little bit of everything for him. My hope was to become a producer. A lofty dream, especially in those days.

Max had been working on *The Seventh Veil of Salome* for about three years when I went to visit my brother in Mexico. Many Americans had decamped there because of the Red Scare and the blacklisting at the studios. My brother had not been singled out as a Communist but had instead departed on his own, which saved both of us many headaches. It was bad business to have a Communist in the family back then, but my little brother was smart enough to say he was moving to improve his health, quietly evading any inquiries. For my part, I believed in paying my dues, working hard, and not calling any undue attention to myself, which meant staying far and away from any Commie meetings even if I was sympathetic to the writers and directors caught in the whole HUAC mess.

When I left for a long holiday, the casting issue had not been resolved. Max had hired Clifford Collins to play the soldier Marcellus and Richard O'Donnell, on loan from Paramount, would have the role of Josephus, the king's advisor. But Salome remained a question mark.

Max was taking a big gamble with *The Seventh Veil of Salome*. William Dieterle had shot his own take on the story of the Biblical temptress two years before, with Rita Hayworth in the lead, no less. Normally this would have killed our project immediately, but Max was a major director back then, and he had a lot of pull. Plus, he thought he had a fresh angle on Salome, something that would cash in on the sword-and-sandal craze yet differentiate the product.

Hollywood was changing in the fifties. The studio system was beginning to falter; a new generation of actors was invading the screen. Studio executives had discovered teens watched flicks. They wanted to see Marlon Brando in a fitted t-shirt, not stare at Clark Gable.

There was a different breed of actors streaming into Holly-wood. They were a cool new type of talent who were producing surprising hits and living differently. They frowned at the studio's fixers and their stodgy rules. James Dean, rather than courting the gossip columnists, could be found at Googie's, having coffee with Dennis Hopper and "Vampira" Nurmi. Meanwhile, Marilyn Monroe had founded a production company and moved to New York for a chance to study with Lee Strasberg. This had once been unthinkable. It was an exciting time!

Max envisioned *The Seventh Veil of Salome* as a flick for the fans of this new crop of performers. "Beatnik John the Baptist" is what screenwriter Joe Kantor called it as a joke, but it wasn't far from the mark. There would be the huge sets and dazzling cos-tumes people expected from any Biblical epic, but also the sensu-ously handsome and sensitive Orlando Beckett—who felt like a combo of Montgomery Clift and Farley Granger—for the role of Jokanaan. He was young, still a contract player who hadn't quite become a star, yet bankable.

Vaughn Selzer was swooping in from New York to play Agrippa, Salome's cousin. This had been a bit part until Selzer read for it and Max told Kantor to write the kid more lines. Like Brando, Selzer was unwilling to enter a long-term contract, he'd had his break in theater, and he walked around in jeans and t-shirts while looking like a million smoldering bucks.

Clifford Collins, a decade older than his castmates and already an established actor, brought with him classical Hollywood glamour. He was debonair, smooth, vain, and beloved of Louella Parsons. He knew how to work the old system even as the younger kids were trying to tear it apart.

There's a story that studio head Fred Dressler asked Max, "So who's Salome gonna fuck?" and Max replied by saying, "All three of them, at the same time." I don't know what Fred said to *that*; it sounds a little crass for Fred. On the other hand, for all his muttering about family values, Fred liked dollars more than he liked modesty.

At any rate, there we were, building sets, securing cinematographers, signing up secondary cast members, and we still didn't have a girl.

Max had written a list of what he wanted. She would be a fresh face. She'd be exotic. *Really* exotic. A dark-haired Spaniard, or an Italian. No Rita Hayworth bullshit. Rita Hayworth's dad was a Spaniard and her red hair color was a dye, but Hollywood had tamed her too much. Max didn't want that kind of girl, bleached and blanched.

I suggested Yvonne De Carlo, who'd done many Technicolor pictures and had the raven-haired tresses I thought he'd like, and he yelled, "Canadian! Not a fucking Canadian!" One of our scouts met Joan Collins in London, and he sent footage from *Land of the Pharaohs*. Joan was painted a chocolate brown for the film, and Max immediately jumped on the phone and berated the scout. That was exactly what he didn't want.

Max also demanded that his Salome be able to project raw sexual allure and danger. Prettiness wouldn't be enough. Oh, and she also needed to seem innocent at times, a vulnerable maiden caught in a web of deceit and destruction. Two sides of a coin.

It was a tall order, and one reason why I headed to Mexico was to forget about our desperate need to find an actress. Fred Dressler had gone from being irritated by how long this project was taking, to sweating and worrying, to yelling. We needed a Salome so the costume designer could stitch the costumes on a body.

Anyway, off to Mexico I went to see my brother, and while I was there I had a terrible toothache. My brother told me there was a dentist who spoke fluent English and worked for many of the Americans living in Mexico City and gave me his address. I took a taxi and sat in a neat reception area that was attended by a young woman with her black hair pinned back in a practical bun.

Well, I wasn't a talent scout, but I knew potential when I saw it. The girl was adorable. She reminded me of the lushness of Dolores del Río when she'd arrived in Hollywood, but she also had a bit of Audrey Hepburn's enchantment.

A soldier's fortunes rise or fall with those of their general. My general was currently trapped in a swamp. I thought I had found a way to pull him out of it. If I proved my worth with this picture, my title could be changed to that ever-elusive designation of assistant producer. It was how Joan Harrison had climbed up the ranks, going from Hitchcock's secretary to one of the few women producing films in Hollywood.

I phoned Max and told him there was a girl I wanted him to see, and she'd be coming in from Mexico. In those days, it wasn't that hard to get a ticket to Hollywood. Scouts would look at Broadway plays, nightclub acts, beauty pageant winners, and models who sold anything from butter to face creams. The wannabes would be evaluated, perhaps screen-tested. Sometimes we flew in potential performers from faraway places, normally from Europe. What was more unusual was that the girl in this case would be auditioning for the lead.

The chance of a contract was slim, and actors normally started with bit parts, then moved their way up. Yet, sometimes, a major find was made in seconds: Audrey Hepburn was signed up for the lead in *Gigi* after being spotted in the lobby of a hotel, without having ever set foot on Broadway, and within two years she was off to films and a major star.

Like I said, the girl reminded me of Audrey, with those big eyes and a wistful expression on her face. Such a discovery could be a true show of my sharp instincts.

What experience did the young Mexican lady have? She'd taken dancing lessons, could play the piano, and had appeared in a few plays during high school. She worked in her father's dental practice.

Her name was Francisca Severa Larios Gavaldón, and she was twenty-one years old. Her family and friends called her by her nickname, Vera.

We named her Vera Larios.

Vera

SHE'D SLEPT well the night before the audition. It wasn't until the morning, after she'd slipped into a simple dress with a wide brown belt, that she began to doubt herself. It was her mother's question that did it.

She came down the stairs, and her cousin Cecilia gushed about her hair and her makeup. Her aunt Prisca looked unimpressed, but then she didn't think much about movie stars and auditions. Her mother gave Vera one long, piercing look and shook her head.

"Is that really the dress you're going to wear?" she asked.

"What's wrong with it?"

"It makes you look common, honey. And the sandals! Really. Wearing sandals like you're the maid."

Vera stood there with her hat in her hands, feeling her face growing warm with anger and shame and knowing her mother would have liked to see Lumi auditioning. She'd always preferred Vera's little sister. Lumi was fair, like their mother, and Vera took after their father.

"Dad gave them to me," Vera said.

"What does your father know about shoes?"

"I'd like to wear them, for luck."

"Well, it's not as if we have time for you to change," her mother said, shaking her head. "The driver is already in the car outside. I knew we should have asked your cousin Federico to drive us there. Now we can't make them wait."

"Good luck!" Ceci yelled as Vera hurried out the door. Her aunt Prisca didn't say anything, tight-lipped as usual.

Vera didn't know her cousins or her aunt well. Her mother's family was from Durango, and during the Mexican Revolution some of them had drifted north, to the safety of California, while her mother made her way to Mexico City. There, her mother had nurtured hopes of a singing career. Instead, she'd married a dentist who also hailed originally from the north of Mexico. José Larios spoke good English, having grown up near the US border, and used that skill in his practice. That he was dark of skin was unfortunate, and that their first child—Francisca Severa, whom everyone had called Vera since she was a toddler—was swarthy like her father's side of the family was regrettable. Which is probably why, within a year of Vera's birth, Lucinda had given birth to Lucinda Mariana, who was quickly nicknamed Lumi. Lumi's reddish-brown hair, her pale skin, her dimples, were the delight of her mother, who began arranging for dancing, singing, music, and poise lessons for her little one.

Vera had been exposed to these extracurricular activities, too. Since Lumi, despite her good looks, couldn't play an instrument, Vera learned to play the piano to accompany her sister during their family recitals. And since Lumi needed a dance partner to practice at home, Vera learned the steps, too. Lumi needed to take acting or voice lessons? Then Vera should tag along, to keep an eye on her little sister.

Lumi was awfully good at these activities, and she had more charm in her pinkie than Vera had in her whole body. What Vera possessed instead was a good grasp of English, courtesy of her father, and also knowledge of Italian and German, due to her love of opera. She excelled in her typing classes in school, while Lumi couldn't be bothered to learn shorthand or how to fiddle with the typewriter.

That was how she ended up behind the counter at her father's practice, answering the phones and handling reception three days a week. When there was a lull at work, she turned on the portable radio and tried to find a station that broadcast opera, or else she flipped through the pages of the newspaper and looked at what films were playing that week. She especially enjoyed getting lost in tragic love stories. Drama made her heart sing. The paintings she liked the most were the lush portraits of the Pre-Raphaelites. In her room she kept a small reproduction of Waterhouse's "The Lady of Shalott" and an impressionistic view of Xochimilco as painted by Joaquín Clausell, both of which appealed to her romantic sensibilities.

"You know, we have talent flowing through our veins," her mother said, sitting in the car next to her and taking out a small compact mirror to admire her face. "We're related to Ramon Novarro, and he was the most handsome leading man in Hollywood back in the day. Vera, don't fret."

"I'm not fretting, Mother."

"You are. Stop tugging at that belt."

Vera placed her hands atop her purse. She'd been given a page to memorize and was told to also prepare for a "personality" test. Her agent had said to look natural, which was why she'd picked the simple dress and sandals. Only now she tried to catch a glimpse of herself in the rearview mirror and wondered if she shouldn't have selected a showier outfit, heels, nicer jewelry. Lumi would have known what to wear.

Stop it, stop it, she thought and looked down.

She went through the lines again.

"It is the heat that numbs my tongue. It is not my fault. We should not have gone out," she whispered.

Her sister was popular in school. Vera, less so. She tended to stare off into space, to drift into dreams as she sat wide awake at a desk. The girls thought her odd because of this. Her silences contrasted with Lumi's vivacity.

She tried not to look at Los Angeles through the window, tried not to track their route, and when they reached the studio— a stucco fortress that contained administration buildings, wardrobe warehouses, a commissary, a prop shop, and a myriad of sound stages—she kept her eyes on the page between her hands.

"It is the heat that numbs my tongue," she whispered, and then the driver was opening the door, and she saw Isadora Christie standing next to a four-story building, smiling. Vera's agent, Luke Mahoney, stood next to Vera. He was a lanky young man who'd worked at Zeppo Marx's agency. Zeppo had once been an actor, performing with the other Marx Brothers, but he was now an agent who represented a whole stable of stars. Luke Mahoney's client roster was unimpressive, which was probably the only reason he'd agreed to represent Vera. The bigger agents had shrugged when she'd phoned them. There were pretty girls aplenty, and most of them without accents.

"Welcome to Pacific Pictures," Isadora said. "You look lovely, Vera."

"Thanks," she said.

She couldn't help but think that Lumi would have looked lovelier. But her sister would never be a star. When Lumi had turned nineteen, right around the time when it seemed she might get a break, that she might make it into pictures, she'd married a young accountant who lived down their street. Their mother had threatened to have the marriage annulled immediately, and then she wailed when Lumi said she was pregnant. Actually, the word "pregnant" had not been uttered in their house. Their mother said Lumi had disgraced herself, although she only said it once and never repeated it again.

Lucinda smiled at her daughter's wedding and told all her

friends and relatives Lumi was marrying a bright young man, and this wouldn't put a damper on her acting career. Six months later, Lumi was a mother.

Lumi didn't tell Vera she was getting married before her boy-friend asked for her hand in marriage, and she didn't discuss her pregnancy. Vera, for her part, didn't pry. There was something hard in her sister's gaze when she announced her engagement, something raw. As though she'd challenged their mother to a duel and won.

Sometimes Lumi came to the house with her little girl in her arms and Vera laughed and played with the baby, and Lumi used that time to leaf through the movie magazines their mother left around the house, but she never looked at them with interest any-more.

"You'll be meeting with Roberta Sellmer. She'll handle the personality test, and then Max Niemann will pop by and watch you do a reading," Luke said.

"I can watch, of course?" Vera's mother asked.

"Definitely, it's been arranged," Luke said as they followed Isa-dora inside the building. Vera felt as if she were crossing through a magic doorway into a land of myth. This was the place where films were made, where the actors Vera and Lumi had whispered about late at night became the heroes of epics and adventures.

"Will they be filming me?" Vera asked.

"Yes. You shouldn't think about it. If Max wants to, he'll give you direction. Otherwise, pay attention to Roberta, not to the oth-ers. Got it?"

Vera nodded. She stood by a wooden-platformed set, which consisted of a chair, a window, a desk. It all looked modern, not like the period film they would be shooting. Around her people adjusted bright lights, moved a camera, fiddled with pages. Fi-nally, she was asked to go onto the set and stand next to the chair.

A man stepped in front of her with a slate in his hand and held it up to the camera, then stepped aside. The crack of the slate was still ringing in her ears when a woman spoke. She asked her name, where she was from, what she liked to do in her free time.

"I like music," Vera said, trying not to stare at the people around her or at the camera, attempting to focus on the person speaking to her, like her agent had said. "Opera. Maria Callas . . . when she sings it's beautiful. I saw her on stage four years ago. She sang the part of Aida."

"Very well, Vera. Can you walk around? Hold that vase? Please turn your head."

She swiveled, walked across the stage, and sat down. She heard someone asking for a medium shot. She looked left, then right. A door had opened and someone had come in. It was a mustached man who stood with his arms crossed, regarding the scene. Perhaps it was Max Niemann, perhaps not. She could see her mother and Isadora and her agent. Her mother clutched her handkerchief in one hand.

Sit at the table, someone said. Stand. And she did, moving like a marionette. A man who had been standing by the side of the stage joined her, and Roberta said they would have him read lines with her. The bit parts she'd had in plays had been with people she knew well, friends and classmates. She'd never had a reading with a stranger, jumping cold into a role. He hadn't even spoken his name, and she didn't know whether she should extend her hand in greeting. She clutched the pages instead.

They went through the pages twice. She remembered the lines, she didn't even have to glance at the pages a single time, but had no idea if she had done it well. There was no direction, just whispers and the movement of the camera, or the shuffle of feet. The man she was speaking to looked bored. She didn't know if he was an actor or a staffer who had been assigned this cumbersome task. Maybe they tested girls every day, and he simply wanted to fetch lunch.

"Do you have any acting experience?" the man with the mustache asked, his arms still crossed against his chest.

"I was in plays in high school and appeared in a staging of *La Celestina*," she said. "And my sister . . . I . . . I had a silent part in a film."

Lumi had entered a contest. It had been a promotional event for a sardine company. The winner appeared in a flick with a "major movie star." Lumi had two lines, and they'd agreed to let Vera tag along. Their mother had acted as though Lumi was the next Silvia Pinal. She'd thrown her a party and bought her a new coat.

The amateur production of *La Celestina* had been her most important role. It was the one time she'd acted alone, without shadowing Lumi. She'd played Melibea. Eight shows and two months of rehearsals during the summer. She assumed her mother would be pleased, but Lucinda didn't think much of it. Arturo wasn't a fan of it, either. He didn't believe married women should act, nor was he impressed with her interest in music. Instead, he praised Vera's cooking and her penmanship.

"What dances do you know?"

"I've taken rumba, tango, waltz, and foxtrot lessons," she said.

"Please dance the waltz with him."

Two crew members hauled the furniture off stage, leaving the wooden platform bare.

There was no music, which she thought odd, but Vera didn't dare to protest. The man who had read lines with her now stepped forward and took her hand. She waltzed with him like she had waltzed with her sister, her feet gliding across the wooden floor. It was a simple chore that lasted but a couple of minutes before the man she thought was Max Niemann spoke again.

"Please dance the tango."

She'd danced the cha-cha with Arturo when they dated the year before, and she'd been good at it, but the tango she had not practiced in a long time. She'd danced it with her sister, or followed the steps in her room alone. She was not used to dancing with a boy.

Vera took a breath.

Vera stepped back, creating a space between her and the man. He looked confused. They'd been asked to dance, after all. Then she met his eyes and gave him a nod. Because that was how you began to dance a tango. It was the proper way: you had to ask your partner, there was that cabeceo that initiated any dance.

It was the man who was supposed to nod first, but she nodded at him.

The man seemed to understand the cue. He stepped closer, raising his left arm, offering his palm up, and she raised her hand in turn, allowing him to wrap his hand around hers. Then they took a side step to the left.

You must feel the tango in your gut. That's what their dance teacher had said. Vera tried to feel it there, in the pit of her stomach; she tried to feel the music that didn't exist, conjuring an invisible orchestra, her hand tight against the man's hand, her eyes burrowing into his.

The palm of his hand rested on her back, against her spine. Her left arm rested lightly on his shoulder. Body to body, chest to chest, they moved across the stage.

She thought of an evening she'd gone dancing with Arturo. He'd asked her to marry him, she'd demurred. Then she'd wept, alone in her room.

She moved with the man, following his lead, trying to synchronize her body to his. Tango was a silent dialogue. There was a smoothness to the steps with this dance, and she knew that she was making small mistakes, stammering without speaking. Here and there she'd lost him, lost the flow, and yet as her foot moved parallel to the floor, as he held her tight and she held her head up high, she thought there was grace to their steps.

"Very well. That's enough. Step down from there."

They stopped and drew apart. The man who'd been watching her with his arms crossed turned to speak to someone. Isadora motioned to Vera, and she walked toward her and her mother.

"What do I do now?" Vera asked.

"The driver will take you back to your aunt's home," Isadora said and shook her hand.

"You did well," Luke said. "They should get back to us in a day or two."

Vera nodded. In the car, her mother was quiet, but Vera knew what she was thinking: she'd been too stiff, too awkward, she'd bungled her lines. She probably didn't photograph right. Lumi would have won them over. Lumi was beautiful, she had a tiny nose and delicate eyebrows. Vera's nose was wider and her eyebrows were thick.

When she listened to operas, sometimes she became their heroines. She was Brünnhilde, Violetta Valéry, or Tosca. This was the extent of her abilities: a wild imagination, a capacity for emotion. This was likely not sufficient.

Vera looked down at her lap.

Later she sat in Cecilia's room while they drank Coca-Cola and turned on a portable radio. Ceci was sixteen, and she had a huge stash of movie magazines, which she spread across the floor. Vera looked out the window, watching as her uncle and her cousin got into their car and drove away.

"Where are they headed?"

"They're going to play cards. We used to live in Boyle Heights and our friends lived a couple of blocks away, but now my dad and my brother have to drive there to see their friends. It's annoying, but my mom says Montebello is better for us. More exclusive. My dad had to say we were Spanish to the real estate agent."

"Why?"

"They don't like selling to Mexicans. My mother likes it here. Being Spanish sounds nicer, anyway. I wonder if the movie folks will let you say you're Mexican."

"I don't think you can hide it."

"You'd be surprised."

Cecilia pulled out a box from under her bed and handed Vera a magazine.

"My mother doesn't let me read *Confidential,* but I buy it any-way. It has all the juicy stories. Can you read all the magazines you want in Mexico City?"

"Yes."

"It figures. You know, my mother doesn't let me go to the mov-ies without a chaperone."

"I used to chaperone my sister sometimes," Vera said.

"My mother says girls don't go anywhere in Mexico without a male relative or an old aunt. She doesn't want boys to get fresh with me, so I'm forced to take my brother everywhere I go. Have you dated much?"

"There was a boy I went out with for a few months, but we stopped seeing each other," she said, remembering Arturo.

"What happened? Did he break your heart? Did you break his?" Ceci asked, putting her magazine down and staring at Vera with delight.

Before Vera thought what to say her mother was poking her head in the room.

"Mr. Mahoney called. They want you at the studio tomorrow."

*

FRED DRESSLER'S name appeared on a little plaque on a mam-moth walnut wooden door that opened into a large office with gilded mirrors and tasteful paintings. It was like walking into a museum; there was the feeling that everything in the room was part of an exhibit.

Behind an enormous black desk with two telephones set atop its shiny surface sat Fred Dressler, a balding, short man who re-garded Vera with a quirked eyebrow. Isadora and Maxwell Nie-mann, he of the distinctive mustache, were already seated. Vera and her agent occupied their spots in the two chairs that had been set aside for them. Vera's mother had wanted to come in, and she wasn't pleased to be left waiting in the anteroom, but Luke Ma-honey said it couldn't be helped.

There was an official round of introductions, at which point

Maxwell Niemann, who still seemed to prefer to spend his time with his arms crossed, nodded at her, and Fred Dressler asked his assistant, who was standing by the desk and had handed him a folder, to step out.

"Do you know what I do here, Miss Larios?" Fred Dressler asked, and Vera, accustomed to having her mother go on long tirades, wisely understood that she was not supposed to reply and instead looked attentively at the man. "I make stars, that's what I do. It's the same thing my colleagues do. They made the 'Oomph Girl' and the 'Sweater Girl,' and many more."

Fred Dressler leaned back in his black leather chair; he paused. Perhaps he expected Vera to ask who was the "Sweater Girl" or to applaud the talent of Lana Turner. But again, she was quiet. Next to her Luke Mahoney fiddled with his hat in his lap, giving her side-glances. Maxwell Niemann seemed remote.

"A young woman called Rossana Podesta arrived in the United States recently. She's an Italian girl who has been hired to play Helen of Troy by Warner Brothers. She has been chosen over Elizabeth Taylor and Ava Gardner for the part. She doesn't even speak English. And do you know why she was chosen? Because she's new. *New*, Miss Larios, is the name of the game. And you definitely are new. A little too new, perhaps."

Vera looked at Dressler as he smirked and opened the folder, holding a piece of paper up and giving it a quick read, then discarding it. "In the old days we had the benefit of time. We started by taking pictures of our actresses, placing those pictures in the magazines, giving them bit parts. But the world moves faster and faster. James Dean is in two films this year and getting top billing with Taylor and Hudson on his next flick. Top billing! That kid is twenty-four and no one knew him last year. But young people want young faces, and Henry Fonda won't do any longer."

Dressler picked another page, then turned it over. Then he began sliding photos across his desk. "You tested well, Miss Larios, but we only have two, maybe three months to prep you for this shoot, and I'm not sure if I'm able to make that gamble. An unknown foreign actress in the lead for one of my major pictures. What do you think?"

"I'm not sure I can convince you, sir," Vera said at last. "I know a lot of work goes into a movie and I have no real experience. But I've always loved this role."

"Always?" Dressler asked, looking confused. "The screenwriter is still putting the finishing touches to the pages. You haven't even seen the whole script."

Vera's mother had chided her for her performance during the audition. She said she was too shy; she tried to coach her on the way she should behave. Vera thought perhaps she should smile now; she worried that her face was serious and her tone somber. Yet she couldn't help herself.

"I mean that I've always loved Salome. I don't know your movie script, but I know Lachmann's libretto and I know Strauss's music, and I think I know what it all means. *Ah! Ich habe deinen Mund geküsst, Jochanaan*," she said, with the same solemn tone she had employed when answering a teacher's question as a schoolgirl.

"That's nice, but we're not shooting Strauss," Niemann said, turning to her agent, who looked back at the director with anxiety that was verging on panic. The director turned to her. "Now tell me what it means, if you can. And I don't want you to quote anything."

Vera sat in her chair, silent and still. Max Niemann's voice was unkind and hard, and perhaps it might have been best if she offered no reply. But her mind had conjured an honest answer and she spoke it.

"Gustave Moreau drew a hundred sketches of Salome. Her passion haunted him. That's what it is," she said, carefully picking her words. She looked at the director, and he looked back at her with interest, unfolding his arms and grasping the arms of his chair instead.

"It's passion. It's madness on the stage. The intensity of feeling that gets under your skin. It's chasing a moment you'll never regain. It's loving, for the first time. When you love like that, I think, you'd like to tear your heart out. Salome cuts off John the Baptist's head, but he already ruined her. He stabbed her heart."

They were quiet. When she glanced at Dressler, behind his desk, she could see he was frowning again. Her agent was practically crushing his hat between his hands. Max Niemann drummed his fingers and, unable to maintain his cool composure, he spoke with impatient vehemence.

"Come on, Fred. I must have her," he said.

Fred Dressler rested his elbows on the desk and nodded. "Very well, Miss Larios. And very well, Max. The girl is yours."

Salome

SALOME WALKED through the gardens of the palace, observing the white peacocks as they spread their feathers and lounged under the lemon trees. A servant held a parasol above each of the girls' heads, shielding them from the sun's rays.

Berenice and Mariamne walked at her side while Salome ate the seeds of a pomegranate one by one. She had spoken little that morning while the girls buzzed around her, sweet as honey and noisy as bees. She wished to swat them away but couldn't find the strength for it. She'd slept only three hours the previous night, tossing and turning in her bed while the moon filtered through the green curtains of her chamber. She'd thought of the prophet, of Jokanaan. She'd seen him preach twice more, swaddled in simple brown robes. But though she'd lingered after his speech was finished, she had not dared to speak to him yet, even though she longed for a few words with the man.

"I heard your cousin travels with the proconsul and will be here during the tetrarch's birthday celebration," Mariamne said. "Is it true?"

"I've heard nothing of the sort," Salome replied.

"They say he is a favorite of the emperor, and much beloved by his sons," Mariamne mused.

"He is also heavily in debt. Best you keep your pretty hands to yourself."

Mariamne huffed and snatched a little fan from an attendant, fanning herself faster.

"Is it true your mother has hired fifty dancers for the tetrarch's birthday celebration?" Berenice asked.

"I wouldn't know. Those matters are for her to arrange," Salome said, popping a pomegranate seed into her mouth, letting it rest on her tongue.

"Might you dance during the festivities?" Berenice continued.

Music and dance brought joy to Salome's heart. Her father, Archelaus, had been a man who loved music and dance more than politics. That, they said, had been his flaw. Salome believed it had been no flaw of his own that had doomed Archelaus, and that instead his miserable ending had been determined the moment Herod walked into his throne room and smiled at Archelaus's wife. Now the tetrarch watched Salome with his keen eyes, smiled at her, too, and she did not wish to dance for him.

Salome swallowed the pomegranate seed. "What inane questions you ask. I told you to amuse me and all you do is fatigue me," she said acidly.

"You're in a foul mood today," Berenice muttered.

A thin man with gray hair, accompanied by a servant, was walking toward them. He wore a voluminous tunic and above it a mantle. A square of cloth was draped above his shoulders with telltale blue tassels hanging from each corner identifying him as a Jew. Though the clothing was simple and unadorned, the man had a proud, serene face, which signaled his rank more than the signet ring on his right hand. This was Josephus, advisor to the tetrarch.

Josephus bowed his head. "Almati, may I have a word with you?" he asked.

"You may. Leave us," Salome said. Her attendants bowed their heads and retreated. Josephus did not need to use any verbal command with his servant; the young man stepped away automatically.

They walked down a path bordered with tall palm trees. Ahead of them was a patch of creamy narcissuses and beyond that a pool where fish swam in lazy circles. Her father's palace had magnificent gardens, and she remembered that the lilies there looked as pale as silver in the moonlight, their sweet scent growing stronger after dark. The gardens of Herod Antipas could not compare to those of her childhood, but the palace of her childhood was lost.

"I hear your mother wants the preacher Jokanaan tossed in a dungeon."

"He rails against her. You know my mother, she cannot stand any criticism," Salome said lightly, even though her pulse quickened at the mention of the man's name. "She'll forget he exists in a fortnight."

"Yet she wishes for you to speak to the Lord Tetrarch about him."

"Your spies are well paid. Perhaps she's said a thing or two about that."

"Your mother thinks her problem is the preacher, but she would have an angry mob at her gate should she arrest him. Jokanaan is beloved by many. You must know that."

"Then I suppose he is safe, since you will it," she said as she moved two steps ahead of him, then whirled around to stare into the man's eyes. She did not like the presumptuous tone he was using with her.

"You venture to the market frequently, almati," Josephus said, staring back at her.

Salome's gaze skirted away from him. Josephus stepped forward, and they began walking again at the same pace. Apparently, Josephus's spies stretched beyond the walls of the palace. She ought to have known he'd been watching.

"Have you told my uncle?"

"There is nothing to tell, and yet that does not mean I am unconcerned. We live in perilous times. Your mother fears the preacher undermines the tetrarch's authority, but the greater danger is your cousin."

"Then Agrippa really is traveling with the proconsul?"

"Yes."

They had reached the pool of water, and Salome looked at it. Her heart was unsettled, but she only nodded and pressed her lips together.

"Your mother wants you to join her and a small number of courtiers for dinner tonight."

"You'll be there?"

Josephus nodded. "She is nervous. You must soothe her."

"And will the tetrarch be there, too?"

"Him, too. Speak even more sweetly to his ear."

"I see. You must like this prophet if you wish me to speak sweet words to the tetrarch," Salome said stiffly, for Josephus understood her distaste toward her uncle and stepfather. It was not only the memory of her father's death that made her toss the pomegranate into the pool of water, but the taste of humiliation. The conflict had cost Salome her rightful seat. As her father's only child, she would have been heir to the throne of Samaria, Judaea, and Idumea. But in his lust and myopia Herod had allied himself with the Romans to unseat Archelaus and lost her family the territory.

"I am not a friend of this man," Josephus said.

"Then?"

"Prefect Pontius Pilate prefers to solve all problems by beating people with clubs, but it is not a wise choice. Such actions might be costly for the tetrarch. Your uncle should not be imitating him."

"What do I care what the tetrarch does for sport?" Salome replied. "And if he wants to imitate that Roman pig, let him roll in the same mud and excrement."

But she liked Pontius Pilate even less than her uncle. It would not do if the tetrarch was weakened and the Roman prefect gained more power as a result.

The fish in the pool had been scared by Salome's projectile, but now they began to swim around again.

"Forgive me, I am rude today," Salome said with a sigh. "I'll

attend the dinner. I'll be pleasant and smother my mother's com-
plaints. I have no quarrel with you, Josephus, and I know your
advice is always sound."

"You're very kind," he said, inclining his head at her, but then
he looked at her and his eyes narrowed a little. "If you will take
but one more piece of advice from me, dear child: do not venture
into the market again."

Salome was surprised by this command. Josephus was usually
more subtle when he spoke; such bluntness was uncharacteristic.
Her instinct, for one moment, was to heed his words. After her
father's fall, it had been Josephus who was like a father to her. She
had grown up admiring his intelligence and sense of justice.

She knew, as he looked at her, that he sought to protect her as
much as he hoped to protect his own people from strife. Yet even
all the affection she held for this man, whom she considered great
among all men, was nothing compared to the burning passion of
her heart.

"I will not promise you that," she said and turned around, following the path that snaked around the pond and losing herself
between the fragrant lemon trees.

*

THE DINNER was served in Herodias's antechamber, which was
decorated with images of musicians playing the flute, the tambou-
rine, and the lyre. The banquet hall where the tetrarch received
visitors was decorated with floral patterns and featured no human
figures nor animals, for this would have offended Jewish sensibilities, but in the privacy of the lady's rooms the dictum was ignored.

The dinner party was small, and aside from Salome's mother
and her stepfather consisted of Josephus and several of the palace's
highest-ranking stewards. They all sat around a low table and reclined on couches. The topic at hand was supposed to be Herod's
birthday party, but Herodias kept downing the wine and motioning for a slave to refill her cup, and the more she drank the more
her tongue strayed.

"Have you heard the latest insult that mendicant preacher tosses at us?" Herodias asked. Upon her brow she wore a golden circlet inlaid with white pearls. "He calls me an adulteress and claims our marriage is invalid. He says we are accursed under the eyes of his God."

"There is a preacher who babbles at every street corner these days," Herod replied, reclining against his cushions and keeping his gaze on his own cup of wine as he lifted it to his lips. "At least this one does not presume to perform magic. The one they call Jesus says he can cure diseases with a touch."

"That is unquestionably the work of evil spirits," Herodias said.

Herod waved a hand dismissively, the rings on each of his fingers glinting under the multicolored lamps. "That is the work of a swindler, same as Jokanaan. He makes his living by collecting alms, and to do that he must please the rabble with vulgar proclamations and mad tales. Let these preachers entertain the scum of the streets if they wish to."

"Jokanaan belongs in the dungeons."

"They say he is a boy of, what, twenty-three?" Herod asked, turning toward Josephus.

"Twenty-one, sir."

"There you have it. He probably doesn't even possess a beard yet. You'd have me toss a pup in a cage."

"I'd have you chain a rabid dog. Don't you remember what the rabble is capable of? Pontius Pilate hung golden shields with a carving of the head of Caesar upon the walls of his palace, and the Jews called it idolatry and threatened to storm the abode. For five days they rallied in the streets, yelling in rage and scratching at the walls."

"Pontius Pilate is a fool who does not understand this land nor its people. The Jews were bound to be offended by such a shameless display."

"That is what Jokanaan calls you: a shameless man," Herodias said.

Herod slammed his silver cup upon the table, staining the pale tablecloth with drops of wine as red as blood.

Salome, who had not spoken until that moment, took her small fan from the hands of her servant and waved it lightly in the air. "How dull these preachers are with their talk of angry gods and curses! I cannot even tell them apart, and I doubt the Jews care for them, either. My uncle is correct: Jokanaan is a swindler and best ignored."

Herodias glared at Salome while Herod turned toward her with a smile. When she was a child the tetrarch seldom smiled at Salome, seldom looked at her. She'd thought perhaps she reminded him of his dead brother. The girl was kept at a distance. Yet, now that she had grown into womanhood, the tetrarch's eyes lingered on his niece. The previous year, when Salome had last danced for the court, she'd recognized, for the first time, that same zealous look that he had given Herodias once upon a time, when he'd come to Archelaus's palace and coveted his wife.

Now the covetous look lingered, became commonplace whenever Salome sat at his table, and she tried to avoid dinners and meetings with the tetrarch. Yet here she was.

"Your daughter is right," Herod said.

Salome smiled back at him, her fingers tracing the feathers of her fan, swallowing her distaste.

"Shameless, incestuous, and a usurper. He'll yell this for all the world and Rome to hear," Herodias said, unwilling to be silent.

"Usurper!" Herod said, shoving his cup away. "How dare you repeat that word!"

"It is not I who said it!"

Herod pointed a finger at her. "Do not think I am a complete fool, Herodias. You write to Agrippa, I know it, and if Rome should hear anything it would be through your missives."

Herod disliked Agrippa as much as he had disliked the young man's father. There were whispers, though they were muffled, that once upon a time Agrippa's father had been a favorite of Herod the Great. Herod Antipas, incensed at the thought of his brother-in-law gaining more power at court, had hatched a plot that resulted in the execution of Agrippa's father.

"If I write to your nephew, it is to maintain a cordial relationship with the boy. Tiberius is fond of him, and he has grown up in the company of Tiberius's sons. You may have little love for your sister, but her son is a rising star at court."

A servant took the spilled cup away and brought a new one, filled with fresh wine.

"My sister is a vicious viper, but you may have a point," Herod conceded.

When Herod the Great died and his lands were divided into four, his daughter was granted Jamnia and some meager lands surrounding it. Jamnia was tiny compared to the vastness of her brothers' territories, but it was a bustling port. Now that Herod's finances had become strained as he fought a never-ending war with King Aretas, he had hoped his sister might lend him the necessary gold to continue his campaign. Yet she had refused.

"Dear uncle, don't think of her. We are supposed to discuss the preparations for your feast," Salome said.

"Yes, once again the girl is correct," Herod replied.

Despite everything, the tetrarch seemed soothed, and the dinner ought to have continued with good cheer, Jokanaan and any worries forgotten; but Herodias had consumed too much wine, and Salome had underestimated her state of inebriation. The wine emboldened her.

"After all, Agrippa might marry Salome one day," Herodias said, speaking clumsily, as if she had not heard a word her daughter had spoken.

"Marry! When you've given me no heirs?" Herod asked, his cheeks growing red with outrage. "So her children might have a claim to my throne?"

"I meant only—"

"You are a barren cow who should learn to keep her mouth shut!"

Salome pressed the peacock fan against her face to hide her

shocked expression. She had seen her mother and her stepfather quarreling before. They had long arguments, but Herod most often bent to his wife's will, and he was cool in his anger, turning distant and evasive rather than hot and fiery. But lately his attitude to his wife had changed, and perhaps Salome should not have been surprised to witness such an explosion.

"The preacher is right to call you a whore."

"My mother is a lady, sir, and widow to a tetrarch!" Salome said as she shoved the fan away and glared at her uncle.

Herod's face was iron as he looked back at his niece, yet Salome saw a flicker of dangerous thirst ripple across his face.

Herodias sat with her back straight, her eyes fixed upon her husband. She stood up in one smooth, elegant motion and turned to Salome.

"Come, daughter mine, the hour is late, and I grow tired."

Salome stood up, bowed her head to the tetrarch, and they departed. As they walked together, followed by their handmaidens, Salome whispered in her mother's ear.

"Mother—" she began, but Herodias cut her off with a furious whisper.

"The preacher is a great danger, and yet you speak against me in front of my husband when you should echo my words?"

"The preacher is nothing—"

"And then you antagonized him rather than help my cause."

"*You* antagonized the tetrarch by mentioning Agrippa."

"Agrippa must be mentioned if Marcellus is to be offered as a viable alternative."

Salome looked at her mother in surprise. The woman caught Salome's wrist, her fingers digging into her skin. "I am not blind, Salome, nor am I a fool. My husband wishes to seed his destruction, but I will not allow it."

"What do you mean?"

Herodias stepped back, quickly releasing her daughter, and clasped her hands beneath her breast. Her eyes were bright, and her voice was low. "Go to bed. We will speak tomorrow."

*

SHE WENT to see Jokanaan preach again, despite Josephus's misgivings, despite her own nerves. She went without a handmaiden, dressed in a simple outfit one of her servants might wear rather than her shoes inlaid with pearls and her silk dresses. A coarse veil hid her face.

She listened to him speak, and when the crowd thinned and he walked away, she followed him past the street of the textile merchants, past drinking dens and sellers of candied fruit who loudly hawked their wares, past a bathhouse, and into an insula of the Roman style that was now popular in the city.

The main gate opened onto a central courtyard with a well, but Jokanaan's lodgings were not on the ground floor. Instead, he took a narrow staircase that led him and Salome up, toward the area where the cheapest rooms were to be found.

She followed him down a hallway that was so dark she could hardly see where she was headed, and when a dog barked behind a shuttered window, she almost lost her step. She went on, blindly, and caught but the faintest glimpse of a door opening and closing. One ray of light spilling into the hallway before the darkness swallowed the sun.

She moved slowly until she stood before this door, and, breathing in, she knocked. He opened and did not seem surprised by her presence, allowing her in without a word.

His home was but a single room, with a table, a chair, and a clay cup. In a corner there was a mattress filled with straw and next to it a wooden chest. A window let in a breeze and some light.

"You've ventured far," he said.

She had thought she would be nervous in his presence, grow mute with timidity, yet her lifelong training had given her the gift of poise. There was no stammer, no anxious sigh. "You do not know me, so how can you tell where I come from?" she asked.

"You masquerade as a servant today, but I've seen you in the dress of a high lady."

"How could you recognize me if I veil my face?"

"By your eyes," he said simply. "Why have you come?" he asked with frank curiosity.

"To warn you. You question the tetrarch's marriage; you call him a usurper. Such words will not be tolerated. Cease in such declamations."

"I repeat the truth that God speaks to me. Herod Antipas has slain his brother and by laying with his brother's wife committed incest. He sits on a stolen throne, painted in blood, his soldiers paid with pilfered gold."

"The tetrarch will have your tongue for that."

The young man seemed unimpressed. His voice was steady and confident. "You cannot frighten me. Tell your lord that I follow a higher Lord than him, and speak his truth, not that of Rome's lackeys."

"You think Herod sends me?" she asked, her hand resting on the back of a chair.

"Who else?"

"Herod would not care to issue such warnings. But Josephus worries about your fate."

"Ah, Josephus, who advises the usurpers and the vipers," the handsome preacher said, suppressing a laugh. Up close, she could see he had flecks of gold in his eyes. They were green and gold and brown, finer than jewels from Palmyra.

"What do you mean?"

"Herod and his kin were imposed on us by the Roman emperor. But the empire will crumble, and we shall be set free."

"You defy the emperor's will?" she asked, and suppressed a laugh of her own.

"I do. Herod and his family are worms who gnaw at spoiled meat."

She had been more amused than outraged, but his insult jabbed at her pride. "You speak to Salome, daughter of Herodias and Archelaus. Granddaughter to Herod the Great. Great-granddaughter of Antipater. I am of the most royal blood of Idumea," she said, and as she spoke she removed her veil and her hair covering.

But Jokanaan did not seem intimidated by this revelation. He looked at her with icy composure. "Then, Salome, know that the cry of your family's crimes has risen to the ears of God. Cast away your riches, bow your head before the Lord. You are still a girl, and have no full understanding of sin. The Lord will forgive you."

She sat down by the table and scoffed. "A girl? You think yourself so much older and wiser than me? They say you are twenty-one; I am the same age. If I am a girl, then you are a boy," she said, reaching for the clay cup and tracing its rim. "How long have you preached?"

"The Lord came to me four years ago, as I slept. It was as if a sword pierced my heart, and then a voice whispered in my ear and I awoke. Now I do his bidding."

"How can you be sure it was not simply a child's dream?" she asked.

At last, a crack of emotion appeared on his face, and he was offended. "It was no child's dream, but a revelation. The Lord has spoken to me many times since."

"That is good and well, but could you not preach without mention of my uncle or my mother?" she replied, placing the cup back on the table. "Your God does not require you to mention them each and every sermon."

"Herod Antipas killed your father and profaned his bed, yet you embrace your uncle with a smile and kiss your mother on the cheek."

Salome stood up abruptly, clutching her hands, her back to him. He'd wounded her; his words were like a slap against her cheek.

"What else do you think a girl alone is supposed to do? Raise an army and lay siege to a fortress? No. Those *are* the dreams of children."

She turned to him again. He was pensive, his initial curiosity now laced with disquiet.

"When war broke out between my uncle and my father, my father had me sent to my aunt's palace at Jamnia for my safety. My mother remained at his side. She wrote to say all would be well, and eventually she wrote to say I was to return to her. The war had ended, and my aunt explained my father would be exiled."

Salome looked down at the folds of her dress, at her hands laced beneath her breast. "I thought this meant Mother and Father and I would be reunited in another city. But instead, I was taken to my uncle's palace where I was informed my mother had married again. I was not to correspond with my father, who was sent to Gaul.

"Six months later my father drank aconite," she said. "He killed himself."

She did not weep. Trained as she had been in courtly graces, she could school her face into a mask of marble. Seldom did she allow sorrow to show, veiling it under iron rather than silk cloth. But the darkness of her eyes did cry out, and such was this emotion that the young preacher stepped forward, clutched her hands, and gave her an astonishing look.

It was like being touched by fire. In an instant she recognized the look on his face. After all, she'd had a chance to witness it each morning in her hand mirror since the first time she'd heard him preach: it was love. Not the common love of men and women, but the passion of fated lovers. It was written in the stars and might have been foretold by sages. Love that boiled, that cleaved, that annihilated.

She thought she'd faint and clutched him to maintain her balance.

"You wish to kiss me," she whispered.

But he stepped back, as if fire had truly burned his hands, and she stumbled. When he spoke, there was trembling despair in his voice.

"No, I shall not. Come not near me," he said. "I've been chosen by the Lord."

"You will."

At that he shook his head. "Never. Leave me."

"Then I will kiss you, one day," she said, breathless, and stepped out into the narrow dark hallway, feeling the tug of fate in her blood and not knowing it was the harbinger of tragedy.

Pierce Pratt

NANCY WAS attractive. She could have been Salome, no doubt about it. But she kept making dumb choices. The men she hung out with were no good. She ran with a fast crowd and was friends with crooks, booze hounds, and pill poppers. Before Benny Alden, there were other shady characters. She dated Johnny Stompanato, the mobster who was knifed by Lana Turner's kid. Is it that surprising what happened in the end?

Bad crowd and lousy habits. She drank too much, so to stay thin, she took Dexamyl. She gobbled those green pills up like candy. Of course, lots of people were doing uppers and downers. Judy Garland popped forty Ritalin tablets a day like it was nothing. Errol Flynn liked to put cocaine on the tip of his penis—he said it enhanced the sex—and had an awful heroin habit.

But those were stars, and in those days there were fixers who made sure these things were not known. They had people to protect them, even to fetch them drugs. Nancy was nobody, and she spent too much time at parties and too little time worried about getting roles.

You had to work the club circuit, get your photo in the pictures. Jayne Mansfield was an expert at "accidentally" exposing a nipple at every party in town. Vikki Dougan made a career out of showing her rear in her custom-made backless gowns.

But Nancy would go to a club, meet a no-good B-movie actor, and next thing you knew they were walking out the door and going somewhere cozier, often to do drugs or get rip-roaring drunk.

The vice squad was no joke back then. When Robert Mitchum was arrested on a marijuana charge, he received probation and went right back to work. But Lila Leeds, who'd done bit roles around MGM and had a main part coming up, was run out of Hollywood.

Nancy had a mean streak, especially when things didn't go her way. She'd be sweet as molasses, and then you'd make a mistake and she was slapping you and scratching your face. She punched me one time. Then she apologized, said I riled her up too much. "I get too hot in the head, honey," that's what she'd say.

I saw her on and off for about a year. I was used to temperamental actors, so her outbursts and her drinking, although annoying, were not enough to steer me away completely from her.

We didn't have an exclusive relationship. I was dating a lot, too, but I was still surprised when she said she was serious about Jay Rutland. Not so much because Nancy was serious about someone, but because Jay didn't seem like her regular crowd.

Well, okay, fine. I figured the girl was moving up in the world. She was finally taking my advice and dumping her lowlife friends and that Benny Alden. You ask me, none of what happened was Nancy's fault. It was Benny's doing.

He gave me the creeps.

I met him one time when Nancy had a party. I'd heard about him, like you hear about shady folks in Hollywood, one word here and another there. I knew he was a dope dealer.

I was sipping a drink and talking to Nancy, and this man glared at me. There was something coiled inside that guy, held tight, as he watched me with his hooded eyes. Nancy said he'd knifed a man back in New York and I believed it. She laughed when she said it, too. She thought it was funny.

That was the trouble with Nancy. She got a kick out of such characters. She was a jaded, hard creature. Attractive and mad, which was part of her appeal. It was a sizzling combo, at times.

I was surprised when one time she told me she'd been a married housewife. I don't recall how it came up. Maybe she was doing an audition for a detergent brand, who knows. But she said she used to diligently starch her husband's shirts and iron his slacks and cook his favorite foods. I asked her what happened, and she shrugged, told me she simply got tired of it and left the guy.

I could believe it. Nancy was the kind of girl who could dump you without a word. You'd come home one day and there simply wouldn't be a meal in the oven and the lights would be off and your wife was gone.

Nancy

NANCY SAT by the window, sipping her drink, while Karen fiddled with the portable radio and Tessa read the cards for Cathy. Betty was painting Marsha's nails a bright pink.

She was thinking about a girl dancing in a room strewn with purple-and-red cushions to the sound of flutes and drums.

"Aren't you going to get ready?" Marsha asked. "We got ourselves an hour before we need to be at the movies."

It was nearly seven, and Nancy was still in her day dress and her flats. Normally she'd be dolling herself up like the others, applying rouge to her cheeks between taking sips of rum. Instead, she kept staring out the window, kept thinking about a dancer before the court of a king.

"Don't talk to her, she's sore 'cause she got that little part on that Bible movie," Karen said.

"Why would she be sore about that?" Marsha asked.

The spell was broken. The dancer had vanished. "Because I have to be a slave who carries a parasol, that's why," Nancy said, turning away from the window and glaring at Marsha. "It's not real acting, it's standing. And they're giving the lead to an ugly spic who hasn't even been in anything."

When Pierce had first called and told her the good news, she'd assumed he meant she was getting the role. Instead, he said the part of Salome was already cast, but he'd secured her a bit role. The problem was she'd phoned her father the week prior to that, told him she was going to be in a flick. She'd been hoping to impress him, but it wasn't impressive anymore. It was basically the same damn gig she'd obtained when she'd had the six-month option.

She was a fucking extra. Her old man would have a laugh about it.

If only Pierce hadn't been such a smarmy liar! He'd sworn the employees at the casting office loved her headshots and her screen test was solid. It all felt fine. Then, suddenly, the director made up his mind from one day to the next, and he'd gone for a Hispanic honey no one had heard about.

Pierce had been lying through his teeth, that's what had happened. She'd never had a chance.

"Her picture was in the paper today," Karen said, turning to Marsha. "'Vera Larios. The Mexican Liz Taylor, the sizzling sensation,' they say."

"Sizzling tortilla face," Nancy replied, looking at her liquor glass, a quarter full. Her father had probably seen that same story already and found out Nancy wasn't going to be Salome after all.

She shouldn't have mentioned the title of the picture, but she'd been excited, Pierce had sounded sincere, and she had screen-tested. She'd told her old man that she was in the running for the lead in *The Seventh Veil of Salome*. She'd said she practically had a contract.

The problem was when she talked to her father, she tried to fill the silences. Desperately, she spoke too much, because he spoke so little.

Salome.

She'd told him she was going to be Salome, with a gauzy dress that went from a deep orange to pale yellow and bells around her ankles. Salome, carrying the head of John the Baptist on a silver platter.

She didn't even know how to pronounce the last name Larios. Nobody did. What a joke.

Nancy stood up, dumped her glass in Tessa's kitchen sink, and moved toward the door, elbowing away Karen, who let out a loud "Hey!"

"Where are you going?" Cathy asked.

"For a walk. It's stuffy in here," she muttered.

Nancy hurried down the stairs, and when she reached the front entrance of the building she found Benny standing there, leaning against a car. He was having a smoke.

She wasn't surprised to see him. Nancy had been artfully avoiding Benny. Whenever that happened, he eventually came around to find her. It was about time he showed up, but it didn't please her to see him even if she'd been expecting he'd stroll around the block any day now.

She walked toward him, arms crossed. "You didn't say you'd be dropping by. I'm headed out with the girls tonight."

"I thought it might be the boys. You've been ditching me lately, making excuses."

"So what?" Nancy asked with a shrug. "We're no proper nothing."

"That's the issue. I'd like it if we were a proper something. I keep telling you we should get properly serious about this. I'd take care of you; we'd have a house and a pool and maybe even a couple of kids. You know, married bliss."

Nancy thought about Theodore and her three-year stint as Mrs. Livesey. It had started well enough, she supposed. After her hopes for a career as a child actress fizzled and she packed her bags and went to live with her mother and her mother's new husband, Nancy threw herself into the experience of being a regular teenage girl. She never liked school much and instead focused her energy on socializing and having a merry time. One day, she walked into the drugstore and caught the eye of the owner's son, the good-looking, pleasant Theodore Livesey. Not much later, shortly after her graduation, the eighteen-year-old and her boyfriend married.

With his dad's help, Theo bought a little house that came with a lovely kitchen where Nancy was happy to whip up his favorite treats. She was in a daze the first few weeks of her marriage, giddy with joy. She mopped the floors and arranged flowers in a vase, which was swell until she realized Theo hardly noticed the cake she'd baked or the way she'd folded the napkins so they looked like swans. After seven months she was bored stiff. Another four months and she'd started sipping a few too many brandies from the cabinet her parents-in-law had given them as a wedding gift.

Tedium. That was Nancy's life. Tedium each day and each night. Theo didn't look handsome when she had to stare at his face every morning as he read the paper and buttered his toast. But she gritted her teeth and made multicolored Jell-O, peeled potatoes, collected and organized coupons in a drawer. She styled her hair, powdered her face, slipped into dresses that emphasized her bosom.

Until one day Theo came home and said he'd slipped. He'd cheated on her. He'd spent three months fucking one of the employees at his dad's pharmacy where he worked. Nancy knew which employee it was: a freckled, flat-chested, frizzy-haired, ugly girl whose name tag always looked crooked.

Theo apologized, he said he had to come clean, he said he didn't know why he'd done it and he wouldn't do it again. Nancy told him she forgave him. In the morning, while her husband went to work, she remembered that ugly bitch. That two-bit whore. He had cheated on her with that hag. It stung.

Nancy had been dissatisfied in their little house with their multitude of appliances and their cheerful curtains with a flower print. But she had put her head down, completed her chores, cooked the meals, and smiled.

It had been Theodore who cracked. Not Nancy. It should have been her who ran hollering out the door months ago.

The full wave of the humiliation struck her like a tsunami. She left Theodore. She smeared mustard over his reading chair, set his clothes to wash with a packet of blue dye, cut his ties and tossed them in a blender, stabbed his pillow thirteen times.

That had been married bliss, and remembering it Nancy

couldn't do anything but laugh so loud Benny frowned, grabbed her by the arm, and squeezed hard, pulling her to the side.

"What the hell is the matter with you? You think it's funny?"

But she only laughed louder. Benny squeezed tight, until she shoved him away, her laugh turning into a snarl. "What are we going to live on in that house with the pool, Ben? Are you going to deal dope while I put the kids to bed at night?"

"I'll quit that."

"Right."

"You don't believe me, but I'm crazy about you. I really am."

That's what every two-bit crook had told her, and none of them had meant it. She suspected Benny did mean it, but it didn't please her. The words had long lost their power, and coming from a guy like Benny she couldn't think they were worth much to begin with.

Nancy reached into his jacket pocket for the crumpled half-pack of cigarettes she knew was there and held up her cigarette as he lit it with weary, suspicious eyes.

"Kent Shaw says you're running around with that Jay Rutland."

"Kent's an idiot."

"Doesn't mean he's a liar. You twicin' me?"

"Maybe I have, maybe I haven't," she said. She'd been seeing Jay for weeks now, although she'd been careful not to let Ben catch wind of it. Or so she thought.

"I find that guy near you and I'll cut him a new asshole," Ben said, his voice low, as he tipped her chin up to get a good look at her eyes.

She took a puff of her cigarette and gave him a contemptuous grin. "That's what you say about every guy, Benny. I've danced this dance before."

"Yeah? Then you know you've nothing going with that rich kid. Don't get any ideas. You're too cheap for that sorta fellow."

"What do you know?"

"I know cheap, baby."

"Fuck you, Benny."

"Not while you're fucking him. Come and look for me once you're over that brat."

She blew a little smoke from the corner of her mouth and tossed the cigarette away, then hurried back inside the building without another word. When she reached her floor, she heard the loud noise of the portable radio and the girls' laughter drifting toward her. Nancy headed back to her apartment and locked the door.

She poked her head out the window to see if Benny was still downstairs, but he'd left. There was a bitter taste in her mouth, from the booze and the cigarette and something else. Rather than joining the girls, she pulled out a bottle of good gin and drank alone. Tessa had only cheap hooch and Nancy didn't want any of that.

She wanted champagne flutes and her name up in lights.

Cathy came knocking a little while later. "Hey, Nancy, you comin'?" she asked.

Nancy didn't answer. For what? she thought. To venture to the movies and get picked up outside the cinema by a few loud fellows with no prospects and no brains? Men like Benny, at best men like her useless ex-husband or that rat-faced Pierce Pratt.

"Nancy?" Cathy said again, and Nancy kept quiet, kept drinking her gin slow.

"Let her be, her royal highness is throwing a tantrum," Tessa said.

The girls muttered among themselves; someone laughed, and their voices drifted away. She sat there, drinking, smoking, flipping through the pages of old movie magazines. She phoned Jay, but his line was busy. When she tried him again half an hour later the line was still occupied.

Nancy changed into a red dress, applied a fresh coat of lipstick, grabbed her purse, and hailed herself a cab.

She rang the bell and waited until Jay came to the door. He was already in his pajamas and didn't look pleased to see her.

"Nancy, what are you doing here? I have a meeting early in the morning."

"I thought you were up. Your line's been busy," she said, sliding into his home before he could think to object.

"I left the telephone off the hook so no one would wake me."

"Too bad," she declared, tossing her coat and her purse onto his couch and grabbing him by the hand. "You'll have to stay up a little longer."

"Nancy, it's no joke—"

"Take off those silly pajamas," she said, letting go of him and marching toward his bedroom.

"What?"

"Have you ever wanted to see the dance of seven veils, Jay, darling?" she asked. Her voice was loud as she took off one of her high heels, then the other. "It's old, exotic. I'll tell you what: it's not a Mexican dance. No maracas!"

"Where are you going?"

"To your bed."

"You're drunk."

She laughed a quick, rehearsed laugh that she'd perfected for such occasions and tossed her shoes aside.

"This is not funny."

Nancy shrugged. Once she reached the room, she unzipped her dress and let it pool at her feet. She looked over her shoulder at Jay, who was leaning against the doorway staring at her with a dour expression. He scratched his head.

"Nancy, you're welcome to stay the night, but I'm headed to the guest room. Okay?"

"Sure you are," she muttered, reaching for the hooks of her bra, her fingers fumbling the job.

It took her forever to finish getting undressed, and by the time Nancy looked toward the doorway again, Jay had vanished. She considered going after him but instead walked toward the bed and slid under the covers.

She couldn't remember why she'd wanted to see Jay, or why she'd even phoned him. He was the furthest thing from Benny, maybe that was it. Who knew.

When she woke up it was to the sound of a vacuum cleaner. Nancy grabbed one of Jay's robes and opened the door of his room. A maid was sliding the appliance down the carpeted hallway. The woman was old, but her dark skin reminded Nancy of Vera Larios. This was another Mexican cockroach.

The maid looked up at her, and Nancy closed the door.

She went into the en suite bathroom and took a long shower, leaving three towels on the floor for the maid to scoop up. In the kitchen, she riffled through Jay's refrigerator, nibbling at pieces of fruit and pouring herself a half glass of orange juice. She left these items outside, also for the maid to deal with.

Nancy opened the massive glass door that led to the back of Jay's house and followed the purple flagstones past a white gazebo, toward a turquoise swimming pool. To the left of the pool there was a cabana hut that served as the changing room, along with lounging chairs and a table with a wide yellow umbrella. Beyond the pool, the path continued and led down a wooden staircase, past avocado trees and a stretch of unspoiled wilderness.

Nancy disrobed and lay naked on one of the lounging chairs. She wanted to work on her tan, but she also figured it would make for a fine greeting if Jay were to come back, poke his head outside, and find her stretched out naked like that. He hadn't seemed too happy the previous night, but that could be fixed.

There was nothing Nancy couldn't fix with a few kisses and sweet words.

After an hour had passed and Jay had not shown up, Nancy ventured back into the house. The maid had finished her cleaning and vanished.

Nancy went into Jay's study, looked at his vast collection of books, and glanced at the titles on the spines. Jay's furniture was modern, expensive, all teak and walnut and clean lines. Nancy couldn't see the use for a study, but she did like the look of it.

The study connected to a piano room, and this in turn led to the vast living room with enormous windows. A well-stocked bar trolley of white walnut with brass details and a glass top was tucked behind the couches, which were assembled to allow a good view of the large double-door walnut cabinet with a turntable and radio. A carefully curated selection of records, most of them jazz, served as the bulk of the wall décor. Nancy liked Dean Martin and Sinatra. She couldn't understand what Jay saw in the music he bought.

She turned on the radio. As her feet moved around the soft rug and she flipped through an issue of *Life* that she'd picked from the study, she pondered what it might be like to live in a place like this, far from her cramped apartment with the hot plate and the rickety fan.

She tossed the magazine on the couch, lit a cigarette, and toyed with a heavy glass ashtray, turning it between her hands. She wasn't too cheap for this sort of place and this sort of fellow. Benny had it wrong. In fact, she felt right at home in a big house with a pool, and Jay was glad to wine and dine her and buy her flowers. And she was sure he wasn't going to stop at flowers. Guys like Jay could buy their girlfriends jewels, furs, clothes. Real presents. He might even secure a nice apartment for her, better than the one the guy with the fish and the wife got for her. Or he might buy her a car.

She'd heard stories about guys like that who'd spend big on a gal, and Nancy didn't come cheap, no matter what Benny said.

Stupid Benny. She was never phoning him back. He could go rot in an alley for all she cared.

Jay walked into the living room as she was setting the ashtray back on the coffee table. He didn't seem surprised to see her there. "Hello, Nancy," he said, hands in his pockets.

She smiled at the sight of him. There was something opulent about Jay Rutland, like she was gazing at a museum object that should be kept under glass. His closely fitted jackets and his good looks were delectable.

"How was the meeting?" she asked, her voice cheerful.

"Much ado about nothing. Are you feeling better? You were drunk."

"Sorry about last night," she said, stepping toward him and

sliding a hand down his tie and giving it a playful tug. "Sometimes I feel I'll fall to pieces, you know? And I get a little mean."

Jay sighed and grasped her hand. "Nancy, you're a lot of fun, but you and I, we're so different——"

"That's what you want, isn't it? First time I met you, that's what you said. That you were looking for some fun," she said quickly. She'd had vicious rows with all her boyfriends, it was a habit. The trick was to simply minimize the incident and not let them dwell on it. Erase it like it never happened.

"I did say——"

She began working the buttons of his shirt. "And you said I was exciting."

He attempted to brush her fingers away. "Yes, but——"

"We're young, and it's boring being alone when you're young. That's the other thing you said. That you were feeling lonely." She looked up at him, her lips curving into a wide smile. "You'll never be lonely with me, baby."

Jay looked like he maybe had an objection, but she slid her fingers against the buttons of his trousers and he swallowed his words. That was one thing that he at least had in common with Benny and Theodore and the other guys she fooled around with. They were simple creatures. This knowledge filled her with a sense of triumph, although for a moment it also made her hand go still, the sting of that bitterness again hitting her, before she shook her head and kissed him hard.

Cecilia Gavaldón

GOSH, SHE was a sweetheart! Maybe that was the problem. Or maybe it's that she was confused. That might be it. Vera came from a different place. She didn't understand the rules.

My parents still remembered the riots of '43. Sailors went around Los Angeles beating Mexican men. They pummeled boys who'd done nothing except wear a fashionable zoot suit. They called Mexican girls "loose." Blacks and Mexicans in East LA could swim only on Wednesdays—that was the day the pools were drained and refilled. To buy a house in the new suburbs they were developing, you had to say you were Spanish. That's what my mom wrote on our application. Spaniards.

They thought we were filth. They said we were inherently criminal. We had to be careful and watch out for ourselves.

Back in Mexico City, my cousin was a dentist's daughter who lived in a nice middle-class neighborhood. Her father fixed the teeth of a whole bunch of American immigrants. There were embassy employees among his clientele and a few movie people who'd gone south to avoid the blacklist. The Kilian boys, whose dad worked at Televisa, were getting braces back then, and they knew Isadora Christie, who first discovered Vera. That's how that happened.

Anyway, this meant my uncle made a decent living. He was a dentist by trade, but he loved the arts. He was a big opera buff, and he'd take her to classical music concerts or to see famous tenors perform. Vera's mother made sure her girls knew the etiquette manuals from top to bottom. They had fashionable dresses, shoes, and hats. Their brothers, twins who were twelve when Vera moved to Los Angeles, attended a private school. Their dad drove a Ford station wagon.

Vera wasn't a debutante, as they liked to say in the press, but she also wasn't the type of girl who'd ever heard the words "spic" or "wetback." When she looked around, Vera thought she was like everyone else because that's what she was used to feeling.

This meant she lacked a certain insulation. I'm not saying she was foolish, but she was a bit naïve about what awaited her at the studio and what people thought of her.

She didn't know how to deal with boys, either. I must admit, back then I was boy crazy. I had a huge crush on Tab Hunter, but I also managed to get my hands on Mexican magazines that had stories about Jorge Negrete and Joaquín Cordero.

I couldn't understand why Vera was shy with men. My mother

was strict—she wouldn't let me go to the movies without my brother—but I convinced her to let Vera and me go together, since she was older. One time, when we were in the lobby of this cinema, two boys tried to invite us to a party. Gosh, they looked swell! But Vera excused herself and dragged me home.

Boys tried to talk to her, and she'd say two words to them. So quiet, that girl! She'd be sitting in a room and you'd forget she was there because she was *that* quiet, and very still. I'm not sure how to explain that. The stillness. She'd be thinking, staring off at something, humming. My mom said she was a bit funny in the head. She also said Vera had been engaged, but I couldn't believe it. The few times her ex-boyfriend came up in conversation Vera clammed up. The closest I got to learning the full story behind him was when Vera told me her mother was still angry at her for breaking the engagement, which is entirely understandable.

I think that's why Vera went to Los Angeles. There's no doubt my aunt wanted her daughter to be an actress, and Vera was dedicated to the role of Salome. But I think ultimately Vera was trying to escape her past.

She was this delicate, ethereal creature. Poised and quiet. I couldn't believe she'd broken any engagement. My mother said the church had even published the wedding banns! Can you imagine what people must have said? Such an embarrassment. I would have never shown my face again in public, mark my words!

That a girl like Vera would do such a thing was unimaginable. But then my mom said it's the quiet ones who are trouble, and she was right.

Vera

VERA, STUDIOUS by nature, immersed herself fully in the task of becoming Salome while the studio cranked up the well-oiled machinery they used to manufacture stars. She was assigned to Dan Quiterio, one of the top publicists at Pacific Pictures, who was supposed to mold her image. The man decided the best course of action was to sell her as mysterious, exotic, and unattainable. Rather than flogging every newspaper and gossip column with her picture, Dan wanted to keep her out of the public eye. Vera was to go to acting and dancing classes, and whatever wardrobe fittings were necessary, but she wouldn't attend parties and receptions or mingle with other actors.

Rather than imagining Vera as a hot-blooded Latina like Lupe Vélez, he pegged her as another Dolores del Río. Aristocratic and refined, that would be Vera's image. When Vera told him del Río had actually been a wealthy high-society lady before making her debut in Hollywood, while she was a former receptionist who had worked for her father, the publicist shrugged.

Vera spent the bulk of her days in a three-story building that contained a dance studio on the ground floor and several offices above that served as the basis of operations for the acting coaches, voice coaches, singing instructors, and tutors at Pacific Pictures. When she wasn't practicing her lines or working with a choreographer, Vera took refuge in a small library that housed reference materials. She often sat by a window that had a view of "Dodge Town"—the nickname for a stretch of street on the back lot that had facades of saloons and posts for horses, and which was used to shoot Westerns—and read a book. Or else she had her meals there, since Dan had declared the commissary out of bounds for the time being. It wouldn't do if the mysterious Mexican actress were to sit down and drink a Sprite next to everyone else, at least for now.

She hummed to herself when she was alone, a melancholic melody that she was toying with in her mind. Sometimes she hummed songs she'd heard on the radio, ballads about falling in and out of love.

Luke Mahoney took her out to lunch her first week on the lot and tried to give her tips on how to work with Max Niemann.

"He's specific about his direction. He'll tell you exactly what he wants. He might even line read the scene for you," her agent said. He wore a suit that didn't quite fit him, and he looked awfully young. His mustache was more a bit of blond peach fuzz than a true mustache. "Repeat every word using his same inflection and he'll love you."

"Won't I be a bit stiff if I'm imitating him?"

"I doubt it. He's been doing this for ages. He cut his teeth with silent flicks, you know? He directed Norma Talmadge, I think."

"Clara Bow," Vera said. "In 1926. I looked up info on Max in the studio archives. He didn't direct her, really. He was an assistant director on set. He was quite young."

"Look at you, you're a regular Sherlock Holmes," he said cheerfully. "Anyhow, the man is a little temperamental with his actors, but he'll make you a star."

"That's what the publicity people say."

"Believe them. Ah, what else? Smile at him, always. He likes that."

This remark reminded Vera of her mother, who liked to tell Vera to look pleasant at all times. *Smile, Vera. Laugh, Vera. Say thank you, Vera.*

The days went by. Max Niemann swooped in to see her a few times, Isadora Christie by his side with a notebook as he remarked on this or that. He often talked to and questioned her acting coaches or her dance instructor rather than her.

"How's the kid doing?" he asked.

She felt rattled when he stared at her, smiling with effort, but after a while she understood he was seeing her in an abstract way, almost as if she were a drawing he must color in. His instructions, barked to Christie or someone else, often were about the hairdo he wanted for Salome, or how Salome should move. She noticed he enjoyed her malleability, the easy way she took direction. She was used to obeying, and he was used to commanding.

Around them, the picture kept taking shape to a steady, invisible rhythm. Black-and-white wardrobe tests had led to tests shot in color. Carpenters erected palace walls, painters created facades of reddish-yellow bricks, and catering planned the many meals that would be served to the extras who would be decked in sandals, togas, and armor.

Vera sent postcards and photos of the city to her sister. No letters, just a few words in her small, delicate handwriting. Lumi didn't like long letters, and Vera wasn't sure what she should say. She still felt as if she were masquerading as Lumi, as if she wasn't quite deserving of this opportunity.

She listened to records in the evening, reading the script while opera played in the background. Sometimes she didn't read the script; instead she opened the battered copy of Flaubert's *Three Tales* she'd found at a used bookshop, or recited poetry while her cousin looked at her in amusement.

"Aren't you shooting a film?" Ceci asked.

"Of course."

"You should be reading *Hollywood Connection.* They have the best gossip in town. But don't tell my mom I buy it."

"I won't," Vera promised and sat with the book resting on her chest, trying to picture a palace, the whisper of scarlet curtains, and the distant tune of a lonesome flute.

*

DAN QUITERIO arrived after Vera had finished eating her lunch and put her tray away, just as she was about to open a small volume of Gabriela Mistral's poetry. She had not followed Ceci's suggestion of picking up *Hollywood Connection* after all.

Dan was fortyish, wore round-rimmed glasses, and always carried a clipboard with him. He had an air of dynamic efficiency that was echoed in his quick speech pattern.

"I talked to Max and he agrees it's time to start pushing you into the limelight. I have an invitation to a party for you."

"We start shooting soon," she said, surprised. "I thought he wanted me to focus on my preparation."

"Working at Pacific Pictures means generating publicity. It's part of your preparation. Your date will be Simon Gilbert. Argentinian, has been with us for two and a half years. He has four American pictures under his belt. 'The Singing Gaucho' is what we're calling him. Rising star, pleasant fellow. You'll look lovely in photos together," Dan said as he handed her a picture.

Simon Gilbert's publicity photo showed a grinning man with a mustache and a guitar in his hands.

"The party is for Miguel Montaner and will be held at his cottage. Maybe you know him, he's a musician. Mexican, like you. Plays at many clubs. He cut a hit record a few years ago and composed a couple of songs for RKO. He's with us now. Simon will pick you up at your house at nine in two days. The columnists attending the party will be Hedda Hopper, Louella Parsons, and Sidney Skolsky. I'll be there, too, along with the studio photographer. Don't take a picture unless I've authorized it; we want you posing with the right mix of people. Sarah Lane has several dresses she needs you to try on for the party, so you should head there after this meeting."

Vera didn't know what to say. She stared at Dan for a minute until he looked up from his clipboard.

"Shell-shocked?" he asked.

"A little. I thought maybe things would proceed like now, with me out of the papers and no parties."

"We've been teasing the public, Vera. But at some point, we have to drop the veil," he said. "Simon and you will dance a couple of dances, we'll introduce you to people, and we'll have you home before midnight, like Cinderella."

"You make it sound easy."

"It is easy when you have me in your corner. Want me to walk you to Sarah's?"

Sarah Lane was a tall, elegant woman of about fifty who served as the head women's wardrobe mistress and who knew every actress's exact measurements at any given time. Under her watchful eye, dresses, shoes, and wigs were catalogued and collated, missing buttons replaced, and alterations quickly made.

Vera found Sarah slightly intimidating, but she greeted her and her assistant with a smile.

"I have three outfits set aside for you," Sarah said as she opened a door to allow Vera into a changing room. "Dan said you should look like a princess."

The dresses on display had all been used by the major studio stars for movies, screen tests, or other functions. They had tags with the names of the performers who had worn them, and she was immediately overwhelmed by the sight of such glamorous designs.

"Try them on," Sarah said.

Vera tried on all three dresses, but her favorite was clear from the start. She was drawn by a white silk décolleté dress embroidered with translucent crystals that nipped the waist and swept into a full skirt. Sarah agreed it was the best look for her.

Back at home, when Vera unwrapped the carefully packaged dress, shoes, and jewelry, her cousin Cecilia squealed. Vera's mother and aunt were more measured in their praise. Vera's aunt remained unsure about these Hollywood parties. Her mother's objection was the color of the dress.

"You know how it goes: flies in milk," her mother said, shaking her head. "Women with dark skin don't have the complexion for white dresses."

Lumi was constantly dressed in cream and pink. Vera supposed her mother would have rather seen her sister in the dress, her hair well coiffed and her skin several shades paler than Vera's.

"The studio likes it. I'm going to the party with a real gaucho, what do you think about that, Ceci?" Vera asked, trying to forget her mother's barbed comment.

"I've seen his picture and he's swell," Ceci said. "Is he going to come in to meet us?"

"He should come in to introduce himself if he has any manners," her aunt said. "Who ever heard of a man who is taking a lady on a date and doesn't come in to meet her family?"

"It's a studio-arranged event, Aunt Prisca."

"They don't teach them how to begin a courtship here in Los Angeles," her aunt continued as if she hadn't heard Vera.

Vera didn't want to think about courtships. Inevitably, that made her remember Arturo, sitting in her parents' house, asking for her hand in marriage. Then, Arturo and her, alone, kissing, and that empty feeling in the pit of her stomach, that ache and hollowness that made her turn her head away from him.

She finished getting ready, her hair piled up with the assistance of her mother's artful fingers, her makeup subdued. She wrapped a stole around her shoulders when the car honked. She bid her family goodbye before her aunt Prisca and her mother could insist on meeting the young actor who was picking her up, and jumped into his car.

Simon Gilbert had the matinee idol smoothness that her cousin Ceci adored. His suit was perfectly tailored, his skin tanned to the exact shade of brown the studio found desirable, and his voice was expertly modulated. They shook hands, and she thanked him for escorting her to the party.

"Why, it's arranged, my dear," he said. "No need to thank me."

"All the same, it's nice of you to do it," she said.

Their conversation, as they drove up a winding road toward Miguel Montaner's home in Bel Air, focused mainly on movies they'd both watched and mindless chitchat. Simon Gilbert told her he'd originally started his career doing three-minute Snader Telescriptions with his "gaucho" act before securing a contract with Pacific Pictures.

"Korla Pandit got his break with Snader. So did Liberace," Simon explained. "My work was filler, but I snagged a movie part. And here I am."

"Were you ever nervous shooting your first movie?" she asked.

He laughed. It was a good, full laugh, like his voice. "Yes! I have an ulcer from it. I had to take an Alka-Seltzer on the hour."

Montaner's "cottage" turned out to be a house with a red-tiled roof, surrounded by sycamore trees, at the top of a steep road off Stone Canyon Road. It was more modest-looking than any number of elaborate, garish faux Tudor and French château—inspired monstrosities lining the streets, though inside it exuded the same glamour as any other movie star's abode, and it was packed to the gills with singers, dancers, and actors.

Dan Quiterio had timed their entrance, and when Simon and Vera walked into Montaner's living room the party was in full swing. Several people glanced in their direction, pausing to admire Vera and Simon, including a man in a tan suit with a martini glass who took out a notepad and scribbled something as they walked by him.

They were immediately greeted with a warm hug by the host. Vera had never seen the short man with a receding hairline, but she did recognize the woman standing next to him. She was Marla Bahia and had appeared in several comedies, mainly doing dance numbers. While Montaner was ordinary, even bland-looking, Marla towered over him, an Afro-Brazilian twenty-something beauty in a yellow turban, her arms decked with bracelets. Why, she'd been in musicals with Tito Guízar! There she was now, a couple of paces from Vera.

"May I introduce you to the 'King of the Marimba,' Miguel Montaner?" Simon said as Vera shook the man's hand. "And here is the 'Chica-Chica Girl,' Marla Bahia."

"The ridiculous names they come up with!" Marla said, airily shaking her head.

"At least you're not the 'Singing Gaucho,'" Simon pointed out. "I'm from Buenos Aires. I never even wore a poncho until I moved to Los Angeles."

"Well, 'Chica-Chica Girl' is still silly. It's stupidly repetitive. You want a drink?" Marla asked, pointing toward the next room. "It's impossible to throw a large party in this house, but I think Miguel likes forcing people to feel like they're trapped inside a sardine can."

"Why is that?" Vera asked, as they slipped into a small annex where a curved corner wet bar was studded with tumblers, glasses, and bottles. She could hear music drifting from another room: a live act was under way.

"His theory is that it feels more exclusive. Sometimes there are so many guests they can't even slip inside and must stand outside in the gardens, peeking through the windows!"

"She exaggerates," Miguel said. "What do you want?"

"I don't know. I hardly go to parties," Vera confessed. "A Coke? What would you have?"

Marla laughed and waved to the bartender. "Two gin and tonics!"

After a few minutes, Miguel handed Marla and Vera their drinks. Vera said a polite thank-you, and the four of them drifted into the room with the music. The performers were a duo, a man on the guitar and a woman singing, both of them standing atop a small platform. Marla was correct, there was hardly any space to stand.

"Dan Quiterio says you're beginning *The Seventh Veil of Salome* next month?" Miguel asked.

She nodded, smiling shyly. "I can hardly believe it. It feels so strange to suddenly be starring in a big picture."

"Not much experience?"

"None."

"It was pretty much the same for me. My background is in nightclubs," Marla said. "Miguel also came from the club circuit. He sings, but never even read a script before making his film debut."

"I can't say I'd read a movie script before, either, and on top of that I'd never carry a tune," Vera said. "I'm afraid I'm rather green."

"The studio must have seen something special in you," Simon assured her. "They auditioned half of Hollywood, after all. How do you like Max?"

"He's very professional," Vera said politely.

Someone bumped into Vera, and Marla grabbed her by the elbow and nudged her aside until they wedged themselves next to a small table with an ashtray and a couch, which seemed a strategically sound position to observe the people around them.

"There! That's better," Marla said. "I tell you, if a clown steps on my dress like last time, I'm going to dump my whole drink on his head. The costume department gets furious if one stitch is out of place, but then they encase us in these tight gowns that'll rip at the slightest motion. I like your dress—nice earrings, too."

The man in the tan suit was scribbling again; he looked at Vera, then at Marla. Vera glanced down, then touched her earrings.

"Thank you. Do they have actresses attend many parties like these?" Vera asked.

"Parties. Premieres. Hotel openings. Whatever the publicity department wants," Marla said, sipping her drink. "I'm in an awful musical comedy right this instant, and to spur interest in it they have me here dressed as a banana to be photographed by the press."

"I don't think you look like a banana."

"Ha! You're being nice, but it's either a banana or Tweety Bird. Look at the feathers on the neckline of this dress."

"Who is Tweety Bird? Is she a singer?"

Marla chuckled. "You know, the little yellow cartoon bird that's chased by the cat."

It took her a couple of seconds to grasp what Marla was saying. "Oh! We don't call him that in Mexico," she said nervously. "You must think I'm silly."

"No one's going to quiz you on cartoons. It's fine. I didn't realize at first 'exit' doesn't mean the same as 'éxito.' There I was, staring at a door, wondering why it said it would lead to literal success."

The women laughed. Miguel Montaner and Simon Gilbert had begun an animated conversation with two curly-haired men who looked nearly identical, except one of them carried a ukulele under his arm.

"Who's that?" Vera asked, glancing in the direction of the man in the tan suit with the martini glass, who had drifted to the other side of the room. "He keeps looking at us."

"That is a piranha," Marla said, raising a lofty eyebrow as she sipped her drink. "Ronald Wilson. You know *Confidential* and

those trashy publications that go after movie stars? He writes for
those rags. Calls himself a journalist, but he's really a money-
hungry asshole. He works with this lowlife called Wallace Olrof
who often takes pictures to accompany his stories. He's tried to
smear Simon for ages. It's his hobby."

"Smear how?"

"Last year there was a rumor that Simon had attended certain
parties for men only. You get my meaning? And that at some of
those parties he danced with Orlando Beckett. Ronald hounded
them for weeks. Wallace was practically waiting behind every
bush to snap pictures."

Vera had heard about places in Mexico City where men danced
with men, but this was so quietly whispered that she wouldn't be
able to pinpoint where they took place or what type of people
went to those functions.

"What happened?" she asked.

"Nothing. No one would confirm the story. But it doesn't mean
it wasn't annoying."

"Was there any truth to it?" Vera asked, watching as Orlando
Beckett greeted Simon and his circle of friends. They were laughing.

"Would it scandalize you if there was?" Marla asked, now raising her eyebrow at Vera.

She paused to consider this. Men were not supposed to like
men, that was simply one of those dictums everyone knew. In the
papers and the magazines that peddled crime stories at the newsstands around Mexico City, Vera had spied headlines about raids
of "deviants." Here, in Los Angeles, it was the same, and yet it
seemed unfair, even if Vera's mother and her aunt Prisca would
have thought it scandalous for her to say so.

"They're so beautiful," Vera said softly. "If they were together,
I think . . . I just think love is beautiful, it's the most magnificent
thing there is in the universe."

"Aren't you the romantic! Maybe the last romantic in Hollywood."

She thought, shyly, about the operas that she adored, or the maidens with long hair that Rossetti had painted. How she'd watched with delight as two lovers kissed on the screen and mouthed their dialogue.

"I'm sure that's not true," Vera said, blushing. She took a sip of her drink, cautiously glancing in the journalist's direction. "Do you think he'll write something cruel about Simon tonight?"

"I doubt it. He's probably more interested in me. They went after Ava Gardner and Sammy Davis Jr., claimed they had a fling. You can imagine the result: they're banning her films in the South because of it and MGM is furious. Wilson is fishing for a story about me and a white Southern actor. You can dance samba and they'll clap, but they'll frown when the Black performers think they're the same as the white people."

Before Vera could say anything, a broad-shouldered man with his hair combed straight back over the top of his head had drifted toward them with a wide grin and a loud "Hello!" It was Clifford Collins. He wasn't alone, either. At his elbow there came a platinum blonde whom Vera also recognized: Donna Fowler. They were both experienced actors who had appeared together in a couple of films. Although Vera had spied Orlando Beckett around the lot from afar, until now she had not laid eyes on Clifford Collins, who would play the role of Salome's Roman suitor.

"Why, if it isn't the 'Chica-Chica Girl'!" Collins said.

"Hello, Clifford. Nice to see you," Marla said, politely but without warmth.

"And who do we have here? The Princess in the Tower! Have the studio heads really let their captive out of the dungeon? This is the first time I've seen you anywhere. You're more guarded than Fort Knox, darling."

Collins extended a hand, and Vera shook it. "I'm glad to meet you, Mr. Collins."

"Clifford," he said, throwing her a roguish grin. People said Collins had a resemblance to Clark Gable, but Vera thought he looked more like Errol Flynn before excess began to mar the Australian actor's face. He wasn't exactly the type she'd picture in the role of a Roman soldier—there was something much too brash and modern about him—but he was a big star. "Or Cliff will do. What are you gals drinking?"

"Gin and tonics," Vera said, showing him her glass.

"But you've hardly had a sip," he pointed out. In his left hand he had an almost empty glass. Donna Fowler also had a glass, which she finished drinking and set aside on a table.

"I'm not much of a drinker."

"Cliff will be terribly disappointed. He likes a girl who can hold her liquor," Donna said.

"I'm so clumsy. I'm also glad to meet you, Miss Fowler. I'm Vera Larios. Mr. Collins and I are going to be in *The Seventh Veil of Salome* together," she said, extending her hand in the blonde's direction.

The woman shook her hand limply and smiled. "I know you, darling. I read that story your publicity guy placed in the papers this month. You're supposed to be the new face of Hollywood. I suppose ethnic types are quite popular right now. Who's that Puerto Rican they have at 20th Century Fox who's going to be in *The King and I*? And there was that little Mexican who was in *Vera Cruz*? Sara Something," Donna said distractedly.

"Sara Montiel. But she's Spanish," Vera replied.

"Isn't it the same?"

"It's not the same being Mexican as being Spanish, no. It's like saying France and England are duplicates."

"But you are a Mexican?"

"Yes. My mother's family is from Los Mochis, my father—"

"I was in Mexico last year," Clifford said. "Went fishing. Caught a huge marlin. The women there are awfully pretty. You're gorgeous, my dear. What did you do before coming to Hollywood?" he asked, so quickly that Vera didn't quite know how to answer.

"I . . . well—"

"You know what I find funny?" Donna asked loudly. "It's how Mexican girls stand. They're always with their backs very straight and their tits pushed out. Why do you think that is?"

As if to illustrate her point, Donna pointed at Vera's bosom and laughed. Vera blushed, her cheeks warm with humiliation. She couldn't even think what to say. All she could do was stare at the woman.

Marla raised an arm, as if waving to someone. "Excuse us, I think Simon is looking for us."

Marla grabbed Vera's wrist and pulled her away, until they reached a hallway and Vera let out her breath. Her hands were trembling. She'd seldom felt so low, so mortified.

"I forgot to warn you about the other piranhas," Marla said.

Vera shook her head and hugged her arms. "That was cold and cruel. Why . . . why was she like that?"

"Donna is a racist pig. She's not the only one, either. Besides, Clifford's a womanizer. She takes it out on the girls, not on him."

"I don't even know him!"

"But you're going to be in a picture together. She probably thinks he'll go after you."

"Aren't they dating?"

"For five years. And he still won't propose. That's also what probably has her seething. That and the fact that they wouldn't let her audition for the part of Salome, even when her boyfriend is the romantic lead."

"They didn't? Really?"

"No! The director says an ironing board has more acting skills. I heard it from Isadora Christie," Marla said mischievously.

Vera pressed a hand against her mouth to muffle her laugh.

"Thanks for that," she said. "It'll sound silly, but I saw you in pictures when I went to the movies with my sister. We tried to copy your dance numbers after we were back in our room and I always said you had to be nice in person. And it's true."

Marla smiled. "You're a nice girl, Vera. Stay like that. Now let's dance with one of those hunky actors who were looking in our direction," Marla said, and they headed back into the room.

Vera did dance, partnering first with Simon Gilbert, then with the twin who didn't have a ukulele, as well as several other men.

She joined a conga line when Marla pulled her in. Eventually, she drifted outside and stood next to a large pond covered with a tapestry of water lilies. The music drifted through the open windows. The vibrant conga had given way to the slow, moody voice of a woman singing "Isn't It Romantic?"

Vera pressed her back against a tree, humming the tune and looking up at the silvery moon glimpsed through the branches.

A splash of water and a male voice made her turn toward the pond. "Damn!"

"Are you okay?" she asked.

A young man in a white jacket and a pale blue shirt open at the neck looked at her and smiled nervously. "I dropped my lighter. I can't see a thing with all these plants floating in the water."

Vera drifted closer to him and knelt by the pond. It was dark in this part of the garden and it was indeed difficult to discern anything, but she reached into the water and brushed the water lilies aside. She was rewarded with a glint of metal in the dark and pulled out the lighter and handed it to the man.

"Now to see if I can get it to work again," he said, holding the lighter upside down.

He stepped toward the tree where Vera had been lounging and dragged the lighter against the bark with quick strokes until there was a spark and a flame bloomed.

"Eureka," Vera said.

"Indeed," he agreed and laughed. "Do you want a cigarette?"

"No, thank you."

He produced a cigarette and pressed its tip against the flame of his lighter. The moonlight, filtering through the tree branches, showed her his face clearly for the first time. He was young and good-looking, and there was something open and friendly in his eyes.

"Are you a model or an actress?" he asked. "Everyone here seems to be one or the other."

"An actress. I'm in a movie that's going to start shooting soon. A Biblical epic."

"Which one?"

"*The Seventh Veil of Salome.*"

"I know a girl who's in that," he said. "She's one of the extras. It sounds like it's going to be a huge production with big sets and a large cast. Have you been in many big movies?"

"It's my first film."

"Congratulations! I'm Jay Rutland, by the way."

"Vera Larios," she said. Her hand was still wet from the pond, so she nodded at him, and he nodded back. "Are you an actor?"

"I'm a musician. Kind of. I have a lead about a gig at the Captain's Table on La Cienega, but who knows."

"What instrument do you play?"

"Piano. The gig at the Captain's Table would be for a jazz trio," he said, stretching up an arm and holding on to a branch. "It's hard landing a steady anything. Too many good musicians, all angling for the major clubs."

Vera placed her hands behind her back and looked up at him. "Maybe you'll get a break soon and I'll see your name in the papers."

"Wouldn't that be something?"

He laughed amicably. The moonlight struck his face like a Fresnel light, haloing him, and giving him an otherworldly air. A breeze made the leaves rustle, and the music drifting from the house was a dreamy murmur. Neither of them said a word.

"Vera!" someone yelled.

She turned her head. It was Dan Quiterio, pointing to the house.

"That's the studio's publicist," she said. "I have to run."

"It was nice meeting you. I'll look for your name in the papers, and you look for mine, okay?"

"Yes," she said.

"Good luck."

She hurried back toward the house. Dan greeted her with a swift hello, said something about the studio photographer needing her, and she turned around, one quick motion, to look back at the young man under the tree. He had stepped forward, also heading toward the house, hands in his pockets, cigarette dangling from a corner of his mouth. His eyes were on her, and he smiled in good-bye.

She dallied for a few seconds while Dan kept walking and talking. She smiled, feeling lightheaded, her fingers brushing the beads that decorated the bodice of her dress. Then, she picked up the hem of her skirt and climbed up the half dozen steps that led to the back porch.

Salome

WATER DRIPPED down a section of one of the walls of the interior courtyard, like a make-believe waterfall, and the columns here were painted a dark green, as if to imitate the vegetation of a lush oasis. Salome leaned against one of these columns, observing the courtyard with its floor of yellow and purple tiles from a balcony.

Her cousin Agrippa was arriving a day ahead of the proconsul. That Agrippa had ventured on his own could be interpreted as a discourtesy, for it added wrinkles to the greeting protocol, or it could be a kindness if he had special information to relay to his family. It was, either way, exactly the kind of behavior Salome expected of her cousin. He caused tremors wherever he walked.

"Will he be housed in the guest quarters next to the proconsul or the family quarters?" Salome asked her mother as they watched Agrippa stroll across the courtyard in the company of Josephus. He had only a minimal entourage consisting of two slaves. The rest of his servants and belongings would no doubt be arriving the next day.

"He ought to stay with Lucius Vitellius and his men, seeing as he is practically a foreigner. It is disgraceful," Herodias said.

From the angle where Salome stood, she could not see her cousin's face, but he was dressed in the Roman mode, with a toga. One might have expected him to wear different attire before entering the tetrarch's palace. There was something either bold or naïve about his choice. More likely the former. He probably wished to remind his family of his Roman connections.

"Rome raised our family to power," Salome said.

"Herod the Great understood how this game is played. One cannot bow too eagerly to either the Romans or the Jews."

"Will we be hosting him this afternoon?"

"Josephus has instructions to show him his rooms," her mother said. "Later, the tetrarch and I will offer him a gift of wine and honey."

"And I?"

"You will be busy practicing on the harp."

Salome frowned. Her mother wished to control the meeting and keep Salome from learning what was said. This did not surprise her, but it did irritate her. "Why can't I greet him? He is my kin, too," she said.

"The tetrarch might be upset with Agrippa. Your presence might enflame his temper even further."

"You only wish to have me at court when I am of use to you."

"You do not yet understand the ways of men, Salome."

"I understand the tetrarch well enough."

Herodias narrowed her eyes at Salome's words, but she did not add anything else.

Salome spent the afternoon practicing the harp in her room, as her mother had ordered, but when the hour of night was near, she went to the courtyard with the waterfall. She walked by the potted palm trees in the company of her handmaidens and sat on a bench close to the waterfall.

Shortly after, Agrippa arrived. He was once again in the company of his two slaves and still dressed in Roman garb.

Agrippa was but a couple of years older than Salome. When she had been sent to her aunt's house, he had still been a boy whose voice had yet to break, a devilishly smart child who liked to play pranks on his cousin and pinch her arms when she irritated him. He had turned into a sophisticated-looking man, his cheekbones sharp, his mouth set into a cool smile.

They said he looked like his father, that genial, handsome man who had once been so beloved by Herod the Great that he thought of him as a son, and thus enraged Herod Antipas.

"Salome, it has been long since I last beheld you. Won't you show your cousin your face?"

He addressed her in Latin, rather than Greek, which was the common tongue of the court. Her Latin was perfectly acceptable, as were her Hebrew and Aramaic, but she thought this choice on his part was another annoying reminder of his allegiances. Agrippa was almost entirely Roman, despite his birth family. Instead of replying in Latin, she therefore stuck to Greek.

"Dear cousin, it has indeed been long," she said, removing the wispy bejeweled veil she seldom donned at court. That she had worn it that evening had been for the sake of striking a more dramatic pose, just as she had let herself be seen in the courtyard, knowing one of his slaves would inform his master that his cousin was nearby. The courtyard, after all, was not far from his quarters.

"You are as lovely as ever," he said diplomatically, switching to Greek.

"You mean as when you teased me and called me skin and bones?"

"Did I, truly?"

"You made me eat mud cakes. You said you'd cooked them yourself. Then you said if I didn't eat them, I'd be a coward. When I had a stomachache, you denied it was your fault. You were a convincing performer."

"What a thoughtless boy I was. But I seem to remember that once or twice, when we dueled with wooden sticks, you cruelly poked me in the belly and even once hit me on the head."

"If you hadn't fed me mud cakes, perhaps I might have been sweeter."

"Most gracious cousin, a vast amount of your appeal was always your delicate cruelty. Shall we walk together?" he asked.

Salome motioned to her handmaidens, bidding them to scatter away. They would remain nearby, in the shadow of the pillars, but out of sight. Agrippa's slaves were similarly dismissed.

She rested her hand on her cousin's arm as they walked. "I was distraught when your mother said you couldn't greet me today," he said. "I so desired to see you."

"Why? Did you wish to feed me mud cakes?"

"My, you do carry a grudge, don't you? But I won't complain. The anger seems to burnish your eyes with a special glaze. You are beautiful, Salome."

Despite his trite words, she knew at least this sentiment was true. When she removed the veil, a satisfied smirk had streaked his face. One should not underestimate the power of beauty. Her uncle had fought a war for the woman he coveted.

"I would have imagined they'd taught you better ways to praise a woman at court, Agrippa," she said. "No matter, tell me, has your journey been pleasant?"

"And I would have thought they'd showed you how to fish for information in a more efficient manner, Salome," he replied. "I doubt that you are standing here in such a delicious blue silk dress simply because you felt bored, or that you are terribly interested in knowing about how my mount lost a hipposandal before reaching the palace."

"Very well," she said. "What did you discuss with my uncle and my mother?"

"Not much. I told them my mother sends her greetings. She also indicates it is time I took a wife and proposes that we be married."

"They say you have debts from picking the wrong gladiator at the circus."

And debts from living an existence so lavish people wondered if Agrippa thought himself one of the emperor's children. She'd heard he played dice with Drusus, attended the chariot races with Claudius, and wasted his money on elaborate feasts for both. They even said he paid for Caligula's whores at the best brothels in Rome.

"Every young man has debts."

"But your debts are extravagant. They offend our uncle. The tetrarch, he has no doubt turned you down," Salome said with a satisfied smirk.

"He has not."

This gave Salome pause. She looked up at her cousin in surprise.

"He demands a payment. An impossibly high one. Since my mother has not funded his useless war and the construction of his monstrous new city, he asks to draw blood in this manner."

"He asks for a dowry. Then he insults you and denies you at the same time," Salome concluded. She wondered whether her mother might now press for a marriage with Marcellus.

"At his peril. The emperor is displeased."

"Why?"

"I imagine you already know why. The city he has built in his honor? It is a costly failed venture. The Jews despise it."

The tetrarch, hoping to imitate his father, Herod the Great, had launched a grand construction project and built a new city and named it after the emperor. But Tiberias was built atop a cemetery, and the pious Jews refused to settle there. Herod had been too bold.

"Then is it that and that alone which has turned the emperor away from the tetrarch?" she asked.

"The war with King Aretas is a thorn in the tetrarch's side."

King Aretas, lord of the rock-cut city of Petra, would never forget the way Herod Antipas had slighted him, yet Salome frowned. "It has been this way for a long time. There must be something else. What?" she asked as Agrippa rested lazily against a column.

"You'll know tomorrow, once Proconsul Vitellius arrives. There is to be a small reception for all of us, I'm told."

"Don't be silly. Tell me today."

"I'm not used to doling out information without payment. I've told you more already than I told our uncle," he said, extending a hand and catching her wrist so that he might pull her closer to him.

"I'm not used to being denied," she said, granting him a fetching smile, cocking her head in the way that made Marcellus and many other youths stare in wonder.

"How funny. I'm the one who usually says that," Agrippa replied and tipped her chin up. "Kiss me twice and I'll give you an answer."

"I'm no fool; tell me and I'll kiss you."

"No," he said with an aloofness that made her realize he wasn't interested in kissing her. He was merely measuring her reaction, hoping perhaps a maidenly blush would color her cheeks. If she'd been attracted to him, he might have used this in his favor.

She could see why Emperor Tiberius and his children had found the young man pleasing. He had a proud, patrician bearing and a delicious natural cunning. Yet this did little to enflame her. She had no desire for anyone except the beautiful prophet.

She stared Agrippa in the eye, and he stared back at her, both of them scrutinizing the other. Agrippa, seized with what was a mixture of quiet admiration and perhaps exasperation, let out a laugh.

"I should know better than to duel with you, lovely one. You're still good at swinging a stick. Wear another blue dress tomorrow. Vitellius will be much impressed when you remove your pretty veil."

"Good evening, beloved cousin," Salome said and stepped away from him, motioning to the handmaidens who were waiting quietly in the shadows of the courtyard.

Vera

THE COMMISSARY was a medley of strange sights and sounds, as cowboys and odalisques chatted with one another and commandeered tables. There were foods that Vera had never tasted before—roast beef and gravy, macaroni and cheese—next to piles of salad and baked potatoes. Mounds of shimmering Jell-O provided a touch of color. The commissary was decorated like a French café, with starched white tablecloths and paintings of the studio's biggest stars lining the walls.

This, Vera's publicist had said, was gossip central, and everyone gathered in flocks. Publicists at one table, supporting players at another, and so on.

Vera wasn't sure which table she should sit at and she stood, helplessly looking around, until Marla waved at her. Vera moved toward her, realizing with a sigh of relief that Marla was sitting with Simon Gilbert. That made two people she knew. The third person at the table was a skinny twenty-something man in a rumpled suit wearing a pair of round glasses and working on a crossword.

"You made it!" Marla said. "A little bird told me this is your first day on set."

"Technically yes, but I'm not shooting today," Vera said. "They have a big crowd scene scheduled."

"Well, at least it gives you an excuse to explore the wonderful cuisine of the studio. What are you having?"

"Ah . . . roast beef, I suppose," Vera said, looking down at her plate. She had blurted the first thing that came to mind when it was her turn to order.

Simon made a face. Vera looked at him. "What?"

"The roast beef is an abomination," the man with the crossword puzzle said, "as is most food on the lot. Nothing's kosher, either. That's why I bring my lunch. This place is worse than a Christmas at Grossinger's."

Vera noticed that the man indeed had a brown paper bag next to him, presumably containing his lunch.

"Kosher! Since when do you care about that? Every three weeks you're at Scandia's having smoked pork chop," Simon said.

"Every three weeks the studio wants rewrites on one idiotic script or another. And I only go there if you pick up the tab," the man said with a shrug. "If I were you, I'd stick with the Jell-O. It's unlikely they can make that as tasteless as everything else."

"You're a culinary snob."

"Dear Simon, I don't like to eat things I can't recognize."

"You can't recognize mashed potatoes?"

"I wouldn't give those to a chazzer," the writer said dryly. "You know what I'd really like? For the studio to put me up at the Marmont. They have a good, hygienic kitchen."

"Why would they put you up there when you live in town?" Simon said and rolled his eyes. "Can't you walk two blocks to get a burger? There's a diner right down your street."

"I saw a roach run across the floor there one day. I'm telling you, Vera, bring your sandwich. Most places are filthy. Poke your head into a kitchen and witness the culinary depravity. Canter's on Fairfax is the only place in town to get a decent bagel, and I trust the Tick Tock Tea Room. Other restaurants, you'll grow a tapeworm a mile long in your guts."

"You're going to scare the girl off," Marla said, shaking her head. "Vera, meet Joe Kantor. He's the screenwriter of *The Seventh Veil of Salome* and an absolute whiner."

"The latest screenwriter," the man said, pushing his glasses up the bridge of his nose with his index finger as he scribbled on his newspaper. "If I'd had this gig from the beginning, we wouldn't be in this mess. They're making me write more lines for Agrippa."

"No surprise. Vaughn Selzer is going to go big this year," Simon said.

"Maybe, but you can't trust theater actors. Their training is always wrong for film. I suppose I'll have to think of an exciting speech for him in the third act and do it fast."

"I haven't read the ending yet," Vera said. "The script I have is missing those pages. It says I dance, and then there's a blank page."

"That's still a work in progress," Joe said. "The censors, you see, are having a fit over a few lines. Although they've missed a whole lot of subtext."

"You're always railing against the code," Simon said with a sigh.

"Why shouldn't I? Why should anti-Semitic trash like Joseph Breen be allowed to mark my pages with his little blue pencil?"

"Breen's not even working there anymore."

"Breen, Shurlock, it's the same. All the people at the PCA are schmucks."

"There's no way around them."

"I know that," Joe grumbled.

"What lines are the censors objecting to?" Vera asked.

"Sexy ones. It's always the sex that gets noticed. You can have Christ nailed on the cross and bleeding like a hemophiliac and they won't mind, but give them one good line about the blackness of your abyssal eyes and they'll start barking like rabid dogs." The writer paused, looking at Vera intently. "You do have very pretty eyes. I should use that line." The writer unscrewed a thermos and poured himself what looked like tea. "Ah, almati, I see your Roman general approaching."

Vera sat up straight as Clifford Collins stopped next to their table. He was indeed dressed in period garb, attired as a Roman, with a sword at his waist. Marla had told her they'd shrunk Marlon Brando's undershirts so they'd cling more tightly to his body, and Vera suspected the costume department had taken similar steps with Clifford Collins's wardrobe. His bronze-colored cuirass was perfectly sculpted and showed an idealized muscular chest ornamented with the head of a horse.

"There you are! I've been looking for you all morning," he said, smiling at her.

"I'm sorry, I didn't know," Vera said. "Does Mr. Niemann need me?"

"It's nothing work related. I want to take you to Ciro's this weekend. Eight, Saturday."

She disliked the way he spoke, with a certainty that indicated he would not be rebuffed. His matinee idol smile struck her as too bright, too hard, and although she felt shy replying, Vera managed to shake her head.

"All my appearances have to be approved by the press office."

"You won't have any trouble with the press office. Saturday at eight."

"Still, I'll have to check with the press office and see about it," she said firmly.

The smile was eclipsed. He frowned. "I don't think that's necessary."

"The girl's trying to follow protocol," Simon said. "She doesn't want Danny Q giving her grief. Come on, Collins, you know how the publicity folks get when anyone goes over their heads."

"Are you working for the press department now, Gaucho Boy?" Clifford asked, glaring at Simon.

Simon leaned back in his chair and smiled at Clifford. "I'm repeating what I was told. Danny Q wants to build publicity for my role in *Valor and Glory*, and he thinks featuring me and Vera together at clubs will help with that. It'll push her name out there, too."

"*Valor and Glory*," Clifford said, his hand resting heavily on the pommel of his prop sword. "Fine, then laugh and enjoy your lunch. I'll see you around the lot, Vera."

"You don't want to sit down and have a bite?" Simon asked innocently. "The Jell-O is top-notch today."

"I've lost my appetite," Clifford muttered.

When the actor had walked away, Simon broke into laughter and so did Joe. Marla rolled her eyes at the men.

"I didn't understand the joke," Vera said.

"Simon was picked over Clifford for *Valor and Glory*, and Simon here has been having fun reminding him of that fact," Marla said dryly. "He's still sore about that and you know it."

"Marla, he's an idiot. A couple of half-decent movies dressed as a pirate, and the man thinks he's Mr. Irresistible. He's not," Simon said dismissively. "He's a discount Casanova."

"Or Herod, waiting for the princess to dance for him. A no-goodnik, at any rate," Joe said. He scribbled a few letters and looked intently at his crossword.

"Whatever he thinks he is, he's got pull, and you'd be smart not to be prancing and showing off in front of him," Marla warned Simon.

"You dislike him as much as I do."

"But I don't show it like you do," Marla said, and she pulled the corners of her mouth into a smile. "Show your teeth and grin, smear a bit of Vaseline to make that smile stick. That's the way it's done."

"The Singing Gaucho chuckles at danger," Simon said, and he took a straw, moving it as if he were handling a tiny sword while Marla rolled her eyes at him.

"Don't be like him, Vera," Marla said with a sigh. "He's a child."

*

SHE TOOK her cousin Cecilia to the movies. Ceci reminded Vera of her sister. Before Lumi married, the girls had shared secrets late at night and walked around the city arm in arm. But now that Lumi had a child and a husband, there was distance between them. Vera supposed it was natural that Lumi acquire new responsibilities, but she also feared something fundamental had shifted between them, even before Vera had departed for Hollywood.

Cousin Ceci was excited about the outing because she normally had to go with her brother, and they didn't like the same movies. He'd drag Ceci to a Western when Ceci wanted to watch a romantic film. Vera took her cousin to the show she wanted to see, and Ceci was delighted by the prospect of having a soda after the film. Aunt Prisca didn't think Ceci should be at those teenage hangouts, sitting in a red plastic booth or tossing coins into jukeboxes.

Everything was swell, as Ceci liked to say, until they stepped out of the soda joint. A couple of towheaded young men stared at them with interest.

"Hello, good-looking!" one of them said. "Where are the two of you headed?"

Vera did not reply. She pulled Ceci with her, silently urging her to walk faster. The two boys laughed.

"Brownie, where you going?" one of them asked.

They turned the corner and moved at a brisk pace. Behind them, the man kept saying ridiculous, offensive words, and all they could do was keep walking. Finally, Vera stopped under the awning of a hat shop and looked behind them. The men had left.

"Vera, are you okay?" Ceci whispered.

"I'm fine," Vera said. She took out a handkerchief and dabbed at the corners of her eyes.

She'd had men catcall her back in Mexico City, but this seemed worse. Rawer. A double affront.

"They're pigs," she said, looking again down the street to make sure the boys were not lurking nearby. "How dare they?"

"Please don't tell my mom about this, Vera! She'll make us bring my brother next time. Or she'll say we didn't dress proper. She'll be so mad!"

"Dress proper? I'm wearing a skirt and a blouse, you're—"

"She'll say it's too tight a skirt."

"It's not any tighter than any other skirt," Vera said, gesturing at the women that were walking by them.

"But when you're a Mexican girl . . ."

When you were a Mexican girl everything was a come-on, Vera thought, even though Ceci hadn't said it. The way you walked, the way you breathed became an invitation. She bit her lower lip and clutched her purse tight.

"They'll never let us out again!"

"Hush, I'm not going to tell her," Vera assured her cousin.

Ceci sighed with relief.

*

SHE COULD hear her brothers playing in the background while her father spoke. The telephone couldn't quite capture the warmth of his voice, yet she smiled as he told her about his week. Then he asked to speak to her mother, and Vera passed the phone. Her mother didn't like Vera talking to her father because it was expensive to call long distance, but also because he was beginning to press her mother about her return home. Vera's mother kept saying she needed to be around to manage their daughter's career, while her father thought Vera could manage on her own.

Vera sat in the living room while her mother muttered and shook her head and talked about seizing the moment. When the bell rang, her mother used it as an excuse to hang up.

Vera sat on the couch, carefully going over her lines.

"But it's darling!" her mother said.

Vera looked up. Her mother walked into the living room with a huge arrangement of pink roses.

Vera's cousin, who had been sitting by Vera's feet leafing through a magazine, immediately raised her head, curious. Her aunt also poked her head from the kitchen.

"Who's it from?" cousin Ceci asked.

Vera's mother placed the flowers down on a table and opened the card. "Clifford Collins," she read out loud and looked at Vera with delight. "A major star!"

"Wow, he's sending you flowers," Ceci said.

Vera stood up; she took the card and carefully read it. It said: *Talked to the press office and they think Ciro's would be perfect for a date. Saturday at 8, Clifford Collins.*

Vera tucked the card back in its small envelope and stared at the roses while her mother began wondering what dress she might wear on such an occasion. She thought back to the boys who had catcalled her.

*

THE TRIUMVIRATE of Los Angeles nightclubs consisted of the Mocambo, the Trocadero, and Ciro's, all sitting on a stretch of Sunset Strip favored by the wealthy and famous.

Everyone was beautiful at Ciro's, from the hatcheck girls who handled the mink coats and other embellishments the patrons lugged around—Yvonne De Carlo traveled with her pet monkey—to the cigarette girls in their short skirts, to the restaurant's official photographers, and finally the guests.

Their beauty was enhanced by the soft peach light, which the club owner had picked to ensure a flattering glow illuminated the room, but there were plenty of natural and artificial good looks to go around. Well-coiffed movie stars and aspiring starlets, decked in ermine and diamonds, or more modest paste jewelry, frequented the 3,000-square-foot club and its small dance floor, ensuring a steady supply of pretty faces and dashing profiles.

Ciro's was designed for the famous to be observed: its dramatic long flight of stairs led down to the tables and the dance floor, allowing everyone below a look at arriving guests. Hedy Lamarr stepped down those stairs, in a cape that swept to the floor, with a diamond pasted to her forehead. Lana Turner, in clingy dresses, liked to walk in with a long stole wrapped around her shoulders.

As Vera walked on the arm of Clifford Collins, attired in a simple yet elegant black dress with a square neckline and a fitted waist, she was aware of the glances in their direction and kept a calm smile plastered on her face even as her heart drummed erratically inside her chest.

Marla had told her Clifford Collins was a big wolf, top grade, but so far he'd hardly spoken a word to her, too busy nodding and smiling at the people around them as they made their way to their table. Thrice he'd paused to talk to someone, introducing Vera as "the newest discovery at Pacific," then continued his march, which, Vera thought, resembled a Roman triumph.

They were ushered toward a booth, and when Vera sat down

and looked around, she was struck by the scent of perfume and cigarettes, the sight of women throwing their heads back and laughing, the purr of voices washing over her. A man, not far from their table, winked at Vera, and she quickly busied herself with the menu. She felt, much as she had at Miguel's birthday party, unprepared for the occasion.

"You seem to know everyone here, Mr. Collins," she said at last, placing her menu down.

"Most Bankable Actor as voted by *Screen Magazine* two years in a row," he told her. "But call me Clifford. I can't have my co-star calling me 'Mister' anything."

"That's an impressive achievement, Clifford. Did you always want to be an actor?"

"I wanted to sail yachts and get dates with pretty girls. Being on the covers of magazines helps one obtain both without having to study arithmetic and pursue a boring degree. By the way," he said, placing both elbows on the table and smiling as he leaned forward, "you made me grovel before Dressler to obtain this date with you. Girls normally like to be photographed with me, you know?"

She was aware Clifford Collins had essentially demanded to go on a date with her. Dan Quiterio had sounded a little affronted when he told Vera that this "date" was mandatory, that Mr. Dressler had asked for her specifically to accompany Mr. Collins.

Vera didn't know if Dressler was accustomed to issuing such edicts in the name of his most profitable stars, but she understood that there was no exit clause for her and had accepted the invitation as courteously as she could. She didn't like the way Clifford was bringing it up. It made her feel ashamed, as though he'd purchased a meal and ordered it delivered to his room.

"I was told I should focus on my role," Vera said. "I also thought your girlfriend might object to any dates."

"Who? Donna?" He laughed. "Look, Donna and I have an arrangement. We obtain a lot of column inches when we are together. That's what being here is all about. Tomorrow they'll write about you and me, and it'll sell papers."

"You only want to go out with me as a publicity stunt?"

"No, darling: the other way around," he said, catching her hand between his own.

A waiter approached them, asked for their order, and she slid her hand away. Clifford knew what he wanted, barely glancing at the menu as he spoke, while Vera asked for suggestions. Once the waiter departed, Clifford lit a cigarette, and Vera sipped her mineral water.

"The trick is to play the publicity card all the time," Clifford said. "People can become famous with a single photograph or three minutes on camera. Learn how it works and you should be able to make a career out of it. Especially with your looks. Donna is not wrong: ethnic types are all the rage right now."

"It's a little demeaning when you say it like that."

"What? Ethnic? Darling, you sure as hell don't look like a good, decent, all-American gal," he said. "No, you're a bewitching little—"

"Girl who stands with her tits sticking out?" she asked.

Clifford smiled and shook his head. "Now, don't be offended. I'm saying you're no Grace Kelly. Turhan Bey is no Gary Cooper, and he does fine. You have to know your angle."

"And your column inches, I suppose. I thought the hard part was learning the lines."

"That's the easy part. Max said you did a bit of theater in school."

"Yes, and afterward an amateur play," she said.

"Well, I bet you at the end of the play the boys in the audience were not remembering your lines, but your strut."

Again, she thought of the boys who had catcalled her and held her chin up proudly. "I never asked them."

"No need. I'm telling you. You have that sashay only the Latina girls have, the swinging hips. It's a gold mine, even if you can't say 'howdy' without tripping over the words."

"But I don't trip over the words, Mr. Collins," she said coolly.

"Hypothetically, even if you couldn't," he told her, giving her a wink. "Everyone's saying you're one of Max's stunt castings so he can get more press. A brilliant new discovery! A diamond in the rough! But there's nothing wrong with stunts, darling. Where would we be without the machinations and publicity games of the studios, hmm?"

"I suppose we'd be brushing up on our arithmetic."

He laughed at that and clinked his glass with her own. The conversation switched, thankfully, from her suitability as an exotic import to other topics, and although Vera never felt truly comfortable sitting with Clifford, she at least found herself less on edge. In the middle of the evening a photographer approached their table and snapped a picture of them, as Clifford had said would happen, and Vera held her smile in place.

"Stick with me, darling, and you'll do all right," Clifford told her and again clutched her hand once the photographer turned from them. Although she slid her hand away, Vera was sure he would soon be grabbing her again. She thought it was as the screenwriter had told her: Clifford Collins was waiting for Salome to dance for him.

Kenneth "Kent" Shaw

GOD, YES, I knew all sorts of folks back then, because I was playing the club circuit around Los Angeles, and that requires an enormous amount of socializing. It also requires stamina, and I'm not saying it as an excuse, but one big reason why I got hooked on dope was because it helped me keep playing. It doesn't help in the long run, though. By the end of the decade my ass was like a pincushion from shooting up and I was still a broke trumpet player trying to land a steady thing.

Anyhow, I heard about Benny through the club circuit. He knew lots of musicians, lots of actor types. I think that's how he first bumped into Nancy. An actor was buying dope off him, and Nancy was tagging along. Something like that.

By the time I met Benny, it seemed like they had been an item for a long time. They had a funny dynamic, to say the least. They brawled. They exploded. They engaged in full-on war. Nancy would slap Benny, he'd twist her arm, then she'd call him names and he'd reciprocate with an equally colorful list of insults. Looking at them when they were like that, you'd think they despised each other.

Nevertheless, Benny was smitten with her. Nancy seemed much cooler toward Benny. I think he had this idea that he could make her love him. That if only he tried hard enough, Nancy would love him back. He told me she was the only gal for him. He wanted to marry her, which was nuts because Benny certainly wasn't the only guy for Nancy. Half the time she was going around with other men behind his back, and the other half she did it right in his face.

The thing is, if Nancy had loved Benny back, if she'd agreed to marry him and buy a house with a white picket fence around it, Benny would have lost interest quickly. It was the thrill of the chase that had him hooked, and maybe it was also the idea he could reform Nancy. That he could somehow change that fast-living girl into something close to a nice gal.

But there was no way Nancy was ever going to be the nice girl next door. She had discord in her bones. She loved to tease Benny, loved to make him jealous, loved it when he made a scene and lost control. Then she'd berate him for it.

She'd tell him to fuck off, or maybe he'd tell her to get lost. Then two weeks later they'd be sitting cozy together.

Benny despised Jay Rutland. I didn't tell him that Nancy was seeing Jay, but Benny found out anyway, and he was in a foul mood for weeks. It didn't bother him that Nancy slept around. He was used to it. It was the fact it was Jay. He felt threatened. Jay's money and class were immensely appealing to Nancy, and Benny knew that.

Nancy loved fine things, and Jay was exceedingly fine. Top-notch.

Nancy and Jay. Damn.

I did warn Jay that Nancy was bad news. He laughed it off and told me Nancy was fun. Which, granted, she could be. She was quite a looker. But underneath it all there was something ugly and mean, and you really didn't want to get too close to her. You especially didn't want to cross Nancy Hartley. God help the person who incurred her wrath.

Nancy

IT WAS the first week. The first week Nancy had to watch as Vera Larios, dressed in her Salome costume, pranced around the set. The first week Nancy had to hear her declaim lines with her faint accent, staring around with her lost eyes. The first week of people murmuring "Miss Larios" as the spotlights were angled to best flatter the dark-haired girl's swarthy complexion.

It should have been Nancy with the dressing room, with the makeup and the assistants fawning over her. She had pictured herself in that costume, pictured herself talking to that director, she had dreamed and planned and hoped, only to end up standing next to a crop of extras, staring at a girl, newly arrived in Los Angeles, stumbling her way through a set.

"Her screen test wasn't even good," she told Cathy as they ate together in the commissary. "Pierce told me they showed it without sound to the studio heads."

"Why would they do that?" Cathy asked.

"Because of her voice. Because of her accent."

"She does sound a little funny."

"Try a lot."

"Clifford Collins is all over her," Cathy said, looking in the direction of a distant table where Vera sat. Collins was standing next to her, in his Roman costume, chatting her up.

It should have been Nancy at that table; it should have been

Clifford Collins talking to her; it should have been her movie and her first major role. She was Salome! Beautiful, cruel, ruinous Salome. Why, the dance alone should have assured her the part! Nancy could dance. All those early lessons, all that training, had not gone to waste. She hadn't been another Shirley Temple, but that didn't mean she couldn't be a star. She had the face and she had the drive and damn it, that should have cinched it for her.

It was a first week of hell, and even though the weekend was supposed to bring Nancy a respite, even though Jay's pool awaited her, tantalizingly cool for a late afternoon dip, even then Vera Larios managed to ruin it all.

Jay was looking through his record collection and humming to himself while Nancy rested on the couch, smoking a cigarette and lazily flipping the pages of the paper, when she chanced upon a photo of Clifford Collins and Vera Larios sitting in a booth at Ciro's.

Nancy sat up straight, her breath so hot it scalded her. It was bad enough that she had to watch that cheap tart walking around the studio lot, but now there was the paper, loudly proclaiming the attractiveness of Clifford Collins's date and reminding readers that soon they would be able to enjoy her on the big screen, in the role of Salome.

"The little bitch," Nancy said, loud enough for Jay to turn his head.

"Sorry?"

"That actress. Vera Larios," she said, tossing the newspaper aside. "You'd think Clifford Collins would want to have a prettier date. She has a face like a tortilla, all flat."

"That's rather mean."

"She's insufferable! You should see her on the set. She acts like she's above everyone else, and she hasn't even shot her first film yet."

Jay picked up the paper, glancing at the page she'd been looking at, then unfolding it. His eyes flew over the picture's caption.

"She seemed pleasant when I met her," he said. His voice was soft and amiable. Something about that softness made Nancy immediately rear up.

"When did you meet her?" she asked.

"The other day at Miguel Montaner's party," he said. An easy, innocent retort that nevertheless prickled her ears.

Miguel Montaner, who was in movies. She pictured Jay in one of his expensive jackets, chatting up and dancing with pretty girls, all charm and wit. Or else telling jokes to other young men, maybe even playing the piano for the guests.

Nancy had never been invited to one of those parties, the kind that columnists wrote about in the magazines, nor did she venture into clubs on the arms of movie stars, like Vera Larios did. But Jay Rutland could attend those gatherings; he might even be photographed laughing next to a budding star like Vera Larios or shaking hands with Miguel Montaner.

Success would be swift for Jay. He already had a foot in the door, and within weeks she expected there'd be more parties, more meetings with actresses, more of a world Nancy could only glimpse from afar.

He wasn't willing to share that world. She'd thought a wealthy boyfriend would come with expensive gifts, but all Jay had bought her were flowers and a few meals. All Jay knew to do with his money was waste it on records. All he liked to do was drive with the top of his car down, listening to the radio.

"Didn't I mention it? I thought I did," he said, still innocently, and yet every word was like a dagger. "I went over with Kent Shaw to see about a gig at the—"

"No, you did not." Nancy squared her shoulders, tossing her cigarette into a glass ashtray. "I guess you wanted to have fun with Kent and his starlet friends. Vera Larios! Did you meet anyone else?"

"I . . . no, I was talking to musicians."

"And Vera Larios. Who is such a pleasant girl," Nancy said as she walked in front of Jay and examined his face with microscopic intensity.

"I was there trying to make contacts. I talked to that girl for five minutes. We should go for a drive, Nancy," Jay said. "We can listen to the radio while the sun sets."

He was truthful, and yet there was a detail that made her flinch, for, beneath his bland words, Nancy spied a true interest in and attraction toward Vera Larios. It was the way he stood, trying to look casual, his eyes evading her own. Maybe even the way he had picked up the paper, his fingers careful upon the page. His intonation, attempting to sound careless, even his suggestion of a drive, was like a murder weapon at a crime scene.

And there was the fact that until this moment Jay had not mentioned meeting Vera Larios. Since Nancy was working as a bit player in *The Seventh Veil of Salome*, it would have been natural for him to tell her he'd talked to the star of the picture. But he had not said a peep, as if he had not wanted Nancy to know about that introduction.

Of course, Jay Rutland could technically talk to Vera Larios and a dozen other women if he wanted to. They'd gone out for weeks, yet there was no formal arrangement between them. This served to only irritate Nancy more. Other men might have thought to install her in a nice apartment, to afford her a certain secure spot at their side, but either Jay Rutland was too stupid to suggest a love nest, or else he thought she didn't warrant one.

Nancy was not his girlfriend; she was not really even his lover. She was a girl who came around some days, who sucked his cock and fucked him by the pool.

All at once this relationship, which she'd thought comfortable and pleasing enough, seemed to her cheaper and more bothersome than before. At least with men like Pierce Pratt she knew where she stood.

"You didn't think to take me with you? You figure I don't need to make contacts?" Nancy asked.

"I think you're doing okay. You're in the Salome picture."

"I'm nobody in that picture," Nancy said, furiously remembering the way Vera Larios had looked on the set the previous day, wrapped in a dress of yellow and orange, as she laughed together with Orlando Beckett.

Jay folded the paper and sighed, tossing it aside. "Kent managed to get me invited, but I couldn't bring you along."

She glared at him, hands on her hips. "You never take me anywhere."

"Nancy, we went out yesterday."

"Not anywhere that matters," she said, thinking of Jay's stupid drives and his stupid picnics and his smoky little clubs and the awful jazz music on the portable record player, as if that constituted a good time.

"This was about work."

"What work? You're a pathetic fool who thinks he's a musician because he can play 'Chopsticks'!"

Jay's face turned hard. He looked as if she'd punched him. She wished she had done that. Every cell in her body demanded a vicious fight.

"I'm going to the studio. Why don't you let yourself out?" he said with a cutting simplicity that hurt deeper than a blow.

It was as easy as that for Jay. He'd lock himself in his office, maybe play music on his portable record player, type a few letters on his typewriter, then emerge once Nancy had vacated the premises and drive himself to a fancy restaurant for supper. Without a care in the world.

Jay could simply walk away.

Nancy, meanwhile, would have to get herself back home, back to her apartment with a rickety fan, to eat a meal out of a can. Jay could go to Ciro's that night. He could drive his convertible, hand the keys to the valet, then walk in and stroll past the booth occupied by Clifford Collins and Vera Larios. She might even recognize him.

She might even invite him to join them for drinks.

Jay could do all of that, and Jay might, without blinking, without thought.

As Nancy looked at him, with his shirt open at the neck and his glossy side-parted hair, with his easy good looks and his easier money, she felt a mad, burning hatred for Jay Rutland. She felt like that about Benny sometimes, for entirely different reasons. But the emotion was the same, a poisonous, sharp jab of rage that made her hands tremble.

"Don't you dare go away," she told him, but Jay was already strolling out of the living room.

He was humming, of all things. A cheerful tune that made Nancy grab the heavy glass ashtray and hurl it at his back. Jay let out a yelp and turned around, staring at her in open-mouthed outrage.

"You hit me!" he said at last. "For fuck's sake, you hit me!"

"Don't be a baby," she said, rolling her eyes at his aggrieved voice. He sounded like she'd swung a baseball bat at his head. She'd tossed plenty of things in Benny's direction—dishes, clothes, a vase—and he didn't squeal like a little kid. Benny tossed the stuff back.

Jay shook his head in disbelief.

"You can't take a joke, Jay? I was playing around," she said with mock laughter. "Come on over, I'll put ice on it."

"Get out!" he ordered.

Nancy, who had felt like breaking something, like burning a house or tossing furniture out a window, was rewarded with a pernicious joy. To hear that little rich boy wailing in distress brought a smile to her lips.

"Fine," Nancy said, scooping up her purse from the couch and putting on her sunglasses. "It couldn't have hurt that much, you know? Act like a sissy, what do I care."

The rush she felt as she walked out of his house was worth Jay's indignant face. How she loved that feeling! That feeling of being in control, of hurting and twisting and mangling. It was better than booze or dope.

Later she'd regret her behavior. Later she'd have to figure out a way to patch things up with Jay. But right then and there she was gleeful and decided to go dancing. She'd phone a couple of the girls, or she might call Benny instead. She'd worry about Jay Rutland's feelings and his bruised back later. Much, much later.

Salome

HEROD ANTIPAS sat upon a chair made of wood and inlaid with mother-of-pearl. His father, Herod the Great, had sat upon a throne of gold. But Herod had been a king, with a crown upon his head, and he'd ruled over a true kingdom, not just one-fourth of it.

To the tetrarch's right was his wife and to his left Salome. Agrippa was placed next to his cousin. He had slipped out of his Roman clothes into the traditional crimson robes of the Idumean nobility, his waist cinched with a jeweled belt and his feet encased in slippers embroidered with gold thread. Salome's dress was also red, the color of saffron, and around her neck hung a garnet of immense size.

Salome did not think the tetrarch could be too happy to have his nephew with them, and yet he was a member of their family, and thus he was afforded a spot of honor for this reception with the proconsul.

There was much banging of the drums, and then the doors to the audience chamber opened. Lucius Vitellius marched in with his retinue of eleven lictors. Marcellus, who had also escorted the proconsul in his journey to the palace, smiled at Salome. She ignored this gesture, instead focusing on the Roman politician before them.

Lucius Vitellius wore a toga with a broad band of purple running down the front of the garment to signify his rank, although his expression alone would have clued anyone to the importance of this man. Despite a dusting of gray upon his temples, his face was less lined and worn than that of the tetrarch, even though Salome knew Vitellius was a handful of years older than her uncle.

The war with her father and then the drawn-out conflict with King Aretas had left their mark on Herod Antipas.

The customary introductions were made in Latin for the sake of their guest. Vitellius seemed bored, and although he looked at the tetrarch and his wife, and although he nodded at Agrippa in greeting, he paid little attention to Salome.

"I trust your journey has been pleasant," Herod said.

"It has been long," Vitellius replied.

"I hope you enjoy your stay with us. Your quarters will provide much needed rest."

"I will rest in your palace today, and then I journey to Caesarea."

"You head there at once?" Herod said, sounding frankly surprised.

Caesarea was where Prefect Pontius Pilate resided, in the palace with magnificent lilies that had once belonged to Salome's father, and Pilate was no friend to Herod Antipas. Had Agrippa known this was the proconsul's intention? Was this the secret he would not reveal the previous night? Salome glanced at her cousin, but he was looking at the proconsul with a neutral face.

"An important matter has arisen," Vitellius said simply.

"In a fortnight it shall be my Lord Tetrarch's birthday," Herodias said. "We thought you would be our honored guest during this celebration. We have planned special dinners and performances to keep you entertained until that joyous date."

"I will return for the tetrarch's birthday celebration, fear not. But tomorrow I shall hear the one they call Jokanaan the Baptist preach, and then I continue on to Caesarea."

"What do you want with him?" Salome asked.

At once the eyes of all the courtiers turned toward her. Herodias stared at her daughter. The question was too frank to be asked out loud. She had spoken without thinking. Now the proconsul looked at Salome with interest.

"I've been told he preaches the rule of his God above all and begrudges Rome its taxes," the proconsul said.

"What man does not begrudge the tax collector?" Salome replied, her voice playful. "I could tell you a dozen jokes about them, and two of them quite bawdy."

"That may well be truth, but I'd like to hear his preaching all the same. I like to listen to such speeches with my own ears."

"That is a wise choice. Perhaps Prefect Pilate might tell you a funny tale of taxes while you're in Caesarea. They say for the building of his aqueduct in Jerusalem he took funds from the Jewish temple, causing a veritable panic. They say a hundred Jews complained about the matter, and he clubbed them all until they went quiet. On second thought, I do not think that is such a funny tale after all," she said.

To put in question Pontius Pilate's judgment was to question Rome, and yet Salome spoke with a light and brazen tone. She wished, desperately, to distract the proconsul from the matter of Jokanaan, and also to point to the faults of the prefect, who would no doubt speak ill of the tetrarch and of her family.

"The lady has an interest in politics. How delightful," Vitellius said, then he turned to speak to her uncle.

There were smiles and rigid pleasantries, until the proconsul took his leave. Afterward, Salome went in search of Marcellus. She had no trouble finding him and pulled the Roman to sit with her on a carved stone bench that ran along a wide hallway.

"Do you truly intend to take the proconsul to Caesarea so that Pilate may gossip about my uncle?" she asked. Normally she might have been coyer, addressing the matter in an oblique way, but she was altered. Her thoughts flew to Jokanaan, and she was also tortured by the fear that her family might be in danger.

"I am escorting Vitellius, as he has requested," Marcellus said. "It is not a choice I make."

"And you'll also show him the preacher?"

"That is not my choice, either."

"Vitellius might want to harm him after he hears Jokanaan railing against Rome," she said worriedly.

"Have you turned so pious that you are now concerned about the welfare of a beggar preacher?"

"No," she said quickly, her tone cool, attempting to mask any twinge of emotion. It would not do if Marcellus could divine her true interest in Jokanaan. "It doesn't mean I'd like the man clubbed and beaten. Vitellius is clearly ill-disposed to the tetrarch. You might have sent word this was the case."

"He does not confide in me, although he seemed friendly with your cousin when I saw them together."

"Agrippa," Salome muttered, thinking of the young man who could both play the part of a Roman and seem like a Herodian prince, as he had that day. Mutable. Dangerous.

"Your uncle has been living in a perilous position for some time now. His long war with the Nabateans has cost him too much blood and gold. His marriage to your mother is prohibited by the Torah," Marcellus said. "Your father was well liked, but your uncle is not."

"You think I am not aware of this?" Salome replied.

Her father! A playful and pleasant and charming man. Though not to Herodias, who had watched in muted anger his numerous mistresses, his carousing, building a tall fortress around her heart. Until Herod Antipas had come to the court of Archelaus and smiled at his pretty wife.

Damn her uncle and his lust, damn him and his thirst for power. Yet, he was her kin, and his destruction might mean the destruction of Salome, too, for the triumph of Roman men like Pontius Pilate would mean the inevitable diminishing of her own household.

"My family has a villa in Ostia where we breed horses," Marcellus whispered, his hands drifting close to her waist. "There are lovely woods and meadows and a stone path that snakes through the main gates. The bedrooms have a view of the sea. I've told you about it before."

"You have," she said, unwilling to provide him with something other than a terse couple of words. But there were other matters that troubled her now. She brushed his hands away.

*

SALOME HAD been summoned to her mother's antechamber as an afterthought even though this gathering was clearly of importance. The tetrarch was there, as well as his wife, along with Josephus. Mannaeus and Chuza were also present. These men constituted Herod Antipas's most trusted advisors.

Josephus was speaking when Salome walked in, swathed in her dress the color of saffron, though her hair was now undone, falling loose behind her back.

"Sejanus has eroded the emperor's authority, and might indeed be able to dethrone Tiberius. It is not a time to make rash decisions," he said. Josephus looked tired and grim as he spoke. This argument must have been going on for quite a while.

"It is not rash," Herodias replied. "Jokanaan threatens the tetrarch's rule. He mocks my husband and me. If such a man is allowed to roam the streets and spread his bile, then Vitellius will think us ineffective rulers, and Pontius Pilate will make sure the proconsul knows how efficient he is when it comes to handling the rabble."

"Pontius Pilate is Sejanus's man," Josephus said. "And that problem might take care of itself if we simply wait."

"And should Sejanus seize the throne?" Herodias asked. "What then? Pilate will have even more power to do as he wishes."

"Arresting the preacher will only anger the Jews."

"That is true, yet remaining immobile cannot help our cause," Mannaeus said. "The Nabatean king has invaded Perea. The tetrarch's position cannot be further weakened by evil talk and dissent in the streets."

"If the preacher was arrested, it would be a show of strength and quell any of Pilate's criticisms," Chuza added.

Salome did not know if Herodias had bought the support of these men, or if they had come to agree with her position on their own, but it was clear that great forces now threatened Jokanaan.

She thought, for a moment, to intercede on Josephus's behalf and call for caution, but the tetrarch spoke.

"I have listened to you all and will render a decision tomorrow morning. For now, you may leave us. I have called for my niece and must speak with her."

The men bowed their heads and departed, Josephus throwing Salome one quick, questioning look before he stepped out.

"It has been a worrisome day, Lord Uncle. I hope it may turn more pleasant," Salome said politely.

"I hope so, too," he replied. "Sit."

Salome sat across from her uncle, looking toward her mother, who watched her by the tetrarch's right, her brow decorated with a diamond.

"Your cousin Agrippa has asked for your hand in marriage. Your mother, however, wishes to solidify our ties to Rome."

Sextus Marcellus and his quaint villa, she thought. Her mother must have advanced him as a plausible groom, as she'd told Salome, hoping that the tetrarch would find him more palatable. Agrippa would pay no bride price, but Marcellus and his family were wealthy. Perhaps the tetrarch thought to refill his coffers with their assistance.

"I do not wish to tie ourselves to Rome in quite this fashion, especially at a time when imperial change might be at hand," her uncle said. "As for Agrippa, I have asked that he pay a bride price, which he of course cannot afford. But the matter is bound to be brought up again since he appeared quite keen in his proposal. No doubt his mother has enumerated your many good qualities. More than that, I'd say he is as infatuated as a green boy."

The tetrarch reached for a cup and took a sip, his eyes fixing on Salome over its rim.

A green boy? Agrippa had not appeared as such when she'd spoken to him. He had seemed cool and cunning. Why would he have displayed himself in such an open fashion for her uncle?

"He has only seen me for a few minutes," Salome said, and laughed.

"You've made a powerful impression on him. He pressed his suit once more today, after our meeting with the proconsul."

"What did you tell Agrippa?" she asked.

"I gave him the same answer as before: he might be an appropriate groom, should he be able to secure the funds I've indicated. Perhaps, too, if you find him pleasing."

"Then you are not completely opposed to him?"

"Your cousin wishes to spend time with you, to court you, and we are eager to allow it," her mother explained. "Agrippa may not be Roman, but he lives in their midst, and he is privy to many secrets and machinations. We wish to know what he knows."

"You wish me to spy on him," Salome replied. "You wish me to report on what he says."

"Yes. And what did he say to you, when you walked together in the courtyard?" her mother asked. It was not surprising that Herodias was informed of Salome's movements in the palace, and she'd known this question would be asked, yet Salome lowered her eyes for one moment, thinking through her answer.

The emperor is displeased, that was what her cousin had said, yet Salome stayed her tongue and shrugged. "He said I was pretty and asked for a kiss."

Herod Antipas's face turned hard at these words, the frown upon his brow carved deep. Herodias seemed curious rather than offended.

"I declined, of course. I would not let myself be kissed by a man I hardly know," Salome said with false modesty, for she had told the young preacher that she desired his mouth without compunction.

"Perhaps he might speak more interesting things next time," Herodias said. "You will repeat everything to us. This will be no real courtship, it is merely a tool. You understand?"

"Of course."

Herodias seemed content with this, while Salome's uncle sat drinking and simmering, his eyes fixed on her with an intensity that made Salome shiver.

"Lord Uncle, what will be done about the Jewish preacher?" she asked, moved by a deep and terrible emotion that forced her to speak when she did not wish to attract his attention, when she wished to simply step out of the chamber in silence.

"I must think on it tonight," her uncle said.

Herodias placed a hand on her husband's arm, and Salome noticed the beauty of her mother's dress, the finery of the diamonds she wore, the thickness of her black tresses, which hung over her shoulders. There was something triumphant in her demeanor, as if she knew the battle she had long fought had already been won. Yet the tetrarch's gaze was distant, turning only to Salome.

"Play the harp, Salome," he ordered. Herodias looked at her husband in surprise.

Rather than demurring, as she was wont to do, Salome stood and went to the place where her mother's harp awaited. Her finger rippled across the strings, wringing out a lonesome melody. She played a love song, her voice sweet yet ripe with yearning.

The tetrarch was entranced while Herodias looked at her daughter with barely repressed rage. But Salome raged, too. Her mother thought only on ways to use her, as if she were a puppet that could be made to dance to the woman's tune. And there was also the matter of Jokanaan, which troubled her deeply. If he were to be imprisoned, it would be because Herodias had pressed for it.

When Salome finished playing her song, she bowed her head to her uncle and her mother. The tetrarch dismissed her. She walked out of her mother's antechamber with her heart beating fast, as if she'd toyed with a tiger, sneaking a hand into its cage. Perhaps she had.

Salome motioned quietly to the handmaidens who awaited her. They walked together to her rooms in silence.

A few steps from her doorway, next to a colored lantern that hung low on a golden chain, stood Agrippa, lounging with a shoulder against a wall and watching her with cool eyes.

"I would have thought you would be with your Roman friends, drinking wine and playing dice," she told him.

"As you see, I have been awaiting you."

"You may go in," she told the handmaidens, who quickly stepped inside the rooms.

Once they were alone, Salome turned to her cousin, who was still attired in his princely crimson clothes that matched the hue of her own gown. The jewels on his belt caught the light, sparkling green and blue.

"You were summoned by our uncle," Agrippa said, "no doubt to discuss my presumptuous marriage proposal. I make quite the lovestruck, zealous suitor. The tetrarch likely thinks me a fool."

"Why?" she asked, carefully surveying his face.

"Would a man not be rendered helpless by your beauty?" he replied, brushing a lock of her hair with the backs of his fingers, barely touching her. "The blackness of your abyssal eyes beseeches me."

"Not when that man is you," she said, eyes narrowing. "What game is afoot?"

"How suspicious you are, little cousin. What have I ever done to you?"

"Nothing, but you give me no reason to trust you."

"I see. I will gift you a token of trust. Yesterday you wanted to know what has turned the emperor away from our uncle. Quite clearly it has been me," Agrippa said smugly. "I've whispered in his ear for a long time. The tetrarch is likely aware of this, which would naturally mean he might not be inclined to allow me much contact with you. But, if he should think his nephew besotted and simpleminded when it comes to women . . ."

"Then he might allow you to speak freely after all, thinking he's found a weakness in your armor. They wish me to spy on you, but you *want* me to spy," she said and was frankly surprised by Agrippa's devious mind, which had predicted and outsmarted their uncle with ease.

"Yes, I hope they think you are spying on me and that we be given leeway to speak and act thanks to this blunder of theirs. You see, the game I play is the game of crowning kings."

"I could march back into my mother's chambers and tell her what you've said. The tetrarch might have your head for hinting at those words," she whispered, a little intimidated by the arrogance of this man. "It is treason to covet the tetrarch's position."

"I do not covet the tetrarch's position: as I said, I speak of kings and crowns."

She looked at him wide-eyed, understanding his meaning. Their grandfather had been king, ruler of all the four lands. She clutched his arm and pulled him deeper into shadows, away from the soft glow of the jeweled lamp. They were alone, and yet this matter had such colossal implications that she sought the refuge of darkness.

"You've gone mad?" she asked, her voice so low it was like the rustle of a moth's wings.

"Of course not. I'm simply a man on the rise."

"And why do you think I would help you rise anywhere and turn my back against my uncle?"

"We have many things in common, Salome. Our fathers, for example. Yours took his life in despair. Mine was strangled by our grandfather, but only after our uncle Antipas whispered about my parents' disloyalty to the king. Do you know why my mother was spared? It was only because I already nestled inside her womb. Herod the Great had some pity, after all. But I shall have none for our uncle Antipas."

As they stood in the shadows of that hallway, Salome thought that she truly saw her cousin for the first time. Before, she had thought him a handsome, smart youth. But now she peered beneath his veneer of sophistication, unveiling an ugly, angry core. Oddly enough, looking at him, she found herself thinking back to the beautiful preacher. Not because the men had anything in common, but because she sensed their destinies were about to become irrevocably entwined.

Vera

I'M A LUCKY GIRL, she told herself. She did this every day. When she rose and readied herself for the studio she remembered how lucky she was to have this job. She rehearsed with the choreographer, went through costume changes, sat still in a chair so the makeup artist could work on her face, stood under the glare of the lights, said her lines a dozen times until the director was satisfied, read the new pages that had changes, smiled at everyone on set, and whenever that smile melted, she reminded herself, *I'm a lucky girl.*

But at home it was more difficult to feel lucky. The specter of her sister lurked there. Vera's mother would talk about Lumi over dinner. When Vera's cousins asked what she'd done at the studio that day, there was always a handy story about Lumi. Lumi had been a natural at dancing or Lumi could always take a good picture.

"Wouldn't Lumi have looked stunning in that dress?" Vera's mother asked, passing around a newspaper that showed a picture of Vera and Clifford Collins at a club.

Clifford Collins. That was another reason why Vera was a lucky girl. The actor seemed to like Vera. Even on the days when he was not needed on set, he showed up and chatted with her. He'd taken her out for dinner several times; they'd been photographed together, which increased her profile. Clifford was successful, charming, and handsome. When they'd danced, he squeezed Vera a little too tight, and although she gently brushed his fingers away, his hand often strayed toward her when they sat together, gripping her own hand, or sliding against her knee. She offered her cheek for him to kiss in public, when he pressed her for it, then turned quickly away because she didn't quite like Clifford, not like that, not in any way other than as a colleague. And sometimes she felt vaguely uncomfortable in his presence, when his arm slid against the small of her back.

Wasn't she a lucky girl? And would a lucky girl have any cause for complaint?

But the heat was growing suffocating, the days felt longer, her mother's comments sharper, the director's demands drained her, and sometimes Vera didn't feel lucky at all. But she was doing well, she was! Yet there was that gnawing doubt in the pit of her stomach that she tried to chase away with a steady smile and a calm facade.

One afternoon, when she was able to leave the studio early, she stopped at a record store near Sunset and Vine. The aisles full of beautiful music soothed her, and her fingers danced across the album covers. She picked a record, asked a clerk if she could listen to it, and headed toward the back, where there were rows of listening booths.

Distracted, thinking about the studio, her mother, Clifford Collins's increasingly amorous advances, she opened a door to one of the booths without paying attention and found herself face-to-face with a startled young man.

"This is the wrong— I didn't realize it was occupied," she said quickly, and then just as quickly she recognized him. "You're Jay. From that party."

The young man nodded and smiled. "Yes, I am. You're Vera."

"That's right. What a funny coincidence," she said.

He was handsome and affable, and for a moment she stood there, simply admiring him, and he seemed to do the same.

"What are you listening to?"

"Oh," she said, flipping her record around and showing him the cover. "Renata Tebaldi, opera. And you?"

"Chet Baker. Jazz."

They looked at each other, both smiling. Vera turned her head toward the other booths. "Well . . . I should listen to this."

"Do you want to use this booth?" he asked.

"I can't kick you out of it."

"No, I mean, put your record on. We'll listen to it together."

"The employees won't mind two people squeezed in a booth?"

He laughed. "During lunchtime you see four teenagers

squeezed in these booths trying to dance to their favorite singles. Come on."

Vera stepped into the booth. In some stores there were headphones, and in others you could record your own voice for a few cents, but this booth with its posters pinned on the walls and its narrow seat simply offered the chance to listen to a few records without further complications.

They sat next to each other. Jay began playing her record. He didn't try to chitchat with her while the music swelled, and she was thankful for that. Some people didn't listen to music as much as use it as background noise. You really shouldn't treat someone like Tebaldi like background noise. Tebaldi's voice was majestic, expressive, almost indulgent, capable of exquisite phrasing.

After a while, Vera told him to put his record back on, and they both listened to Chet Baker as he sang "My Funny Valentine." Later, they exited the booth and headed toward the front of the store.

"How did you like your Tebaldi?" he asked.

"She's magnificent. And Baker was poignant. I don't usually listen to jazz, but he sounds devastatingly earnest. I like that," she said. "Do you ever listen to opera?"

"Can't say it's my regular thing, but I liked your record. Hey, what if I buy it for you?"

"I couldn't let you."

"Why not? It's not a big expense."

"Well, okay, but you'll have to let me buy your record."

At the cash register they paid for each other's music. As they were exiting the store, he turned to her. "Want to get a soda?"

Vera paused, considering the way Clifford Collins kept pursuing her and wondering if this young man would try to place his hand on her knee, as Clifford had. Or perhaps he'd turn rude and mean, like the boys who had accosted her and Ceci the other day.

"You must think I'm talking like a teenager," he said quickly. "It doesn't have to be a soda."

"No, a soda's good," she said, laughing, seeing how mortified he looked.

Schwab's was the logical choice. It was not only a pharmacy with a soda fountain but a haven for up-and-coming actors, Hollywood hopefuls, and never-beens alike, crowded with actors, screenwriters, production assistants, and extras either ordering another cup of coffee or sipping a milkshake. There were real chances to spot movie stars at Schwab's because the Garden of Allah and the Chateau Marmont were both nearby.

When they stepped in, the place was popping with customers. People were running in and out of phone booths to take important calls, lighting their cigarettes or elbowing each other at the counter. Starving actors would nurse a soda for hours there, hoping to be discovered, like Lana Turner had supposedly been discovered, perched upon a stool looking pretty, although the actual venue where the discovery in question took place had been the Top Hat Café.

Vera and Jay did not attract much attention as they found a spot at the soda counter and placed their order.

"How did you start listening to opera?" he asked.

"My dad. He plays it at home in the evenings, and I developed a taste for it. What about you? How did you discover jazz?"

"I started listening to it five years ago. A friend had a few records, I borrowed them, and it became a big love affair. My mother hates jazz, she thinks it's senseless noise. She's probably okay with opera."

"Chet Baker is moody," Vera said. "That song you played, it was like a dream."

"Yeah, it gives you goose bumps how he sings. It's lyrical."

Vera sipped her soda, her fingers toying with her napkin, folding it and running a nail along a crease.

"You've always liked music?" she asked.

"My mother arranged for piano lessons since I was a little boy. She expected me to learn certain skills, I suppose. Like playing tennis, speaking French, the piano. She didn't expect me to get

serious about it, though. How do your folks feel about your acting?"

"My mother had her heart set on my sister being an actress
since she was a toddler. She arranged for all kinds of lessons, and I
learned, too. I can play the piano, you know? I used to play and my
sister danced during family reunions," Vera said, her fingers
lightly pressing against the counter, evoking the keys of the piano.
"My sister has a beautiful voice, and she's refined. She's lovely. I
don't think anyone expected I'd be the one obtaining a film role."

That's why she didn't phone Lumi, why she only wrote postcards. Vera feared she'd usurped her sister's life. What was worse,
she thought other people would begin noticing this soon.

"I'm certain she is lovely, but so are you," Jay said.

Vera gave him a sideways glance and smiled. "Thank you."

It was his turn to sip his soda and toy with his napkin, ripping
little strips off the edges.

"What do you do for fun?" he asked. "Besides opera."

"Not much lately. The film I work on is a full-time obligation,
and even in the evenings I sometimes fulfill publicity engage-
ments," she said, remembering Clifford Collins and his hand
pressed against the small of her back. "I like to read, and sometimes I cook."

She also sat alone and played a record. She turned into Elektra
and avenged her father's death. She was Mimi, wracked with disease. The characters were friends and confidants. The music was a
balm. But she couldn't tell him that, nor that sometimes she
dreamed she was Salome in a palace with lapis-lazuli tiles. It was
the kind of talk that Arturo had found off-putting and that her
mother disliked.

"Are you a good cook, or do you burn the toast?"

"I'm good. My grandmother taught me. What do you do for
fun?" she asked, sliding her hand down the side of her glass and
wiping away a water droplet.

"I tried to teach myself how to fix a drink and can make an

awful martini. I bought a book about cigarette tricks, but I'm not good at that. Oh, and a magic trick book. But I'm terrible at it."

"That's a pity. You have no skills," she said, but she was smiling and so was he.

"I'm a bum. I like to drive my car and I'm okay at it. Let's see . . . I have a swimming pool, and I'm an excellent swimmer. I used to dive in high school."

"I never learned how to swim."

"No kidding. I should show you the basics sometime."

"Water is terrifying."

"If you're living in LA you need to be able to swim. You're bound to be invited to a pool party."

"I'm not much for parties. Do you socialize a lot?"

"I try to hang out with people. I don't think it's healthy staying cooped up in my house playing piano from dawn until dusk. The thing is, before I moved here, I couldn't wait to get out of my family's house. Now I'm away, and I feel unmoored. I miss my brother. We used to play tennis on the weekends and then we had brunch. I always had grapefruit juice and eggs. He ordered these gigantic slices of ham and slathered his toast with a pat of butter. I miss that. It sounds silly because I'm twenty-four and I should be okay being away from home, but on Saturdays I want to dive for the phone and talk to him all day long."

Jay looked wistful as he stirred his soda with his straw. Vera thought of her sister and how they used to trade gossip late at night, or head to the weekend matinee.

"I eat dinner with my family on the weekends. We're having chilorio tomorrow. Would you like to join us?" she asked.

She'd never invited anyone over to her aunt's house. She wasn't even sure she should without first asking for permission. But she had the impulse to ask him. It felt like a challenge, both for herself and for him.

"Great. That sounds good."

"Do you even know what chilorio is?"

"No."

They laughed. She took out a pen and smiled, scribbling her address and phone number on the napkin. "If you change your mind, give me a ring, just so I know not to set a plate for you. If I don't hear otherwise, I'll assume you'll come," she said as she handed it to him.

"I'll be there. What's your favorite color?" he asked, carefully folding the napkin and tucking it in his pocket.

"Yellow."

He asked to drive her home, and she said no thank you. As they walked together and she hailed a cab, Vera felt suddenly shy, yet happy. She didn't feel like this when Clifford Collins wined and dined her. Then again, she didn't quite like Clifford. He was pushy, brash. Everything was a performance with him.

Back home, Vera tried to quickly explain she had invited a friend over, offering scant details about him, thinking this was the best course. It only incited increasingly pointed questions from both her aunt and her mother.

"Where did you meet this boy?" her mother asked.

"At a party. I saw him today, and we chatted. I didn't imagine it would be a problem if we had an extra person over."

"Easy for you to say," her aunt grumbled. "The table's hardly big enough for six, and now we must make room for a seventh. I don't even have dishes that'll match for seven."

"Aunt Prisca, I don't think he'll mind if there's a dish that looks different."

"It's not like he'll say it to our faces. But he'll mind."

"I thought you had a date with Clifford Collins this weekend," her mother said.

The next day the story repeated itself, now with her aunt and her mother grumbling in the kitchen. Vera lent a hand, hoping the women would appreciate the gesture, but Vera's mother kept elbowing her away, swatting her hand and saying she should do something else. Vera relented and helped her cousins with the tablecloth and the silverware.

"You have them in a frenzy," cousin Ceci whispered.

"I don't know why," Vera said.

"You're inviting a boy without him first introducing himself to the family. It's bold!"

"Ceci, that's not odd, not in LA."

"Maybe for white girls it isn't! You bet I can't bring nobody home. Did you do that back in Mexico City? Did your boyfriend just drop by one day?"

"Arturo?"

"Yes!"

Vera remembered how carefully Arturo had pursued her, first ingratiating himself with her mother with gifts of candy and flowers. Then the serious, formal introductions between both their families, and the day he'd asked her father for Vera's hand in marriage. In a way, Arturo's persistent chase reminded her of Clifford Collins, and she frowned.

"I don't want to talk about him."

"Vera, you're so mysterious. When are you ever going to tell me something about yourself?"

"You know plenty of things about me," Vera said as they folded cloth napkins.

The result of such prodding and muttering was that by the time Jay Rutland arrived Vera was a bundle of nerves. She checked her makeup four times. When her cousin, who had been sitting by the window, spoke up, Vera practically jumped in the air.

"Wow, he has a convertible!" Ceci exclaimed.

Cousin Federico quickly rushed next to Cecilia's side and looked out the window. Vera peered over cousin Ceci's shoulder. There was indeed a convertible parked in front of the house, with the top down. It was painted a glossy red with a white interior. Jay Rutland descended from it in a tweed sport coat and a blue-and-yellow shirt, a small bouquet of yellow tulips under his arm.

"He looks so fine!" Cecilia said. "Dad, you better put on the tie, this guy likes to dress like Cary Grant!"

"Don't make a fuss," Vera said. Although, truth be told, Jay did look nice, bold in his clothing choice, perfectly put together, his hair impeccable. Young and modern and utterly confident as he strutted toward the door.

"Nobody said it was going to be a formal dinner. Why the linens and the good dishes?" her uncle asked as he peered into the dining room. "Looks like we're celebrating someone's first communion."

"Get your tie!"

Vera decided it was best if she greeted Jay and quickly went to the door, ushering him into the dining room. Vera's mother and her aunt Prisca came out of the kitchen while Cecilia yelled that she had to change her shoes.

"Mom, this is Jay Rutland. Jay, this is my mother, Lucinda," Vera said. "This is my aunt Prisca."

"Hello, Lucinda and Prisca," Jay said.

Vera's mother expected to be greeted with "usted" and "señora." The use of her first name had the effect of making her face turn to granite.

"We'll put those flowers in water," her mother said, quickly snatching the tulips and taking them away.

The house smelled of onion, spices, chiles, and warm tortillas. Vera suspected that Jay had thought he'd be served chili and seemed surprised by the pork dish that was placed in front of him. But he ate without complaint.

"What do you do for a living, Mr. Rutland?" Vera's mother asked.

"I'm a musician."

"A *real* musician? Do you play concert halls?"

"No."

"Then you're not a musician after all."

Jay chuckled as he poured himself a glass of tamarindo water. "I started playing a couple of nights a week at a nightclub."

"Your parents are okay with this? Clubs in Mexico City can be full of unsavory characters," her mother said. "All those rumberas in skimpy costumes, with their feathers and their sequins."

"I'm twenty-four," Jay said. "My parents don't really mind where I work."

"I could be forty-eight, and my mother wouldn't let me play at a nightclub," cousin Federico said.

"That's because you're going to be an accountant," Aunt Prisca said. "Like your dad. He has a good, steady job."

"Twelve years, same job," her uncle said. It was one of his rare interjections. He usually limited himself to reading the newspaper or doing a crossword puzzle while everyone else talked. Cecilia claimed he'd once been an excellent dancer, good enough to win contests, but Vera believed that had to be an exaggeration. "What instrument do you play at those clubs?"

"Piano. It may sound silly, but when I moved to Los Angeles I thought that I'd have a steady gig within a month. It hasn't quite worked out like that."

"I suppose you're an optimist by nature," her mother said archly. "How do you afford a convertible working so little?"

"Mother, please," Vera said. "You can't ask the man how much money he has in his bank account."

"In Jane Austen's novels they tell you how much the men earn each year," Cecilia said.

"You like literature?" Jay asked, turning to her cousin.

"They assign the books in school. They're fine, I suppose."

"Are your parents also musicians?" Vera's mother asked.

Vera gripped her fork tight, praying her mother would stop with that line of questioning. She'd stupidly asked Jay over because she liked him. She'd thought maybe her mother might be nice to him. She ought to have known better.

"My father runs the Rutland Navigation Company." Jay took a sip of water. "My mother is bankrolling me. She gave me a year to get started in the music business, and I moved here. I suppose I'm exploring the world. Like Vera."

"Vera's not exploring. She's working," her mother said. "They're impressed with her at the studio."

The studio. That was all her mother could think about. When

Vera's father phoned it was the studio this and the studio that. The letters were all about the studio, too. Now her mother would spend the next half hour explaining to Jay the plot of *The Seventh Veil of Salome*. Vera was incapable of listening to her drone on.

"Jay's a fan of Chet Baker," she said. "I bet you've met some interesting musicians in Los Angeles, Jay. And the dancing! They probably dance at your club."

"Sure they do," Jay said. "Depends who's playing, but they've got a dance floor."

"I used to dance," her uncle said proudly. "I won a few of those marathon dance contests back in the day. One time I faced off against a hundred and forty contestants!"

Her mother glared at Vera. She'd been foiled in her attempts at interrogating the young man, and Vera steered all conversation away from her mother's favorite topics, instead talking of cars, music, Los Angeles. Her uncle looked more animated than ever. He even took out his records at one point and started showing Jay a few steps, much to the amusement of his children.

Vera's mother asked her to help her bring out the dessert, and they headed into the kitchen. Vera fetched the plates from the cupboard while her mother shook her head.

"He's all wrong for you, Vera. A lazy boy without a care in the world. Wherever did you meet him? No matter. You're not inviting him here again, you hear me? Better that you stick to a reliable man. Someone who can do something for your career. Like Mr. Collins," her mother said, concluding her monologue.

"Clifford Collins works with me."

"Movie stars have romances all the time. Otherwise, it wouldn't be reported by the magazines."

"I don't like Mr. Collins."

"Do you like this Jay Rutland? He might wear good suits, but he lacks manners. I bet he hasn't read the *Manual de Carreño*."

"Why would he read a Mexican etiquette book to eat chilorio on the weekend?"

"Because we're not peasants."

Vera sighed but did not reply. She remembered that one of the dictums of the manual was that there was nothing more inappropriate than a child arguing with their parents. If she talked back, her mother would think it was further proof of Jay's deficiencies, which were rubbing off on her.

"Boys like that are only after one thing, Vera."

"What are they after?" Vera asked, irritated, unable to muffle her reply.

Her mother frowned. She had taken the flan out of the refrigerator and placed it on the small kitchen table, practically slamming the dish down.

"Your sister ruined her chances at a movie career. You're not going to do the same thing. You're not going to toss your future down the drain because a boy with a convertible said you're pretty."

Her sister. There was no way to escape Lumi's shadow. Vera felt like smashing the plates against the floor and hurling the forks across the kitchen. Instead, she quietly grabbed the plates and took them to the dining room.

After dessert and coffee, she walked Jay back to his car. He had his hands in his pockets and was humming a tune as the sun went down.

"What are you singing?"

"That? Sorry, I never know when I'm doing that," he said.

"It's fine. I do that. My mother hates it when I'm humming around the house."

"It's 'These Foolish Things,'" he said. "I've got the song stuck in my head. I suppose it's harder to get a song stuck in your brain when it's an aria?"

"You'd be surprised. 'Habanera' can be catchy. Did you like the music my uncle played? Next time I'll play you Tito Puente. You should listen to him and Noro Morales. A few others, too. You might find the rhythmic pattern of Latin American music interesting, in juxtaposition with jazz."

"The trouble is I like jazz because you can improvise. The timing is more rigid with Latin American musicians."

"But that pattern adds inherent tension to the music. Being able to identify what'll come next creates drama."

It was funny talking about such things with him. She'd discussed music with her teachers when she was growing up, with her father, but her sister had little taste for exploring the intricacies of what lay behind a catchy tune, and Arturo was not artistically inclined. He thought her love of opera and her interest in acting were, at best, childish impulses that would fade once she was a wife and homemaker.

Jay seemed thoughtful, carefully considering her words. He leaned against his car and looked at her. She knew everyone was probably peering out the windows at them, waiting to see the young man depart, and therefore Vera kept a polite distance between herself and Jay, arms crossed.

She glanced quickly at the house, afraid she'd be summoned inside any second now. "I'm sorry that my mother was nosy."

"She's a sweetheart. You should meet my mother. Her hobby is telling me how disappointing I am."

Vera thought about her sister and bit her lip, glancing down. Jay took out a cigarette and lit it, offering her one, but she shook her head.

"I had a swell time. Besides, now I know what chilorio tastes like."

"You hated it."

"I didn't! Maybe we could have lunch next week. I can't make anything but baloney sandwiches, but I do have that pool."

She looked at him, uncertain, guessing how her family would react. Her mother would have plenty to say on the matter of a date. Vera doubted her aunt Prisca would be any nicer. She could always keep any future dates to herself, but she kept thinking about the fiasco that had been Arturo. Then there was the studio to consider, her busy schedule.

"I should be honest with you. I'm not sure I should be dating anyone right now. Things are . . . complicated. I shouldn't have invited you to come over, but, I don't know. I thought it would be fine. Friendly, but . . ."

She trailed off. He inclined his head in apparent agreement. "I get it. Now it's my turn to be honest. I was seeing someone not so long ago, and the breakup is fresh. Logic would say it's a bad idea to jump into anything else."

"Right."

They lapsed into silence. "I had a good time, though. Maybe we could be friends?" she asked.

"That would be the healthy option," he said with mock serious-ness and extended his hand. "Platonic?"

She shook it. They both laughed.

"Okay. Then we'll have lunch. Like friends do."

"Yes," she said.

He jumped into his car and waved goodbye. Vera stood outside for a couple of minutes, her heart already beating too fast for this to be merely "friends" getting lunch.

Vera smiled to herself and slowly made her way back into the house.

*

"I CAN'T believe they booked all of us in the afternoon and the white girls in the morning. It's demeaning," Vera said, looking around the fake swimming pool at the other actresses who were lounging there, waiting for the photographer and his assistant to call them over.

The photos were supposed to run with a story about rising stars at Pacific Pictures. Cheesy shots of girls in swimsuits, holding beach balls, laughing together. It was that type of pictorial. Vera had not realized it was color coded until that day. The photogra-pher was shooting two blondes, a redhead, and a brunette. The group of women waiting for their turn, the afternoon shift, was composed of Marla, Vera, and Clarice Chung. They had been in-formed that a guy in a gorilla suit would be featured with them and that the first group was running late. They could fetch lunch, if they wanted. Clarice had elected to do that, while Marla and Vera stuck around attired in their leopard-print suits.

Despite Vera's major role in a Pacific Pictures movie, she was little more than an imported trinket the publicity department nudged in one direction or the other. Maxwell Niemann was more interested in ensuring she wore the perfect bra to her costume fittings than analyzing her delivery, and Clifford Collins seemed to think of her as an accessory he could flaunt around nightclubs. She didn't find him attractive, but the man couldn't or wouldn't take a hint.

"At least they don't have us in coconut bras and clinging to the leg of Tarzan," Marla said with a shrug. "We're the 'barbaric' beauties. Bet you ten dollars that's the headline they use."

"Don't joke like that."

"Who's joking?"

"Marla, you're impossible," Vera muttered, kicking away one of the beach balls that would be used in the shoot in frustration. "Don't you care how they show us to the press? It's mortifying."

"It's in the contract. We must do publicity shoots."

"It's fine if they demean us, because we have a contract?"

Marla glared at Vera. "You want to talk about demeaning, imagine strutting around with a bone tied to your hair. I had to do *that*, you know? We're in different categories. If the studio wants it, they'll have you play other main roles. You'll get to do a Western and die in the arms of your lover. But I must be in musical numbers that they can cut if they screen them in the South."

Marla grabbed her purse and took out a cigarette, quickly lighting it and staring at the two blondes and the redhead, who were linking their arms together and laughing. "I have a kid back home, and this pays the expenses. I'm only a second-rate Carmen Miranda. Carmen's Portuguese, you know? That's the reason she'll always get better billing than me. Because she's a white girl strutting around in a banana hat dancing the samba, and I'm three shades too dark for the taste of most casting directors. I know what we're doing here."

"I didn't know you had a kid," Vera said.

Marla nodded. "She's back in Brazil. My mother takes care of her."

"How old is your daughter?"

"She's five."

"What's her name?"

"Zélia."

Vera was quiet. She touched Marla's arm. "I didn't mean to snap at you. I'm not feeling like myself."

"Yes, well, we all have our problems." After a minute Marla gave her a cautious sideways glance. "What's the trouble?"

"Clifford Collins," Vera said. "He's pushy, and I don't want to be going out on dates with him, but he keeps asking and I keep having to say yes. I know I should feel grateful that people like me, that I have this film . . . Marla, it doesn't matter, there's no excuse. I shouldn't be rude to you. I'm sorry. You're a good friend and a very talented performer."

"I don't know if I believe you."

"I mean it, honest," Vera said, nodding with such vehemence that Marla smiled and shook her head.

"Cross your heart and hope to die, Vera Larios?"

"May lightning strike me if I lie," she said, solemnly raising a hand and pressing it against her chest. "That's what my sister and I used to say when we were little."

"You're still little. You're a little girl, and you're too damn sweet to stay mad at you. Do you know that?" Marla said, even though she could not be more than a handful of years older than Vera.

"Too much sweetness isn't good, either. Empalaga, like my mother says."

"You'll have enough time to grow cynical. Be sweet now, I say. Talking about sweetness, what happened on that date of yours? Did you kiss the boy?"

"He's only a friend," Vera said, running a hand over her bathing suit strap and smiling a little.

"Aha. That's why you called me right after you bumped into the guy."

"I phoned you because I invited him to have supper with my family, and I was nervous."

"Precisely."

"We had lunch."

"And?"

And she wanted to see him again and again. For lunch, for drinks, for dinner, for breakfast. She liked him very much, even though she shouldn't be interested in a man that quickly. It seemed reckless to head down that path.

Vera shrugged and Marla gave her a mischievous smile. "Well, you better find out if he kisses decently, and do it fast. There's nothing worse than a pretty boy who can't kiss right. What a waste of time!"

"How do you know he's good-looking?"

"By the way you're blushing."

"There comes the gorilla. His costume isn't that impressive," Vera said, as a young man in a costume walked past them with a mask under his arm, providing her with a convenient digression.

"There comes the guy with the coconuts," Marla added, pointing to another man who was dragging a large bag, which indeed seemed to be bulging with coconuts. "And don't think you're distracting me. Do you plan to kiss him on your next date or what?"

"I don't kiss gorillas," Vera said seriously.

They both broke up in laughter.

Nancy

IT TOOK a few days for Nancy to realize she'd made a mess of things, but then she was not one to glance in the rearview mirror. Once she did look, she told herself she'd patch it up with Jay. She was always getting into fights with the men she dated, after all. She'd smashed a plate on Benny's head one time, for Christ's sake.

Nancy figured there was no sense in tiptoeing back in shame to his house, so she slipped into one of her nicest dresses, painted her lips a bright red, and donned a pair of staggeringly high heels before knocking on his door.

When Jay opened the door he stood ramrod straight, eyeing her with suspicion.

"Hi, Jay," she said. "Hope you're feeling better."

"Why are you here?" he asked.

"I'm coming to see how you were doing."

"You hit me with an ashtray," he replied flatly.

"I hope it didn't leave a bruise."

"Damn right it left a bruise."

The best way to get out of trouble, in Nancy's experience, was to never admit to a wrong. If she bumped into someone, she was likely to blame the person for bumping into *her*.

She sighed. "Look, Jay, sometimes I lose my temper, okay? But it doesn't mean I don't like you."

"It doesn't mean I'm going to take it," he replied.

"You're not going to cut me loose like this, are you? At least let me come inside so we can talk," she said. "I hate standing outside like I'm a door-to-door saleswoman."

Her voice cracked under the strain of his exasperated eyes, and she clutched her hands together, nervous. She'd thought he'd let her inside without much of a fuss. At least, she'd hoped for this.

Jay's face softened. "What you did was awful, Nancy," he said, sounding hurt.

"Jay, people fight—"

"Not like that. I know a rotten deal when I see it."

"A deal? Like what, like I'm merchandise with a defect?"

"I don't mean it like . . . Look, it's not going to work. I'm not the guy for you."

"You mean I'm not the gal for you," she replied quickly, the words tasting like vinegar.

"I can't be brawling with someone I'm going out with," Jay said. "You should leave."

"Don't be cruel. I can't even say sorry because you're ready to shove me away. I can't really tell you anything because you won't hear that I'm sorry even if I hire a plane to write it in the sky."

He was still blocking her way, one hand at the ready to slam the door in her face, but doubt shone in his eyes. "Nancy—"

"Come on, Jay," she said in a low voice and stretched out a hand, touching his cheek. "You're not really going to kick me out, are you?"

She thought this would do the trick. It usually worked. A touch, then another, then a kiss. All wrongs forgotten. But she realized at once that she'd miscalculated. Jay jumped back as though he'd been scalded with boiling water. He pressed his lips together before shaking his head.

"Goodbye, Nancy," he said with cold self-possession and closed the door.

She stood there for a couple of minutes in shock before she slammed her palm against the doorbell. "Jay," she said. "Jay! Open up!"

He didn't open. Nancy scoffed, took three steps back, thought about pounding the door with her fists, before she turned around and strode off, clutching her purse tight. Her heart was hammering in her chest.

She'd fucked up. She had. Big-time. Maybe she should have admitted she'd done something wrong. But she couldn't bring herself to honestly ask for forgiveness. Her father said to never show them you'd slipped. When she forgot a step in a dance number, when she didn't hit a cue, he said to always leave them thinking it was on purpose.

Honesty had never served her off the stage, either. Honesty led to vulnerability. Like with her husband. She had loved him, back in the beginning. The first months of their marriage she'd spent in a daze, caring for his every whim, lavishing affection on him.

But Theodore grew bored with her quickly, secure in the knowledge she loved him.

The trick was to always love less, not more. When you loved more, you were weak. Nancy was no chump. She'd been taken in that one time, fooled by Theodore, by that cute young husband of hers, only to discover beneath the facade there was nothing but a weakling and a cad.

You were honest with men and they ate your heart, then spat it out. You couldn't let them see the naked self beneath the mascara and rouge. You couldn't let them find you curled up and small in the middle of the bed.

Fuck Jay Rutland. He was a pansy, a wimp who couldn't even stomach one quarrel. Mr. Drama, acting like she'd hit him with a shovel or run him over with a car. She expected a man to take what she had to give. Even idiots like Benny wouldn't run crying if she slapped them.

Fuck that rich playboy with no balls.

Yet, as Nancy went to her apartment and sat in the darkness of her room, curtains pulled tight, smoking and drinking cheap liquor, she couldn't help but remember that Jay was handsome, happy, and brimming with life. Lush, like fine leather. Harmonious, like a pleasant melody.

Why did she have to hit him? Why did she relish the succulent taste of cruelty in her mouth even as it turned her stomach?

As the hours passed, the sun fell, and the light drifting in under Nancy's curtains became the glow of streetlamps and neon signs. She lay in bed, taking a drag and looking at the ceiling.

A knock on the door made her lazily raise her head. She stretched her body, catlike, thinking that maybe it was Cathy wanting to go to the movies or for a drink. As she stood up and opened the door, she even thought, for one second, it might be Jay. Wouldn't that be something? Jay, coming to apologize to her in her apartment.

Instead, she stared into Wallace Olrof's face. He was wearing that horrid olive-green suit jacket he adored and a matching tie. His hair was slicked back with too much Vaseline, and his smile was too broad, like the mouth of a frog.

"Hey, Nan. Mind if I come in?" he asked.

"Why?"

"I have a business proposition."

"I don't have business with you," she replied, slowly pushing the door shut, but Wallace shoved it open again.

"I heard that you're working at Pacific Pictures in that big Bible picture. *The Seventh Veil of Salome,* ain't it?"

"Yeah, a nothing of a role. Now leave me alone."

"Nah, don't say that. I'm certain you look great in one of those harem outfits. You wore something like that for me for a session once, remember? Or rather, you wore very little. Your friend Pierce Pratt know you used to model?"

Nancy took a drag of her cigarette and stepped aside, letting him in. She was wearing a yellow robe, cinched loosely at the waist. As Wallace walked in, she grabbed a glass that she'd been drinking from and took a sip.

"How do you know Pierce?"

"I know lots of folks in town," Wallace said as he sat down on one of the chairs and eyed her unmade bed, which was only a few paces from her wobbly dining table. It was hot inside the little apartment even with the fan on, and Wallace took out a handkerchief and wiped beads of sweat off his forehead. "Anyway, it doesn't matter how I know him. What matters are those pictures. Pacific has a strict morals clause. Pictures like that wouldn't reflect well on a new hire."

"You said they were for a private collector."

"The prints are safe and sound with a collector. But I have the negatives."

"You're one shitty sleazebag, Wally, but I didn't think you'd ever stoop so low as to blackmail one of your models."

"I have bills to pay, toots. And word on the street is you have a rich boyfriend."

Who could have clued him in on both Pierce and Jay? Cathy might have blabbed about her gig at Pacific Pictures and even mentioned Pierce. But she would almost swear that it had been Benny who talked about Jay Rutland.

She took another sip of her liquor, knowing if she said Jay had dumped her it would get back to Benny. She didn't want him to know. He'd rejoice.

"Benny send you?" she asked, setting her glass down on the table.

"Why would he do that?"

"I don't know. Maybe you two cooked up this scheme to punish me."

"Benny doesn't have a clue."

Nancy sat down on the bed, thoughtful. "How much do you want for those negatives?"

"Six hundred."

Nancy laughed. "You really think I have that kind of dough?"

"All I know is you finally nabbed that gig at Pacific Pictures. A real studio. A foot in the big tent."

Yeah, right. She was a nobody, one of many girls who were squeezed into billowing dresses and sandals each day. She had the privilege of walking behind Vera Larios in a few scenes. Most days, she simply stood on the sidelines, watching. Handmaiden Number Four. That was Nancy. Okay, maybe she'd opened her mouth at a party or two, hinting at bigger and better things. But she'd been drunk when she did that, dreaming out loud. Tracing a future, like one traces the lines in a constellation. Wishing upon stars and all that crap.

"I don't have that much cash," she said as she put out her cigarette in the ceramic ashtray she'd left by the pillow. She leaned back on her elbows, a motion that had the effect of loosening her robe and showing off a large expanse of her chest. She shot him a languid look.

"You're a gorgeous gal, Nan."

"Thanks."

"But I need the money, not a quick fuck."

Nancy stood up and splashed him with the liquor in her glass. Wallace yelled and then stared at her furiously as he wiped the lapel of his jacket with his handkerchief.

"You're a piece of shit."

"Listen, Nan, those dirty pictures get out, you'll never make it in the movies."

"It doesn't matter. Marilyn Monroe's nude pics were leaked to the press, and she's still a star."

"Hate to break it to you: you're not Monroe, baby."

Nancy thought about smashing the glass against his smug face. But the bastard was right. Pierce Pratt wasn't going to defend her if the studio tried to enforce the morality clause. This was the closest she'd ever gotten to steady work. It might not amount to anything but another lousy short contract, but it would never turn into a real opportunity if those pictures were shared.

"I'll be back," Wallace said.

After he closed the door Nancy ended up tossing the glass against a wall. It left a trail of brown liquid that dripped to the floor. The fan whined, and she sat on the bed, hugging her legs. She never should have taken those pictures. Her dad had warned her against that sort of thing. But she'd wanted the extra dough to buy a jacket with a rabbit fur collar she'd seen in a department store.

Nancy chewed on a nail and tried to think who could lend her the money to pay off Wallace. Her first thought was Benny, but then she'd have to make up with him, and he'd feel smug. She'd have done the same if the tables were turned.

Her second thought was Jay Rutland. God, Jay! If only she hadn't quarreled with him. But she had, and he was furious.

No one would do. No one. She found a new glass and poured herself a drink.

That was another thing her dad didn't like about her. The drinking. It probably reminded him of her momma and the fights they used to have. Nancy's mother drank quite a bit. Her dad, too, back then, although he had been sober for years now and he liked to lord that over others.

Her dad never minded the pills, though. Thin and pretty. That was the way a girl should look, and if a little Dexamyl helped achieve a slim waist, who cared.

She didn't want to think about her old man, nor Benny, nor that Jay Rutland. Still, her mind kept going back to the pretty boy, perhaps because he was different from her other boyfriends. A little classier. The kind of man her dad might have been impressed by.

Why did she have to be mean to him? She could have played it all honey and sugar. But there was always something inside her needling her; there were razors hidden under her tongue waiting for the day when she could inflict a mortal cut.

She'd hated him a little since the moment she met him.

But she wanted him, too, even if he seemed a bit too full of himself to her, a little too bright and chipper. The kind of person who has never known a bad day in his life and whom you'd like to shove into a puddle.

Vera Larios was like that, too. That smile she always wore, perfect and refined. Nancy wanted to shove her in front of a truck, not just into a puddle.

Nancy drank. The neon lights outside blinked a bright red. She found the telephone somewhere under the sheets and dialed.

"Hello?"

"Jay, it's Nancy," she said.

"It's late. What is it?"

Are you happy without me, Jay? she wanted to ask. In that big house, with its swimming pool and the fancy piano and that red convertible parked up front. *Have you missed me, Jay? Does anyone ever really miss me, ever really care?*

Maybe if she said she was sorry and really meant it, he'd tell her to stop by. Maybe, but it hurt to even think about such a thing.

She didn't speak, her lips trembling, trying to think of how to explain herself. He sighed, loud and clear.

"Nancy, go to sleep," he said and hung up on her.

Salome

THE STARS shone like diamonds embroidered upon a veil dyed with indigo, and the moon was a scythe of silver, slicing the sky. Salome walked swiftly across the vast hallway with columns that had capitals shaped like water lilies. Her dress was the yellow of amber and honey, the sleeves billowing as she moved. Behind her came her handmaidens in white dresses. They looked like two pale moths chasing after a golden butterfly.

"I'm telling you it's true, I heard it from a guard an hour ago," Berenice said.

"She's lying. She invents these tales to get attention," Mariamne replied. "Salome, your mother awaits you. We will be late!"

"Did you tell him to meet me here?" Salome asked.

"Yes," Berenice said. "But Mariamne is right. Your mother—"

Rumors swirled, swift as sparrows, yet on this occasion discretion must have been preserved, for the details were scant and she must know the truth. Salome waited for no more than a few minutes, yet it felt like hours, her heart hammering in her chest, until Josephus emerged from behind a column.

"Almati," he said politely. "You wish to speak to me?"

Salome gestured to her handmaidens and took Josephus's arm, pulling him away a few paces, lowering her head.

"Josephus, is it true? Has the preacher been jailed?"

"He was taken at dawn and placed in the palace's dungeons."

"I didn't think my uncle would truly arrest him," she said, rubbing her hands together and turning her back to him. "How long does he intend to keep him here?"

"The tetrarch hopes to show off his prisoner to the proconsul, when Vitellius returns."

"A show of strength, I suppose. All for the sake of the Romans. How stupid are men, acting like roosters! He is not in any real danger, is he?" she asked, whirling around and looking at the man once more.

Josephus hesitated. "I would hope not. Yet this arrest might endanger your family. Once the people know the tetrarch seized Jokanaan, there will be turmoil."

"You must be able to do something about it."

"Might *you* be able to do something about your mother?"

"What can I do? She despises him and will not relent."

"You might be correct. Perhaps, then, Jokanaan might bend a little. I must speak to him," Josephus said wearily.

"Take me with you," she said quickly.

"What good would that do?" Josephus asked, surprised by the request.

"I wish to speak to him, too. Will you guide me to his cell?"

When Josephus didn't reply she clenched her hands into fists. "If you don't take me to him, I'll ask the tetrarch to do it."

"What foolishness nestles in your brain, almati?"

She bit her lip, thinking of the burning coal that seared her breast. "You cannot command me as you might command a servant. I wish to assist you, but I wish to see him, too."

"Hush, child," Josephus said, glancing at her handmaidens, who stood at a polite distance yet looked curiously at them. "Dismiss them."

"Tell my mother I will attend to her in an hour's time," Salome told the girls.

Berenice and Mariamne looked at her in confusion but nodded. Once they were gone, she turned to him. "We are alone."

"Your mother will not like this," Josephus warned her. ·

"I'll appease her later."

"You are foolish, Salome. We might wait until tomorrow."

"No, now, take me to him now."

He sighed yet relented, and spoke to his young servant, who had remained politely hidden in shadows and now bowed to Salome. The path to the dungeons took them beneath the palace, into a region that was alien to her. The walls of the hallways were of black stone, and black were the flagstones beneath her feet, and black, too, were the iron sconces that held torches. They passed cells infected with a darkness so thick that even the lantern the servant boy held with one hand, to further light their way, would not have been able to dissipate the shadows. From distant corners there came whispers and the tinkering of chains. Salome pressed her veil against her face to both shield herself from any curious onlookers and muffle the stench of human excretions.

Finally, they reached a cell that was larger than any they had passed. The servant boy held up his lamp, and Jokanaan turned his face toward them, blinking. He sat on the rough stone floor, dressed in the same simple vestments he always wore, with no ropes to bind him nor any bruises on his face.

"Josephus," he said as he stood up, and then when he noticed Salome he said nothing. His eyes fixed on the young woman with a terrible intensity before he lifted his gaze and turned to the older man. "You've brought a noble lady with you."

"The tetrarch's niece, Salome," Josephus said with a slight inclination of the head. "I believe she's heard you preach."

"Perhaps she has," Jokanaan said simply. He wrapped his hands around the iron bars of the cell. "But why is she with you?"

"Why are you here, almati?" Josephus asked.

"To see if you were well and to listen to your side of the tale," Salome said politely. She could not speak the truth, that she had been driven there by a furious affection for this preacher who was a stranger and yet closer to her heart than any other man.

"My side of the tale? You mean to ask why I was arrested? You know why. Because Herod is a tyrant and an impostor," the young man replied, his voice light, like a truant who dismisses his punishment. Yet his eyes were weary when they looked at her. Was it the cell or her presence that upset him? Salome could not tell, and she remembered how flustered he had been when she'd promised she'd kiss him one day.

"What is it that you hope to accomplish, Jokanaan?" Josephus asked angrily. "You've courted the ire of the tetrarch and of the priests alike. You've alienated your allies and your friends, and for what?"

"For the sake of truth. We bow to the Romans and to the te-trarch as if he were king, but there is only one king and that is God. He has spoken to me and I have seen his face——"

"No one has seen the face of God."

"But I have! A Messiah is coming. The Son of the Lamb——"

"Jokanaan, I swore to your father that I would protect you, but I cannot if you continue to defy the world in this way," Josephus said urgently.

The preacher laughed, his hands falling by his side, and shook his head. "You have never believed me."

"I believe in keeping the peace with Rome, a peace that you have threatened for far too long."

"Someone is coming who is mightier than your emperors and your lords. Someone is coming who will not be stopped by the shield or the javelin."

"You do not remember the old days," Josephus said, exasper-ated. "When Herod the Great and Antigonus waged war against each other, the land was scorched and pillaged. The women were raped, children put to the sword. Jerusalem and Joppa were be-sieged. When noblemen wage war, it is *us* who bleed. If the Ro-mans lose their faith in Herod Antipas, we shall pay the price."

"And have you no faith in the Lord?"

"I have no faith in you. You are a child, Jokanaan. A child who refuses to understand the shape of the world. We must go, almati," the man said, turning to her. "We've spent far too much time here."

"And you, princess. Have you no splinter of faith?"

"I worship Koze, Baal, and Uzza."

"But you believe in nothing," he said simply.

Salome stepped forward, her fingers brushing one of the iron bars as she looked at the young man. She opened her mouth, then closed it again, unable to conceive an answer.

He said nothing to her, his eyes like a weight of iron upon her shoulders, and Salome followed Josephus up through the winding hallways. She thought he would interrogate her, ask for the reason she was so keen on speaking with the prisoner, but Josephus did not ask. Instead, she spoke.

"You know his father? Is he also a preacher?"

"His father is a merchant. He thought Jokanaan had a scholar's brain and sent him off to learn in Jerusalem. He comes from a good family."

"What happened?"

"You heard him. God spoke to him. He renounced all earthly delights and began preaching, begging for his supper, and wearing clothes of camel's hair."

"But such a thing is ridiculous. It is as you said: it is impossible to see the face of his God, and he also spoke of a Messiah."

"The anointed one to be the king of God's kingdom."

"Your high priest cannot be pleased about this."

"Caiaphas grows weary of prophets."

"And you are weary, too."

"Resisting the Romans is madness. What will brandishing a sica and killing a few men do for us?"

"And Jokanaan would have the Jews wielding weapons?"

She wished to know more, but Josephus looked tired and shook his head, waving her away. Salome ventured to her mother's chambers alone, a hand pressed against her neck, her brow furrowed.

When she arrived, Herodias bid her to sit next to her on the balcony, and Salome fell upon plush cushions, head bowed, her heart still heavy with the weight of the preacher's eyes on her.

"You've taken your time."

"I am sorry, Mother. There was a matter I had to attend to."

"With Josephus?"

"Yes. He said we have a new prisoner."

"Dragged into the dungeons a few hours ago. The tetrarch finally heeded my words. No thanks to you," Herodias said pointedly.

"I said nothing against you."

"You've said plenty."

"It's a folly to bring him here, Mother."

"It's a folly to have him out there, spreading his venom. Anyway, the matter is resolved, and now all you must do is keep your mouth quiet in the presence of the tetrarch."

A slave carrying an earthen bowl full of dates stepped from behind them and placed the dish on a low table. A cool breeze made the curtains behind them flutter. Herodias tossed a date in her mouth.

"He is only a preacher," Salome protested.

A boy, she thought. He was only a boy. He ought to have been carousing with his friends, studying scrolls with a budding scholar's determination, or pursuing a pretty maiden. Any of those paths would have been natural. His imprisonment was an abomination even if he shouted against Rome. Why, at times she also despised Rome, even if Roman generals and emperors had helped her family establish a dynasty.

"Your little preacher wants to incite a rebellion. Would you like to see the House of Herod brought down? The tetrarch deposed and replaced by Pontius Pilate?"

"Like my father was deposed?" Salome replied angrily, thinking of another young man who had been unjustly punished.

"Your father was a fool."

"Yes, a fool for loving you, for trusting you, for—"

"A fool who was too busy playing his music to manage a kingdom. A fool who preferred to spend his days cavorting with his mistresses rather than attending to matters of state," Herodias said.

Salome remembered the handsome, grinning man who used to carry her on his shoulders and taught her how to ride a horse, and shook her head.

"Is that why you hated him? Because he loved others? Because he didn't love you anymore? Because he recited bad poetry?"

"You remember your father with the eyes of a little girl. I remember him as a woman," her mother said.

"I remember when Herod came to my father's court," Salome whispered. "I remember how you smiled at him."

"Do you remember this, too?" her mother asked, pulling at a strand of her hair, a jeweled pin falling to the ground. On her temple there was a scar. "This was your father's doing. That one time, when a diamond scratched my brow as he hit me. No. You don't remember. You didn't see. Little girls can't see the wickedness of men."

"Stop," Salome whispered as she stood up and leaned against the balcony's rail, her eyes on the stars that pinpricked the night.

"You think I disliked him because he declaimed poetry, or he plucked at the lyre? He humiliated me."

"Stop!"

"You were the one who wished to speak about your father."

Salome's hands were upon the rail. "I wished to speak about your ambition. You seduced Herod, your own brother-in-law. You set aside your husband. The preacher does not lie: you sinned." She turned around, her eyes bright with tears. "You'd imprison a man for speaking the truth and eat dates and drink fine wine while he sits in a cell."

"Because he'd cut my tongue if he could. And he'd cut yours, too, daughter. Pontius Pilate would do the same, and even that cousin of yours who asks so passionately for your hand in marriage must not be trusted. They're all our enemies, Salome."

"You have no faith, no faith in anything, in anyone," she said, falling upon the cushions again, running her hands through her hair, and thinking of the preacher's beautiful eyes. He was alone beneath the earth, in the darkness of his cell, and might remain there for months, perhaps years, if her mother willed it.

"Faith. That is the foolishness that has you in such a state? Dry your tears, silly girl. The servants will see."

"Let them."

"Don't be childish. We must speak of your uncle's birthday feast. He wants you to dance during the celebration."

"Does he?" Salome asked, her voice a whisper.

"An ancient dance to impress the guests. One that can only be danced by an expert. The Dance of the Seven Veils," Herodias said, plopping a date into her mouth.

Salome's voice was no longer a whisper; it was the sound of a petal brushing against a cheek. Barely a whimper escaped her mouth. "Mother, *no*," she said.

This was indeed an ancient dance, one that was rarely performed due to its complicated movements and elaborate dress. Yet the technical prowess required was not what gave Salome pause.

When Herod had visited his brother's palace, Salome's mother had danced the Dance of the Seven Veils for the court. Ever since then, it had become their dance. The dance she danced for Herod Antipas.

"It is merely a dance."

"It is not! You'd make me his whore. Your husband, my own uncle!"

Salome made a movement as if to stand, but Herodias yanked her down. They stared at each other. "Don't be stupid. I do not seek to place you in my husband's bed. Quite the contrary. I wish to arrange a good marriage for you with Marcellus. You'll head to Rome and live in comfort there. You'll birth him sons, and one day, when your uncle must name an heir, he'll recall your child to his side."

"But the dance, then why?"

"The preacher is a thorn in our side. It is not enough to imprison him: he must die."

She remembered now that on the occasion of a feast, when her mother danced, it was customary that she ask for a gift from the tetrarch as a reward for her superb dancing. Now Salome finally understood what she wanted: for Salome to demand the execution of Jokanaan. Herodias must have already asked and been refused. Now it was Salome's duty to repeat the request.

"The preacher is right: you are wicked," Salome said.

Herodias's fingers closed around one of the dark, velvety dates, crushing its flesh. Juice trickled through her fingers. She reached for Salome's face, holding her chin in place.

"We are women. All we can do is survive."

"No," Salome said, shoving her hand away. "Not like this."

She stood up and swept past the billowing curtains. Herodias spoke again.

"Herod stopped loving me a long time ago. The war has made him weary. There was also the matter of his succession. I have not given him children. I birthed a single girl. I'm certain your preacher would say my womb is accursed due to my marriage to my first husband's brother.

"But do you know the real reason why I cannot give the tetrarch any sons? When you were small, no more than three years old, my womb grew heavy with a second child. But your loving father was in his cups, and he didn't simply slap my face. I lost the child. I lost all children after that."

Salome stared in horror at her mother, searching for a lie. There was none. Herodias looked at her with a tired but honest smile.

"Little girls can't see the wickedness of men. But women must," Herodias said with disgust, as she wiped her stained fingers against the folds of her dress. "Survival, my daughter. It is our lot in life."

Dan Quiterio

BACK THEN, columnists were gods and you had to tiptoe around them, careful with what you revealed and what you concealed. Part of the publicity department's job was to feed the fan magazines information and pictures; the other part was planting stories with the gossip columnists or stopping them from printing bad news. Louella Parsons, Hedda Hopper, Sidney Skolsky, they all had their targets. Hopper despised Communists. The whiff of a pinko made her salivate.

A budding actor's career could be destroyed in one column inch because a friend of a friend of a friend said maybe the actor owned a copy of *The Communist Manifesto*. It's a parasitical business, the entertainment beat, and a downright cruel game most days.

The worst of the lot were the crummy writers spinning poison for the rags. *Confidential* printed an exposé about Desi Arnaz frequenting prostitutes, *Hush-Hush* ran a story about Marilyn Monroe blowing her lines in London and having to shoot a scene twenty-nine times during the making of *The Prince and the Showgirl* because she was plastered. The humiliations were big and small, but they stung.

Ronald Wilson was a dirt peddler extraordinaire. He did work for *Whisper, Uncensored, Top Secret,* you name it. His most frequent purchaser of dirty stories was *Hollywood Connection*. Wilson had a predilection for outing gay men and finger-pointing at Commies. You want to talk low? He was scum.

Wilson didn't always write badly about everyone. He was friendly with certain actors and seemed to favor Clifford Collins, which is how he became interested in Vera. When production of the movie began, Clifford squired her to several events. It's not something I had planned; I wanted her to be seen with Simon Gilbert, but Clifford had gotten it in his head that he would date the girl, and it was obvious he was going to have his way.

The coverage was positive, at any rate, and even a sour little gnome like Ronald Wilson seemed to be charmed by the girl. My advice to Vera was to keep everything public and casual. You know, be friendly, but avoid any nightcaps with the guy. He was a cad, I knew it, and there was his long-time girlfriend in the wings to think about.

I figured he'd go on a few dinner dates with Vera and then start chasing after another starlet. I figured she could handle the guy.

It turned into a disaster.

Vera

RICHARD O'DONNELL told her about Babylon. It was when they were sitting together, between takes, shooting the scene where Josephus takes Salome to the dungeons with him. Assistants fluttered around. Max Niemann was yelling instructions. He loved to yell. All his sentences were barked out. When he spoke softly you were in trouble.

"It had all been left behind at the lot. The white elephants and the plaster columns. The staircases and the scaffolding. Griffith's Babylon, moldering on Sunset Boulevard. Until the night the crew from *Gone with the Wind* burned it down. They passed those old ramparts off as bits of Atlanta. That's Hollywood magic: peeling, crumbling movie sets that the fire marshal declared a hazard and were set ablaze in Technicolor."

Richard looked the part of a patriarch, distinguished and seasoned, and when he was relaxing between takes he still spoke with a slight accent even decades after decamping from Belfast and trying his luck in California. His coolness contrasted with the anger of the director. Then again, Vera supposed he'd worked with his share of egomaniacs.

"Were you on Griffith's set?"

"Of course. Everyone was. They needed a huge crowd, and they paid well. Every extra got two dollars a day. I was twenty-three and it was a fortune." Richard sat back in his canvas chair as they watched Niemann making agitated gestures to his assistant. "How old are you?" he asked.

"Twenty-one," she said.

"Everything's only beginning for you," he said wistfully.

Is it? she wondered, as the white-haired actor took a drag from his cigarette. But that's what they said. The publicity people and her colleagues and her family. Lucky girl.

"Okay, you two, there you go," Max Niemann said, clapping his hands, making Vera jump out of her seat.

One take, two takes, three takes, four. The day was repetition, hitting her mark, turning her head, finding the light, holding that pose, say it again, say it louder, say it softer, say it now. The continuity photographer almost collided with a script girl. High above their heads someone was adjusting a light. It was strange to pretend to have a private conversation while a hundred people watched. It exhausted you.

When she slipped into her dressing room and unclasped the long trailing cape of her costume, Vera could hardly recognize herself beneath the black eyeliner, the red lipstick, and the shimmering golden necklace heavy across her chest. The woman sitting in front of the vanity, looking at herself in the mirror, was alien to her.

There came a knock, and before she could respond Clifford Collins was opening the door and letting himself in. She saw him in the mirror and wished to sigh, but smiled a small, polite smile instead. She had been hoping for a few moments of solitude.

"Hello, Clifford, I didn't know you were on the lot today."

He moved around the dressing room with the grace of an elephant, stomping his feet, picking a magazine and then discarding it. He made her think of a child banging a drum for attention or one of those windup monkey toys with clanging cymbals. She hoped he wouldn't stay long.

"I'm not. I came to see how you did with that old ham," he said, now grabbing a newspaper, scoffing at something he read, and ridding himself of that, too.

"Richard? He's lovely."

"He used to be silent film royalty. Right up there with John Barrymore. He's a has-been now, Max only gave him the part as a favor," he said, leaning down behind her and looking in the mirror, checking his hair, which was flawless anyway. "Hey, how about we go to Ciro's in a bit?"

"It's a Wednesday."

"And?"

"I'm supposed to be on the lot at five a.m. sharp. I'll look awful if I stay up tonight."

"Makeup can fix any dark circles."

"Mr. Niemann will have a fit if he knew I was carousing before a close-up."

"Mr. Niemann! You talk like he's the pope."

"He's our director," she said firmly. She was used to obeying the rules and doing as she was told. Max Niemann had said Vera must always arrive on set well rested, and she intended to do so.

"He's my friend, Vera. I go hunting with the guy. Trust me, he won't care." Clifford's hands slid upon her shoulders as he smiled at her in the mirror.

"There's no time to ask *my* friends. Marla will be busy with that new number they're setting up for her, and Simon has a dinner date," Vera said, standing up and stepping away from the vanity.

Clifford took her out frequently, but she tried to ensure it was in the company of other actors. She was cordial, but not overly friendly. It was a skillful dance she'd danced with him for weeks, although she feared the notes in this ballet were growing strident.

She unhooked an earring and placed it atop a table, wondering how she might best guide him out of the dressing room. She tried to treat him with poise and decorum, as a lady should. Vera didn't fancy Clifford Collins, but she couldn't be rude to him.

"That's the whole point, honey."

"What point?" she asked as she took off the second earring.

"Getting to have you alone for a bit," he said, stretching out a hand and running it down her arm. Vera shrugged away from his touch as elegantly as she could.

She shook her head and took two delicate steps from him. "I don't really want to be alone——"

Such evasive actions generally served her well, as she twirled away from him or slid aside, but not this time.

Clifford was in front of her in a second. He caught her arm again and pulled her toward him. He leaned down to kiss her, and she automatically offered him her cheek, as she'd done when they'd posed for pictures. His charming mask melted away at once.

"Now, look here, little girl, I like the chase as much as any red-blooded male does, but this has gone far enough, do you understand? I've wined and dined you and bought you flowers. We've had our share of dances and dates. You damn well know where this is headed."

"I like you, Clifford, but not like that," she said, attempting to speak as politely as possible even if the words seemed to rattle in her throat.

"You think I'm an idiot you can have on a leash?" he asked.

He put his arms around her and kissed her on the mouth. Vera tried to push him away, to utter a protest. Her mother loved talking about manners, but nowhere in the etiquette manual did it say what to blurt when a man tried to press his advances.

"Clifford, stop it," she said, but he kept trying to kiss her as she slammed her palms against his shoulders, attempting to shove him aside.

"Don't be a tease," he said against her mouth.

He pinned her against the wall of the dressing room and kept a tight grip on her waist. She thought about the two boys who had catcalled her and Ceci outside the soda shop. Clifford Collins was a pig, just like them.

Vera bit down on his lip. Clifford let out a loud yelp and jumped back, rubbing his hand against his mouth. He stared at her in mute outrage, as if he wasn't quite sure what had happened, before yelling.

"You crazy bitch!"

"You attacked me!" she yelled back, all attempts at poise and decorum vanishing.

"Look, you prude, I don't know what backwards shanty town you grew up in, but that's called a kiss. Plenty of girls would be taking off their knickers rather than putting on this ridiculous Virgin Mary performance, so why don't you calm down and start behaving properly?"

"In my backwards shanty town, Mr. Collins, *your* behavior isn't proper. You should leave," she said, crossing her arms.

"You're not serious," he scoffed.

"I'm very serious."

Clifford Collins ran a hand through his hair, staring at her with scornful eyes. His voice, when he spoke, was a scorching, maddening growl.

"You kick me out and you'll have yourself an enemy."

Vera took a deep breath and her lips trembled, but she held her head up.

"Get out," she said, pointing at the door.

"You're going to regret this," he said before slamming the door shut.

*

"I SHOULD tell the director," Vera muttered, looking at her cup of tea. She wasn't wearing any shoes, and she knew her mother didn't appreciate it when she looked like this, with her clothes a little rumpled and her hair askew.

A movie star needed to look like a star every hour of the day, that's what her mother said. But they were sitting in her room, with Vera perched on the bed, the cup between her hands and her head slumped, looking nothing like a performer and everything like a girl. Her mother sat on a large armchair, eyeing Vera warily.

"What good is that going to do?"

Vera glanced up at her mother in surprise. "He should know. What Clifford did was inappropriate."

"They'll think you can't handle yourself. Besides, you've been going out with him often."

"Because he pressured me! The studio head practically sent a memo about it!"

"I'm only saying it's easy to misinterpret intentions, especially when you change your mind as quickly as you do, Vera."

She placed the cup on the night table by the alarm clock and looked at her mother cautiously. "What do you mean?"

"Arturo."

Vera tucked a strand of hair behind her ear and wet her lips. "What does he have to do with anything?"

"You break an engagement like that . . . it makes you look flighty. Vera, the way you behave with boys sometimes—"

"Arturo and I should have never been engaged. I accepted him to please you."

"You'd been seeing him for a year, and you were happy when he asked for your hand in marriage."

"No, *you* were happy. You thought it was only right that I would marry before I turned twenty-one. In fact, that's all you thought I was good for: to be married off."

"Now you're going to say marriage is a bad thing. I suppose you want to end up an old maid like your aunt Gertrudis? Fifty-five years old and the woman has had one suitor in her lifetime."

"Mother, I was trying to tell you about Mr. Collins; what do I care about Aunt Gertrudis?!"

"Really, Vera," her mother said, sounding mightily affronted, "the way you talk these days. Raising your voice at me? You were not brought up that way, and as for Mr. Collins, you can't go tattling about him."

"It's not tattling if he was groping me!"

"Vera, you'll only make trouble for yourself. Calm down and be a professional!"

Vera bit her lip and shook her head. She could feel the tears welling in her eyes and rubbed a hand against them.

"Look at your face. Vera, stars don't cry. Stars are not weak. Do you think Grace Kelly or Ingrid Bergman walk around the lot sniffling, whatever their troubles may be? If you go cry in front of that director, he'll laugh you off the lot."

She closed her eyes. Downstairs the phone was ringing. Ceci yelled.

"Vera! It's that Jay Rutland calling!"

"Let her take a message," her mother said.

Vera didn't reply; instead she hurried downstairs, plucked the handset from cousin Ceci's hands, and pressed it against her ear.

"Jay?"

"Vera, you know how you said you wanted to learn how to swim? There's a pool party this weekend."

"Where?"

"At my place. Small crowd, all of them good people. I do owe you a lunch, since we had to cut the last one short."

She'd lunched with Jay twice before; on both of these occasions she'd had a good time, even if the last lunch had been a quick cup of coffee before she had to return to the lot. If every time she went out with Clifford Collins it had felt like a chore, each meeting with Jay had been a breeze.

Vera glanced at her mother, who had come downstairs and was eyeing her critically. Ceci was also lingering by, no doubt wondering if she was going to head out with Jay again.

"Can you pick me up?" Vera asked.

*

THE CROWD was indeed small and amusing. Five people, all of them musician friends of Jay. Jay fixed everyone cocktails, and they lounged around the pool. Vera did not swim, dipping her feet in the water instead. It was odd, being there with other people. She spent all her time with actors from the lot or with her family. Talking with folks her age about something other than script pages and studio gossip felt alien. It took her mind off Clifford Collins and his unpleasant words, at least for a few hours.

Although she'd told Jay that she could spare only an hour or two of her time, she found herself lingering as the others said their goodbyes until she was the only one left. Jay asked if she wanted to go inside to listen to records and cool down for a bit.

She followed him back to the living room, but paused to admire his piano. "She's a beauty," Vera said, leaning appreciatively over the keys.

"If I don't make it on the West Coast I'm going to miss this baby," he said.

"Why do you say that?"

"My family gave me a year to make it over here and I don't think that's nearly enough time. I was cocky, thinking I could strike it big."

"Doesn't everybody who comes to Los Angeles think they can make it big?" she said, her finger falling against a key, pressing it gently. "Why the West Coast, anyway?"

"West Coast jazz is the hippest," Jay said, hands in his pockets. "It's light like a feather. Art Pepper, Shelly Manne, Wardell Gray, and Sonny Criss, they're West Coast. I love the music back east, don't get me wrong, but I was curious to see what was happening here. You ever hear about a place and want to see it with your own eyes? Or in my case, hear it?"

"I wanted to see California."

"There you go. Besides, it's the farthest from my mother I could get."

Vera sat down at the piano bench. Rather than a swimsuit she was wearing shorts and a yellow blouse. Jay also wore shorts and a Hawaiian shirt with a pattern of bright blue and green leaves. She tried another key, repeating the note three times, before her fingers began to move, knitting together a melody.

"Hey, you weren't lying when you said you could play," Jay said, leaning against the piano and looking down at her hands.

"I told you I was the accompanist for my sister."

"Sure, but I thought you played 'Greensleeves.' This is much nicer. What's it called?"

She had toyed with several titles, tinkering with the idea of "Love," but she didn't want to say it in front of him and shook her head with a smile.

"I haven't named it."

"It's yours?"

"It's not a difficult tune," she said, almost apologetically. He laughed.

"It's clever." Jay was tapping his foot against the floor and humming. After a minute he sat next to her on the bench.

His hands flew upon the higher notes, echoing and comple-

menting her, matching her pace to perfection. After a little while
he began moving the melody in a different direction and she
began matching him.

"This is what I like about jazz, you know," he said. "Improvisa-
tion. Working together."

"It's not jazz, though."

"No, it's Vera Larios Piano Concerto Number One. Is this the
only tune you've composed?"

Vera shook her head. "I used to write them when I was younger.
My sister was so good at everything and it felt like all I was good
at was the piano."

"You could compose again, you know? Get sheet music and pin
this stuff down."

"My mother would hit you if she heard that."

"Why?"

"There are no lady composers, silly. That's what she'd say. Besides, I'm supposed to be a fantastic actress."

She said the words lightly and smiled even though the memory
of her mother's frown made her want to wince. Music was not a
serious pursuit for a lady and besides, Vera had no real talent. Only
twice had her mother been proud of her: when she was engaged
and when she obtained the role of Salome. Vera had ruined the
engagement, and she feared she'd ruin her chance at an acting
career, too. People might say everything was beginning for her,
but Vera wasn't so optimistic.

"If you told them at the studio you can play, they'd have you
doing musicals in a jiffy."

She laughed at that, a trace of bitterness tainting her lips, but
when he raised an eyebrow at her she smiled. "Maybe I won't tell
them. That way it can be our secret," she said.

"What's it called, really?"

"I told you. It doesn't have a name."

"Every time I compose something I name it, even if it's something stupid. I have a piece called 'Yolk' and another called 'Egg.'"

"Were you hungry that day?"

He chuckled. "Probably. What were you thinking when you came up with it?"

The melody was slowing, returning to the first few notes she'd played, soft and sweet. She'd come up with this piece late at night, while the moonlight streamed through the window of her room back in Mexico City and the crickets chirped in the interior patio of their house. When there was no one left awake but her, with a hand on the curtains, looking for the stars that hid behind clouds.

"I was thinking about the opera I'd been listening to and that final act when Aida died in the arms of Radamès. Tutto è finito. Right before bed. Truthfully, I didn't want to go to bed. I wanted to keep hearing music in my head all night long."

"It's sad. But then dying in your lover's arms must be sad."

"I suppose 'Yolk' and 'Egg' are happy songs?"

"If you combine them and add 'Onion' you get an omelet."

His hand brushed hers for a second as he moved his fingers against the keys, increasing the tempo, producing a jaunty series of notes that matched the careless way he spoke.

"Why don't we call it 'Blue'?"

"No! I'm not naming it after a color."

"'Blue Mexico,'" he proposed.

"'Blue Babylon,'" she said.

"Why Babylon?" he asked. "*Aida* is Egypt, *Nabucco* is Babylon."

"No, it doesn't have to do with Verdi. I was thinking about the real Babylon earlier today. Okay, not the *real* one, but the Babylon people have imagined. They built a huge set of plaster and wood for *Intolerance* and tried to re-create Babylon. An actor on the movie I'm in, Richard O'Donnell, he said the towers were two hundred feet high and the carved elephants were thirty feet. How do you represent Babylon with notes?"

"If you ask Verdi, with the assistance of flutes and oboes."

"Then it won't work with only a piano and no oboes in sight. No, we can't call this piece 'Babylon,' it has the wrong ring to it."

"We're back to Vera Larios Piano Concerto Number One."

"Concierto Para Piano Número Uno."

He mumbled words that hardly approximated what she'd said. She laughed again. Their hands stilled. She glanced at him, and he turned toward her. "It really is good," he said seriously, the small smirk he tended to wear on his face fading. "It tugs at the heart."

"Thanks," she said, resting her hands in her lap and looking down.

Jay was quiet. It was funny, they'd spent the whole afternoon noisily chatting and sipping drinks with his friends, eating sandwiches and telling jokes, and she'd loved that youthful chaos and carelessness. But she liked this even better, the quiet of the evening washing over them like the waves kissing the shore.

She was awfully busy these days; she hardly had time to appreciate either silence or music, nor the simple pleasures of sitting still while a cool breeze brushed across her back. He didn't try to fill the silence or to criticize her, as others might; Jay simply sat next to her on the piano bench, and they remained in amicable muteness.

Sometimes it was like this, she thought. You met someone you could just sit next to. Everything else ceased to matter but that solitary bubble, shielded from the chaos and the discordant rhythm of life.

She wished, for one fleeting instant, to tell him that the piece was called "Love," but then she thought better of it and only turned her head and smiled.

Nancy

NANCY'S FATHER was stylish. She appreciated that. Back when he'd been a tap dancer, he'd dressed in perfectly tailored slacks and shirts, his hair slicked with Vaseline, shoes shined so bright she could see her reflection in them. Even Valentino didn't look as good as her old man in his prime.

Charlie Hartley was not featured on posters anymore, and his name did not evoke recognition, except among the bookies who operated on the Sunset Strip, but he still dressed like a star in the making, with a white jacket and a carnation on his lapel. There were ten thousand bookies in town. Some had scanty operations, setting up shop in crummy card clubs or holed up in a stinking office the size of a closet, while others dined at the finest eateries and rubbed elbows with movie stars with a penchant for gambling, like Mickey Rooney.

The riffraff of the world was eternally pouring into Los Angeles, and Charlie Hartley tried to stand out between the lowly bookmakers, callow bug boys, crude racketeers, black market operators, and small-time confidence men.

Her dad didn't want to look like any little candy store or deli bookie. Even if that was what he was, eternally holed up at Vanna's with a cup of coffee and a slice of pie.

Strive for the top, that was her dad's motto. It was the reason she worked so hard when she was a kid, dancing until she had blisters on her feet. Her dad also taught her to dress well, to look the part of a star. When she was a little girl, her outfits were starched and ironed to perfection. Maybe that was why her mother left, because she was tired of stitching and starching and ironing so her husband and her kid could look pristine.

Anyway, Nancy still cared a great deal about her looks, and she'd picked her white coat with the fancy brass buttons and done her hair nicely, choosing the voluminous curls and heavy side-parting that her father deemed the classiest. She strutted into the small diner in her white heels and white gloves, past the display case with glistening pies and the busboy who gave her an appreciative look, until she reached the booth farthest from the door.

Nancy stood in front of her father's table where he sat thumbing through a book, with a folded newspaper at his left and a slice of lemon meringue pie on the right. He only ever had a few nibbles of pie, instead preferring to drink cup after cup of coffee.

She slid into the seat in front of him. "Shakespeare again?" she asked.

"Marlowe," her father said, without raising his eyes from the page.

Nancy never took up reading, but her dad loved Shakespeare and all those old playwrights. Back when he nurtured hopes of making it as an actor, of dipping his toes into film or theater, Charlie Hartley had feverishly memorized lines from *Hamlet*. Once in a while, he could still be coaxed into declaiming a soliloquy, like he'd done around their dinner table.

At least if he was reading, it meant he was in decent spirits. When he was in a foul mood he couldn't open a book. Maybe she'd be lucky, and he'd be flush with cash that week and feeling generous. Sometimes she'd caught him like that, and he'd bought her a steak dinner or face powder. But when he was irritated her father became stingy and wouldn't dispense a nickel.

"How've you been, Dad?"

"Fine," he said, turning a page. "What are you up to?"

"I'm working at Pacific Pictures. Just like I told you. In that Salome picture, remember?"

"The one with the little Mexican tomato in the lead, isn't it?"

He must have read about her in the papers, seen her picture, like Jay had. They were trying to push that girl big, talking about her dates with Clifford Collins and her appearances at swanky clubs.

Why couldn't Nancy make it into the papers? When she was a kid, she thought it was because the market for child performers was fiercely competitive, but as a woman it hadn't been any better. Yet when she compared her face to the faces on movie posters, she thought she looked better than many other girls. Definitely better than swarthy Vera Larios.

Nancy placed her purse on the table and her hands atop it. "Yeah."

"Is she any good?" he asked.

"Not much. She has a stupid accent."

"Some men have a hankering for those Tijuana chippies," her father said simply. His eyes were still on the page.

A waitress brought Nancy a menu. Nancy slid it aside. She wasn't there for the bad coffee. She was hoping her father would ask her another question. He didn't, immersed as he was in his book.

"It's going well over at the studio. I'm only signed for six months, but I bet after this flick is over they extend a new contract. A real good one."

"That's nice, Nancy," he said, although his voice was flat. He was hoping to rid himself of her. Perhaps he was expecting someone to stop by and pay off a bet. Nancy wondered if she shouldn't take the hint and return another day. But she couldn't wait.

"Thing is I have a few expenses right now," she said, trying to sound casual.

"You know that red doesn't work well with your complexion. You should switch back to blond," her father said, his voice still devoid of any emotion. It was a clear indication she should beat it and make her exit. She didn't.

"Didn't you hear me? I have a few—"

"I heard you," her father said, finally looking at her. He shoved a bookmark with a green ribbon into his book and clapped it shut. "I'm not sure what you want from me."

"I need a loan."

"Again."

Nancy regretted the other occasions she'd asked her father for cash. Most of the time, she'd spent the money on impulsive purchases. Perfume, or a new pair of heels. Now she had a real emergency, and she hoped he'd be lenient and wouldn't think too much about the money she still owed him.

"For what amount?" he asked.

She hesitated, wondering if she should ask for the full sum or half, and then try to see if she could come up with the rest on her own. Her father might be willing to advance her a more modest amount. Would that sleazy photographer accept half? She doubted it. If he was cornering her, it meant he required the dough.

"Six hundred."

"What do you need that for?"

"Expenses."

"No girl needs six hundred dollars for expenses. Are you gambling? Because if you are——"

"No! You'd have heard of it if I was."

"Then what? You planning to buy yourself a mink coat or some other stupidity? You're always wasting your cash."

"I have to look good, don't I?"

"Get a fellow to buy it for you."

Nancy gripped her purse tight. "I don't need it for a coat."

She debated whether to tell her father the truth or to conceal it. She knew he'd be furious. He'd always warned her off such pursuits when she started modeling, told her that a girl who wanted to make it into pictures couldn't be dipping her toes in a sewer.

If he discovered what she'd been up to, if he heard about the nude pictures, he was sure to call her an idiot, no better than a hick who'd scarcely stepped off the bus. It was the kind of muck you couldn't rinse.

"It's important," she said at last.

"How do you plan to pay it back?"

"I told you. I'm going to get a real fat contract. I'm going to nab a lead role."

Her father grabbed his fork and stabbed the pie but didn't eat a morsel. "You know what the hardest part of my job is? It's the evaluation. Every time someone places a bet with me, I must figure my extension. I must protect myself. And I have to say, Nancy, I wouldn't extend much credit to you."

"What are you saying, that I won't pay you back?"

"Yeah, exactly."

"I'm working. I'm at Pacific Pictures. I'm going to make it big."

"If it was going to happen, it would have happened for you already."

Nancy scoffed. "You can't know that. What do you have, a crystal ball? You're no talent scout."

"I have plenty of experience with talent scouts. I dragged you to all those auditions when you were a kid, didn't I? That was when it was time to strike, when you were a girl and they could mold you at the studios. But you didn't want it bad enough and exited stage left. Now it's too late."

"I'm twenty-six, not sixty," she said, thinking back furiously to those fruitless days. She hadn't made it, all right, but who could blame her for quitting at thirteen? Besides, she'd gotten back on the horse; she'd returned to Los Angeles.

"Too late, Nancy! You've been swirling around town for, what? Three, four years now. That's a century in Hollywood."

"You're always exaggerating."

"I know it. I worked the circuit," he said proudly.

"You barely worked anything."

"What's that supposed to mean?" her father asked, his face going sour. "I worked the circuit. I had bookings all around the country back in the day. Kansas City, Grand Rapids, you name it. I did what you couldn't do. All those dance lessons and singing lessons and dresses I bought. For what?"

Nancy remembered it perfectly well. The exhausting times when her father packed her into the car and drove her to meet agents, or the dresses he picked for her so she could look presentable. But she also remembered years before that, when Charlie Hartley was still trying to make a name for himself, when it was him memorizing lines or standing before the bathroom mirror.

"You could never make it in the movies, Dad. It doesn't mean I won't."

"Why? Because you can apply mascara and curl your hair? You have nothing special."

Nancy's face hardened. Her father hadn't said that when she

was a child. He'd looked at Nancy with expectant eyes, weighing each one of her good qualities, from her eyes that looked so similar to his own, to her mother's cheekbones. But at some point, he'd lost his faith in her, for no good reason, either. Nancy didn't think she'd changed, that she'd grown uglier or danced worse or lost any of her grace. Yet one day her father must have spotted a defect, like noticing a crack on a teacup. He'd never been able to see her as a whole being again.

"I have something. I'm going to prove it to you one day. You can keep your money, I don't need it."

"Good."

"I really don't. I don't need you, either. Never did. You haven't done one God damn thing for me ever since I came to LA."

"Get out of here, Nancy," her father said with chilling detachment, like she was a stranger he was shooing off. He adjusted the carnation in his pocket and looked down at his book, opening it to the page he'd marked.

She remembered how fine he'd looked when he was her age, twenty-something and smiling for the crowds. She remembered the headshots he had taken, with his hair parted, and the carnation on his lapel. And that one shot with both of them together, she sitting on his lap, mugging for the camera. Little Nan Hartley and Charlie Hartley. Tapping together to a lively tune. A team. That's what her father had called it. Destined for fame, surely for Hollywood. The both of them. Now he tried to pretend none of that had been real, to erase those promises, but she recalled everything he'd said about fortune, about recognition and her name in lights.

Nancy stood up, snatching up her purse, and walked out of the joint. The midafternoon heat hit her as she reached the door, and she paused for a second, wanting to rush back in and beg her father for that loan. Explain to him it was dire need this time, tell him to have pity on her. But she knew the old man would only be disgusted by such a display.

She had to try someone else, and as she set off down the street, walking quickly, her lips pursed. The only name that came to mind was Benny Alden. Of all people, Benny.

Minnie Wells

I WORKED at *Hollywood Connection* since the beginning as an editorial assistant. You can't understand what it was like before these so-called "gossip" magazines hit the newsstands. The studios controlled every aspect of an actor's life. They also made any unpalatable stories go away. Eddie Mannix, Howard Strickling, these were fixers who arranged for abortions and quickie divorces. They knew who to bribe and who to intimidate in order to provide audiences a glamorous picture of their stars.

The "gossip rags" exposed the real Hollywood, a place where Errol Flynn liked to watch his guests having sex through a two-way mirror and Eddie Fisher brought three floozies up to his hotel room. Not exactly the Norman Rockwell fantasy they tried to sell you.

Was it right? It wasn't right when the studio heads were sweeping away pictures of the prostitutes some of their actors liked to beat up, I'll tell you that. It wasn't fair when a studio contract meant you'd never have to stand trial for driving drunk and running over a poor idiot.

I'm going to say it: yes, it paid. Paid decently, too. So what? People were hungry for this dirt. When *Confidential* reported that Maureen O'Hara was caught practically having intercourse with her Mexican lover in Grauman's Chinese Theatre, row thirty-five became something of a local attraction, which must have been embarrassing for O'Hara, but if they hadn't reported on it, someone else would have.

Our interest in Vera Larios was the same interest we had in any other actress. There wasn't a specific directive about her. Ronald Wilson wrote a lot of stories about a lot of folks. I don't know if Clifford Collins was his informant about some of the things that were happening on set, but that wouldn't have been a crime, either. Plenty of people blabbered, and all actors have their petty feuds.

What was going on between those two? I don't know. But you also must understand Hollywood in the fifties wasn't exactly the most feminist place in the world. Heck, we didn't have the word "feminist." Pretty girls were propositioned year-round, and no one thought to run to human resources.

Smart women, like Ava Gardner, latched on to a powerful guy. Mickey Rooney kept Ava safe from the creeps back when she was starting out. Vera Larios seemed to be following the same strategy, walking arm in arm with Collins. Then, suddenly, poof. It's the Cold War between those two.

It's not enough to be pretty, or even talented, in Hollywood. You also need to have brains. Vera Larios didn't. Instead of befriending Collins, she did something to turn him off.

Okay. Maybe there was a bit of a grudge there, and Collins milked his contacts to get back at her.

But what were we supposed to do, ignore a scoop? *The Seventh Veil of Salome* was an important production with a large cast. Ronald Wilson was doing his job, writing about the production, and if things had taken a bad turn, that was even better for our sales.

Everyone loves a taste of failure. Everyone wants to see one of those beauty queens knocked down a peg. When the trial happened, we had to take pictures. We had to do interviews. We had to be there. If we didn't do it, someone else would have. We didn't have anything against her—it was a story.

Vera

"YOU KNOW, at MGM they have chicken soup with matzoh balls. Kosher soup. Here, they give us clam chowder three days a week,"

Joe said as he stared at the bowl in front of him. "Damn hash-house food."

"What's wrong with clam chowder?" Marla asked.

"First of all, it's not kosher. Check Leviticus. Not that this has ever stopped me from munching on a lobster, I know. But I recognize these clams from yesterday, and I saw that meat loaf on Monday when it was called 'hamburger special,' that's what's wrong. They're trying to starve us."

"Eat your lunch, Joe."

"Eat my lunch. How am I supposed to do any work with this in my stomach? It's an abomination. I wish Simon was around to take us to eat a proper meal."

"He has to pack his bags for Rio and figure out the storage issue."

"Simon's going to Brazil?" Vera asked. "For how long?"

She'd recently posed for a few photos with Simon for the movie magazines. The studio regularly distributed such images to keep their actors in the public eye. He hadn't mentioned anything about a trip, although he had said he was having people over on the weekend and she should drop by.

"Six-month tour," Marla said.

"I thought he had that new movie coming up," Vera said. "He was doing hair and wardrobe tests the other day."

"They have to stash him abroad until it blows away," Joe said as he raised a spoonful of soup to his mouth, but then put it down.

"What blows away?" Vera asked.

Marla gave Joe a look, and Joe looked back at her. The woman scooted close to Vera, her voice low.

"Ronald Wilson finally convinced someone to talk about Simon. The story should be appearing in *Hollywood Connection* in a couple of weeks. The studio is sending Simon on a musical tour, but they really want to deflect attention as much as they can."

"Why didn't you tell me sooner?"

"We only found out this morning," Joe said.

Vera sat there, stunned. "Do you know who's talking about him? I thought no one was willing to be quoted."

"I'm guessing Clifford Collins pressured someone to spill the beans," Joe said. "He's had it in for Simon for months now."

"Why?"

"Simon beat Clifford for a role."

"*Valor and Glory*?" Vera asked incredulously.

"That one. And then Simon rubbed it in his face, he even did it in front of you, Vera, remember?" Joe said, waving a spoon at her and then looking down again at his clam chowder. "Clifford is a good friend of Ronald Wilson. I'm guessing he went for drinks with the guy and told him he had info on Simon. Clifford has many pals on this lot, and some of them must have had gossip to share."

She remembered that time Clifford had come to the table where they were sitting and Simon had made what amounted to a joke. Was that what had precipitated this? Was he *that* petty?

"God," Vera said, rubbing her temples.

"What?" Marla asked.

"It's . . . I made Clifford angry the other day."

"Are we talking a little angry or big angry?" Joe asked, and he spread his hands as if to measure the rage in inches and feet.

"Big."

"You better find a shield and a sword, kid. Like any Roman general, he's good at siege tactics."

"Stop it, don't scare her," Marla said, slapping Joe's hand and turning to Vera. "Clifford's malicious, but he'll forget about it quickly."

"You're probably right," Vera muttered, and she clutched her hands anxiously. "God, I shouldn't be worried about myself right now. What about Orlando? Is he mentioned in the story?"

"No, luckily. Only Simon and 'anonymous' associates and sources. The usual stuff they love to print."

"Barely coded innuendo and spite," Joe said. "It'll sell plenty of copies."

"What'll happen to him?"

"Simon will be back in a few months," Marla said. "People love him. It's the same speed bump as with Van Johnson; there were rumors about him and some actors a while back, but MGM hushed that up."

"Mayer married him off," Joe reminded her. "But Van's a good American boy, you know? It'll be different with our gaucho."

"Quiet," Marla told him firmly. "It's not going to ruin him, and you're not going to trouble him with any pessimistic talk when we get together on the weekend. It'll be fine."

"Abi gezunt," he said with that biting tone that was the equivalent of a roll of the eyes.

"You're not going to say a single cynical word. Understood? Joe, look at me, understood?"

Marla stared at him, and Joe sighed. "I wouldn't dream of it."

*

VERA WAS resting against a slant board to ensure her long blue dress wouldn't wrinkle. Above her head, in the catwalks, crew members were busy adjusting the lights. From the corner of her eye she could see Clifford standing next to the director and hear his booming laughter. Max Niemann laughed back.

They were shooting a love scene that day. Marcellus, the Roman soldier who desired Salome, had returned with the proconsul and rendezvoused with her in the hallways of the palace. She'd committed the lines to memory and understood the scene perfectly. Yet she couldn't stop fretting.

The assistant director called for quiet, the sound recordist called for speed, the clapper boy enthusiastically yelled out the scene number, and there came the loud clap.

Take one. She stood with her back to Clifford. He turned her around, holding her by the shoulders. One line, another.

"Salome, you drive me mad. I burn with my need for you."

Then him embracing her. She should have been able to do it. She knew the script; the scene was brief. Yet every second was an agony. Clifford held her too tight, his hand strayed from her waist, he practically shoved her back. Take one and two and three. Small things, and yet not so small, over and over again, which made her trip over her words. His eyes were hard on her, and then when she made a mistake and they had to do another take he delivered either a booming laugh or a look of contempt.

It was not two actors on a sound stage, finding their way through a scene. It was a merciless enemy delivering blows. She was near tears when the director yelled out in exasperation.

"Cut!" he said, waving his arms. "Cut, cut, cut!"

Max Niemann stomped toward them. He stared at Vera. "What the hell is wrong with you? You're supposed to be swooning in the man's arms. You look like you're in a horror film, for fuck's sake."

"I'm sorry, Mr. Niemann."

"You're supposed to kiss the man, Vera. Kiss him, not flinch!"

"I'm sorry," she repeated, trying to blink away the tears. But her voice trembled, and she sniffled.

"What's the problem?"

"Mr. Collins," she whispered, but then she remembered how Clifford had said he was a good friend of the director and how chummy the two of them were on set that morning. She drew in a breath. "It's a difficult scene," she concluded.

"You have half an hour to compose yourself. Fucking amateur." The director shook his head in exasperation and stomped away. "We're breaking for half an hour!"

"Keep taking deep breaths, doll," Clifford told her as he brushed past her.

*

ON THE weekend she caught a ride with Jay and went to see Simon. He lived in a Tudor-style house with a splendid brick facade located close to Hancock Park. The living room was paneled in dark mahogany and had coffered ceilings. The backyard consisted of a lovely little garden that was thick with vegetation.

"I lease it from an actress who built it back when talkies were starting out," Simon said, as he handed her a glass of wine. He wasn't having wine; instead he smoked and drank a cup of coffee. "I need to find a house sitter or sublease the damn thing. I'm afraid my plants will die a merciless death."

"You have so many of them," Vera said, looking around appreciatively. "I loved our interior courtyard in Mexico. We had canaries and all sorts of plants, even a little fountain. You don't get that here in American homes."

"I know. That's why I have a dozen ferns spread around," he said with a sigh as he leaned against the fireplace mantel and looked around his living room. It was still early, and not that many guests had arrived yet at his bon voyage party. "You should look at the garden later, it's very nice. My piano, it's lovely, too. Of course, Marla doesn't like it because there's no pool. Well, who needs a pool when I'm going to be in Rio, right? I'll go swimming every day there."

"I'm sorry about that," she said.

"What? About the tour? It's Hollywood. Cary Grant and Randolph Scott could live together in Santa Monica, but that's only because they were 'bachelor roommates' and Cary is worth too much money. The rest of us, we must evade gossip."

"It's cruel what Collins did. And over what? A crummy part?"

"He's an asshole. Always was, always will be."

"He's not a good actor, either."

"Wooden," Simon said and smiled. "Orlando says he's giving you trouble on set?"

"Definitely," Vera said as she toyed with the stem of her glass and sighed. She'd done seventeen takes of that stupid scene with Clifford. By the end of it she thought she would scream.

Although Vera was tired, she was glad to be at Simon's party. It kept her mind from wandering into dark places for too long. Lately she'd pictured Salome, veiled, wrapped from head to toe in silk, as

if resting inside a cocoon. But the fabric of the cloth was too heavy,
it was too tight around her body, and Salome suffocated. If someone peeled away the wrappings, beneath they'd find only a gleaming skeleton. These morbid thoughts melded with images of
carnage. The Baptist's head on a tray, but also Salome with her feet
cut off, dancing on stumps. Or else she recalled the last scene of
Strauss's opera, when the princess is crushed to death under the
shields of soldiers. In her mind, Salome was like a beetle, shimmering and frail, and she saw her body brutally mauled by the
tetrarch's men.

Simon took a couple of puffs from his cigarette and a sip of coffee, then placed the cup on the mantel. "Your date seems nice," he
said, looking at Jay, who was talking to Marla and Miguel. Joe
stood next to them, not really chatting; he merely seemed to be
nodding. Joe raised a glass in their direction, and Simon raised his
glass in turn. "New boyfriend or casual fling?"

"Not a boyfriend," Vera said, blushing. "My mother doesn't
like him."

"How come?"

"I think she wants me at the studio working all the time with
no boys in sight. Sometimes I can't stand . . . the living arrangement," Vera said. She'd meant to say "her," but had managed to
catch herself before speaking like that.

"You should lease my house and come live here. Get a space
away from the family. Two bedrooms, a den, this lovely living
room, and I won't gouge you on the price. How about it? Want to
take over Gaucholand?"

Vera laughed. "I couldn't."

"Why not? Look, if Joe stays here, he's never going to water the
orchids."

"I'm beginning to think you invited me so you could tempt me
with your swanky house."

"Vera, you've peered into my dark heart," he said and sighed.
"I'll miss this silly town and my stupid ferns."

"I'll write to you every week until you're back," she promised. "I'll take photos of your plants and mail them to you."

"You sound like you're sending me off to war. Joe's bombastic lines must be rubbing off on you. We'll have to make a romantic drama when I come back."

"What kind of drama?"

"Something where I don't have to sing. How about I play a bullfighter?"

"Have you ever been near a bullfighting ring?"

"No. But I like the way those matadors look in their tight costumes."

They laughed. Jay was walking toward them. Simon whispered mischievously in her ear. "Your 'not boyfriend' is coming to find you," he said, and she blushed once more.

Later, as the party filled up, Jay and Vera walked in the tranquil garden behind the house, all voices and bright lights shrouded from them. The stars were out, and she felt at ease after a week that had been trepidation and suffering. She had not only struggled in her scene with Clifford, she'd danced poorly during the choreography sessions and floundered in scenes with other actors.

"You seem far away tonight," Jay told her.

"Sorry, I'm thinking about work," she said.

"It must be fun to be at that big studio."

"It's wonderful. I'm lucky," she said automatically and with such good cheer Jay should have been fooled by her carefree words. Yet perhaps the fact that it had been such a long week, or the two glasses of wine she'd had, conspired to make her voice splinter. A slight wobble gave her away.

Lucky girl.

Maybe that luck was turning.

He looked at her curiously. "But?" he asked.

"It's . . . I do like filmmaking. I like the whirlwind of it, how busy everyone is, the energy you feel on a set. Or, when I'm rehearsing a dance and they play the temporary music, I get excited trying to imagine what the final score will be like and what it'll feel like once it's on the screen. You know, when the real magic happens, when image and sound come together. God, the movie business is a jolt of electricity sometimes, it really is.

"But there are also many expectations. From the studio, from the audience, from my mother. I'm always being watched and judged. I feel like an interloper, like this isn't supposed to be my life. My mother, she never expected I'd do anything like this."

"What did she assume you'd do?"

"Not this! This was supposed to be my sister's life, and I . . ." Vera trailed off.

She sat on a wooden bench, quiet, and Jay sat with her. The air was perfumed with the scent of roses and jasmine; it made her think of home.

"Sometimes I miss Mexico," she admitted.

"You want to go back?"

"No," she said quickly. "I like California. It's exciting being here because I feel I can become someone new. Or maybe not someone new, but I might be able to discover who I am. But it's also terrifying for the same reason. For example, I've been think-ing about what you said, about that melody I wrote."

"About composing?"

"Yes," she said, nodding. "I even scribbled a few notes the other day at lunch. It's madness, isn't it? I'm an actress. Can you try to be two things at once?"

"Hazel Scott's a classical pianist who plays jazz. Swinging the classics, like she says. I suppose she's not doing that well these days due to HUAC and all, but that gal can wow you with her playing. She's dynamite."

"I don't know if I'm dynamite, that's the problem."

"I'm supposed to be working for my dad's company right this minute. That's what everyone wanted. My mother, most of all," he said, frowning. "What did your family want for you? Before Hollywood happened. You say this was supposed to be your sister's life."

"Everyone always said she was the pretty one," Vera said, looking down at her hands. "They thought she'd be a movie star. They thought I'd marry. I was, in fact, engaged."

"What happened?" he asked curiously.

"I broke it off."

"Was he a bad fellow?"

Vera raised her eyes and smiled sadly. "No, he was perfectly nice," Vera whispered, standing up and stepping away from Jay rapidly. But she felt him behind her. He didn't speak. Perhaps if he'd asked a question she wouldn't have talked, but the silence enticed her. "He courted me the way you're supposed to. He introduced himself to my folks, took me dancing, drove me to the movies. He asked me to marry him. The first time, I told him I wasn't sure how to respond. The second time, I accepted.

"Only I still wasn't sure about it. It's just that he'd told my mother that he'd asked me to marry him after that first time. She insisted I should accept him. That's why I agreed to the wedding. I couldn't think of a single reason why I should say no, but I kept wondering if I'd made the right choice.

"Then he invited me to his apartment. He had a pretty place, a charming bachelor's pad. I knew he wanted me to sleep with him, and I did. I went over there four times. When I was leaving that fourth time, he kissed me goodbye. And I realized I felt nothing at all. We'd had sex, but it hardly mattered. We could have as well have been napping. He kissed me, but if he'd simply shaken my hand, it would have been the same. I didn't love him."

She'd thought it would be like in the operas. That it would be passion and grandeur and magic. That she would be moved, emotion thundering through her veins. But Arturo had never roused any real excitement in Vera. She remembered looking at his face after they'd had sex and thinking that this was the face she would see each morning when she woke up and each night when she went to bed. This filled her with dread. She should have been elated to be married. Instead, she shivered when she counted the days on the calendar.

"I wanted to love him; I couldn't. I had to break the engage-ment. The invitations had already been printed and mailed, the wedding banns had been called. My mother almost died of shame. But I couldn't picture myself day after day having to pretend, hav-ing to wear a mask, living a life without love."

Jay was standing next to her, arms crossed. He nodded, thought-ful. "I suppose you can't force it."

"No, you really can't. It should be alchemy. Magical. Effortless. At least that's what I imagine. What do I know?" She frowned. "Have you ever been in love?"

"No," he said. "I've had a childhood sweetheart, a serious girl-friend, a foolish dalliance, but I don't think I've ever crossed that line into love."

"Quite the playboy, then."

"Hardly! The childhood sweetheart was Mildred Teale. Two years together in high school and my date to the prom. Nice, but kids' stuff. She married a friend of the family last year. Then I dated a little in university, but to be honest I was terribly busy and falling in love with music, not women. My mother set me up with Bridget Mills of the Mills and King Company junior year, and that lasted nineteen months."

"It sounds formal."

"It was. I mean, it wasn't an engagement, but my mother would have loved that."

"Why didn't you get engaged?"

"Bridget was a charming girl, but she wanted me to stop think-ing about music and secure a solid job behind a desk. I felt a bit like you: like I'd be buried alive."

She supposed it was an accurate description. She had been bricked behind a wall as if she were the heroine in a Gothic horror story.

"Bridget and I broke it off. She was glad about it. She'd grown tired of me. We still talk sometimes; she's a smart gal, but not the gal for me."

"And the foolish dalliance?"

"That," Jay said, wincing as he rubbed the back of his neck, "was plain lust. Nancy: model and actress, very attractive and very volatile. It was a bad idea from day one. You only dated that one boy you were engaged to, or did you have your lustful bad choice, too?"

Good girls were not supposed to talk about lust, and here she was discussing such things with Jay. She should slap him or change the subject. Then again, good girls were not supposed to have sex with their boyfriends or admit to anyone that they'd committed such an indiscretion, and she'd done that. If her mother or her aunt should hear Vera talking, they'd faint. Luckily, the dear ladies were not there.

"We went to an all-girls' Catholic school and after classes we had many lessons. Plus, my family is a typical Mexican middle-class family: chapada a la antigua."

He repeated the phrase. "What does that mean?"

"Old-fashioned. In Mexico, we talk of gente bien. The well-to-do. And if you want to be like the gente bien then you have to be a bit old-fashioned or everyone will make a fuss. But here everything is new and young people roam free."

"We have our codes, too. That was brave, what you did," he said, sounding serious. "Breaking that engagement off. I don't know what I would have done if the invitations were already in the mail. To be honest, I might have given the marriage a year simply to keep my mother from killing me."

Vera chuckled. "My mother thinks it was stupid. That I was a stupid girl, always had been, with my head in the clouds. You know, sometimes I feel if I can finish this movie and dance that wonderful dance sequence, and she sees me on the screen . . . I think I'll have proven her wrong."

"I think you will."

Vera watched him and smiled. "I tell you too many personal things," she said. "It's impolite."

She didn't even understand why she did it. It was excruciatingly easy to talk to Jay, but she couldn't say what made it easy.

The way he looked or sounded soothed her. She felt anxious with others, or chose to clothe herself in armor when speaking, but with Jay she let her defenses melt.

"Says who?" he asked.

"Etiquette manuals. My mother is huge on etiquette."

"She can't beat mine."

A burst of loud laughter from the house made them turn their heads. Vera looked at her wristwatch. "It's getting late. If I don't head back soon, my mother and my aunt will think I was behaving naughtily with you."

"What a wicked imagination they must have."

"You know what I mean."

"Tell them we haven't even kissed," Jay said lightly.

"I know we haven't kissed. It's a platonic friendship," she said in the same tone.

"Will we, ever?" he asked. His words were a caress, which gave her pause.

Vera looked at him, handsome and smiling in the moonlight. Jay had an effortless charm in the daytime, but at night, when the stars were out and the darkness polished his features, he was lovelier than any man she'd ever met. She remembered how she wanted to perish when the tenors sang at the opera, how the emotions lacerated her skin.

Pure feeling. That's what the music had granted her and what she'd not been able to replicate.

He looked back at her.

She inhaled sharply, her hands fluttering up to him as she lifted her chin and kissed him. Softly, at first, then with true vigor. He wrapped his arms around her. They lingered like that, their kisses growing languid until finally they parted. He ran his hand through her hair.

"You're making it difficult to be your platonic friend," he whispered.

"Maybe we shouldn't be friends," she whispered back.

They had started playing music in the house. She couldn't hear the lyrics. They vanished in the shadows of the garden. But she could hear the slow hum of the melody as Jay pressed kisses down her throat, then captured her mouth again. They drew apart. There were laughter and giggling nearby as people ventured into the garden.

They laughed, too, held hands, and rushed back into the house. In the living room they joined the dancers moving their feet to Nat King Cole's "Too Young." Vera looked up into Jay's face and smiled.

Salome

SHE HAD not seen the preacher again since her visit to the cells in the company of Josephus, though her mind kept returning to him. Or, rather, her heart returned to the young man's side, flying as quickly as a dove, as each dawn spilled into her room.

Berenice and Mariamne looked at Salome curiously, wondering about their lady's nervous pacing and her fretting. It was not like Salome to spend her days in her rooms, her tresses unbound, her eyes far away.

"Does your head ache? Do you want a cup of water with a spoonful of honey?" Berenice asked.

"Don't be silly, she needs a cup of mint tea," Mariamne said.

They tried to ply her with a plate of sliced oranges and a bowl of white almonds and silver dishes with multicolored sweets. Salome shook her head. The girls whispered, and she assumed that Herodias would soon pay her a visit and demand to know what Salome was doing, languishing in her rooms for days now.

But it was not her mother who barged into her chambers. Agrippa arrived one evening, much to the consternation of Salome's handmaidens, who tried to tell him that their mistress was feeling unwell as he boldly stepped forward, walking through her antechamber and into her room.

Crimson curtains suspended by bronze rings surrounded the large, low bed where she sat propped on plush cushions, and when

Agrippa swept the curtains away the rings tinkled. Salome was not attired for receiving guests, bare of jewels and clad in a sleeveless linen dress.

Mariamne came behind Agrippa, fretting and mumbling. "He pushed his way in, he says—"

"Cousin, I have come to keep you company as you convalesce. They tell me you have a terrible headache that won't cease. Perhaps I might know a good remedy. Would you like me to tell you a story?" he asked solicitously.

Salome did not bother reaching for a shawl to cover her shoulders, nor did she rise from bed. Instead, she looked her insolent cousin in the face.

"Fetch tea and let it cool by the window," Salome told Mariamne, and the girl nodded, slipping away.

"Fetch sweets, too," Agrippa said. "I won't abide tea without them."

"You come here as boldly as a lover with his mistress. My mother will be incensed."

"She won't mind, since she wishes you to spy on me."

"I do have a headache. Perhaps you ought to come back another time."

Agrippa sat on the bed. "The proconsul returns tomorrow, and then in three days' time we will celebrate the tetrarch's birthday, yet they say you might not attend. Are you nervous about performing in court? I heard you are an exquisite dancer."

"I am. And what of it? I am not a trained monkey to entertain you," she said, leaning on an elbow and tossing him a peevish look, but he kept smiling, ignoring her mounting irritation.

"Not me, but our uncle."

"What exactly do you want?"

The tinkling of the iron rings and the rustling of cloth announced the return of Mariamne, who placed a lacquered tray with three serving dishes by the bed. Each silver dish was filled with a different kind of sweet. The girl bowed, giving Agrippa a nervous smile, then departed.

"I want a kingdom, obviously," Agrippa said and popped a square of poppy-flavored bread into his mouth. "Our grandfather was not a tetrarch, he was a king. I'll be one, too."

"Roman wine has poisoned your brain," Salome said acidly. "There is no kingdom. It was cut into pieces."

"Our uncle has no heirs. I, by virtue of my lineage, have a better claim to these lands than any other man. Jamnia is my mother's and of course that makes it mine. To the rugged north our uncle Philip rules Batanea, Gaulanitis, Trachonitis, and Paneas, but he is sickly and is not likely to last the year. Samaria, Judaea, and Idumea should be yours by the right of your father's blood. You are Archelaus's only child. The people still remember him fondly."

Salome flinched at that, thinking of what her mother had said about her father, painting him a monster.

"What if I am his only daughter?" she asked. "Pontius Pilate rules where my father did, and when our uncle Philip dies a Roman will also be sent to govern there. Should our uncle Herod perish, it will be the same."

"I do not jest when I say your father is still beloved by many. So is my own dead father. Meanwhile, our uncle Herod is despised for his useless war, and our uncle Philip is a weakling. They would place wreaths of flowers upon our heads and cheer our names if those old fools were to vanish."

"They will not vanish, Agrippa, and if you cut off our uncle Herod's head, they'll say you are as bloodthirsty as he is. They won't cheer for you when you look like a common murderer. I doubt Rome will assassinate him for you. Our uncle still has friends. The emperor himself has favored him, and Pontius Pilate is firmly clinging to his seat, too. He would not cede it to you."

"Pontius Pilate has obtained his power from Sejanus, and Sejanus has gone too far."

She moved toward him, flinging a cushion aside until their faces were close together.

"What do you know?" she whispered. Until now Agrippa's words had been nothing but the speech of a braggart, but he looked certain of himself. If Sejanus was indeed teetering on the brink of destruction, and if he were to take Pontius Pilate with him in his fall, that might mean a chance to retrieve the lands her father had governed.

"I know if you marry me, we can restore our fractured lands into a single kingdom," he whispered back. "You can be queen and I can be king. A throne, Salome. A real throne and a real crown upon our heads, not the diadem they let our uncle Herod wear."

Not even her own father had worn a crown. The crown had been Herod the Great's, their mighty grandfather. He had ruled over the cities of Alexandrium, Hyrcania, Jericho, and Machaerus, bringing into bloom the promise of an eminent dynasty that his own ambitious father, Antipater, had once dreamed. Shrewd and ruthless, Herod the Great had been so admired that even Rome trembled and was awed by the man. His crown, his kingdom, now broken into four pieces like fragments of smashed pottery, was a shadow of what it had once been.

And although it was nothing more than whimsy and foolish talk, she sighed.

"A crown," she said, her voice faint, and fell on her back, staring at the decorated ceiling of her room, with its pattern of blue triangles and hexagons upon a yellow surface.

"A kingdom. With cities built to our measure and armies carrying our standards. Think of the immense avenues and the temples, of the statues erected in honor of our fathers who were hideously wronged," Agrippa said as he sank onto the bed next to her, murmuring in her ear. "Think of the coins minted with our likenesses on them, and the philosophers and poets that would flock to our court. No more petty wars against King Aretas, or delirious debts owed to foreign princes who have funded battles that were always meant to be lost."

"That's funny, coming from you," Salome said, and snickered. "You're the most indebted man in Rome."

"No, I am the most intelligent man in Rome because the emperor's sons attend my parties and the most influential senators drink my wine."

"Then it's not true that you lavish money on the best brothels in the city?" she asked, turning her head and smirking at him.

"Of course I do. I pay to have the workers there spy for me, and I pay to keep my friends happy."

"And you are so pure of heart you never indulge in a tryst with a pretty meretrix or a dashing concubinus?"

"Flesh for the sake of flesh is a waste," he said, but as Agrippa spoke, he leaned on his elbow and bent down to look at her, as if he might kiss her.

"If you try to seduce me again, it will amount to the same as the first time we spoke: the answer is no," she said, and pushed him lightly away so that he fell back upon the sheets and was now the one looking at the ceiling while she looked down on him. "You can stop with your silly stories if you think to use them to get me to bed with you. Promise me jewels or pearls or ten crowns, bah! You're the same as all the boys who think they can curry my favor with a tall tale. Be gone, Agrippa. My head still aches."

She stood up and parted the curtains. On a low table of inlaid jade and emeralds, by the balcony, her handmaidens had left two cups of tea. She could hear them tittering now in the antechamber, probably wondering if their mistress was in a lover's embrace. Instead, she lifted the cup to her lips.

"Why would you think it a tall tale?" Agrippa asked. He had plucked another sweet from the bowl and popped it in his mouth as he drifted toward her. "Pontius Pilate will fall."

"Let's say he does and you are correct. That still leaves us with our uncle Herod firmly perched upon his seat. Pontius's ruin might even benefit him. Why wouldn't he petition the emperor for the territories he once coveted with the Roman prefect out of the way?"

"The emperor is not going to give anything to a man who is facing a bloody revolt."

"What revolt?"

"Haven't you heard? In the streets, the Jews speak angry words. A holy man has been imprisoned in a deep dungeon, and all he did was preach the truth."

Salome, who had been smiling, swallowed a mouthful of tea and was silent. She had heard. They didn't whisper only in the streets, but also in the palace. Jokanaan the prophet had been kept in his cell for ten nights now. During those nights she lay still, as if the sheets upon her bed were a burial shroud, and traced the shadows that drifted upon her wall with weary eyes. In the daytime, she had counted each hour and listened to each rumor that drifted her way.

The Pharisees, longtime enemies of Rome and of the tetrarch, spoke of a tyrant who trampled upon the innocent, and their voices echoed down busy streets. The Sadducees, who might normally be more conciliatory, burned with rage, too. Vociferations were common, as was the clang of soldiers' shields as they pushed people away and silenced dissenters.

Caiaphas had sent word, quietly, that the prophet must not be released, for he would spark a riot, although Josephus feared a riot might break out if Jokanaan was not set free soon. Herodias had ordered the court astrologer to study the heavens, hoping his augurs would assure the tetrarch that the prisoner must perish. High-ranking officers added their counsel and asked for the insolent preacher's death.

Her cousin spoke urgently, his voice low. "If the prophet were to die, imagine what would happen: chaos, madness, the city ablaze. All of Rome would know what a worthless ruler our uncle is. He would be replaced."

"Then, by right of marriage to me, you would demand my father's lands, too."

"No." He shook his head. "By your right alone, you'd be crowned queen of Samaria, Judaea, and Idumea. I would be a consort king."

By her right alone! The eagerness that she had not felt when

Agrippa looked at her in bed now enflamed her blood. A queen regnant, able to command armies and order magistrates. The thought of it made her dizzy, yet she set her cup of tea down and eyed him with distrust.

"Why would you ever consider that? You said you want a kingdom, yet you'd allow me to keep a fourth of it?"

"I want a dynasty," Agrippa said, and he took her hand and pulled her out onto the balcony, where he leaned forward against the railing. "We are the seeds of a mighty tree. Our children will rule it all," he said and extended an arm, sweeping it across the sky.

"You're bold."

"So are you."

She rubbed her hands against her arms and looked down at her bare feet. The elation he'd conjured was quickly dying and turning to ice. It weighed her body down, made her soul heavy, and she could hardly raise her head when he spoke and delicately touched her chin.

"You must fix your hair and change into splendid clothes. Our uncle will send for you when I leave your chambers."

"How can you be certain?"

"He'll be curious and jealous. What improprieties could the young would-be lover commit behind the privacy of silk curtains?" Agrippa wondered. "I'd want to know."

Clever Agrippa, she thought. It had been ten nights and Salome had lain alone and quiet in her rooms, far from court, far from her uncle's eyes.

*

HEROD SUMMONED his niece. She did fix her hair, but not because Agrippa had counseled as much. She thought if she looked weary her uncle might want to know why. She preferred to avoid such a line of questioning.

The dress she picked had a high, stiff collar embroidered with pearls and was severe in cut. It gave her a solemn air. When she walked into her uncle's reception room, Salome immediately bowed her head and swept a hand against her chest.

"Lord Tetrarch," she said, her eyes fixing on the mosaic of lions decorating the floor.

"Come forward."

Herod, who was sitting on a wide couch with carved legs in the shape of more lions, beckoned Salome with his right hand, and she raised her head and obeyed. "Agrippa has paid you a visit. What did he say?"

Her cousin was indeed canny, having calculated their uncle's reaction with ingenious precision. Salome felt both impressed and annoyed by his wits. "He came to push his suit, even though he cannot afford the dowry you request."

"Of course he did," Herod muttered. "The effrontery of that boy never ceases. What else?"

"Not much else," she said. The lie was easy since she had decided she would not reveal any of Agrippa's machinations to her uncle. At least, for now.

"He spoke to you for a long time."

"He likes to hear himself talking, and he was trying to woo me."

Her uncle nodded and stood up. "Your mother would like to see you married to Marcellus. You've spent many days alone in your rooms. Have you been pining over him because he is away?"

Herod was watching her carefully. Salome cursed herself for her melancholy and isolation. It had brought up too many unwanted questions and attention.

"My mother may like the Romans and their ways, but I know that the choice of a husband must be made by the tetrarch."

"Well spoken," he said. He curved his lips into a smile, and his eyes fixed on her with that fierce intensity she detested. When she stood in his presence in the dining hall she could step out, but now, alone, in his chambers, all she could do was lower her gaze and wait.

"I wish for you to dance for me during my birthday feast, Salome. It would impress my guests. Yet your mother says you will not."

"It's a long dance."

"I know. But I'll give you a reward if you do, as is customary."

Pearls or emeralds, perhaps. A golden bracelet. When her mother had danced the Dance of the Seven Veils she'd received such trinkets. It was the tradition, but Salome desired nothing except for the mouth of the preacher deep in the cells of the castle.

Her uncle must have noticed her skepticism, even though her eyes were downcast and her expression was neutral. "Perhaps you wish for a grand prize? Something out of the ordinary. Ask me for your heart's desire and you shall have it."

"My heart's desire," Salome said, scoffing and raising her eyes, sure that the tetrarch was jesting. But when he spoke his face was made of stone.

"If you dance at the feast you may ask of me what you will. I promise to give it you, even unto the half of my kingdom."

She turned from him, her heart beating faster. "Will you indeed give me whatever I ask?"

"I swear it by my life, by my gods. Do you wish for me to swear it before the court? I shall," he said, and the tetrarch stepped close to her, until he was standing behind Salome and his hand fell upon the young woman's shoulder, pulling her toward him so that her back was pressed against his chest. "By my crown, Salome."

You have no crown, she thought. *Our kingdom is shattered, and my father is dead, and you have no true throne.*

"It will be a remarkable feast, and I want you to shine like a diamond in the midst of all our honored guests. I'll have actors from Crete and singers from Carthage. The Jewish preacher will be marched out in chains of bronze for the proconsul to see," Herod murmured in her ear.

"You'll bring him to the feast?"

"It'll be a show of power."

Jokanaan. How she longed to see him again, and yet how she had resisted the impulse to flee deep into the dungeons in search of the young man.

In her startled state Salome barely reacted to the touch of the tetrarch's hands upon her shoulders, sliding down her arms. "What is to become of him?"

"I have not decided yet," he said with a sigh. "He is either a holy man or a fraud. How restless the Jews grow about him!"

"He's seen the face of God," she whispered.

"Come now, forget about that fool. Will you dance for me, Salome? You are exquisite, the most charming woman at court."

Salome stared down at the floor with its great lions, their mouths open, mutely roaring. She fixed her eyes on their fangs and stood still, trying to remember her father's face, his voice. But he'd been dead for so long and all she could recall was her cousin's whispers, urging her to treason.

"I'll dance, Tetrarch," she said, pulling away from him, "but you must remember your oath. You'll give me what I wish."

Before she could say more, he'd spun her around, and they were facing each other. The tetrarch smiled, pleased by her answer. "What do you want as a reward?"

"I won't speak it yet. You must wait until the feast. Unto half your kingdom, you've said."

"Precious Salome, will you wish for a citadel?" he asked, his hand resting on her waist for a moment, possessive and firm. He had never dared as much, but then she had never allowed him this nearness. She evaded the tetrarch, stepped aside; it was a nimble choreography. Now she stood still, thinking of the beautiful preacher whom she loved.

"No," she said. "Nothing so fanciful." Then, finally, she disentangled herself from his grasp, smiling with a false, cheerful ease. "It will be a wonderful birthday feast."

"Indeed."

She bowed her head and bid her uncle farewell. He responded with a nod and a smile. Salome remembered when he'd first come to her father's court, in his armor and his cape, looking like the prince from ancient tales. She remembered how her mother had looked at him with admiration, and her ladies had whispered muffled compliments.

But now there was little left of that strong youth. Instead, she stood before a gray satyr whose eyes burned with a poisonous yearning.

Agrippa was right. Why should they remain under the control of tyrants and fools? Why should they do the bidding of old men with dark desires and foul breath? Why not strike, strike now, strike somehow?

Yet as Salome hurried out of the chamber she recalled Agrippa's other words, his plan: that the preacher must die. She closed her left hand into a fist and pressed it against her chest, feeling the wild thumping of her heart.

Lillian Kelly

NANCY WAS the most glamorous girl in school. The rest of us, we were stumbling around, feeling awkward, trying to figure out how to paint our lips or what shoes to wear, and there she was, looking like a film star.

She loved movies. She was always reading about actors and actresses. She tried to imitate their mannerisms or adopt their poses. She talked about the people in films like she knew them personally. Wasn't Franchot just darling in his latest film? Whatever possessed Hedy to wear that awful skirt? You'd think she'd been having cocktails with these folks the night before.

She did my hair a few times in the style of famous stars. She had a real talent for hairdressing. I used to tell her: you should open up a salon, Nancy. I have some fine pictures of us together, dolled up and ready to go out for a school dance.

She acted older than the rest of us, wiser. She was special. Everyone thought so. I wasn't surprised when she married Theodore

Livesey, even though they hadn't dated that long. He was the best that could be had—not only handsome, but a member of one of the most respected families in town—and that was what Nancy wanted. She wanted the best.

You should have seen her those first few months after the wedding, buying herself dresses, gloves, and hats so she could look good for Theo. Picking the perfect curtains that matched the perfect rug. Cooking meals fit for a king.

She was a great cook. She loved to have people over and make canapés and fix cocktails for everyone. She was a charming hostess, wonderful.

After her divorce, we sort of lost touch. I did see her once when she was living in Los Angeles. This must have been almost a year before, you know, the incident happened. We went out for lunch. She still looked like Nancy Hartley. She dressed nicely, did her makeup well, and her hair was impeccable. But she appeared tired and worn.

She was twenty-six, but sometimes she angled her head one way and you would have thought her ten years older. I think the world hardened her, made her grow up faster than she should have.

That last time we met, she talked about Hollywood people the way she used to. Monty Clift has been doing this and all that. I remember feeling sad when she spoke. Because she was trying to impress me, trying to make me see how she knew this person, how they were close, but I could tell it wasn't true. She sounded like when we were in high school and she collected issues of *Photoplay*. She was still dreaming the same dreams a decade later.

Nancy

SHE MET Benny late at night. She couldn't have done it in the daytime. Their relationship was knitted together in the safety of shadows. Under the glare of the sun, she might have thought better of it. But the stars muffled good sense and prudence.

When Benny opened the door, he wasn't surprised to see Nancy.

He let her in; they went to his room. She felt annoyed by how sure of himself he seemed. As if he'd circled this date on the calendar weeks before and predicted she would show up. Then again, that was the way they dealt with each other, wasn't it? There was an awful clockwork mechanism that joined and separated them.

She disliked kisses on the mouth. It was one of the things that had annoyed her about Jay. How much he enjoyed kissing, holding hands. Benny knew this. Benny kissed Nancy on the neck, which was fine.

Then he touched Nancy and murmured against her skin. She lay down on the rumpled bed but didn't make a move to take off her clothes, and he stretched next to Nancy until she grabbed his face and shook her head.

"What's the matter, doll?" he asked.

Benny could be sugary sweet, lavishing tenderness and compliments. That's why she'd taken an interest in him. When she told him she wanted to make it as an actress, Benny believed her. Others nodded their heads, but Benny was one of the only people she'd ever met who responded to her words with real conviction, saying she would make it big one day. Men pretended to be nice, heaped false praise on Nancy, eager to fuck her, but Benny could be honest.

"I have a huge problem, Benny. Wally Olrof wants me to pay him six hundred dollars."

"What for?"

"He put the bite on me."

"How? What's he got on you?"

"He took nudes of me, promised they were private. Now he says if I don't give him six hundred bucks, he'll show them to the folks at Pacific Pictures. They'll kick me out if they find out about that sort of gig, they will. All over that cheap crook."

Benny frowned. "You let Wally take nudes?"

"It was ages ago. I'd forgotten about it. A gal's got to make a living, right?"

"You could have asked me for the cash," he said, although they both knew that was a lie.

Benny made money but he also burned it quick. Maybe it was

the liquor that emptied his wallet, maybe it was that Benny was the type of guy who would never score big. He was destined for the little leagues, a small-time criminal who was going to seed quickly. She could see his ruin sketched on his face, recognizing the faint worry lines that would soon turn to deep furrows. His body was losing the nimble physique she'd found attractive when they'd first met poolside ages ago.

Back then, when Benny had been nameless, merely a good-looking stranger who asked her out to dinner, she had been able to fantasize that he might be someone special. A Prince Charming ready to squire her away to happiness. She'd learned better, quickly. Benny was another nobody with a few good lines and a car. He was never going to achieve anything because he didn't care to rise above mediocrity, and he didn't have the capacity even if he did try. Benny was a dead end.

"I can ask you now, can't I?"

"Six hundred," Benny said, shaking his head. "Why haven't you told that Princeton chap to lend you the dough?"

She wished he hadn't mentioned Jay Rutland. The thought of him made her frown. "You know I broke it off," she said.

"Didn't know nothing. I've been keeping out of your way, seeing as you don't want me no longer," he said, attempting to appear apathetic although the slight hitch in his voice gave him away. He'd been thinking about her and Jay; he'd probably been driving himself crazy over them.

"I never said I didn't want you."

"You did, Nancy."

"You called me cheap, Ben," she replied, wishing she didn't sound so damn wounded by it.

He scratched his head. "Didn't mean to hurt you."

"You did. You always know how to hurt me."

The rawness of her response made Benny stare, and for one moment she felt like dissolving in sobs and hugging him. Then she straightened up, remembering why she'd gone there. The six hundred. She'd better get it.

"Maybe you're right. Maybe I should ask Jay for the money."

Benny's room was draped in shadows, but she could see his eyes clearly enough. There was an angry, hard resolve in them. He stood up, grabbed a jacket. "Come on," he said.

*

WALLACE OLROF, unlike Benny, was not nocturnal, and when Benny knocked on his door he took his time opening. He rubbed his eyes, yawning theatrically as he looked at them from behind a thin door chain. He had put on a tattered gray robe and a pair of matching slippers.

"Ben, Nancy. What—"

"Let us in, buster. We got business," Benny said.

"It's after midnight," he said, yawning again.

"It's urgent and it'll be worth your while."

For a moment Nancy thought he wouldn't let them in, but then Wallace blinked and nodded, undoing the chain and shuffling aside. He looked at Nancy curiously, a speck of disdain in his eyes, before motioning to them.

"Let me put the kettle on," Wallace muttered.

They walked across his living room, which Nancy remembered well from the time she'd come over to have her picture taken. He'd had her lying on that blue couch in the corner, her legs in the air. Six hundred dollars. The bastard hadn't paid her nearly enough for those dirty pictures, and he wanted six hundred bucks.

Wallace stumbled into the kitchen and flicked on a light switch; the kitchen was illuminated, revealing its stark ugliness. Wallace's sink was full of dirty water, and he had dishes soaking in it. The linoleum floor was scratched and littered with crumbs. The little kitchen table pressed against the wall had an ashtray packed to the brim with cigarette stubs.

Wallace filled the kettle with water and set it on a burner. "What's so urgent?" Wallace asked.

"Nancy said you're wanting six hundred dollars for a bunch of old pictures you took of her."

"That's a deal between Nancy and me."

"I've come to settle it."

"You're going to pay the six hundred dollars?" Wallace asked.

"Fuck, no."

Wallace looked at Benny in confusion and opened his mouth, probably to protest or ask a question, but before he could utter a sound Benny punched him in the face. Wallace stumbled back and Benny hit him again, his fists sinking into the man's belly. Wallace almost toppled over, before grabbing on to the sink. Benny clutched Wallace's hair with a firm hand and forced the man's head into the dirty kitchen sink, splashing water and rattling the dishes there.

Wallace struggled, attempting to loosen Benny's hold on his head, but Benny was bigger than the photographer. Why, Wallace was nothing but a skinny little shrimp wrapped in his gray robe. When Benny pulled him up, Wallace sputtered and gasped and tried to pull himself away from the man's hands with no success. In the process of attempting to dislodge himself from Benny's grip, he'd managed to lose one of his slippers.

"Where do you keep the negatives?" Benny asked.

"You're insane! I'm not telling you anything!"

"You better."

"Fuck you!"

Benny dunked Wallace's head underwater again, rattling the dishes, sending a cup and a glass crashing to the floor. Wallace was screaming, but it came out as a muffled gurgling. He was trying to push Benny away, but Benny persisted in his task, his brows knitted together as he pressed the man down and held him there.

Nancy had seen Benny getting mean with others before, usually when a guy owed him money. But she'd never seen him quite this furious. It scared her enough to make her clutch the chair next to her, but she didn't speak a word urging him to stop. She clamped her mouth shut, remembering how that piece of shit photographer had treated her.

Benny stepped away, and Wallace was finally able to raise his head out of the water. With shaky legs he stood next to the sink, soaked, his eyes wild. Benny lifted the kettle and slammed it against the photographer's torso. Wallace screamed and fell to his knees. Benny raised the kettle again, this time aiming for the head.

"Where are the negatives?"

"Living room. White box next to the books," Wallace said. He spat on the floor.

Benny threw the kettle against a wall and stomped into the living room. Nancy followed him. Benny pushed a bunch of books aside, and there was the box. He went back into the kitchen where Wallace was moaning. He immediately quieted when he saw Benny. Nancy leaned against the doorframe, and Wallace stared at her. She stared back, her chin held up high.

Benny opened the white box, which was filled with negatives, and tossed it on the kitchen table. Then he rattled a drawer open and another until he found a box with matches. From the cupboard he took a large salad bowl and brought it to the table.

He grabbed one of the negatives and held it up to the light. Then he tossed it in the salad bowl, along with the others.

She had a sudden desire to look at the negatives, to gaze again at her image imprinted on the film as if to ascertain it was really her, or to remember the exact way she'd posed. But what would that do?

Benny struck a match and lit one of the pieces of film. It curled a little as the flame ran down its side. The burning film had an acrid, unpleasant smell. She recalled, morosely, that Jay Rutland had taken a couple of snapshots of her with his camera. Casual shots like the ones every couple took, back when she thought they might be a couple. And she also thought about her ex-husband, who had paid for a session with a local studio photographer for a series of glamorous pictures of his young wife.

She remembered her glee when she saw the final shots, how she had admired the line of her neck and her sexy eyes. More than once, when Theo was away at work, she'd taken out the shots and looked at them reverently, trying to imagine them printed in a magazine or the newspaper. She had even asked Theo if she could have more pictures taken, and he had wondered why she'd want to do another shoot when she already had those photographs.

"I think the pictures are good, and maybe I could model," she said. "When I was little my daddy wanted me to act, and maybe modeling is not the same as acting, but it's close enough."

"Nancy, what a thought!" Theo said, chuckling. "What a silly thought!"

Maybe it had been that day, when her husband laughed, that she had begun to hate him and their little house with its pretty curtains and the baking dishes and the china they'd been gifted for their wedding.

Well, what did Theo know? She'd modeled, yes, she had, for a few catalogues and even for the likes of a slimy photographer. Dressed in a plush coat and also stark naked.

Benny had never asked to take her picture. If he'd asked, she would have said no. Then again, she felt that perhaps the reason he hadn't bothered to voice this request was that he believed he could always have her in the flesh. He didn't need Kodak film to remember her.

"Is that it? Do you have any more pictures?" Benny asked.

"No," Wallace said.

"If you do, and I find out that you do, I'll hurt you much worse than this."

Wallace was panting. He spat again and shook his head. Benny walked back toward the doorway and pulled Nancy with him. They stepped out, arm in arm.

He drove in silence—though his mouth twitched a couple of times, as if he were thinking of something to say before deciding better of it—and in silence they returned to his home, back to his room, to his bed. Protected once again by shadows, she was able to breathe again as he pulled down the zipper of her dress.

The fabric fell from her shoulders with an effortless ease, and she slid under the sheets. The familiarity of these steps made her wince for one second.

It always ended like this with them, the eternal reconciliation. The beating had been a new and different element, but the rest was the same choreography they'd long mastered. It was comforting, in a way, yet it also irritated her.

A dependency, that's what it was. She wanted to get rid of Benny and never managed it. Then at times like this, shrouded in the sweetness of the night, she would stupidly think maybe they belonged together.

"I'd fucking kill for you, do you know that, Nancy?" Benny asked as he pulled the sheets aside and slipped into bed next to her, burying his mouth against her nape.

"I know," she whispered, wishing he didn't care that much, didn't want her so badly, because then she felt compelled to want him back a little. It would have been better if she hadn't wanted him at all.

That trickle of a feeling incensed her, and sooner or later she'd strike up in rage against him. Because, in the end, Benny wasn't who she desired. Benny was nothing like the poised actors she admired, or the classy studio executives she thought might make good acquaintances. The nagging idea that Benny might be the only person she would ever deserve—a twisted, depraved soulmate—made her grit her teeth. Yet in the end there she was, in Benny's bed, indebted once again to this man, clutching him tight.

Hollywood Connection

Scandal on set! Latin lassie causes "mucho" trouble

PACIFIC PICTURES has been trying hard to promote its newest acquisition, Vera Larios, as a south-of-the-border sweetheart, but turns out the little enchilada is less sugary than we thought.

Larios, who is currently on the set of *The Seventh Veil of Salome*, has been seen palling around Hollywood with co-star Clifford Collins. As many of our readers know, Clifford and Donna Fowler have long been an item. Well, it turns out that this tiny brown temptress has been hard at work, endeavoring to break the couple up.

"Clifford is a gentleman, so he agreed to squire Vera at clubs as a favor to the studio, but then Vera seemed to get the idea that he was available, even though Donna had made it clear he was *her* man. Well, Clifford had to set the record straight, and Vera didn't take it well," a source close to the actor said. "You should have heard her shrieking!"

Apparently, communication between the two performers has been frosty on set, aggravating what many are calling a strenuous shoot. A little bird has told *Hollywood Connection* that the girl can't even say her lines right, and her voice coach has trouble understanding her when she tries to speak two words of English. Then again, Larios wasn't hired for her speaking skills but to show off that bosom. But even that is proving to be a problem.

"Vera is not only demanding, but she also is completely unprepared for the role," the same source said. "Word is recasting might be in the works."

With fears of the flick going over budget and director Max Niemann reportedly having several loud rows with his star performer, you'd think Vera Larios would be concerned about her career, but we hear she's too busy snagging a new man. The fellow in question? Jay Rutland, of the Rutland Navigation Company. Watch out, Jay! This Mexican minx has claws. As for Larios, she might want to spend more time learning her lines than dancing at Ciro's.

Vera

HER MOTHER'S voice had several registers. She was, at this point, a soprano who might have been able to sing the part of the Queen of the Night, her words practically piercing the windows in the living room. Vera figured the entire neighborhood would be able to report on their conversation the next morning.

"'She might want to spend more time learning her lines than

dancing at Ciro's,'" her mother said, rolling up the magazine she had been reading and now brandishing it as if it were a weapon, moving her hand up and down in the air. "This is not good publicity, Vera! It's not proper behavior from a Larios!"

"I told you, you're too soft on her," her aunt said. She was on the couch, knitting and offering the occasional comment. Vera's cousin Cecilia sat next to her mother, with a basket full of balls of yarn on her lap. She knew better than to interject and simply held on to the wicker basket.

"It's only a silly story," Vera said, although she had a lump in her throat. Since she'd learned about the coverage in *Hollywood Connection* that morning, she'd been weathering recriminations, first from the publicity department, then from her director, and now from her family.

"You have an image to maintain, Vera! What will we do if they start talking like this about you? Things are going to change around here. I am too soft on you. Work! That is what you should be doing."

"I'm working," she protested.

"From now on, you will go back and forth from the studio, no parties, no clubs, no dancing," her mother said imperiously and dropped the magazine on the coffee table in front of her. "I'm not going to let you ruin this for us."

"Mother—"

"No. I've had enough. You never finish what you start, Vera. You're too absent-minded, you've always been like that. Every time I stopped at your father's reception room, you'd have the radio on and you'd be staring out the window."

Her mother and her aunt glared at Vera, secure in their power. Vera's first instinct was to look down at the floor and nod, but something welled inside of her. Anger, which she'd carefully concealed her entire life.

Maybe Vera did stare out the window, maybe she did slip into the music and if they played a piece from *Carmen* or *La Bohème* she could lose track of time. But what of it?

She stood up.

"I'm an adult. You can't tell me where I can go and what I can do. You're not my agent, you're not my director. You don't have a say in my life."

At first, her mother did not react, possibly because she couldn't believe that Vera was talking back to her. Respect and obedience were what she had been taught; her frustrations were kept under the skin. The manuals of good manners her mother declaimed, like scripture, demanded it. The middle class rabidly sought decorum. Decency. Even denial. Every single impious, impure thought was to be kept under lock and key, in secret. Emotion was a whisper. But now Vera felt like hollering.

"I don't have a say? I'm your mother! I'm here to make sure you don't ruin this chance, that you don't—"

"You should go home, then. Dad calls and writes asking when you'll go home. Well, you should. I don't need you here to babysit me."

"As if you'd be able to do a thing without me. You're a girl."

"I'm a woman, and I'm getting my own place."

Her aunt dropped her needles, and cousin Cecilia gasped. Vera's mother did not react. She looked as if she'd been turned into a pillar of salt and marooned upon a barren mountain.

"Your own place?"

"Yes," Vera said. "A friend of mine needs someone to take over his lease for a few months. It's a lovely house."

"You can't possibly live on your own. It's not done. What will our friends say? Your father will be livid!"

"I'll tell him tonight."

"No. I forbid it."

"I'm doing it. I want to have a life, and I can't have it if I'm clinging to your skirts," Vera said.

"Raise crows and they'll peck your eyes," her aunt said.

That nasty little dig was typical of her aunt, and it was typical of Vera to ignore it, but she would not let herself be frightened.

"Stay out of it," Vera said, even though she felt like her lip might start trembling.

"Severa!" her mother yelled in a voice that was a perfect imitation of a coloratura, hitting an astonishingly high F6.

*

IT WAS summer and sunny outside, but the set had turned to ice. It was like walking from the Sahara and into Antarctica each day. The pressure of the shoot was fraying her nerves, and she suspected a coup, a fatal blow.

Recasting. That terrible word that had been dangled in *Hollywood Connection*. It haunted her, as did her mother's bitter face.

"Could they really do it?" she asked Marla.

"Depends how much footage they've shot and what they've shot. I wouldn't lose sleep over it."

Marla was leaning against the wall of one of the office buildings and smoking a cigarette. She was in full costume, with a red skirt and matching high heels. Vera didn't smoke, but she also leaned her back against the wall, arms crossed.

"But it happens sometimes, doesn't it? They recast Judy Garland in *Annie Get Your Gun*. Bette Davis has been recast, too."

Marla nodded, airily holding her slim little cigarette between her middle and her index finger.

"But that's different, honey. They recast Bette every time she's being rebellious, and they recast Judy because she pops too many bennies. The important part is the rushes. If the daily rushes are going well, then the rest is meaningless," Marla said.

"I'm not normally invited to watch the rushes. But Clifford gets to see them. He asked to have a few of his lines changed again. He says Joe's script makes him seem too soft, that he sounds like a 'sissy' because he's supposed to cry in a scene."

"Does he want to sound like a prick instead?"

Two men dressed as clowns were walking a dog, and they waved at Marla. Marla waved back.

"If Clifford could, he'd have the picture retitled and centered on his character. He's unbearable, but the director loves him, and the more he likes Clifford's performance, the more he hates mine. He snaps at me all the time now."

"Max snaps at everyone. His temper is legendary."

"But the story in that stupid magazine," Vera muttered. "It's made things even worse with him. And the dance . . . I keep going over the dance in my mind."

"The magazine story is nothing." Marla dropped her cigarette and crushed it under the heel of her shoe. "Keep doing what you're doing, it will be fine. I've seen you working on your choreography. Even overworking."

"It's not just that. My mother hates me because I'm moving into Simon's house. I'm not even convinced it's smart to be on my own. Maybe I should rethink it."

Her mother was wrong, wasn't she? About Vera being hopeless, about dire predictions of failure should she move out and send her mother packing. About the difficulties of making it on her own in the city. She was tossing respectability into the gutter, that's what her mother had said.

She'd been so certain of her choice only a couple of days before, and now Vera trembled.

"Never. You're supposed to watch over the man's plants. Otherwise, Joe gets to kill them all. Last year, he murdered two ferns of mine. Come play canasta at my place this weekend. Miguel and Joe will be there, but we'll also have a special appearance by Ricardo Montalbán and Georgiana Young. They're fun."

They walked together for a few minutes, before Marla's route took her away from the sound stage where Vera was working. Vera hummed a tune under her breath.

She wanted this movie, this role. Lucky girl! That's what everyone had said. Vera wanted to prove to them that it wasn't luck, that it was talent. That she deserved this moment. The way her mother looked at Vera, that mixture between skepticism and resentment made her blood boil. She would have preferred her other daughter in the role, the good one. Yet it was Vera here, now.

Nevertheless, it was too much. All together, all at once, the attention, the pressure, the demands, and she often searching for a respite. A second of clarity. She had no idea what she was doing, where she was headed; half the time she couldn't think. Was she shameless and stubborn, like her mother said, or merely determined and energetic, as Marla told her?

That thread of a melody she was weaving, it kept her sane.

Too soon, Vera was back on the set, the tune interrupted as she was ushered back into her costume, into a headdress, into the elaborate palace made of plaster and imitation bricks, burlap, and wooden supporting panels. Too soon, her director was there, yelling.

"Salome!" he said. "Salome!" As if he'd forgotten Vera's real name.

*

LUKE MAHONEY had wanted to take Vera to the Zebra Room, where everything was, predictably, safari themed, with chairs upholstered in zebra-print fabric and spears on the walls. She managed to convince him to have lunch at Hamburger Hamlet instead. It would be a more casual spot. She couldn't stomach a popular restaurant where they might bump into other actors, or even worse, her director.

Luke skipped over most of the small talk and jumped to business right after they ordered their burgers.

"You got the script I sent, right? If you haven't read it, it's fine. It's a love triangle. You'd play the Indian maiden who is in love with the hero."

"I have it with me, but I haven't even finished shooting *The Seventh Veil of Salome*," Vera said, pulling the script from her oversize purse. "How can I be thinking about another picture?"

"It's the way it works with contract players. The studio wants to get its money's worth out of everyone. You're not going to only shoot one flick a year. *Wild Thunder* won't begin filming anytime soon. You'll have two whole months between pictures before cameras roll."

"It doesn't seem like a great part," Vera said, thumbing through the script. "Great" was a euphemism. From what she'd seen of the script pages, the movie would require her to stand around mutely for the duration of it, or say the most ridiculous, grammatically incorrect sentences.

"Let me be honest. If you start rejecting parts, the studio will warehouse you. You don't want that. It's difficult enough getting jobs for Hispanic actors. There aren't that many roles to go around."

"What about Anthony Quinn? He works often."

"Because folks think he's Italian, and he married DeMille's daughter."

"Katy Jurado was nominated for an Oscar last year."

"And I'll have you remember she played a Comanche princess. Vera, what we need is to have you out there in as many vehicles as we can. Let people see you can do an Indian girl in a Western, then maybe you'll get, I don't know, a Tahitian girl or a Chinese geisha like in *Madame Butterfly*."

"Cio-Cio-San is Japanese," Vera said, looking at her agent tiredly. "Di sua voce il mistero l'anima mi colpì."

He laughed. The waitress placed their hamburgers before them, and he picked his up with both hands and began munching it. "You know what's your problem, Vera? You're too clever by half, and you want everyone to know it."

"Luke, I don't think it's too much to ask—"

"For better roles? No. You can ask, but I'm telling you: ask too much and they'll think you're difficult. You don't want that. Already people are talking about you."

"The *Hollywood Connection* story," Vera said with a sigh.

"Yes. Besides, the trick about this town is that you must strike quick. You're a hot enough commodity right now, but careers can grow ice cold in a few months. I've seen it happen dozens of times," he said, shaking a finger with the air of a professor giving a lecture. "If you take this part, you'll show the studio that you're willing to play ball. That's what we want. Don't kill your career before it even begins, Vera."

Was it what *she* wanted? Vera stirred her soda with a straw and contemplated the hamburger on her plate. She thought of Salome crushed under the soldiers' shields, her body a dark smudge against a marble floor, her blood staining the decorative mosaics red.

*

"WHAT'S THAT?" Jay asked.

"Hmm?"

She turned her head. They lay on a plush white rug in the living room. A forgotten crossword had been brushed to the side, along with a pencil and two empty bottles of soda. The record Jay had been playing had ended, and she had filled the silence with her humming. It was her first weekend in her new home, and she'd felt intimidated by the lonesomeness of the experience. She'd telephoned Jay, he offered to stop by, and had come with records under his arm and a warm smile.

It was not the clandestine reunion her mother and aunt feared. Debauchery, that's what they pictured. Wine, drugs, sex, parties, dirty dishes, mounds of wrinkled clothes, chaos. Cousin Cecilia had told her so. They'd been arguing about her back at the house. Vera's mother was making arrangements to return to Mexico City. Yet she paused in her packing to complain bitterly about her daughter's ingratitude and defects, with her aunt serving as a Greek chorus.

Vera had felt tempted to invite her family over so they might see she had not moved to Gomorrah, but she decided it was best to wait. Her mother might interpret such an invitation as an attempt to gloat about her newfound freedom. If she waited a couple of weeks, perhaps she'd be more tractable. Despite her mother's furious proclamations that she would leave immediately, Vera doubted she'd make it out of Los Angeles in less than a month.

"You were humming."

"I didn't realize it," Vera said, twirling the straw she had used to sip her soda between her fingers.

"Music from your movie?"

"Maybe . . . inspired by it. It's something I've come up with."

"Vera Larios, are you writing music?"

"No! Not really," she said, dropping the straw as if she'd burned her hand.

"Yes, you are."

He grinned at her and she smiled back, feeling shy. "Well, yes, maybe a little. Simon has an upright piano in the study, and I was tinkering with it this morning."

"You'll have to play the whole thing for me later."

"It's not finished."

"Does this piece have a name?"

"Love," that had been the melody she'd written before. This she had dubbed "Passion." "Not yet," she said.

"If it's inspired by your movie you can call it 'Theme for Salome,' and if the flick's a big hit you'll have a major musical success to go along with it."

"I should be thinking about choreography, not naming tunes," Vera said with a sigh. "I feel like I'm going to ruin every take of the dance sequence."

She hardly had time to think this role through, to imagine Salome. She knew she was merely repeating words on a page, imitating emotions. The dance was supposed to be the climax of the film, the moment when Salome is stripped down to her core, and yet she was unsure of what she would reveal on screen.

That little tune in her head helped Vera maintain her focus. It soothed her. She felt as if there was another story that was told within that melody, different from the one the studio was attempting to shoot in bright colors, about a woman who is trapped behind the tall walls of a castle. That story enticed her, made her want to keep stepping forward even as her fears threatened to crush her spine. She remembered how she'd pictured Salome with her feet cut off, still attempting to dance.

"I want it to be right, to be perfect. But each time I think I understand the performance, I stumble. I'm tense. I fear it'll be terrible. Are you ever afraid?" she asked.

"Of spiders and sharks," Jay said, smiling. The jest did not lighten her mood; she shivered.

"No. I mean afraid. Really afraid. As if you'll make a catastrophic mistake and then the world will end." She sat up and wrapped her arms around her legs. "It's hard to explain. I can see the movie clearly in my mind sometimes, I can almost hear the score playing, but other times I think the film is about to catch on fire, and it will combust on the screen, right before my eyes. There'll be nothing but ashes."

"A career up in flames, then," he said and sat up, too. His hand rested on her shoulder.

No, not a career, she thought. But herself, reduced to ashes.

"It's the dance scene that keeps me awake, the moment when they bring the silver plate with the head of the Baptist on it. I've even started dreaming of it, dreaming of blood." She chuckled and shrugged. "I suppose I'm not much of an actress if I get this nervous, am I?"

"You're too hard on yourself," he said, tucking a strand of hair behind her ear.

"But it's hard and sometimes it's awful. My agent wants me to take the role of an Indian girl in a Western and I hate it. It's a terrible part."

"I guess all actors have bad roles."

"You don't get it, Jay. Mexican actors, they're asked to play bullfighters and spicy 'señoritas' and stand in the background."

"But you have a major part."

"I thought it would lead to better things, but the kinds of roles my agent is talking about, they're not better," she said. "They're silly and even embarrassing. On the streets they call us 'greasers'; at the lot we're 'brown sugar.'"

"I've never heard anyone call you a greaser or brown sugar."

"You're not around all the time," she muttered and closed her eyes. He couldn't know what it was like, the little digs she stomached and then the bigger ones. The way she was afraid of making a bad impression or even of attracting attention, because what if it was the wrong kind of attention? In the magazines and the newspapers they described her as a hot tamale, a spicy pepper, a chocolate chica.

She was comestible. A snack. She was also supposed to be fiery, wild, loud. That she wasn't anything like that hardly mattered: they could pretend she was, mold her into someone else. She thought sometimes they resented her at the studio precisely because she didn't embody the traits they had imagined she'd have. Like her agent said, she was "too clever." But if she didn't remember a word in English, her tongue momentarily tied, she became stupid. Silly. All breasts and no brain.

Too clever. Not clever. Thinks too much, talks too much. Hardly says a peep. Haughty but shy.

She felt his fingers ghosting upon her hair. "You don't like California, then."

"I do. I like it. Then I don't like it other times. I like films and then not so much. I want to make music and . . . I don't understand how I'm supposed to be several things at once. That's what I want. To be many things."

Jay lifted her chin with his hand, and she opened her eyes. "When the shoot is over, we should go on vacation. Somewhere distant and exotic. We'll open a map and randomly pick a place. Wherever our finger lands, we'll go there for three whole weeks."

"What if your finger lands in the middle of the ocean?" she asked.

"You'll turn into a mermaid and swim there, and I'll become a dolphin."

"You're trying to distract me."

"No, if I wanted to distract you, I'd do this," he said and kissed her. A long, sweet kiss.

The living room was drenched in sunshine, the light so bright everything seemed overexposed and golden. It was like stepping into a dream. She felt the palms of her hands tingling, goose bumps upon her flesh.

His eyes had turned soft and longing, though he said nothing, did not kiss her again. Yet his want was obvious, as was her own. Fluidly, without hesitation, Vera stood up and grabbed him by the hand, pulling him up so he'd follow her into the bedroom.

Their relationship had not tilted into the physical yet. She'd been afraid it would be the same as with Arturo. That she wouldn't love him enough. But what had been difficult with Arturo came easily with Jay.

It had been awkward, even embarrassing, to make love to Arturo, like attempting to read a manual in a foreign language. Jay unzipped her dress in one smooth motion, then took off her stockings and peppered kisses on her neck. There was something fun about this. It had been tedious with Arturo, an obligation rather than desire.

Jay was *alive*. And so was she when she was with him, the colors turning more vivid, the sounds growing sweeter. The world became immense when viewed through his eyes, full of possibilities, yet never intimidating.

She undid his tie and the buttons of his shirt. When he took out a little box with rubbers and joked that she was corrupting him, she laughed against his shoulder. Arturo had made a fuss about prophylactics; he said good girls shouldn't know about such things.

They laughed more, a little joke, a funny expression. It was a game, it was effortless, like a catchy tune.

It was clumsy, too, for a minute or three, because they didn't know each other's bodies yet and there was an amount of awkward maneuvering, of shifting and rearranging limbs, of Vera now leaning over him to capture his lips rather than the other way around. Such blundering had its charm; it didn't detract from desire.

They were young and unencumbered and therefore it became graceful: the way his hand slid over her thigh, how his mouth pressed against her own. And in turn, her fingers drew a pattern on his skin, the mute scribbling of piano notes, music recorded only in her head played upon his flesh.

It was sincere. The whispered compliments, the gentle tracing of the freckles on his skin. The way he sighed when he said he loved her. Which he hadn't said before, both of them cautious around that one word.

But she did love him and he was beautiful, so she said so in turn. The way he held her, catching his breath, made her heart stutter and everything was right where it was supposed to be. That lock of hair upon his sweaty brow, the texture of the sheets on the bed, even the vase with freshly cut flowers she'd placed on the nightstand that morning. A perfectly framed picture, a flawless moment.

I am loved, she thought. She knew. She was. Her eyes drifted shut as he kissed her, smelling of green and summer.

Salome

PROCONSUL LUCIUS VITELLIUS returned to the palace. With him came Marcellus. He sought Salome immediately, eager to thrust a bracelet he had acquired in Caesarea into her hands. Salome looked at the circle of silver with weary eyes.

"You seem tired, Salome," Marcellus said. "They say you've taken ill since we left."

"They say right," she replied.

"Could it be that you've missed me?" he asked.

If he was trying to flirt with her, he would fail. She was in no mood to entertain jests or to smile coyly. The only reason she'd dressed properly and observed the return of the proconsul from one of the interior balconies circling the great courtyard was that her mother had demanded her presence. She had watched her cousin standing in another of the balconies with his retinue. He had smiled at Salome, and she'd looked away from him, resting her hands on the railing and glancing below at the guests streaming into the palace.

She'd thought perhaps her mother would want her to come down and greet the proconsul and his men, but Herod and Herodias gave their brief welcome and then walked away together. Salome and Agrippa had served merely as decorative items, perched atop their balconies, close but not close enough to matter.

Marcellus had spotted Salome, wrapped in blue and green silks that resembled the colors of a peacock, on the balcony, and he had quickly made his way up there.

"What news do you bring from Caesarea? Have the proconsul and Pontius Pilate become friends?"

"I doubt it. The proconsul was polite, yet distant with the man."

"Sejanus supports Pontius Pilate."

"Yes. What of it?"

She thought of what her cousin had said to her, of the doom that might soon befall both men. But was Agrippa speaking the truth or imagining things?

Salome frowned and chanced to see that Agrippa was smiling and looking in her direction once more.

"I heard Agrippa requested your hand in marriage."

"Who told you that?" Salome asked, standing stiffly as Marcellus threw Agrippa a suspicious look, then turned to her.

"Your lady mother."

It didn't surprise Salome to hear this. Her mother, after all, wanted her to marry Marcellus. If the Roman was made to see that he had competition, perhaps he might pursue her with more vigor. That must be her mother's thought.

"Fear not, my uncle won't allow such a union," Salome said. Agrippa smiled even more blatantly at her before turning around and departing with his men. "What have you heard about Sejanus in Rome? Did the proconsul speak of him?"

"Nothing of significance. There is talk that he is too arrogant, but then that has been the case for a while."

"Perhaps he even abuses his status?"

"He is a man of equestrian rank rather than noble birth; that is bound to make people talk. They are envious."

"His name has been struck into coins. That must rankle a few men."

"Perhaps it does."

"Marcellus, will you tell me nothing?"

He sighed. "Very well. The death of the emperor's oldest son has made him melancholic. He is staying in Capri, and Rome has been left in the care of Sejanus, which irritates and worries some people. That is all I know. Your cousin would have heard more. He has been at court, after all. But, Salome, it is not like you to become interested in such intrigues."

"What should I be interested in, then?" she asked.

He took her hands between his. Salome's handmaidens, who were awaiting her at a prudent distance, whispered between themselves at the gesture. Marcellus stepped closer to her.

"Salome, intrigues carry with them numerous dangers. One must take each step carefully. You are a sweet girl. I wish to give you happiness and peace. If you should not enjoy the thought of my villa in Ostia, then think of other possibilities. I might obtain a post in Alexandria, or else we might retreat to the wild frontier of Gaul. Opportunities are to be found in such places. The possibilities are endless."

Gaul, perhaps to Lutetia Parisiorum, where a semblance of civilization was maintained. She had not thought to ever leave her homeland, and yet his words ignited her imagination. She was not thinking of the same opportunities he was considering; likely he pondered a rise through the military ranks, perhaps even the handling of a province on a nebulous future date.

Salome thought instead of the anonymity distance might grant her. She recalled the stories she'd heard about Albion. In a remote place like that, a woman and a man might be lost and never found. She closed her eyes and let Marcellus rest his hand against her cheek, lost in a reverie.

"Salome, you drive me mad. I burn with my need for you," he whispered against her ear.

She snapped her eyes open and looked at him, disoriented for a few seconds. She'd been thinking of another man, of another voice whispering to her.

"I must go," she told him.

*

GUARDS DID not bar her way. Her access to the cells was simple and swift. She'd known it would be so. Perhaps that was why she had prostrated herself in her room. She did not wish to speak to the preacher again; the longing was a disease and she'd tried to extirpate it. But she still longed. She could finally admit this.

The young preacher sat in the middle of his cell, looking dirty and weary, but when he saw her, he stood up at once. Salome approached him. Her long skirts trailed behind her, dirtied by the muck of the prison.

"You said I believed in nothing the last time we spoke," she told him.

Jokanaan sighed and nodded. "You do not, except perhaps in yourself."

"If I prayed to your God, do you think he might speak to me as he does to you?"

"Perhaps, if you prayed with an honest heart," he said simply, out of habit. He had said such things before. He did not expect prayer of her, or belief.

"What does your God tell you?"

"The Lord says my people must not accept the yoke of Rome, that we must not cower in fear and obey the commands of blasphemers. He speaks of a future and of freedom."

"I dreamed of freedom today. I was awake, but it was as if my soul had escaped my body."

The young man approached the bars of the cell slowly, his eyes fixed on her. "You did?"

"Yes," she said vehemently. "I dreamed, but my eyes were open."

"What did you see?" he asked, intrigued.

"When I was a child, my father told me stories of faraway lands. There was one place that caught my imagination more than others because it was terribly wild and untamed in the telling. It is the land the Romans call Albion, where barbaric tribes huddle in the cold.

"There is rain and mist. The people there live on milk and meat, and they wear the skins of bears and wolves around their shoulders. They dye their cheeks blue with woad, and their warriors tattoo their limbs with the shapes of animals so that they may be endowed with their power."

She sat down as she spoke, and her voice was calm and sweet, the voice of a storyteller, but she did not look at him. She was staring at her hands until at last she raised her head and looked into his eyes.

"And beyond that, even farther north, my father spoke of a huge tract of country where the sea holds sway and passes deep inland. Beyond the place where the Britons, the Caledonians, and the Maeatae gather. There everything is white and there are walls made of ice.

"I saw myself on a ship heading in this direction, and I saw you with me. I saw us walking across the cold white plains of those inhospitable lands. But after much walking the cold receded and the land was green. There were birds of many shapes and sizes, with plumage the color of saffron or as pale as pearls. Ivy tangled around the trunks of trees, and the air was perfumed by many plants. The hills were painted with grass of the lushest green and dotted with yellow flowers. Under a willow the color of malachite, I wove primroses into our hair and there came the sweetest of melodies from a distance; it was music that made the flowers sigh."

They sat in front of each other, so close that their breath might mingle. She could almost feel the shiver that went down his body as he pressed closer to the bars, and to her.

"I saw freedom."

He shook his head at last, as if he were waking from a trance. The languid softness that had invaded his limbs vanished, and he was quick to reply in a matter-of-fact tone, like a teacher correcting a pupil.

"You dreamed of a place, and not of freedom."

"But don't you see?" she replied urgently. "Here, we can never truly be free. But if we were to go away, if we were to escape . . . Jokanaan, I have earrings and bracelets studded with jewels that I could sell to buy passage on a ship—"

"A ship," he replied and laughed without mirth. "Where might one find a ship in the dungeons of Herod? You toy with me. Well, chuckle and enjoy your jest."

"I can secure your release."

"That is even more unlikely than a ship."

"It is not. I know how," she said, and thought about the dance she was to perform before her uncle. Anything she wanted, he had promised her. She'd do it. She'd bare her shoulders and her legs and her breasts. She'd fling herself before the tetrarch's chair and kiss his thin lips. She'd whisper the wicked words he wished to hear into his ear and offer her flesh.

The sarcasm and disbelief in the preacher's face was erased. But rather than looking pleased, he seemed uneasy. How young he looked! Young and scared.

"Come away with me," she said.

"You've returned to torment me?" Jokanaan asked.

"Torment you?" she replied in surprise. "Why would you ever say that?"

"Because it can only be a form of torture to come here and paint such fantasies when I am to be paraded before Herod and his guests tomorrow in chains. Yes, no doubt you mock me."

He stood up, and she imitated him, rising quickly. "I do not! I wish to free both of us!"

The young prophet, now more perturbed than ever, paced back and forth in his cell, muttering to himself, while Salome stared helplessly at him.

"It is trickery, no doubt," he said. "This is a ploy you've devised together with the tetrarch."

"What ploy?"

"It must be."

She clutched the bars of his cell and spoke. "It is not!"

The young man ceased in his restless pacing. One would have thought he'd been tossed into the circus with a pack of lions by the way he looked at Salome. His eyes were wide and alarmed.

"Seek the Son of Man, that is what you must do," he said. "Scatter ashes upon your black hair, veil your face, and head to the sea of Galilee where he speaks to his disciples. Kneel down by the shore and call him and bow at his feet; do that, Salome, and do not think of lands of ice or what may lie beyond them."

"I might be able to save you."

"Only my God may save me. Go to the sea of Galilee, and ask for the remission of your sins."

"It is a sin to want to be free? The tetrarch keeps you underground in a cell, but he keeps me in a different prison of silk and gold. I long for light and air as much as you do."

"I cannot listen to you; I listen only to the voice of God," he said, stubbornly fixing his eyes on the floor.

"And God decrees that you must remain in this cell?"

He did not reply. His face was like granite; he stood stiff and firm in place. She did not know what words to speak, how to convince him to follow her on this mad scheme. She thought to express herself in the most eloquent and rational way, with carefully crafted sentences. Yet, at that moment when she ought to have been her most persuasive, she was unable to communicate with any sensitivity. Instead, she was seized by an intense and terrible yearning.

"From the moment I gazed at you, I loved you," she said, revealing to him not only her naked heart, but the smothering veracity of her vision of distant lands and the freedom they might find there. She had glimpsed, as certainly as a sibyl, the future.

Jokanaan was first surprised, then staggered back a couple of paces, as if she'd struck him. His young face was filled with an awful sadness. He pressed a hand against his eyes.

"The Lord punishes me for my arrogance," he said, his voice thick. "You must leave."

"I do not understand."

"I thought myself exceptional, yet I am as flawed as any ordinary man. I cannot speak to you, I cannot. In my pride, I thought I would refuse you, as I did once before. But this time, it is ten times worse, and the pain I feel is such that I fear it will render me senseless, and I cannot bear to look at you. To go with you would be to betray myself, my God, my soul. You are damnation, and yet I long to be damned."

She recalled that day when she'd first seen Jokanaan preach. Their eyes had locked together, and she'd felt overcome with emotion. She realized it had been the same for him, that in that instant he'd loved her back.

Later, he'd refused her kiss. But by then it had been too late. Love had wounded him, the same as it had wounded her. Their hearts were infected by that longing, and it had only been made worse with each passing day.

If she had met him before, when he was simply a merchant's son, sent to study in the city, would she have loved him at first glance, too? Yes. And if he'd been different, if his limbs had been crooked or his face savaged by the elements, then would love have sprung between them? Yes, too. In every epoch, in every disguise, she would have loved him.

But Jokanaan wouldn't look at Salome. He acted as though she were Medusa and might turn him to stone. He'd have nothing of her. He'd rather die. To him the escape she promised, the green hills with yellow flowers she'd glimpsed, were a torment worse than whatever torture the tetrarch could devise.

Salome fell to her knees, grasping the cold bars of iron for support. When she looked up, she saw that he had lifted his hand and revealed his face. He was looking at her. But it didn't matter now. She'd understood the finality of his refusal the same as he had understood the sincerity of her passion.

He would not seize the future she could offer. Slowly, very slowly, Salome stood up and walked out of the dungeons.

Vera

"WHAT MONTGOMERY CLIFT has, and what we should all be developing, is a sense of 'public solitude,'" Vaughn Selzer said. "It's the capacity to appear unaware of the camera, and to do that you have to disappear into the role. You find the *truth*."

Vaughn had snatched a dish with grapes that had been sitting on a table and was toying with the fruit. They were not supposed to tinker with props or décor, but Vaughn was restless. Handsome, yet a little unpolished, his brashness seemed to make up for whatever deficiencies he might have possessed. His screen test, they said, had been dynamite.

"The problem is you have to be able to deliver, take after take. You can't be burning it all in five minutes," Orlando said with the air of a veteran actor. He had five pictures under his belt and had been reared through the steps of the Hollywood system after being plucked from Ealing Studios. It showed.

The three of them were lounging between a pair of plaster columns, discussing acting. Vaughn was a proponent of "the Method," while Orlando thought it was hot air. Then again, Vaughn came from New York, where the Actors Studio seemed to be all the rage. On the East Coast, promising young actors in blue jeans and with tousled hair had apparently discovered an absolutely American style of acting. Orlando, who was British, was skeptical about such claims. Vera tended to like the wild ideas some of the Method actors espoused, but she was canny enough to understand that she was no Montgomery Clift, and as a young Mexican woman had to tread carefully.

"Anyway, Max loves line readings. He's the one who shows you how the role is supposed to be performed," Orlando said, shrugging. "There's no point in even discussing alternatives."

"But he doesn't line read," Vera replied. "He hollers."

"He'll definitely holler at Vaughn if he keeps asking about his bloody motivation," Orlando said. While other actors were asked to tame their accents and disguise their ethnicities, a British accent was considered posh and appropriate for a period film like *The Seventh Veil of Salome,* hence Orlando's liberal use of words such as "bloody" and his fondness for calling women "birds." He often hammed it up to make himself more exotic, putting on a Cockney accent and saying he'd been a shoe shiner before arriving in Hollywood, although Marla had told Vera that he'd attended a fancy school and dropped out of it to pursue acting.

"I'm supposed to walk in cold to a scene?" Vaughn asked. He petulantly took a grape and tossed it at Orlando, who tossed it back. But the grape missed Vaughn, hitting an extra who turned around and glared at them.

They broke up in laughter. Orlando, who looked like a decadent Byronic poet, could be tempestuous—he was widely considered to be something of a boy wonder, and he knew it. Blond, with tousled locks, and a little too short by Hollywood standards to be a leading man—yet so charismatic nobody bothered to criticize his stature—Vaughn was prone to issue proclamations as though he really were a member of the Herodian royal family. But Vera had discovered that the commonality of their youth smoothed certain differences between them, and their conversations never veered into real conflicts, even if they disagreed, as they did now.

Vera watched as Joe Kantor quickly zipped by two centurions

and rounded the stage, waving at them excitedly. Finally, Joe reached the actors and sat down next to them, looking flushed.

"What the devil?" Orlando said. "Are you running a marathon?"

"I've come from the projection room. Dressler was looking at the rushes today!"

During her time at the studio, Vera had seen little of Dressler. Nevertheless, she'd heard enough about the studio head to realize this was the equivalent of Zeus descending from Mount Olympus.

"What were you doing in the projection room?" Orlando asked.

"Max had me with him; he doesn't like running the reels alone when he's in one of his moods. Isadora Christie was there, of course. Clifford Collins, too. Anyway, no one knew the old man was coming over. He never tells people when he'll be popping his head into a projection room. They ran a couple of things for him."

"And?"

"Pandemonium. He said nothing is popping on screen. He hates Clifford's delivery."

"What about us?" Vaughn asked. "Did he see any of our scenes?"

"He saw one with Jokanaan and Salome, when they're in the dungeons." Joe hesitated as he looked at Vera. "He thinks Salome is not seductive enough. Max complained Vera's not following direction well."

Vera pressed her lips together and looked down at the floor, blushing.

"Sorry, sweetheart," Joe said and patted her hand.

"What does Max know about seductive? The man would have probably asked Alla Nazimova to play the role a second time if she wasn't dead," Vaughn said.

"Who's that?" Orlando asked.

"The owner of the Garden of Allah. She used to be in films before the talkies. They dated, back in prehistory. You didn't know this?" he replied. For all his talk of New York and alternative forms of acting, Vaughn had a keen ear for gossip and history, always eager to know who was who and what was what. He was cannier than Vera could ever hope to be.

"As if I should care what a dusty old mummy was up to thirty-odd years ago!" Orlando exclaimed.

"I need to run," Joe said, interrupting them. "I must rewrite dialogue for Clifford. Director's orders."

"At this rate you'll be writing new dialogue the day before the premiere," Orlando said.

"It could happen," Joe said dryly. "Max is worse than Sturges."

"Didn't you audition for Sturges?" Vaughn asked Orlando.

"No. Douglas Sirk."

She brushed her hand against her temple, wincing. The pleasant prattle of the men had turned strident, and the beginning of a headache was sprouting in the back of her skull.

"Are you okay?" Joe asked, pushing his glasses back up the bridge of his nose and giving Vera a thoughtful look.

"I'm fine. It's only a headache."

"Do you need me to get you anything? An aspirin? Glass of water? Half of the ham sandwich I tucked in a lunchbox this morning like the naughty man I am?"

"No. Go, Joe. I'll be fine," Vera said, smiling weakly.

Joe smiled back and rushed off. Orlando and Vaughn began discussing Charlie Chaplin, who had been ousted from the United States for his Communist leanings. Vaughn knew a guy who had dated Chaplin's latest wife before she moved to California. But Vera wasn't paying attention to their chatter anymore. She bowed her head and bit her lips.

*

"YOU NEED to see Sarah Lane in wardrobe," Max told her when he sauntered back onto the set. "They're going to modify the costumes in a couple of scenes, make the neckline plunge a little more."

"Is this about the rushes, Max?" she asked, smoothing her skirts and trying not to seem nervous. "I can do better. I'm having a hard time finding the character sometimes, but I'll get it right."

"Honey, don't start babbling nonsense about finding anything. I already have enough with Vaughn trying to find his stupid motivation," the director said, glancing wearily at the young actor, who was still chatting with Orlando. "What we need is a sexier costume."

She thought of the moment when Herod's soldiers crush Salome beneath the weight of their shields. Her chest felt like bursting. When she spoke, her voice was hoarse.

"But you're having new dialogue written for Clifford Collins. In fact, you're always working with Clifford, trying to instill confidence in him."

When she'd been given this role, her agent had assured her the director would lead her scene by scene, that it would be fine. And Max had been nice in the beginning, dazzled by his new find. They'd worked well together, she thought. But he'd soured on her, and Vera knew it. She was simply trying to reach the finish line.

Max frowned. "Clifford's part still needs tweaking. *You* need a costume change."

"I need to show my tits more," she said.

She'd been a well-behaved girl during the whole shoot. She was watchful, quiet, respectful, attempting to absorb every bit of information like a sponge. Clifford was difficult, a volatile performer, and Vaughn's stubbornness sometimes edged on the infantile. But Vera, she'd been the perfect pupil, eager to receive a gold star at the end of each day.

Maybe that was why Max seemed so shocked by the caustic reply, then outraged. His eyes narrowed, and he huffed, clutching the script he was carrying.

"What we're shooting here, Vera, is a spectacle. People want to see hundreds of extras, detailed sets, extravagant costumes. They want to look at a pretty girl for a couple of hours and forget their woes."

"But you give Clifford notes—"

"You want a note? Okay, Vera. You play the naïve, young part of Salome well enough. When you're in front of Herod you cower, you recoil and flee. But when it's time to be the seductive, dangerous dame, it's a struggle. Well, you must embody both. And I've said this before. I've told you how to tackle a scene, I've shown you how to play it. Nevertheless, sometimes you're still all over the map. The old and tried ways work; don't start over-thinking it."

He meant the line reading method that Orlando had been discussing earlier. She hadn't thought it mattered much before, but the more time she had spent on set, the more she felt it made her dependent on Max for everything. Vulnerable. You say the line like this, then you pick up the cup like this, then you turn around. Like an automaton. That's the way it was supposed to be done, the way they'd taught her at the studio, the way Max worked. Yet it wasn't nearly enough.

"I don't need spoken demonstrations. I need . . . Max, it's like you don't trust me."

"Vera, movies are not about trust. They're about moving pieces. And right now, I need you to move your little brown ass to ward-robe."

She stared at the director, astounded by his response. Her face felt blazing warm, and she wanted to yell at him, but was unable to utter a whisper. The outrage knotted in Vera's throat, and the incapacity to string words together only made it worse as tears prickled her eyes. Max sighed dramatically.

"Don't start with that," he said and whirled away from her.

*

JAY WAS teaching Vera how to swim. He was patient with her, and although at first she had been terrified of the pool, she was now laughing as she attempted to maintain herself afloat. After much splashing around, Vera finally pulled herself out of the water and began toweling her hair. Jay jumped out after Vera and wrapped a towel around her shoulders from behind, holding her tight. She felt perfectly happy.

But then she recalled what Max had said and tensed up, her body turning to iron.

"What is it?" Jay asked. "You worried about that bum outside? I'll tell him to beat it if you want."

To add to Vera's anxiety, a photographer was following her around. She'd seen him the day before and that morning, when she'd headed to Jay's place, he'd parked his car right across the street. She was certain he worked for *Hollywood Connection* and that they were writing a follow-up story about her. She dreaded what awful headline they would print, what muck they'd invent.

"That would make everything worse."

"They have no right to be chasing you around town. Look how miserable they're making you."

"It's not them."

"Then who?"

"Max Niemann. And Clifford Collins and . . . I feel everyone knows what they're doing and I'm wandering around blindfolded," she said, remembering the humiliating conversation she'd had with her director only two days before.

She'd spent half the night awake after that confrontation, wondering what she might have said differently. Of course, there wasn't anything she could have said that would have mattered, but she hated that she'd simply stood there and started crying. Others had noticed, which had doubled the humiliation.

It was one thing to cry in front of one person and another to have half a dozen extras, an assistant director, and a script girl staring at Vera in astonishment. Orlando had been nice enough to pull her outside with him until she was able to compose herself, yet she'd spent the rest of the day fearing she'd burst into tears.

"Vera, you're doing fine."

She adjusted the towel and was quiet. The water dripped down her skin and hair. She'd come to see Jay because she felt blue, but she was ruining their Saturday. She hated this sickly melancholia that clung to her, making her limbs heavy and her thoughts pitch-dark, but it seemed there was nothing that she could do to exorcise it.

"Come inside. I'll try to fix you a drink."

"Juice is fine, Jay."

"Juice it is, then."

She followed him docilely into the kitchen, leaving a trail of footprints behind. Jay filled a couple of glasses with orange juice and handed her one. Vera pushed herself atop the kitchen counter and sipped her drink.

"I have to head to the club at six," Jay said, gulping his juice quickly and placing the dirty glass in the sink. "Do you want to come with me? I can get you a terrific seat."

She bit her lip, tempted by the offer. She liked Jay's playing, and she was beginning to develop a taste for jazz. But she shook her head.

"Not tonight. I should go over a few lines."

"That means I shouldn't stop by your place after my gig is over?"

"I don't know."

"It's okay if you're busy."

"You ever get nervous about a performance?" she asked as Jay began to run a hand through her hair.

"I was nervous the other night when you went to hear me play."

"Really?"

"Shaking. I was afraid I'd be lousy, and you'd be embarrassed."

"You never look nervous."

"It's all cheap bravado."

"I wish I had bravado," she said, thinking of her sister. Lumi was gutsy. Even when she hadn't rehearsed a tune or didn't know all the steps of a dance, she could perform without worries, while Vera would almost make her fingers bleed from practicing on the piano for one of their family recitals.

Lumi would have never cried like Vera cried. She would have laughed at the director or slapped his face. Lumi was a force to be reckoned with. Vera was meek and dim—they'd all said so when she was growing up, and now Max Niemann was confirming it.

"What did the people at the studio tell you that has you so worried, huh?" he asked, brushing a strand of hair behind Vera's ear.

"I'm not that good, the director says I'm not seductive enough—"

"I think the director is the one wearing the blindfold."

"You say that because you're my boyfriend."

"I say that because you're attractive. And I don't mean just physically; you have an attractive personality, too, and a wonderful sense of style. This little white number you're wearing, it's a smash. I bet if the director sees you in something like this, he'll drop dead," Jay said, running a hand along the bathing suit strap peeking from beneath the towel she'd wrapped around her body.

"The director doesn't believe I'm really fit for anything except maybe standing still. He says he wants a better performance out of me, but his only suggestion is that they alter the neckline of my dress. He told me to run my little brown ass to wardrobe and quit bothering him."

Jay had been lazily running a finger down her neck, but now he stopped. He looked at Vera and frowned. "That's mighty rude. Well, he's wrong. You're good."

"What do you know about acting?" she replied, feeling irritated.

She thought Jay would be irked by the curtness in her voice, but rather than appearing piqued, he looked serious.

"Vera, you'll do incredible things because your heart knows how to dream. It's made me dream again, too. It's silly to say it, you know, but I hear music when we're together. I do. Why, I practically hear a whole symphony when I'm with you!"

The earnest tone he used, almost boyish, made her blush, ashamed by his praise.

"I do, too," she whispered. "Hear music, you know."

"Everything's going to be fine," he said solemnly.

They were both quiet, and she tugged at his hand.

"Jay, you'll make me cry."

"Should I tickle you until you laugh?" he asked, his easy mirth creeping back into his voice.

"You're silly."

"Maybe. At least I'm a sharp dresser. Isn't this sexy?"

Jay's taste in bathing suits ran the gamut from tacky to gaudy. His swim trunks that day had a pink flamingo print that clashed with the bright yellow background of pineapples.

Vera laughed. "No! You look awful!" She spread her arms, and the motion made the towel tumble down.

"Darn. I guess I won't be able to make it in pictures. I better practice the piano some more."

"You should," she said.

"You know, I was supposed to play that new Sarah Vaughan record for you, and we've done everything but play music."

"You have to head to the club at six."

"What time is it now?"

She peered over his shoulder at the kitchen clock. "Three-thirty. But you promised you'd fry a hamburger on that grill of yours."

"I did?"

"Yes."

"I'm not hungry. Are you?"

"Jay," Vera said, admonishing him sternly, but she was smiling. He kissed her, and she felt a delicious spark of pleasure.

Jay pressed closer to Vera, spreading her legs a little so he could fit between them and kiss her some more. It was a difficult endeavor peeling off the wet bathing suit from her skin and making it to his bedroom between so many kisses and embraces, but they managed in the end.

"You're perfect," he said, and the way he spoke, she knew it wasn't merely a careless line. Others might say the same thing, but it wasn't true. Clifford Collins, for example, had complimented her. Same as Arturo.

Their words spilled from their mouths as easily as dandelion seeds were carried by the wind. They disappeared, forgotten, seconds after being spoken.

But Jay meant it. The way he looked at her when they were together, the tenderness he lavished upon her, it telegraphed the truth. His mouth caught her own slowly, and she gave him a gentle push so that he lay flat on his back upon the bed.

It was wonderful when they were joined together, but it was a different kind of wonder when he lay beside her after their lovemaking and she pressed a hand against his shoulder. The world went quiet. Then, after a little while, the sounds returned, and she was able to breathe deeply, to listen, and to hum a tune.

Eventually, Jay rose, took a shower, and began looking for the clothes he'd flung around the bed. She watched him with amusement as he attempted to locate a sock that seemed to have disappeared. When he sat on the bed to put his shoes on, she rested her chin on his shoulder.

"By the way, I might be a bit scarce in a couple of weeks. My mother is threatening to stop by for a visit, and no doubt I'll be forced into chauffeuring duties as she explores the beauty of California."

"Why don't you bring her by the studio? I could arrange for a tour of it. We could have lunch," she suggested.

"I doubt she'd want a studio tour," he said. "She doesn't think much of film people."

"Does she know I'm an actress?"

"She knows," Jay said, though his face took on an uncharacteristic grimness. He shook his head. "Believe me, Vera, you don't want to meet my mother."

"Would she like you to get back together with Bridget Mills of the Mills and King Company?" she asked in jest. But Jay didn't reply, instead looking down at his tie, and she figured she'd guessed right.

"Oh," she said quietly, lifting her chin away from his shoulder.

Jay sighed. He pulled her toward him until Vera was sitting on his lap. "My mother wants me to have nothing to do with California. She has funny ideas about what I should do and what I should like. Yes, she'd be thrilled if I gave Bridget Mills a call, but I'm not going to. And you know why?"

"Why?"

"Because Bridget wouldn't encourage me to keep playing my tunes, and even suggest the idea of recording something."

"You were the one who said Atlantic is moving into the jazz market."

"But you're aiding and abetting me with my crazy ideas."

"I guess it is crazy. West Coasters can't swing," Vera said with mock seriousness.

"Don't you dare," Jay replied, but he was smiling.

"I dare. The sound is too damn sweet," she said.

"You're too damn sweet," he said and tickled her in a spot that had her giggling and loudly protesting in three seconds flat.

She fell back on the bed and Jay kissed her, long and carefully. Against the whiteness of the bedsheets her hair was a glossy river of black, and he held her tightly as she smiled.

Marla Bahia

WE HAD our little group back then. Joe Kantor, Simon Gilbert, Miguel Montaner, and a few others. We played cards at Simon's place every other weekend, and we had parties at Miguel's house. Vera fit right in with us. She was a lovely gal, a hard worker.

It was tough for her, being a newcomer and having to figure how everything worked so quickly, but Vera was doing well. More than well. I know there was talk of recasting, but that was idle gossip, the kind of stuff they print to sell magazines.

A good deal of *The Seventh Veil of Salome* had already been shot when stories about recasting surfaced. Seventy, maybe seventy-five percent of it was in the can. It's hard to eyeball a shoot when you're not on the actual set, but you get a good sense of how a production is running by chatting with the extras or the negative cutters. They'd shot quite a bit.

They were not going to recast. What any production might do is tighten certain parts, maybe retool a scene or two. Even a massive reimagining wouldn't have meant Vera would be fired.

All kinds of productions run into trouble. *Gone with the Wind* went through three directors. *Duel in the Sun* circled through even more hands: seven directors. Selznick rewrote the script of that film every day, which meant nobody knew what lines they were saying. Look at *Cleopatra:* they had to switch from shooting in London to shooting in Rome. It cost them a bundle.

What I'm trying to say is I've seen slow-motion disasters, and *The Seventh Veil of Salome* didn't seem like it was headed in that direction. And the talk that Vera was unprofessional, that she was a bad actress, that's just lies.

I don't think Max Niemann disliked her. But he was an old-school director. He expected actors to behave like puppets and parrot their lines back at him. He didn't like them getting ideas about how to tweak a scene after he'd blocked it out.

That doesn't amount to an insurrection. It's not mutinous to ask a question. Sometimes men think it is. They think a woman should be gagged. Maybe Max saw it like that, I don't doubt it, but that wouldn't make Vera unreasonable.

And the thing was, if we want to talk about unreasonable and dramatic, there were plenty of other people who fit that bill. Clifford Collins, for one. Vaughn got testy, too. And Max, famously, was the kind of man who'd call an assistant director "damn idiot bastard" in the morning, then pat him on the back in the evening.

Those are antics. That's making a spectacle of yourself.

Nancy

THE TWO negative stories about Vera Larios that she'd read in *Hollywood Connection* filled Nancy with joy. She was glad that tamale face was being exposed as the untalented hack that she really was; every cruel barb made her laugh.

On set, the atmosphere was frosty between Vera and Clifford Collins, and the girl was clearly uncomfortable with her director.

Recasting was not only prudent, but necessary. Nancy wondered if she shouldn't give Pierce Pratt a call and ask him what they were saying around his office.

If only Nancy could be seen by the public! If Max Niemann took a chance on her rather than on that silly Mexican girl. If she was seen, if she was filmed in bright colors and with good lighting, Nancy knew everyone would love her. They wouldn't be able to stop themselves.

Even someone like Jay Rutland would want Nancy.

Jay. He was the sour note in this joyous symphony. His name, appended to the end of the stories about Vera, made Nancy want to scream. How quickly that little fool had sunk her teeth into the man.

Nancy felt robbed twice over: first of the role that should have been hers, then of the man she should have possessed. Vera Larios was a first-class thief.

She ended up meeting Pierce for cocktails at the Formosa Cafe. She had picked this location because Benny was coming around her place often again, and she didn't want him bumping into Pierce, not because she was particularly interested in the food or the décor. Noodles and spring rolls had little appeal for Nancy.

But the Formosa was a place where actors and studio employees liked to congregate. It served as the unofficial commissary of Warner Bros., but people from other parts of town liked to swoop in for a mai tai and sit in the dark red booths, chatting until late at night. If you were lucky, you might see Lana Turner or John Wayne milling around.

Tessa had told her there was a fellow who could organize dates at the Formosa, which meant she knew a pimp who did business there. Nancy wondered, looking around the diner, which of the handsome performers whose glossies blanketed the walls used this sordid service.

She'd never stooped as low as Tessa, never sat at a table waiting for a stranger to grin at her and take Nancy back to a cheap motel, but as Pierce Pratt approached her, Nancy frowned before she returned his wide smile.

They exchanged platitudes, ordered more drinks—Nancy had already finished a cocktail by the time Pierce appeared—and soon she was grilling him about Vera.

"They're saying they'll recast her, what do you think?"

"That's above my pay grade."

"Come on, you've heard something. They published those stories about her in *Hollywood Connection*. Sounds like she might be in hot water, don't you think?"

"If you want the whole truth, word is Clifford Collins can't stand the girl. He calls her 'Little Miss Frigid.' If you ask me, she turned him down. Can't have gone well. He's got a big ego, that one."

Nancy toyed with the stem of a cherry, considering this. "Then she really might get fired if he hates her that much."

"It's one thing to dislike the girl and another to ask that she be recast. As far as I know, Clifford's not pushing for that."

"He might," Nancy said.

"Anything's possible, I suppose."

He caught her hand between his and began massaging it. His tone of voice indicated he cared little about Vera Larios's work situation and a lot more about Nancy's availability after they were done drinking their cocktails. Normally she might have flirted with him, patted his leg, flattered him about the cut of his jacket or the tie he wore. But Nancy remained oddly quiet.

Her thoughts were centered on Vera. She wondered if they were running the rushes for Max Niemann and the director was once again disappointed. She wondered if Vera was with Jay at this exact moment.

She thought, fleetingly, about her failed screen test, when she'd had a chance to read for the part of Salome. She wondered, if they recast the part, if she might be able to test for it again. Surely Pierce could arrange it. He had come through the first time, hadn't he? Could be the second time she'd clinch it. She'd simply been too nervous on that first occasion. Her timing had been a tad off.

A second chance. That was what Nancy needed. Maybe she'd get it. Maybe it wasn't too late.

James Dean was discovered when he was parking cars on a lot near CBS. He was no one and then he was a star. Such things happened every day. It could happen to anyone. It could happen to her.

*

VERA WAS moving around the set, trailed by two dressmakers who were armed with needles, thread, and a box of beads, intent on making adjustments before the cameras began to roll again.

Break time. The extras could put down their grape juice, which would be passed off as wine in the film, for a little while.

Nancy watched Vera Larios walk away, off to wardrobe for minor alterations and then probably to her dressing room. They said she had yellow flowers delivered to her frequently. Maybe it was Jay who sent them. Maybe it was another admirer.

Cathy scratched her arm and fidgeted. "I can't believe the fabric on this costume. It'll give me blisters, I tell you."

"It's so hot in here, too," another extra said. She was a young thing who'd been nervous nearly every day of the shoot and complained constantly that it was too hot in the morning and too cool in the evenings. "I wonder how Miss Larios manages to stand around without breaking a sweat."

"After the latest alterations she's hardly wearing anything," said another extra. She was a veteran at the studio, with eight pictures under her belt, and wore an unflattering black wig that made her look like Theda Bara.

Nancy was also in one of the itchy Theda Bara wigs. Her red hair would have looked much better on film. Instead, she had to be filmed with a black blob atop her head. Not that it mattered, because no one would see her clearly; the camera was always drifting in Vera's direction. Tantalizingly near yet a step too far.

"No wonder she's not warm," the older extra concluded.

"It's really a little bit indecent, don't you think?" Cathy said. "Her entire midriff is exposed except for that jewel on the belly button."

"She looks cheap, but then she *is* cheap," Nancy said.

"You don't mean that," the young extra said.

"Yes, I do. She's cheap and she's common. Girls like that, they're everywhere in Mexico. Head down to Tijuana and you'll be able to pick half a dozen of them up for ten dollars. Hussies. Tramps. Chippies. They want you to think she's something special, that she's got a spark, but she doesn't. She's a lousy beaner," Nancy concluded.

There was silence, the women next to her processing the words. The young extra looked aghast.

"Who is a beaner?"

Nancy turned around. Vera Larios stood there. Perhaps she'd forgotten something, perhaps the director had called for her. Who knew. But she was there, staring at Nancy.

She looked hurt and young, like a child who has lost her favorite doll. And sad, terribly sad, her large eyes bright with unshed tears.

Nancy felt bad for a moment, a word that might have been a nascent apology lodged in her throat, but before she could say anything the girl spoke again; this time her tone was firm and her face did not seem like that of an injured child. The eyes were bright with smoldering fury. Vera Larios had raised her head, imperious.

Her queenly face matched the garments she wore; a costume fit for a princess.

"Who is a beaner?" the girl asked again, each word carefully enunciated, daring Nancy to speak. "I asked you, who? Or can you only talk behind people's backs?"

Nancy hated her then. Hated the blackness of her hair and the whiteness of her teeth. She hated each imitation jewel attached to her headdress. She hated her heavy eye makeup and the redness of her lips. But most of all she hated the way she stood, proud and suddenly fierce, in her rhinestone-encrusted dress, daring Nancy to speak.

She realized, instinctively, that if she apologized the girl would probably turn around and walk away in a huff. Irritated, maybe even eager to complain, yet that might be the end of it.

But just as something had flickered inside Vera's heart, making her voice hard, a spark burned inside Nancy, burning equally bright and fast.

"That's what we call your type. Beaners," Nancy said, and even as she knew she was dooming herself with those words, she couldn't help but delight in her ability to say them.

Everyone stood still. Vera raised a hand. Nancy thought she might attempt to slap her with a feeble splayed hand. Instead, a fist connected with her nose, and she was nearly toppled over by the blow.

The extras next to her shrieked. Vera Larios was shoving her down, hard, pinning her against the floor. In the tumult, Nancy didn't know what she was doing. She tried to kick and punch; she screeched. She even bit Vera, her teeth sinking into the girl's arm, before pulling at her hair, tearing off beads that had been carefully woven into her black locks. The beads bounced and rolled across the floor, fake pearls spilling over blue-and-white tiles.

Nancy dug her fingers into the girl's neck, determined to choke her, but before she could squeeze tight, she was dragged away by two extras dressed as Romans. Nancy kicked and flailed, now attempting to attack them, frenetic, determined to kill that little bitch.

She hollered obscenities. People were yelling back at her. Nancy was dragged outside and she immediately threatened to go back in.

A small crowd had gathered outside the sound stage. Stagehands and extras looked at Nancy with wide eyes.

"Fuck you!" she told a production assistant who began mumbling something. "Fuck you all!"

Two startled security guards came running toward her. They spoke low, quick words. Nancy followed them. She was out of breath, sweat dripped down her forehead, and her anger was quickly being replaced with mortification.

She licked her lips and tasted blood. A car appeared, with a chauffeur behind the wheel. It was one of the studio cars that was used to ferry important actors and directors from one place in town to the other. She'd seen such vehicles circling the lot, gleaming under the Hollywood sun.

One of the guards told her to get inside. Nancy obeyed. It made no sense to prolong this departure any longer.

The driver demanded an address from her. She gave it to him.

The car took off. During the ride she imagined herself a famous actress being driven home.

She was dropped off in front of her building. Once she reached her apartment, Nancy wiped her bloody mouth and ran shaky hands through her hair. She contemplated her reflection in the mirror. She washed her face, combed her hair, slipped out of the torn costume she was wearing and into a bathrobe.

She drank, turned the radio on, turned it off, drank some more. The phone rang, and it was Pierce Pratt. His voice was low, a scratchy whisper against her ear.

"You've been fired, Nancy. You're not allowed on the lot again."

"I figured," she said simply. She'd been painting her toenails and regarded the work critically.

"You figured? Did you also figure that I got you the job? That I stuck out my neck for you?"

Nancy wiggled her toes. "That bitch punched me in the face. What did you want me to do?"

"What did I want you to do?" Pierce asked, sounding aghast. "Anything but what you did! Don't call me again."

Prick, she thought. Cutting her off like that: four words and no goodbye. Just like Jay had cut her off, only to take up with that Larios bitch right after they were done. Maybe Jay had already been seeing Vera behind Nancy's back. Maybe he'd been seeing her all along.

Stupid assholes, both of them.

Benny would holler when she told him this story. He wouldn't be offended or scandalized. He'd say that the whore had it coming, he'd ask Nancy if she'd landed a few good punches. They might even laugh about it over drinks.

Benny was like that. Benny understood.

But even though she intended to phone Benny, with each glass that Nancy drank, she began thinking more about Jay in his flashy car. Jay with his walk-in closet stuffed with fashionable suits, neatly boxed hats, silk handkerchiefs, and highly polished cordovan shoes. Jay, who had an office and a pool and all those records lining the walls of his living room.

Jay, who was refined and handsome in a way a fellow like Benny would never be.

Her fingers danced upon the numbers on the phone, dialing Jay even though she had been thinking of Benny for most of the evening.

"Hello," Jay said, picking up the receiver quickly, his smile obvious although Nancy could not see him. She wondered if he'd been waiting for Vera to call that evening, if perhaps he'd been smiling for her.

"You're home," she said.

"Nancy," he said, and she could picture his fading smile, his voice growing hard with the simple mention of her name, just as Pierce's voice had grown hard.

"I wanted to call to wish you happy birthday."

"It's not my birthday."

"Nevertheless, would you still like a present?" she asked.

She'd used that line with Benny once before when they quarreled, and he'd laughed hard. He'd invited her over, and they patched things up over a bottle of whiskey. There was nothing that could divide Nancy and Benny. Not harsh words or even a shove or a punch.

Jay didn't laugh. He wasn't like Benny. He was quiet. "I'm sorry, Nancy. I must go," he said.

"Everyone's gotta go," she said.

Nancy stared at the receiver, blinking, trying to remember Benny's number. Her reflection mesmerized her again. She wondered what she might have looked like if she had been allowed to wear the regal costume Vera had been wearing. She pictured herself with jewels in her red hair and the eyeliner thick on her face. She hung up.

With clumsy hands she applied face powder and painted her lips red. She couldn't fashion a costume like the one at the studio, but she pulled out a white gown from the back of her closet and tugged at the neckline. She draped several necklaces made of cheap glass around her neck and pulled her hair back with a black ribbon.

The woman who stared back at her was Salome, her face slashed with a wide grin. If she could be seen like this, the world would be hers. She knew it; she sure did.

Salome

THE PALACE had grown silent, and his footsteps were stealthy. When he whispered in her ear, his voice was as low as the murmur of bees.

"Salome," he said.

Her nights had been spent restlessly conjuring the face of Jokanaan and thus, for a moment, she thought that the man at her side was the preacher. Eyes half-lidded, she reached for this phantom lover, her fingers splayed against his cheek. But his face was smooth, devoid of a beard, and even with sleep still clinging to her limbs, Salome realized it could not be the preacher. How could

Jokanaan, trapped in a cell, make use of a barber and perfume his skin?

Salome's eyes snapped open, and she beheld Agrippa, sitting on her bed. She sat up.

"I've bribed your servant. Yet it would still be rather embarrassing if you began to scream, so let me assure you that I'm here only to speak with you," he said. "You need not fear that your maidenly virtue, should it be intact, shall be breached this night."

"How dare you?" she replied, her voice a harsh whisper.

"What? Imply that you are not an untouched flower? I'm merely trying to be clear about my intentions."

"How dare you be here, in my chambers? In the middle of the night."

"I could not speak to you during the day. You've been avoiding me."

"I've been busy. I have no time for anyone. I will dance at our uncle's party and must prepare."

"You made time for the Roman and the famous preacher in the cells," Agrippa said. He didn't sound jealous; he was merely pointing out a fact.

She said nothing, which he must have taken for an invitation to make himself comfortable, for he reclined back upon the many cushions scattered across the bed.

"Tomorrow you'll spend all day being readied for our uncle's birthday party. Your mother will be in your rooms, supervising your clothing and your jewels, ensuring you have memorized all the steps of the dance you are to perform. I had to come tonight. Tomorrow, it will be too late."

"Too late for what?" she asked, wrapping her arms around her knees, irritated and yet intrigued. This seemed to be her perpetual state when she was in her cousin's presence.

He'd irritated her when they'd been little, too. He'd been haughty, even as a boy, and he never liked to lose when they played at games of chance, cheating to achieve victory, which incensed her. But when Salome's father had died, it had been Agrippa who had embraced her and let her weep. Herodias would not allow such a thing. Her father had been a traitor, Salome's mother said, and her uncle was a hero. She could not show any sorrow in public upon his passing.

"They'll have the preacher at the banquet, to prove to the proconsul that the rabble does not rule the city streets. That those who speak against Herod are swiftly dealt with," Agrippa said. "Yet, our uncle vacillates. What to do with the man? His favored advisor, Josephus, has begged for leniency. Humiliate the prophet during the party, yes. Keep him in chains, but do not harm this man.

"Your mother and others whisper the opposite: kill this wretch who opposes the rule of Herod. His mere existence is like a dagger hidden under one's sleeve. He is a weapon that might render the tetrarch weak. And our uncle dithers, he does not know what to do. Tomorrow, during the feast, tell the tetrarch that the prophet must die. Tell it for all to hear, and you will tip the scales."

"You overestimate my influence," Salome said stiffly.

"I think not. I believe the tetrarch would do anything to obtain your favor. I believe you've bewitched him. The problem with our uncle is that he is easily overtaken by his baser desires. A man must always aim higher," he said. His fingers were trailing up her arm. She swiped his hand away.

"Then maybe I'll ask the tetrarch to free the preacher," she said.

"That would be stupid. You'll make yourself a whore. Ask him to liberate that man and what will you get out of it? Nothing. But you'll be in his debt. He'll have you pay him with your flesh. If you liberate the preacher, he'll go back to speaking his dissent, and once again he will be imprisoned. And now the tetrarch will know that his pleasure can be purchased easily, that the preacher is your weakness. Again, you'll secure his safety. Again, you'll give yourself to our uncle."

"Not if the preacher goes far away."

She thought about the green lands beyond the distant cold and white plains she'd described to Jokanaan. Lands where saffron butterflies would nestle in her hair and golden fish would leap from the rivers. Magical lands beyond the borders of the maps tucked inside Herod's palace.

"He wouldn't," Agrippa said.

"You don't know that."

"I know his type. He's a holy man who believes in the righteousness of his cause. Why would he run away? When a god speaks to you from the heavens, why would you fear mortal men? A savior of the world will soon arrive, won't he?"

Agrippa was correct. The preacher had rejected her escape plan and rejected her. If Salome asked once more, he'd reply with the same negative. This was clear. His stubborn faith was stronger than iron and granite. Only his god might save him, not her. He'd take nothing from her.

"I didn't realize you'd heard Jokanaan preach," she muttered.

"I make it a habit to keep myself well informed. Which is why I know you regularly visited the man before his arrest. Did he make you believe that he has the gift of prophecy with well-chosen words? Or were you moved by another quality of his? They say Jokanaan is young and comely."

"He is a madman."

Agrippa's mouth, shaped for cruel barbs, curled into a perfect smile. "Yet you want him."

She blushed, fury mingling with shame, under her cousin's sharp, knowing eyes. That he should peer into her heart and discern its yearning struck her as obscene.

"What would you know about wanting? You, who abandon the baser desires in pursuit of a higher purpose," she said sharply.

"Would it please you if I wanted you in that cheap and common manner?" he asked, sounding firm and composed.

Salome did not reply. Quick as a leopard he reached forward, pushing her against the bed. He bent over Salome and gripped her jaw with one hand, making her look into his eyes. There was coldness in the gesture, no fire coursing through his veins.

She'd heard of demons that dwelt in the desert and slipped into the chambers of women at night, much as he had done, but their hands burned like hot coals and their tongues seared the flesh.

"Would it please you if I lavished kisses on your face?" he asked, and his fingers fell upon her neck.

"Don't toy with me," she said, unflinching, unwilling to raise a hand to push him away.

"I might say the same to you, Salome. I've been exceedingly candid with you. In fact, I have never been as honest as I've been when in your presence. I have divulged my secrets and my plans, all in the hope that you might glimpse the glorious future that awaits us, as I've glimpsed it. Jokanaan is not the only one who has the gift of prophecy."

"Drunkards glimpse phantoms and stray travelers in the desert see mirages," she replied with ease. Despite his posturing, his swaggering, she was not intimidated nor moved by him. He was aware of this, as keenly as he must be aware of her secret passion for the preacher.

Agrippa shrugged. He laced his fingers with her own and pulled Salome onto her side so that they might look at each other eye to eye.

"Perhaps you think your Roman suitor might be a better choice than me? You'd be wrong. He might install you in his villa, but what will you be then? Nothing but an exotic trinket he purchased in a distant land. They'll remind you of this fact. That you don't quite belong. That you never will."

"You went away. You went to Rome," she said, wishing the words didn't sound quite as accusing, quite so hurt.

Her father had been the first to leave. The exile who killed himself upon a distant shore. But then Agrippa left, too. He stepped onto a boat with many oars and slipped out of her life. Gone was that clever, laughing child whom she'd chased through her aunt's great manse. Gone he was, to earn the emperor's favor, while she was left behind, silent and forlorn.

He might have fed her mud cakes when they were children,

and she might have hit him in return as they dueled with wooden sticks, but she had cared for Agrippa.

"I've returned. These are our lands, this is our kingdom. You were born to be queen and I to be king," he said. His hand clutched her own with an easy intimacy. She stared at that hand, with its long fingers made to play the lyre. A hand that matched Salome's.

"Far too late and far too changed," she said, thinking of herself rather than him, focusing on the moment she had beheld Jokanaan in the market; thinking of that horrid, hopeless love that had taken root in her heart and was slowly suffocating her.

"I'd have died if I hadn't changed. What do you think it takes to survive at court? More than gold and a smattering of Latin."

"You could have stayed."

"Could I?"

In the darkness of her chamber she couldn't quite see Agrippa's features, but she still noticed the spark of displeasure in his eyes and the tension at the corners of his mouth.

"Ask the tetrarch to kill Jokanaan, and the city will rise in fury. The proconsul will take note of our uncle's inability to rule. Soon, he will be deposed. Anyway, the preacher is dead already," he said. His fingers were tight against her own; it was almost painful. "Whatever you do, he shall die."

"Why?" she asked. Her mouth had gone dry.

Agrippa slid back, releasing her. "You can't believe he'll live. The Romans might have him killed, eventually, if Herod doesn't. His own kin are fearful of the man, fearful of the wrath of Herod and of Rome. But if he dies now, while in the tetrarch's custody, during the tetrarch's birthday party even, there will be a terrible discontent. Riots will break out."

"Something tells me you've ensured that'll be the case," she said, raising an eyebrow at him.

"It's a spectacle," he said, "like the circus."

She turned her head away, staring at coal-black shadows for a moment before looking at him again. "My mother danced for the tetrarch when he came to my father's court. She danced and afterward my father lost his kingdom, but she gained nothing in the bargain."

"Herodias didn't understand the rules of the game," he said.

"What are the rules?"

"Take it all."

"We can't have it all," she said, thinking of Jokanaan in his cell, wrapped in coarse garments, filthy and lean with hunger.

"A crown, a throne, a kingdom. That is all."

"It can't be all."

Love, she thought. What about love? What about the way her heart stuttered the moment she first saw Jokanaan? What about the nights she'd spent in anguished vigil? Or the hours when sleep claimed her and then came the terrible ache of the dawn? What about the mornings she awoke without him once again and wept? What about the pain of his refusal, which was as deep as if a sword had sliced that heart of hers in two?

"What would you know about wanting?" Agrippa said after a while. "I have wanted for so long. I've wanted my birthright and my revenge. What else should I want?"

She, too, had hungered for the same things. She'd wished that Herod Antipas be brought down; she'd dreamed of returning to her father's palace, which was now the palace of that Roman pig Pontius Pilate.

It was only recently that she'd learned new and different desires, hungering for Jokanaan's lips, dreaming of love.

"Another human being, perhaps," she said, if only to contradict him, desperate to cling to a simple, innocent answer.

Agrippa laughed, a lush, low laugh, and grabbed her chin, making her look at him. Their foreheads were almost touching, and his smile was wide.

"Your desires are different? Then be a whore to our uncle and cavort in the dirt. Shame our ancestors, beg and bow low," he said, but without animosity. He spoke with the coolness that seemed to characterize all their interactions.

For some reason his expression made her think of Jokanaan

when he'd rejected her the first time they'd spoken, when she'd promised she'd kiss him one day. Not that the men had anything in common. Jokanaan had been flustered, while Agrippa was poised.

The memory infuriated her. She reared back, like a cobra. "If I had a crown, it would be mine by my own right. Swear it. Upon our blood," she said.

"I said as much already."

"I'll have an oath from you. The tetrarch gave me one. He swore upon his life and our gods, but I'll have you swear upon our blood. Words alone won't do."

"You'll be queen by your right alone. Queen of all the lands your father governed," Agrippa agreed, a hand against his heart. "I swear it upon our blood."

Salome nodded. Without warning she pressed her mouth against Agrippa's own and bit his lip hard, making it bleed. He stared at her, incredulous. She thought he'd react in anger, perhaps he'd bite back.

Instead, Agrippa swept her hair out of her face. He seemed, for once, almost kind. "I do not lie. The Jew you want is dead already, Salome. Sooner or later, they'll send for the executioner. You hunger for a ghost," he said, and when she tried to look away, he held her chin in place. "But *we* might live. Only if we are quick, though. Only if we are together."

She thought once more of her father's magnificent palace with its central garden where the lilies grew so pale they looked like silver. In that palace there was a reception chamber with tiles of blue and white where Archelaus had once sat in the company of his wife. In that chamber Herod Antipas had raised his eyes and beheld Herodias.

"He promised me unto half his kingdom if I danced for him," Salome said in a whisper, the rage she'd felt now turned into something close to sorrow.

He kissed her, but without malice or conniving desire. It was only so that she might taste the blood on his lips. For a second.

"He'll forfeit it completely," Agrippa promised.

Then he embraced her, pressing close to Salome, and she buried her face against his chest, clutching him tight. They had held each other like this when they were innocent children, long ago. Yet even then, she thought, the thread that knit their lives together had been death.

Hollywood Connection

Cat Fight, Mexican Style, at Pacific Pictures

PRESS AGENTS at Pacific Pictures would have you believe Vera Larios is as sweet as molasses, but don't be fooled by her looks, folks. This little dame is a fiery pepper, and she throws a punch as good as Joe Louis.

Pandemonium erupted on the set of *The Seventh Veil of Salome* earlier this week when Vera Larios and an extra engaged in a loud verbal altercation. The screaming match soon turned physical, with Larios lunging at the girl and landing a few excellently placed punches. It's obvious this is not the first time this dame has had a violent confrontation with another gal. Dare we say this might be an experienced lioness?

We don't know what the two were fighting about, but with that hot Hispanic blood running through her veins, there's no doubt Larios seems to be emulating another wildcat of old: the tempestuous Lupe Vélez. The difference, folks, is that Miss Larios is no established box office draw.

Director Max Niemann is apparently distraught by the constant unladylike behavior of his newest star and complains bitterly about her.

"Not only does the girl jump into a brawl as if she were a drunken sailor at a dingy bar, but she's been seen in the most unladylike of embraces with her latest squeeze in the back of a car," a source close to the production said. "It's enough to drive any director mad."

The starlet was placed on two days' suspension, but has she

learned her lesson? As for Vera's latest squeeze, pianist Jay Rutland, we recommend that he watch out. If this feisty kitty gets angry, she might knock him out cold. Meow!

Vera

SHE DREAMED of Salome, in the throne room, before Herod's court, even when her eyes were open. When she was a child she'd been able to dream like that, picturing herself in faraway lands, which had made some of the girls at school snicker. That look she got when she was staring off into space irritated Vera's mother. It made her look stupid, she said.

Now she was dreaming awake again.

The dance haunted her. It was the climax of the film, and Vera still did not know how to tackle it. She understood the choreography, but it was not enough to trace the right steps. Max Niemann was happy when Vera simply parroted the words of the script, but the dance required a deeper meaning. As much as Orlando considered the Method silly psychoanalytic babble, she sensed she must look inside herself for answers.

Every hour of the day there was the anxiety of the dance and now the growing dread of the press and the rumors swirling on set. The scuffle with that actress—Vera didn't even know her name—had many crew members eyeing her with unrepressed curiosity.

Wildcat. That's what they said in *Hollywood Connection*.

Crazy girl. They also said that.

Recasting, that word was murmured. Marla told her it was silly prattle, nothing to worry about. Vera wasn't so sure. Vivien Leigh had been replaced by Elizabeth Taylor in *The Elephant Walk* after she had a nervous breakdown. They'd already shot several weeks of footage when it happened. Could the same happen to Vera? Might her nerves or her anxiousness be cited as the reason for a drastic change?

Vera walked fast, past a small group of extras who were milling around the studio gates. She headed to the Cock 'n Bull. Film people patronized the imitation English tavern—Jessie Wadsworth, one of the few female talent agents in Hollywood, was a regular— but it wasn't the typical haunt of gossip columnists. It was a more anonymous venue than the Mocambo or Trocadero, at any rate, and Vera was trying to avoid the press without seeming like she was hiding from them. That would further incite their interest.

Once Vera's mother arrived, though, she realized her mistake. Lucinda seemed unimpressed by the food options; neither the Yorkshire pudding nor the leg of lamb was appetizing. She asked for a sandwich, which she nibbled at with little enthusiasm.

"I'm not sure what possessed you to order this drink," her mother said, looking at the Moscow mule in its copper mug that Vera had suggested. "You could have come to your aunt's house. I would have cooked for you."

"I didn't want to be a bother."

"Or you might have invited me to that house you are renting. I suppose it's a bit of a mess and you didn't want me to see it."

"I thought it would be nicer if we went out."

This was going to be their last dinner together before her mother left for Mexico. Vera wanted it to be a special evening, but she found herself grimacing and gripping her hands together.

"I guess that Jay Rutland comes around your house," Lucinda said, gently sliding the copper mug away.

"Sometimes. He's a pleasant man, Mother. We have a lot in common. We both love music. We play together on the piano, you know? I quite think . . . well, I think I might—"

"You don't think he's serious about you, do you, Vera?" her mother said, carelessly interrupting her. "A playboy like that."

"He's not a playboy."

"He's not husband material, I can tell you that. A man who earns his living playing a bongo is not fit to be a husband," Lucinda said, raising her eyebrows in distaste.

"He plays the piano, and I didn't ask for your opinion. I like him, that's what matters."

Lucinda clapped her mouth shut and glared at Vera. She felt ashamed of replying curtly, but she had to start drawing firmer lines with her mother.

Lucinda responded as Vera imagined she would, by quickly finding another point of contention.

"Aren't you supposed to be dancing? You have that big dance number soon, and instead here you are, drinking these silly drinks in copper cups."

"I'm practicing."

"You ought to practice harder. You don't have a natural talent for dance, like your sister."

Vera was not surprised by this acerbic comment. But it hurt nevertheless. Vera traced the rim of her mug with her index finger and shook her head.

"It's never going to be enough, is it? I'm never going to be enough," Vera said.

"What nonsense are you going on about now?"

"You know what I mean. Ever since I can remember you preferred Lumi. You said Lumi was prettier, you said Lumi danced better and sang better. I came to Hollywood because I thought you'd finally be proud of me, but you're not."

Vera paused and looked into her mother's eyes. "I'm going to dance well next week and I'm not going to do it to prove to you that I'm worth something. I'm going to do it because I know I can."

*

EXHAUSTION AND remorse. That was what she felt once the strained dinner with her mother came to an end. Vera debated going straight home and sliding into bed, but in this state of mind she knew she'd spend half the night awake.

She decided to visit Jay. In the evenings, there was no guarantee he'd be home. He might be playing at a tiny, smoke-filled club. But he opened the door.

"Vera, Vera," he whispered against her hair, like a prayer, and his arms were tight around her.

"Jay," she said, feeling her worries melting away in the warmth of his embrace.

He looked at her, his thumb sliding across her cheek, examining her with meticulous care. His breath ghosted against her lips; he whispered a word she didn't catch before depositing a kiss on her lips.

"Who is it?" a female voice asked from inside the house.

Jay straightened up at once and looked behind himself.

"It's fine, Mother," Jay said in a flat voice, then he turned to Vera. "My mother arrived this morning."

"You should have said she was coming today. I would have brought a gift."

"She decided to surprise me. I'm sorry, maybe you could come back tomorrow?" he asked, his voice low and quick.

Vera heard the clacking of high heels. "Is that the girl? Do come in," a woman said with an authoritative tone that would allow no negotiation.

Jay nodded, uncertain. He threw her a quick look that seemed almost a warning. Vera stepped inside and took off her coat.

Jay's mother wore a lilac dress with a fancy collar, and her hair was brushed back in a perfect chignon. Her resemblance to Jay was obvious—the same large eyes, the sculpted cheekbones—but she seemed altogether more refined, like a painting that is displayed in a gilded frame.

"I'm Vera," she said and shook the woman's hand. "I'm pleased to meet you, Mrs. Rutland."

"Hello, Vera," the woman said. "Have you come from your studio?"

"She's dropping something off and has to head back home," Jay said. His usual cheerful, easy smile seemed strained and painted on with a rough hand.

Vera looked at him curiously. She wondered if they'd been quarreling before she arrived. She felt as if she'd interrupted something and wondered if she shouldn't make a speedy exit. But before she could formulate a reply his mother took her arm and pulled her toward the living room.

"Nonsense! She can sit down for a glass of lemonade."

"She doesn't want lemonade."

"You haven't even asked her. It's terribly rude to not even ask her to have a drink."

"Mrs. Rutland, I—"

"No, darling, just because my son is a bad host it doesn't mean I'm one. Jay, don't stand there, put away the lady's coat."

Jay obeyed the command, and Vera guessed that on previous occasions his mother had said similar things and he knew better than to argue. Vera was reminded of her own disagreements with her mother and gave him a sympathetic smile.

They sat down in the living room. Jay's mother took out a cigarette case from a small white purse and picked a cigarette with dexterous fingers. Mrs. Rutland motioned to Jay, and he lit her cigarette before sitting down next to her. They both looked at Vera.

She sat with her hands clasped in her lap, feeling stifled even though Mrs. Rutland had said nothing out of the ordinary. She was a little pushy, but then so was Vera's mother. That, however, did not explain Jay's strange demeanor. He looked so odd, which in turn made her anxious.

"Jay says you're new to the film business."

Mrs. Rutland pointed to an ashtray. Jay handed it to her mutely. He seemed displeased; his posture was stiff and awkward. His mother, on the other hand, carelessly lifted her cigarette to her lips.

"I used to work as a receptionist for my father in Mexico City before I came here."

"You hardly have an accent. I suppose your studio has excellent English teachers."

"My father grew up in the North. His English is good, and he taught me."

"I see. Your name, if you don't mind me saying, is pretty. I quite like the Vera part. It's your surname that has me mystified. Larry-oh? God, I can't even pronounce it," Mrs. Rutland said with an airy laugh. She looked at her son, waving her cigarette in the air as if she were trying to trace the letters of her name. "Jay, dear, how do you say it?"

Vera blushed and remembered the party where Clifford Collins's girlfriend had mocked her. This was beginning to feel like more of the same. She looked at Jay, but he was looking at his mother.

"Larios," Jay said dryly. "It's not that hard."

"Yes. Like that. You must forgive me, I don't speak Spanish. I never did like the sound of it," Mrs. Rutland said, pressing her fingertips against her chin and chuckling. "Anyhow, I saw pictures of you in a magazine recently. *Hollywood Connection*, do you know it?"

Vera guessed it had been the story about her fight at the studio. She'd managed to avoid that minefield with her mother, but now she was forced to confront it again in the presence of Mrs. Rutland.

"Yes. They publish silly stories there."

"I know, darling. These gossip rags sell many issues, don't they?"

"I suppose so."

"At least film must provide a somewhat stable salary for a starlet. Jay thinks he can live off tinkering with piano keys."

"He's playing twice a week at a club, and he's working on a lot of original material," Vera said proudly.

She loved to see Jay hunched over the piano, playing furiously fast. But she also enjoyed his slow, careful prodding of each key and the pauses as he annotated a music sheet. When he talked about jazz, his eyes brimmed with an eagerness that made her burn with passion in return, delighted to discuss notes and melodies and styles.

When the talk turned to film and she explained a scene she had to rehearse or declaimed a line from the script, he responded with animation. But music was his favorite domain, and she delighted in this topic since it often lifted her spirits.

"He was supposed to go into the family business," Mrs. Rutland said, softly tapping her cigarette against the ashtray and smiling. "The Rutland Navigation Company. Has Jay told you about the business?"

"I'm certain Vera doesn't want to hear about the business, Mother. And she was dropping off—"

"Jay says he will never sit behind a desk, but after a while all boys are done playing with their toys. It takes a few years to develop common sense. Jay is learning that. Be a dear and get us two big glasses of lemonade, won't you?" Mrs. Rutland asked, throwing him a crisp smile.

"There is no lemonade."

"I saw lemons in the refrigerator, and you can slice them. Really, darling, you'll have the girl thinking you're useless. Go."

Jay stood up, hesitating, before finally heading to the kitchen. Mrs. Rutland leaned back against the couch, her painted vermilion mouth still smiling. Vera didn't know quite how to proceed. She could feel she was skirting dangerously close to a shark but couldn't determine how to best evade it.

"He plays beautifully, Mrs. Rutland," Vera said at last. "He really does. He says he learned from you."

"He learned scales from me, but I didn't teach him to play the kind of noise he likes to play. I certainly didn't tell him to do it in front of an audience, either," the woman said with a dismissive sigh. "Jazz. In California, of all places!"

"There's plenty of jazz in California, Mrs. Rutland. Central Avenue is jammed with great clubs. The Haig, on Wilshire Boulevard, well, it looks really like a shack, but the music they play there is impressive, Jay took me—"

"You like that junk, too, then? I'm not surprised," the woman said, raising one of her carefully plucked eyebrows with disdain.

"It's not the kind of hobby for any of us Rutlands. I suppose Jay hasn't explained who we are, has he? The Rutlands are well respected. We have impeccable reputations. Which is why Jay can't afford to be cavorting with you anymore."

"I'm sorry?" Vera said. She smiled because she thought she'd heard her wrong.

Mrs. Rutland draped an arm over the back of the sofa and gave Vera a critical look. "My dear, I've always believed it's best to be frank and quick about these matters. I won't draw it out: Jay won't be seeing you any longer. You're not the type of girl he'd marry, and as far as mistresses go, I'm not going to approve of one who makes the gossip columns regularly, and drags his name into them, too."

"Damn it, Mother," Jay said.

He was standing at the entrance to the living room carrying a tray with a pitcher and two glasses. He dumped them on a table and glared at Mrs. Rutland.

"What? I told you if *you* didn't talk to her, *I* would," Mrs. Rutland said with a shrug.

"Come on, Vera," Jay muttered, clasping her hand and pulling her up from her seat. "We should go for a drive while my mother sips her lemonade."

Mrs. Rutland's eyes bored into her son's face. "Break it off. Now. You promised you'd do it last week and then you didn't."

"Mother, really! How can—"

"You're lucky I came, Jay," the woman said calmly. "If it had been your father, it would be much worse. You know he really doesn't approve of these Hispanic types at all."

"Beaner," Vera said wryly. "The correct term is 'beaner.'"

"We're leaving," Jay said, before his mother could reply.

He practically growled as they hurried back to the entrance. He opened the closet and snatched her coat out, then stomped toward the detached garage, pulling Vera with him.

"What was that, Jay?" she asked, her voice sharp, not with

anger, but with sorrow. She could see the whole tapestry of their lives coming apart. One pull of the thread was all it took.

"I'll drive you home and we can talk properly tomorrow."

"She said you promised to break up with me last week."

Jay didn't reply. She stopped. He tugged at her hand, but Vera wouldn't budge an inch forward.

"Did you?"

He turned around with a sigh. "I said I would, but I didn't mean it."

"Why would you say it, then?"

"Because she threatened to cut me off. But we don't have to break up. We just have to be more discreet so my family doesn't hear about us."

Vera pulled her hand away from him and stared at Jay. She felt so distressed that she was unable to speak a coherent sentence, and he seemed to have grown mute, too.

"You were going to lie to her? And stash me away somewhere?" she asked finally.

He flushed a bright red. "I was going to omit certain information."

"Lie."

"I wouldn't be able to afford my car or this place if it wasn't for the allowance my mother sends. Without that cash I'd be a bum out on the street. My piano playing could hardly cover my meals, never mind the rent."

"I see," Vera said, clutching the coat under her arm. "That's why you didn't want me to meet her."

"I didn't want you to meet her because she's impossible! Vera, it doesn't have to change anything. We can still do all the things we talked about. We can head on that road trip after your movie's done shooting, I can find gigs at clubs while we're traveling. We'll go away for a whole two months."

He spoke with the same vehement voice he'd used on previous occasions, when they'd taken a drive at night and parked near a little cove, admiring the stars and the sea. Or when she'd rested her head against his chest as they sat on the couch and he played his records. That same tone that promised adventure, freedom, a thousand sights and sounds. But now it sounded hollow.

Vera shook her head. "No, we won't," she said and started walking at a brisk pace.

He went after her, moving with equal haste. "I told you my folks were difficult. You've told me the same, how it's complicated dealing with your mother," he said quickly.

"I'm not lying to my mother."

"It's not lying, it's . . . I want to be with you, really."

"It's lying, Jay," Vera said firmly. "What's your plan? What will you tell them in six months, in a year, in two? Are you going to pretend you're a bachelor every time your parents visit you? Unless you didn't intend to keep it going for that long. Maybe you figured in six months I'd be out of the picture and you wouldn't have to do any explaining. You know us Hispanic types! We're very flighty."

"I don't believe such things. That's my dad."

"You do believe it if you won't stand up to them! My mother doesn't like you that much. But you know what I told her when she said I shouldn't be hanging out with you? I said I didn't care about her opinion. You could have done the same."

"Vera, it's complicated!"

"It isn't!"

Jay spun her around and grabbed her by the shoulders. She let go of her coat, and it fell to the ground. She'd managed to keep herself from weeping, but now she felt herself tearing up as she looked at him.

"It isn't," she repeated, this time in a whisper. "You love someone, or you don't. You want to be with them, or you don't. Everything else is incidental."

"Vera," he said. "What do I have to do?"

She stepped away from him. Two, three, four steps. Her eyes were fixed on his own.

"You take one step in my direction, Jay, and it's because you've decided to be honest. You'll tell your family that you're in love with me and they have to accept it. If they're uncomfortable at Thanksgiving dinner, or they don't like the ring of 'Vera Larios,' you tell them you don't care.

"If you take that step, it's because we're going to be together. Really and truly. I broke off my engagement because I couldn't live a lie, and I'm not going to start living lies with you.

"But if you have any doubts, stay put. I'm not going to love someone in fractions, and I won't be loved in quarters or in halves. You take the whole of me, if you want it. You take that step, Jay, if you absolutely love me."

Jay seemed baffled at first, then something close to fear spread across his face. She realized it wasn't the fear of losing her, but the fear of all the things he'd have to give up if he embraced her. The car, the house, the allowance. His mother wasn't bluffing, Vera was sure of that, and he must know it, too.

She understood why he had looked at her with such care when he'd opened the door. He had been trying to affix her image to his mind, fearing that he might not see her again.

No, *knowing* that he likely would not. For if it came to a choice, he would choose the safety of his family rather than the incertitude she represented.

Vera bent down, picked up the coat, and walked away.

He did not follow her. He did not take a single step.

Nancy

"THE WORLD," Tessa said, leaning over the table and smiling. "The ending of a cycle and the beginning of a new one. There are big changes ahead for you."

The women were sitting at Tessa's scratched old table. They smoked. Tessa didn't have good booze, so Nancy had brought a bottle of whiskey, and they drank from two red glasses. Tessa drank with good cheer and wore a faded cotton dress, her hair still up in rollers. Tessa was rarely presentable before nighttime. Nancy preferred the night, too. It had been only recently, due to her job at the studio, that she'd deigned to wake before noon. Now there wasn't any studio to worry about.

"This here, it's enlightenment. A discovery," Tessa said, tapping her nail against the card.

"Yeah. I'm gonna discover my bank account's empty soon," Nancy said. She wasn't even looking at the cards, although they usually cheered her up. She was staring out the window, at the building across the street, which seemed a duplicate of her own building.

Gray rectangles with smaller rectangles made of glass. Inside them, there sat little people at their tables trying to pass the time, living their insignificant gray lives. Gray. Not Technicolor, like in the movies where people broke into song, fell in love at first sight, or went on overseas adventures. It was black-and-white, this rotten bitch of a life.

"You didn't even like that job."

"Doesn't mean I wanted to be fired. Especially because of that whore."

"You scratched her good at least, didn't you?"

"Yeah," Nancy said, smiling.

Tessa smiled back. They laughed. Nancy rubbed her right foot against the back of her leg, thinking of Vera Larios decked in the Salome costume with a thousand rhinestones and paste jewels. They caught the light and shone like real diamonds, but they were fake. How they'd sparkle on screen, though, and no one would be able to tell the difference. They might even think the rhinestones were prettier than jewels from Tiffany's.

"The Lovers," Tessa said. "A kindred spirit. A soulmate. Trials overcome."

Nancy glanced down at the card with the figure of a naked woman and a man standing in front of a mountain. Above them, an angel spread his hands. To the left of the woman there was a tree with a serpent, a reminder of temptation. Behind the man a tree sprouted and was engulfed in flames.

A loud knock startled them. Tessa opened the door and there stood Clem, Tessa's sometime boyfriend and pimp. He tipped his hat as he caught sight of Nancy.

"Afternoon," he said.

"What you doin' here?" Tessa asked. "I told you we were having ourselves a girls' night."

"Can't time these things, Tessy. I have a fellow who's eager to make your acquaintance."

"What time?"

"In an hour."

Tessa began taking the rollers from her hair while Clem hung his jacket over a chair and sat across from Nancy. He grabbed the red glass Tessa had been drinking from and downed it.

"You're looking pretty this afternoon, Nancy. Are you going out on a date?" Clem asked, giving her an appreciative look.

"No."

"Tessy says things are a bit rocky at your workplace right now. If you ever need extra dough, I can help you make a couple of dollars here and there."

Clem was in his thirties but looked older; his eyes were tired. Tessa also looked older, and as Nancy watched her hurrying to take out the rollers, chatting all the while about the cards, she felt a wave of disgust.

What was she doing there, sitting with that whore and her pimp? Looking at cards and sharing her liquor? Nancy had done such things before and it hadn't bothered her at all, but now she stared at Tessa in horror.

She thought about her father, at a cheap diner, dressed neatly, his hair carefully parted, trying to resemble the performer he'd once been. Nancy stood up.

"You don't need to go yet," Tessa said.

"You have yourself a good evening," Nancy said. She left the bottle on the table, didn't even bother taking that.

She trembled with each step she took to her apartment. Even when she sat down on her bed she was still trembling. Tessa was low and dirty and disgusting. Nancy wondered why it had never struck her exactly how low she was. Clem was the same.

She decided to head out and catch a movie. She took out two dresses from the closet and laid them on the bed. She fiddled with stockings and shoes. Then she stopped, lips pressed tight, remembering the time Tessa told her how she'd found her way to Los Angeles. She'd won a contest. Miss Potato or Miss Orange, something or other. She'd shown Nancy the picture of herself crowned with a sash around her waist, smiling.

How long had Tessa been in California? Seven, eight, or more years? Nancy couldn't recall the number. It didn't matter, she thought, pulling another dress from the closet and tossing it on the bed. But it did.

Nancy had been in Hollywood for almost four years now. In those four years she'd snagged a crummy six-month option and the minuscule bit in *The Seventh Veil of Salome*. She'd also had her picture taken for catalogues and arranged for shots on spec in the hope of landing at men's magazines like *Pageant*, only nothing panned out. And there had also been that sleazy business of nudie pictures.

That was all. She remembered what her dad said: four years was a century in Hollywood.

How long had it taken Vera Larios to secure that role? Four minutes? It was not right when a nobody could sweep into town like that and make it into pictures. People like Vera Larios made it seem simple when it was hard as hell.

It wasn't fair! They'd fired Nancy because of that bitch, and it was Vera who had thrown the first punch. It was Vera who had pushed Nancy to the ground and started attacking her like a savage. But Nancy was the one who was canned.

Now what would happen? The ending of a cycle and the beginning of another—big fucking joke. In a few weeks Nancy would need rent money, and then she'd have to start phoning old boyfriends and associates. Begging for scraps. Maybe even asking another sleazy photographer if he'd pay for nudies.

In another four years Nancy might be letting a guy like Clem arrange dates for her to make ends meet. What would that bitch Vera be up to in four years? Attending premieres. Going to clubs. Smiling shyly for the camera with her stupid, asinine mouth.

There was nothing Nancy could do about it, either. It was like her biology teacher used to say: survival of the fittest. Eat or be eaten. Nancy never had much interest in biology, and the time they dissected a frog she'd mostly let her lab partner tackle the work. But she remembered the scalpel touching a nerve and the leg of the frog kicking. She thought it was funny that the frog was still twitching.

Now she felt like the frog.

If only the director could see Nancy! God fucking damn it. She wanted to be seen, she wanted thousands of eyes fixed upon her face. She wanted what Vera Larios had and she'd never get.

"Drop dead," she whispered, picturing the actress in her Salome gown, glittering under the lights. "Drop dead, drop dead."

She said the words so quickly they became indistinct. No longer words but guttural noises, the type of cries you might hear in a jungle coming from the treetops. The growl of panthers and the howl of monkeys.

"Dead," she said, and she thought how wonderful it would be if that could happen, if Vera would simply die.

*

THE THOUGHT clung to her. It wouldn't leave Nancy, it was becoming a part of her. She pressed her forehead against her windowpane and felt the sizzling heat outside her building. It was equally hot inside. You could fry an egg on her floor. The fan wheezed and turned, never truly cooling the room.

It had been cooler at the studio, no matter what that stupid extra who complained about the temperature said. Even with those big lights hanging overhead it was better than this oven.

She jerked the cord of her phone, hard, and thought about dialing Jay Rutland. For no reason. Maybe to ask if Vera Larios was there and to speak to her. To tell her she should drop dead.

Benny came by with half a dozen carnations under his arm and a bottle of Scotch. They sat on her bed and smoked.

"What's with you?" he asked, pouring two fingers of the stuff into a glass.

Nancy curled her feet under her, shook her head, and motioned for Benny to hand her another of his cigarettes. He lit it and she snatched it quick.

"Told you. They fired me because of that beaner bitch."

"It was pretty funny the way you tell it."

"Yeah, a real laugh fest," Nancy said dryly.

He brushed her hair with his hand, gentle, and Nancy jumped up. She stood in the middle of the room and let the smoke pour out of her lips.

"You know, I was a shoo-in for the part of Salome. They loved my audition. Then Chiquita Banana pulls who knows what strings and she's in. Just like that," Nancy said, snapping her fingers. "They're talking about recasting, you know? I bet if they did, they'd give me a call."

It was far-fetched, but Benny nodded enthusiastically. Far-fetched, yeah, but Pierce Pratt was sweet on her. He'd said she shouldn't call him, but if Nancy rang him up, she bet he'd answer. Maybe . . .

The cigarette burned her fingers. She dropped it and stomped on it. She looked at the floor.

"It's not right, Benny."

"No, it's not."

"I wish she'd drop dead. Bullet to the head."

Benny didn't say anything. He was still on the bed with his cigarette. His face was a blank slate, and his eyes were fixed on Nancy.

"You heard me?"

"I heard you."

"When I think about her, I want to throw myself from the roof-top."

"Don't be stupid."

"I do," Nancy said and she squeezed her eyes shut and rolled her hands into tight fists, pressing them against her temples. "I'd make the papers if I threw myself. I'd make the paper like she does. Not in the entertainment pages, but I'd still be in the paper. I'd be in *Hollywood Connection*. I'd be in *Confidential* and *Hush-Hush*."

"Nancy, don't get like this. I hate it when you get like this. Here, have a drink."

"I don't want a drink, Benny."

"Come on."

She felt blindly for the glass, drank it all, and handed it back to him. Still with her eyes closed, she grabbed hold of the back of a chair.

"Death's a big word, Nancy."

"I know," she said and opened her eyes. "You own a gun, don't you?"

There was silence. He grabbed the bottle and poured her another one, topped himself off. "I own a gun," he said.

Each hour of each day she'd been thinking about Vera Larios. Each hour she'd been hating her. It was no surprise, therefore, when a whole, clear plan formed faster than she could take a drag of his cigarette. In a second, she had the entirety of it.

"I can find out where she lives. You could drive there at night. You have no connection to her, no one would put you at the scene."

"You really want me to shoot that girl?" he asked, but he didn't sound aghast. Surprised, yes. But there was no horror in Benny's voice. He'd done stuff before. They'd discussed some of it, skimmed over most. It wasn't pretty and it wasn't good, so this line of conversation must have struck him as unexpected but not off-limits.

"I'd shoot her myself if I knew how. Fuck, Benny, don't look so worried. I'd shoot her in both legs so she couldn't dance. There, that sound better?"

"It'd be better to beat her with a tire iron if you want broken legs," Benny said.

He is serious, she thought. These were not merely the ramblings of two drunks awake late at night; he was serious. Why shouldn't he be serious, though? And why shouldn't she reply with equal gravity, as befitted the occasion?

"Tire irons look conspicuous," Nancy muttered. "How would you walk behind her into a restaurant with a tire iron?"

"I thought you said you could find her address."

"Yeah. And she might live in an apartment building. Same problem. How do you get past the doorman with a tire iron?"

"She could also have a house. No doorman."

"If anyone saw you, they'd remember a guy with a tire iron," Nancy said stubbornly. "They wouldn't remember a gun tucked away in a jacket, hidden from sight."

Benny walked toward her radio and flipped it on. A crooner was singing about love.

"It's too much," he said as he toyed with the knob that controlled the volume.

"She cheated me. You get even when people try to cheat you, don't you?"

Benny set down his glass. He rocked slightly back and forth on his feet and shrugged.

"I do. I don't normally pump bullets into their legs."

"You pummel them," Nancy said. "Like you pummeled Wally."

"He deserved it."

"She deserves it, too. Sometimes you pummel them, sometimes you knife them. Is a gun that different?"

"It's different when you're talking about a girl I don't know," Benny said, his voice dry.

She was beginning to grow irritated. First he agreed with her, and now he was turning skittish. Nancy didn't like this back-and-forth. Maybe he thought he could impress her by talking about tire irons and guns and then telling her to forget it, he was kidding, no way could he hurt a dame.

"I told you about her because I thought you're the kind of guy who actually does things. You're not just talk like the others, like the phonies," she said.

"What phonies do you have hanging around, honey? Phonies like Jay Rutland?" he asked with poisonous intent.

"Like him, yeah. One big phony with no guts."

"No guts but with dough and a new car. Don't try to pretend you weren't over the moon with the guy."

His eyes were hard. She guessed he'd been tormenting himself about the man for weeks. It didn't matter that she'd said it was over; he must suspect she wanted him back. Well, she wasn't going to assuage his fears.

"Maybe I was and maybe I will be again. Beat it, Benny. Grab your lousy bottle, too."

His face was flushed. She thought he'd either do that, stomping out of the apartment with a curse and a threat, or take it seriously and sit down. He sat down. Nancy pulled up a chair and sat, too, even though she felt so restless she wanted to run around the room in circles.

"If I do this for you, it's gotta mean something," he said.

"It'll mean I can trust you."

"I'm talking about being serious about each other. Only you and me, Nancy. No more running around with other men, no more dropping me and picking me up again. I'll shoot that girl if you want it. Because I love you."

He grabbed her hand, squeezing it tight. She figured he wanted her to say it back, but she chewed on her lip, feeling a pressure inside her chest, but it wasn't that good feeling, it wasn't butterflies in your stomach. It was a rotten, heavy, dark weight she felt whenever she was with Benny. Like it was maybe love and maybe a lot of other stuff, too, that wasn't so great.

But she looked up at him, and she squeezed his hand back.

"I can't live if she's walking around safe and cozy. It keeps me awake at nights, tossing and turning, when I think how she's living it up, starring in *my* movie. It should have been my movie,

Benny. It still could be. They're talking about recasting, and I know they'd hire me if I could audition again.

"If she's out of the picture, then I'll have the role and I'll be happy. We can be different then, Benny. We can have a new car, nicer than Jay Rutland's, and I can dress like we're dancing at Ciro's every night of the week."

"It might not turn out like that. They might get someone else to substitute her."

"Maybe they'll do that. At least I'll have my payback, right? She stole that part from me. I *am* Salome."

God, she really did want her dead, wanted her hurt. Wanted something terrible to happen to Vera Larios. There was this intense rage, this envy, chewing at her heart, and Nancy didn't care if this was madness, she saw no other solution.

"I know you are," Benny said.

They were weaving a conspiracy. Together, in that miserable apartment. There was something exciting about it, and she crawled onto Benny's lap, holding him tight, kissing him. She told him this was something only he could give her, and he knew that was true.

Other guys, men like Jay Rutland, they could trace the bumps of Nancy's spine with their hands, pull down her stockings, cage her between their arms. They could buy her trinkets, maybe an expensive coat. They could even take her on an exotic vacation. But none of them could draw blood for her.

That was him and him alone. And Benny said yes, he would. He'd give her this, which was better than a diamond and pearls, and any nonsense the phonies could promise her.

Salome

THE BANQUETING hall was perfumed sweetly: it smelled of orange blossoms, like a summer garden in full bloom. The tetrarch's table was placed on a platform of sycamore wood, giving it an excellent view of all the other people reclining on sandalwood couches.

The torches made the translucent yellow-green cups on the low table glow with an unearthly hue. Serving girls attired in flowing dresses poured wines from Byblos from the decorated crateras, and young men carried bowls heaped with grapes.

Herod wore a black mantle fringed with golden threads. A golden breastplate, sculpted to imitate the musculature of a young man, rested upon his chest. And upon his head there was the gold diadem covered with precious stones that was the symbol of his power. Next to him, Herodias was dressed in a deep blue dress with a necklace of sapphires gleaming against her throat.

The tetrarch's guests were numerous and varied. There were his advisors and regular attendants, such as the stony, serious Josephus. There was the proconsul with his guards. There were people Salome knew well, such as Marcellus, and others she had never glimpsed before, such as a representative from Jericho who had been seated next to two Thracian merchants. There were high-ranking Jewish men of notable houses, noblewomen with multiple strands of precious pearls around their throats, and even a few adventurous nobodies who had managed to secure through trickery and wiles an invitation to the banquet.

Numerous entertainers streamed in and out of the grand hall. Flautists, singers, jugglers, several groups of dancers. They all played their instruments or swayed to the music; they all smiled and nodded as the guests clapped or cheered them on.

Jokanaan had been dragged to sit among Herod's perfumed guests, in chains, dressed in dirty, coarse clothes. He had been made to sit in a spot from which he could be viewed with ease by the proconsul and his companions, and had been served wine and mouthwatering dishes, but had not touched his cup or tossed a single grape into his mouth. He sat at this appointed spot and regarded the dancers and the guests with indifference.

He did not look at Salome. His gaze did not evade her. It was simply as if he had gone blind and could not see the young woman. He seemed to hear little, too. A harpist played, strumming sweet notes, but Jokanaan paid the musician no heed. He was a stone pillar.

"Will you dance tonight, Salome?" Marcellus asked.

The eyes of the Roman, as well as those of many others, had strayed toward her several times. Salome wore a wreath of flowers upon her head, like a nymph from myth, and a white dress that was becoming in its simplicity. She had not wrapped her neck in jewels, nor did a golden bracelet circle her slim wrist. An elaborate dress or jewels would have made it more difficult for her to change into her dancer's attire.

But she did not require jewels nor complicated coiffures. She was lovely with her crown of flowers; lovelier, perhaps, than she'd ever been. The turmoil inside her heart seemed to make her eyes brighter, her parted lips more enticing.

The gaze of the guests fixed on Salome, but Jokanaan did not look at her.

"She will," Herodias said. "My daughter is the finest dancer in the entire city."

"What kind of dance is it?" Vitellius asked. "I am fond of dancers."

"It's an old dance, is it not?" Agrippa said. "Danced in the Herodian court since the day of our grandfather and before that. It's a queen's dance, meant for royalty."

His voice was pleasant, but his eyes were sharp. Silently they reminded her of her illustrious lineage. *Queen*, his eyes said, although, so far, he had not spoken to her. She had expected he might press his point in low, anxious whispers, but he did not.

"I will perform for my uncle," Salome said simply.

"Yes, that she will," Herod said.

He seemed pleased by her words. His eyes were bright. They often were these days, from the wine. Polished like twin stones, large and dark. Those eyes that followed Salome through the palace, ravenous. The tetrarch reached for his cup and observed her.

With his golden breastplate and the diadem on his head, he somewhat resembled the bold warrior he'd once been, but the memory only stirred discontent inside Salome. In his youth, he'd been comely, and in his youth, he'd killed Salome's father. This she would never forget.

Killed our fathers both, Agrippa's eyes told her.

There came a clanging and murmurs from afar. The harpist's fingers stilled upon her instrument, curious. Proconsul Vitellius frowned, running his hand down the front of his toga. "Whatever is that noise?" he asked.

"Those are the preacher's followers. They come to seek an audience," Josephus said politely. "They've come before and now return."

His followers, or perhaps Agrippa's men? Men paid in twisted alleyways to foster discontent. Not all of them, perhaps only two or three. Yet the right words could sway a multitude to violence. Salome looked at her cousin, who sat at her right. He smiled at her.

"They do not seek an audience. They seek blood," Herodias said.

"They are distressed," Josephus replied. "Many people love Jokanaan."

"They bang shields and screech for love?" Herodias asked scornfully. "I think not."

What would you know about love, Mother? Salome thought. Herodias had gladly traded her first, unfit spouse for a new one with a shrug. Now she meant to trade Salome to remain seated upon that wooden chair that was not even a throne. Herodias's heart was a stone. Yet Salome wondered if perhaps her mother had been right when she turned the softness of her soul into marble.

"The Jews always have a quarrel," Agrippa said. "It takes a firm hand to govern them."

Herod's dark eyes fixed furiously on his nephew. "I govern them in the way that they should be governed. In the wisest way."

"That is precisely what I meant, Uncle," Agrippa said with

mock innocence. "Yet it is difficult, is it not, to govern them at times? This preacher here, for example, says his people should not be taxed, yet what kind of anarchy would descend upon the land if people were allowed to ignore the tribute they must pay? The roads would be untended, and weeds would grow upon the merchants' roads, and how they'll holler about bandits and broken paths."

"Indeed, the merchants will complain at the slightest mishap," Vitellius agreed.

Salome pretended to drink from her cup, but her mouth was dry. She'd hardly tasted the wine. She'd hardly spoken, either. Her gaze drifted toward the preacher, wishing he'd spare her a look. If he looked at her, she would scream and tell the tetrarch that he must be freed, no matter the cost, no matter what Agrippa had said.

If he looked at her, her heart would ignite and she'd be reduced to cinders, but she'd have his love.

"He's a curious fellow," Vitellius said, rubbing his chin and scrutinizing Jokanaan. "I wanted to hear him speak, but before I could meet him, the man was seized. He doesn't look like much of a priest."

"He is no priest," Herodias said. "Simply a lout and a madman with lice in his hair who rambles for the crowds."

"Have you ever heard him preach?" Vitellius asked, turning to Herod.

"I've had reports, which is why he has been imprisoned. The man decries the authority of Rome."

"I heard he also predicts the end of the world. Have you heard this?" the proconsul asked, this time turning to Agrippa, who shrugged.

"The world is always ending for someone or other," Salome's cousin said. "All that matters is who remains afterward."

"I'd expect you to think that way, and you are probably correct. Yet I'd like to hear him speak. You there, preacher, can you share the word of your God with these fine lords and ladies?"

The proconsul sounded merry. He'd had much wine to drink. It was going to his head.

"Do not let him speak," Herodias said, turning toward the tetrarch, her words a hiss, her hand with its long painted nails upon his arm.

But Herod ignored his wife and motioned to a guard, who pulled Jokanaan to his feet, making his chains rattle.

"The proconsul wants to hear the word of your God," Herod said.

There was an inherent taunt and a threat in Herod's voice. Jokanaan had been dragged to the feast for sport, the same way a hare might be released into the gardens for the lords to hunt. A wise man might have kept his mouth shut or attempted to flatter the tetrarch. A wise man might even have begged for his freedom.

Jokanaan looked at the tetrarch, unblinking. He was poised. The chains dangling from his wrists, ugly and heavy as they were, seemed almost the fine jewels of a prince, for he wore them with remarkable dignity.

"Well, then," Vitellius said, drumming a finger upon the arm of the carved chair inlaid with ivory upon which he sat. "I've been told your God speaks to you. I've been told you have glimpsed the end of the world and wish others to know of your vision."

"I have seen that," Jokanaan said.

"And?" the proconsul said as he reached for a bowl laden with figs and plopped one into his mouth.

"Do you truly wish to hear?" the young man asked, looking first at the proconsul, then at the tetrarch.

"Yes, speak up. Speak about your precious God," Herod said scornfully. "If you speak well and you speak prettily, perhaps I might loosen your chains for an hour."

"I speak only the truth."

Courtiers, soldiers, and servants looked at the preacher. Women whose eyes were lined black with kohl smirked, men with perfumed beards that were tinted blue chuckled, the servants carrying heavy amphoras shook their heads and sighed. The harpist had not resumed playing. They all waited for the preacher's words, ready to bark with laughing mockery as soon as he spoke. Because he was such a young man, a man in rags, dirty with his hair uncombed, and what could such a man know about gods and their portents? Only Josephus seemed serious, as was Salome.

"The smoke from a hundred smoldering fires will rise through the air and deposit a blanket of ashes. It will rain ashes for thirty days and thirty nights. Locusts will eat the crops and the fruit will wither in the trees. Women will rend their clothes in fear and men will weep. The walls of palaces shall crumble and cities will burn. The world will be undone and purified," the preacher said.

The horrors he spoke of were numerous and lavishly described, and his tongue was well versed in the telling of such tales. As a result, a few guests spilled drops of their wine, dropped a pistachio that they had intended to eat, stopped their chattering. The architecture of the vast room seemed to enhance the young man's voice, making it boom louder than it had at the market where Salome had heard him preach. A few people shrank in fear.

Then his tone became softer, though it was still easy to hear him. He was clearly a gifted orator and knew how to lead the audience through a narrative, pulling them by the hand like the waves tug at the ocean.

"But then there will come a time of peace and redemption when sorrow and wickedness will be forgotten, when a new world will be formed. Roses will blossom in the desert. Water will spring where there was only rock. The scars of the land will be healed. Lions will lie next to lambs. The people will prostrate themselves before the Lord and praise him for eternity. For there will be no more suffering, no more sin and no more death."

"This you have seen?" Vitellius asked, sounding much amazed.

"I have seen this," Jokanaan said.

Several other guests were also dazzled. A couple looked as if they might clap, pleased by the performance, as they had been pleased by the jugglers, the singers, the dancers. But the preacher was not done speaking.

Be silent, she thought. Because what the man had said was terrible and awe inducing, but it was not treason. It was defiant, but it was not rebellion. Yet if he kept speaking, he'd damn himself. She wanted to clasp a palm against his mouth, yet she knew he could not be silenced.

She also knew he was a corpse, that he'd been one the second he walked into the banquet hall without fear or awe. If he'd cowered, or if he'd begged, if he'd sat at his table in tears, mortified, he might have lived. But he'd walked in like a wayward hero.

Fool, she thought. *How could you, you fool?*

Jokanaan looked at Herod. "I have also seen a ruler with a diadem of gold upon his head, proud and cruel, who will fall to his knees and lie in the dirt, lower than the lowest beggar, lower than a worm. For his sins are many and deep; he rose against his kin for want of jewels and the soft skin of his brother's wife, plunging the land into conflict and bleeding it dry."

He looked at Herodias. "I have seen a scheming noblewoman born of two notable houses who through artifice and cunning caused the misery of many, and who spreads poison with her forked tongue. This woman is accursed, her womb is salted with vice, and she is a great whore, a meretrix. She will be dragged through the streets and flogged, and she will utter many lamentations."

"Silence this vile man!" Herodias exclaimed, turning to her husband. "Silence him, I say!"

"You cannot silence my tongue. You asked for the truth: I have spoken it. Heed it and find salvation. Ignore it and be damned. For the coming of the Lord and the judgment of your sins is at hand."

Herodias looked like a woman who had already been stoned and dragged through the streets; she looked like a wild woman, her nostrils flared. As for the tetrarch in his black mantle with his diadem on his head, he seemed reduced in stature, suddenly feebler. His ornaments, the rings on his fingers, the golden breastplate, even this grand feast to celebrate and commemorate his magnificence seemed instead to highlight his utter insignificance.

"Will you tell a portent about me?" Salome requested, rising abruptly.

Herodias looked at her daughter in surprise. Salome stood rigidly, staring at Jokanaan. He still would not look at her. He had boldly looked at Herod and at Herodias, he had looked around the room and fulminated the attendants with his gaze. He had spared Salome.

"I can speak no portent of you, lady. Yet there are certain paths that are inevitable. It is like this with you. Your path will be marked in blood."

He did not look at her, Jokanaan did not. Agrippa was the one who turned his sardonic gaze in her direction. He did not speak to Salome, but he did not need to.

We are that inevitability, Agrippa's gaze said. *And even he knows it.*

Salome pressed the tips of her fingers against her lips, remembering her conversation with Agrippa the previous night, and the taste of his blood in her mouth. Her heart leaped in her chest.

Everyone was quiet. The noblewomen and Herod's advisors decked in their finery, the slaves standing behind their masters with great fans made of ostrich feathers, the guards whose lances were crossed and who stood at the entrance of the hall. They were silent, as if a great stone weighed them down, squeezing the air out of their lungs.

The tetrarch's eyes were two wells of darkness; his mouth was twisted in a furious snarl, and he gripped his cup as if he might strangle the wine.

"I'll have a dance now," Herod demanded, slamming the cup down.

"I will dance for you," Salome said.

Maxwell Niemann

IT WAS that painting by Gustave Moreau that did it for me. "L'Apparition," it's called. I spied it in an art book when I was twelve years old. Later on, I learned that it was what is called fin de siècle art, but back then I didn't understand the image. Nevertheless, I was fascinated, perhaps because I couldn't comprehend it.

There was a woman, practically nude, her hand held up, and there was a head floating in the air. The blue column and the golden tiles, lozenges of lapis lazuli, the jewels on a crown, emeralds hiding her loins, the blood upon the floor, petals left to rot, the rays of light, the scent of incense and myrrh. It was a nightmare, a dream.

I read Mallarmé's poem "Hérodiade" many years later and thought back to that painting depicting Salome. The virgin-whore. The sexual deviant and devourer. The stone idol.

Salome is a chimera. Part lion, part dove. It's that duality that makes her monstrous, and it's that duality that Vera Larios needed to encapsulate.

Gustave Moreau painted several versions of Salome, but in a movie you only get to show one shot. You can't show the alternative takes. You make a choice with the editor about what will be screened. You get one Salome instead of a multitude of Salomes. She either smiles or she weeps.

I wasn't quite sure which Salome I wanted, and I wasn't quite sure what I wanted from Vera. I can say that now, but I couldn't articulate it then. Possibly, I was too ashamed to put it in words. A director should know everything. I was figuring the ending out, dithering with the script, caught in a haze.

There are flaws in the movie. Beats that don't play well, scenes that should have been trimmed, characters who needed more dialogue. But the dance. The dance resembles that painting. That dance is delirium caught on film. Watch her dance, watch her for three seconds and you'll remain for the whole sequence: you can't take your eyes off her.

Vera

SHE RAN into Joe Kantor late one afternoon, while he was having a smoke behind a sound stage and she was walking around the lot, lost in thought, a melody on the tip of her tongue. He smiled.

"Almati," he said, bowing theatrically. "How does the princess fare?"

"I'm good. I hadn't seen you these past few days. Are you taking your meals somewhere nicer?" she replied, smiling back at him.

"No, the contrary. I'm locked in my apartment eating animal crackers while I work full speed on a new pic, a low-budget noir they'll need quick. I had a meeting today and had to drop by the lot."

"You worked so long on *The Seventh Veil of Salome,* isn't it strange writing something else?" she asked.

"I worked too long on it. And for what? Between the director disagreeing with every other line I tweaked and the censors, she's a shadow of who she was. I had an impressive ending, I did. Now it's all pap," he said, his words with that staccato that characterized him when he was irritated. "Salome repents of her wicked ways in the last reel and accidentally tumbles to her death. I should quit this racket, I really should. I hate most of my writing."

"Could you quit, really?"

"I don't know. I hate cinema. I hate it and I love it. And you?"

"I fear it, at times," she said.

"What an odd answer," he said and chuckled, but he nodded, growing thoughtful. "Ever heard of gilgul? It's the transmigration of souls. Reincarnation. And sometimes the soul of the dead can possess the living. Maybe it's like that with actors. They're possessed for one brief moment, and that possession is what is captured on screen. It's what you see."

"What an odd thing to say," she told him, matching his words, teasing him with her smile. "But then what about cameras stealing souls? Wouldn't I be in danger if I'm being captured on that screen? A bit of my soul could end up there."

"That's what happens in the best of cases. A bit of you ends up there. Maybe a bit of me, too, since I wrote your dialogue. When's the dance?" he asked.

There had been costume fittings and alterations. Rehearsals and discussions with the choreographer. The director had plotted the movement of the camera and the positions of the lights.

"Three days," she said, looking up at the blue California sky with barely a cloud in sight.

"What's bothering you?"

She knew the steps. They were simple enough. For all the talk of ancient lands, the dance was modern. More a tango than whatever dance Salome had performed. Vera could understand music and she could understand rhythm. She could grasp the intricacies of movement.

But she fretted. The dance still escaped her. Its meaning and depths eluded her. She feared it. The shedding of layers seemed to her like the peeling of skin, painful and awkward rather than graceful. There was an inherent vulnerability that seized her whenever she took a step.

"How could Salome dance before all those guests? How could she have the courage to perform? Not only to perform, but to seduce a crowd," she said.

"You're trying to find your motivation?"

"No, it's not the stuff Orlando and Vaughn keep bickering about."

"Then what?"

Max Niemann thought her exotic looks could entice the public. But was that all there was to this scene? To the role? She'd played Salome the way Max wanted her to play the character, and now it wasn't enough.

"I'm missing a note," she said. "Don't you ever feel there's something missing on the page? That's why you revise, isn't it?"

"I revise because the studio heads can never agree on anything," he said with his usual incisive tone.

"With Strauss there are sudden harmonic shifts. It's both alluring and repulsive, but I'm not certain you can replicate that on screen. Not the way Max wants me to dance the scene."

"I know nothing about music."

Vera thought that Jay would have known what she meant. Jay understood the musical oscillation she was talking about, the polyphonic complexities that haunted her mind. But Jay was gone.

"How did you start writing scripts, Joe?" she asked.

"I heard Hollywood was paved with gold and bought myself a ticket to LA. I was only a little younger than you—nineteen, to be exact—and I wound up working on a Poverty Row film. I wanted to write a clever little drama, got assigned to a wrestler flick. Here I am, a veteran of the system at twenty-eight, still peddling the slop the studio heads demand."

"You're cynical, but you must like it."

"Cynicism is my best quality!" His cigarette had burned down to the filter, and he dropped it to the ground. "It's an awfully stupid business, but it has its charm. At the best of times, you catch a spark, and the characters come alive on the screen."

"It's like you could turn off the lights in the theater and you know they'd still be there, going on with their lives," she mused, and she thought back to that sense of solitude that Vaughn and Orlando had been discussing.

He nodded. Then he gave her a look that was almost shy. "You really do look like her."

"Like whom?"

"Like I pictured Salome before I started working on the script."

"Maybe you met me previously, in another life, when I was a princess and you were a cat."

"Only naughty people reincarnate as animals. And wicked murderers become water."

"Why water?"

"So they're always moving, never ceasing, never at peace."

"I wouldn't mind being water. Never ceasing, like a melody without end."

She glanced again at the sky, the clouds.

Joe made a motion, like he was going to immediately light another cigarette, but instead he crossed his arms and looked up at

the sky, too, seemingly interested in the same cloud she was staring at. Then he gave her his arm, and they began walking toward
the commissary.

*

ALONE, IN her house, Vera tinkered with the keys of the piano
and thought of Salome. She thought of Jay, too, and tried to van-
quish his memory. He had sent flowers to the studio, yellow like
she liked best, which she'd tossed away. She wouldn't speak to him.
There were other matters to preoccupy her, and even if there
hadn't been, she couldn't bear to hear his voice.

The dance. Three days, two days. One. She would dance tomorrow. The cameras would roll. The first day of filming of that piv-
otal scene.

Salome dances the dance of the seven veils.

That single line was the only description of the climactic moment in Wilde's play. The script of *The Seventh Veil of Salome* was
similarly sparse: she dances for a few minutes. It sounded easy on
paper, it seemed achievable during rehearsals.

It was, in fact, impossible.

She phoned her sister. She'd sent her letters and postcards.
They had not spoken. There was a quiet, superstitious fear that
had prevented Vera from doing this.

"Is it complicated?" Lumi asked. They had talked for a while
without discussing her work at the studio.

"Not the movements as much as the fact that you have to repeat
the sequence over and over again. Because they'll need a wide
shot, then a close-up, and just like that it becomes more cumbersome."

"But you like it."

"Acting? It's either a rush or a drag. Sometimes I think I'm
doing it all backwards and I'm a fool. Even the other young actors
have more experience than me. Vaughn Selzer has only one picture to his name, but he did a few plays before moving to California. What did I do before arriving here? I worked as a receptionist

and appeared in school plays. I played a shepherdess in the pastorela and was Juliet's nurse. I was Melibea, but Mother thought I wasn't the right type for the part."

"Jean Harlow was discovered leaning against the hood of a car. You'll be famous like her."

Vera remembered this tale; her sister had told it several times. When she'd been little, Lumi had loved to read about movie stars. Later, however, she seemed to grow indifferent to talk of films and Hollywood.

"I never asked, before I left, if it bothered you," Vera said softly.

"What bothered me?"

"Me, coming here. You wanted this, at one time."

"Why would it bother me? I didn't like it anymore, not at the end. Not with Mother pushing so hard for it."

"I know."

"And I fell in love with Lorenzo. She said I'd have to pick. I picked him."

"You were good at it, though. It was easy for you. Every time they turn the camera on me, I fear I'm made of wax and I'll melt away under the lights," she said, twisting the phone's cord.

"How appropriately dramatic."

"I mean it, Lumi."

"You know what I used to tell myself when I was nervous before a performance?"

"But you were not nervous."

"I was. During every pastorela, when we performed *El Tenorio*, and also that time I was Juliet. I used to tell myself they could see me; they might catch every mistake I made, but I could also see them. We were the same, I guess. Vulnerable, the audience and me."

"It is a bit different with a great lens focused on you."

"Maybe that's why I quit. So I wouldn't have to find out the difference. You're brave, Vera."

They talked a little more, drifting from the subject of movies, discussing the city, mutual friends, and Lumi's child. Vera hung up and lay on the couch, the phone resting on her stomach. She hummed, thinking about Salome and also about what Lumi had said about looking back at the audience.

Vera wasn't looking at anyone when she danced. But Salome would. She was dancing for the tetrarch's court, and their eyes would fix on her, but then wouldn't her eyes fix back on them? There was a certain danger in seeing and being seen.

Vera imagined herself as a statue of marble and basalt. She had pictured Salome helpless, pierced by a hundred eyes, and had felt herself pierced, too. But Salome looked, too. Like Medusa, she turned men into stone.

At the end of *Salome*, the last line of the opera, Herod instructed his men to kill his niece. "Kill that woman." Why? Perhaps because she had gazed back. There was death in her face, power in those eyes.

This movie did not end like that. Joe Kantor had written a finale that strayed from Wilde and Strauss both. But embroidered, beneath the lines that the studio had scrubbed clean, Vera sensed that this remained the true essence of Salome.

*

"LET'S RUN through it one time," the director said. "The whole thing."

Conversations died down, the assistant held on to his clipboard, the record player hissed as the needle fell. The music they were using was temporary; the score would be finalized later.

Once the dance was shot the editor would take all the many minutes of footage and he'd cut it. Vera would be fragmented into legs, torso, breasts, hands, legs. Only now, in this moment, could the dance be a whole.

Vera took the spot that had been marked on the floor. The clothes she wore had been carefully designed so that they were fluid; there was an attempt to avoid the awkwardness that came with removing straps and undoing buttons. The Salome of legend would have worn sea-silk; this Salome had been swathed in synthetic fabrics that would show well under the lens, saturated with color.

She first appeared before the courtiers in a blue headdress lavishly decorated with inky-black feathers and silver thread. A blue cape hid her entire body, from chin to toes, and a veil made of pearls obscured her nose, her mouth, her chin. Only her eyes, outlined with black kohl, were visible as she raised her arms, as if reaching for the stars.

In Salome's palace, the palace of the imagination as described by the screenwriter, the ceiling of the chamber where she danced was painted blue and decorated with gemstones that simulated stars. Vera was reaching up, toward the rafters, but she still stretched her fingers to grasp the diamonds encrusted in the ceiling.

She moved languidly, as if she'd awoken from a long dream; perhaps she'd escaped the nocturnal embrace of a lover, freeing herself from his grasp. Her hand pulled away the veil of pearls, showing her face and her painted lips, then she tossed the headdress aside. The cape was also discarded. Two veils gone.

There was practicality in the choice of garments and their removal. The director did not intend to hide his actress's body for the duration of the whole dance; people would be paying to see her, after all. She must disrobe and quickly rid herself of the beautiful but entirely too modest shield afforded by the cape.

Yet Vera removed the cape not only for the director's satisfaction, but her own. She slid out of the embrace of the embroidered cape like the butterfly emerges from the cocoon or the flower opens to the sun.

Beneath the blue cape, Vera wore a purple dress with long sleeves and large silver clasps at the shoulders. The choreographer had called for Vera to take dainty steps, to move her arms as if beckoning the tetrarch, swaying, a smile on her face.

In Herod's palace, the debauched guests, scandalized priests, and avaricious politicians stared at Salome with desire. Herod's palace did not exist, of course, any more than Salome existed. But

Vera glimpsed them nevertheless. The tetrarch smiled back at her through a cloud of smoke; a cloud of incense and sweet perfumes.

On the set, the director looked on with curiosity. The dance was the dance Vera had rehearsed, which the choreographer had designed, and yet it was becoming something different. Movements, learned, repeated, were one thing. Emotion was another. She was chasing after emotion.

They were not especially lascivious, these movements; rather there was an openness to them and a sense of rhythm. The dance was liquid; the movements resembled those of a snake uncoiling and raising its head, then undulating and seeking the sweet melody of a snake charmer.

Vera's hands rippled against the front of her dress, then reached for one of the decorated clasps—they had been shaped like the mouths of lions—sliding her fingers upon them. She took off the left purple sleeve, then the right, exposing her arms. She paused, her hands frozen, then ascending again as she moved faster.

The director's notes called for her to whirl about as if lashed by a tempest and to smile. Vera did whirl, but not with the violent motion that had been intended, but a quarter more of restraint. She didn't smile. Her smile had faded when she undid the silver clasps.

That unsmiling face was, nevertheless, not disagreeable. It was not an unhappy face, nor was it cold. But it was solemn and sharp. Sharper than the director might have intended, like a knife, and yet immeasurably attractive in its cunningness. For Salome was cunning.

At this point, there might have been a natural impulse to speed up. She tamed that impulse, each foot sliding with elegance and certainty, then came one moment of swooning, as if Salome were about to collapse. Her fingertips touched the floor and she pushed herself up, head high and insolent.

In Herod's palace, the spectators, who had roared with excitement, tempered their acclamations. They had been attracted by the woman's dancing, but now they were fascinated. It was not, however, a voluptuous fancy that made them rise from their seats or crane their necks, not anymore. Something else prickled their spine, made them grow faint, even repulsed them for a second, then urged them to clutch a goblet of wine and stare, unblinking.

She moved her shoulders and her hands rose, fingers finding the clasps once more and removing the purple dress, letting it slip away like water upon her body, like the snake sliding out of an old skin. The dress pooled at her feet, and she kicked it away. There was now another dress made of a thin, gauzy material that was exposed to the lights, to the onlookers.

This dress was a gold color at the top, with a plunging neckline that had been carefully designed to show off Salome's cleavage. An orange girdle at her waist was embroidered with spangles, and spangles also decorated the orange skirts of the dress. The little pieces of metal caught the light like stray fireflies.

Salome moved with a defiant grace as the blistering gaze of Herod's court fixed upon her and she gazed back at them, her jet-black eyes searing them, her lips charring the onlookers. The golden dress rippled; it was the color of a flame, and like a flame she shifted, bending a little, almost sputtering, then growing stronger.

She undid the tie of the orange girdle, sliding it away, revealing her stomach and wrapping the gauzy material around her shoulders. The costume designer had glued a circular piece of colored glass onto her navel. The fake ruby was supposed to serve as a modesty shield so that her belly should not be entirely exposed. The effect was the opposite. It seemed to highlight the brazenness of the dancer.

Salome went forward three steps rapidly, moving toward the chair where the tetrarch sat, and extended a hand, as if to touch him, while remaining too far for him to grip her arm. And to grip was what he desperately wanted; to touch, to clutch, to rend. But he also wished to hide his face, just as all the men wished to raise a shield or turn away.

They could not. They stood at the edge of delirium and destruction.

With that same snakelike grace Salome removed the orange skirt, seemingly tearing it into two pieces, and she let the orange girdle fall from her fingers.

Beneath this skirt was a last golden skirt—the seventh veil of Salome—and it was so translucent that it afforded any viewer an almost perfect glimpse of her legs. Without the orange material around her shoulders, the plunging neckline was now exposed.

Yet the part of Salome that was bared the most were her eyes. They had burned before, but now they chilled. There was a wintry desolation in those black pupils. Those eyes enticed, and they also petrified. The pretty painted lips smiled the smile they had been taught, but the eyes spoke a different, darker tale.

Those eyes made the courtiers shrink back. They were too cruel, those eyes. Too fierce. Those eyes might have turned men into stone, and they fixed upon the tetrarch with the brutality and finality of a knife sliding against a throat.

Then she lowered her head, her eyes, and knelt, unmoving. She breathed. She thought she had not breathed since she had begun dancing, although of course she had taken plenty of breaths. There were murmurs and words. A man said something. She didn't hear him.

Max Niemann was in front of her. He was grinning at her.

"Yes?" she asked.

"Interesting choices. There's something almost violent about that routine; it's not exactly like what we rehearsed."

Vera blinked. The film. She'd forgotten it for a little while, her head gone hazy with the motions of the dance. It was like this when she lost herself in music, in operas. When she became Isolde or Leonore for a few seconds.

"It's right for Salome," she said.

"You're going to make it difficult to avoid the censors."

"We are shooting a spectacle, Max. Or have you forgotten?" she asked, guessing he wouldn't like that answer, just as he didn't seem to like anything she did. Yet she didn't much care what he thought, not now. She'd done it, she'd danced it and well. He might dislike it, ask for changes, demand that she slow down or speed up, cut it all in postproduction. That didn't matter. She'd felt the dance.

But he didn't seem irritated; his eyes reflected the daring in her own. "Can you do that again exactly like you did it now? It's useless if you can't repeat it."

"I can dance as long as you can shoot it. Ask me to do it ten times, I'll do it."

His grin was now growing wider. "My dear Salome," he said. "It's going to look magnificent."

*

EXHAUSTION. BUT not the exhaustion she had felt in previous days, not that awful feeling in her lungs as if she were drowning. This was an entirely different feeling, tinged with joy. Everything was musicality, dance, the whirling of her feet, the words of the director. Cut. Take two, take three, take four.

She returned home tired but rose early in the morning with a smile on her lips. Day after day. Then it was the last day of the dance sequence, and when she reached her house she almost sprinted to the door, laughter bubbling from her lips.

Then a man stepped forward. In her haste, still lost in memories of the dance, Vera had not seen him until he spoke.

"Vera," he said.

Nancy

"SHE'S RENTING Simon Gilbert's house," Cathy said, sliding the piece of paper across the table at her.

Nancy looked at the scribbled address with interest. They were tucked away in a grimy grill, sipping sodas and pecking at a plate of fries.

"You're not going to really write to her, are you?" Cathy asked.

"Why not? Maybe I'll send her an apology note," Nancy said with a shrug.

"You're not."

Nancy quickly placed the paper in her purse. "Maybe I'll mail her a can of beans."

They laughed. Nancy pressed both elbows against the scratched table and smiled. "Is she still bumping around like a headless chicken?"

"She's bumping around, all right, but not like a chicken. Nancy, it's obscene!" Cathy said, also leaning forward and whispering. "I was told she did this dance number yesterday, a run-through for the director, and you wouldn't believe how she moves her hips and the way she looks at people . . . It's brazen."

Nancy frowned. She couldn't picture that insipid little chica moving anything in a coordinated fashion. Then again, she supposed her dancing ought to be vulgar. How could it be anything but an oversexed mess? It was fine for those types to dance around with bananas on their heads, but a story from the Bible was a different matter.

"You didn't see it?"

"I'm not in that scene. But I heard it from Leila, she ought to know."

"What does the director say? Has he complained about it?"

"Gosh, I have no idea. But it'll end up on the cutting room floor if it's anything like what Leila told me. I can't imagine how they'd get away with it. Think about what happened with Jane Russell and *The Outlaw*."

What had happened after that flick sat in limbo for years, unable to be released due to Russell's prominent bosom, was that it made its actress a star. Nancy dropped the fry she had been about to eat, furiously imagining that something similar might take place with Vera Larios. But it couldn't. It wouldn't. She'd be no Russell, no pinup sweetheart.

"I'd fire her and recast the part," Nancy said.

"I don't imagine they'd go as far as that. But you bet they're going to make her change the way she's moving. The Hays office won't ever let her play it like that."

Cathy began talking about another flick that they were shooting at a nearby sound stage, a romance. Nancy didn't pay attention. She was still thinking about Salome's dance. The way she would have danced it. The way it ought to be danced.

*

SHE LIT the cigarette, dropping the match in a cup, and inhaled. A neon sign across the street bathed the bed with an emerald glow. She sat at the edge of it. Benny rested a hand on her shoulder, but she shrugged him away.

"You should do it tomorrow."

"I said I'm going to," he muttered.

"You should have done it already. You said you would."

"I told you. I was parked outside her place for three hours and she didn't come out."

"Were you, really?" she asked, looking over her shoulder at him.

"Yeah."

"She would have come out. She would have gone to the studio. Did you go to the right house?"

"I went to the address you gave me. If it was the wrong one, that's on you."

Could be he'd gone to play pool with a few buddies or caught a movie. She suspected, despite his assurances, that this had been the case. That he was getting cold feet. Could be he figured he could string her along like that, promising he'd get to it and never delivering.

He was making a habit of popping by every day and lingering at her side. Maybe that was all he'd intended to happen; he'd stick to Nancy's side and hope she'd forget the plan.

"Do you even have the gun?"

"Yeah."

"But maybe not the guts," she muttered, puffing a plume of smoke. "You're playing me, aren't you? Lousy bum, get out."

She stretched her legs and kicked him in the shins. He gripped her ankle tightly.

"Hey, quit it. I know damn well what to do. I wanted to catch her while she walked by the car, but I guess I'll have to ring the bell."

"I need this, Benny. There's a real chance they'll recast and I'd make the cut. I heard from folks up high at the studio that they want to drop her and this would be the kicker. They'd have to fire her," she said.

The studio "folks" she'd talked to were Cathy Shaughnessy, who had helped her get Vera's address from a friend of a friend. Cathy was not exactly anyone "up high," but Nancy had telephoned Pierce Pratt and spoken a few contrite words. Pierce had sounded detached, but not entirely indifferent. Nancy figured another call, maybe a visit, and they'd be back on friendly terms. Anything was possible.

Of course, she wasn't going to tell Benny about Pierce any more than she would tell him that she had been wondering if Jay Rutland wouldn't be feeling lonely if his main squeeze wasn't around.

"I need a chance, Benny. One lousy chance."

"You'll get your chance, Nancy. You're the best," he said.

Nancy smiled. Benny's enthusiasm was what kept her interested in him. The way he looked at her, you'd think she was already a big star. He was the only one who did, who *knew* she was someone special.

He tried to wrap his arms around her and pull her back toward the bed. She tossed the cigarette away and rested her back against his chest.

"You know what's the first thing I thought when we met? I thought, that girl's someone. That girl's going places. Honey, you're prettier than Betty Brosmer, and they're all gonna see it one day."

"Feels like I'm running in circles sometimes," she whispered,

kneading her hands, thinking back about all the lousy gigs she'd
had and the lousy people she'd met along the way.

Vera Larios never went through any of that. She jumped off a
plane and dashed into the publicity department, just like that.
Snap your fingers and you're a star.

"You'll shoot her twice, right? One for each leg?" Nancy asked.

"Hey, if you want thrice, what the heck. Make it thirty."

She twisted a corner of a sheet. "Don't joke, Benny. Not about
this."

"Fine then. Twice."

Nancy nodded, feeling the press of his body against her own.
But a couple of minutes later she was elbowing him away, reaching for her purse, which lay on the floor.

"What are you doing?"

"I want another cigarette," she said. "Do you want one?"

"Sure."

It was true that she wanted another smoke, but there was also
the nagging, uncomfortable feeling she got when she was with
Benny like that, all quiet and close. It was like an itch that needed
to be scratched.

He lit her cigarette for her, then his own. Nancy looked at the
frayed curtains on her window and the green glow beyond them.

"She's shooting the dance scene this week and it's all wrong.
The way I'd have played the dance scene, you wouldn't have been
able to blink."

"Yeah?"

For Nancy, the dance of seven veils must be beauty and artifice.
A spectacle so grand they'd talk about it for decades to come. The
colors of each veil must be rendered in the brightest of hues, every
gemstone glimmering before the camera. She could hear the por-
tentous music, picture the hundreds of extras in the background.

Bigger, bolder, wilder. There were no limits, in her mind, to the
length of the veils draping Salome, nor the number of diamonds
studding her clothes.

And in every frame, every moment, there was Salome. Salome's eyes, Salome's mouth, Salome's face, Salome's body. Which were, of course, Nancy's eyes, Nancy's mouth, Nancy's face and body.

Nancy transformed into the seductress of ancient times. "Introducing Nancy Hartley" in the title credits. Nancy Hartley on the posters and the marquee. Nancy projected onto the screen.

"Then the scene where they bring her the head of John the Baptist, I'd have made it so there wouldn't be a dry eye in the house. Because, you see, she loves him because she hates him so much, and I can show that."

"It doesn't make sense, that stuff, loving someone because you hate them," Benny said.

Nancy looked at him. He'd leaned back against the pillows and was smiling at her. She didn't like when he smiled like that, his face looking like he knew a secret or a code word that she couldn't guess.

She supposed if he did go through with this, if he marched into Vera Larios's house, she'd be indebted to him forever. He'd have a hold on her even worse than the one that lousy photographer had once had, with the nudes. The thought of which made her want to scratch his face, but the thought of Vera Larios walking around Hollywood like a queen, decked in furs and attending the premiere of *The Seventh Veil of Salome,* was even worse.

"You have the gun?" she asked again, because there was a foul taste in her mouth and she had to say something to wash it off.

"I do," he said.

Nancy shook her head and blew smoke upward, watching it float and dissolve in the greenish haze of her small room.

Vera

JAY RUTLAND looked as he usually did, dapper and handsome, with a shirt that was open at the neck and a charcoal-gray suit. He carried a bouquet of yellow roses in one hand and immediately thrust the flowers forward, offering them to her.

Vera stared at him, clutching her purse, too surprised to attempt a greeting or to even consider grabbing the roses. She swallowed.

"I've called you at the studio, but I received no response so I figured I should stop by," he said.

She knew he had called. Not that it mattered. It was over; she didn't want to listen to his excuses or his apologies.

"Why?" she muttered, quickly opening her purse and fishing out the keys. Her fingers were clumsy; she almost dropped both the purse and the keys in her haste.

"We need to talk."

"There's nothing to talk about."

"Please. Five minutes."

She glanced warily toward the street. There were still photographers chasing after her, trying to build another scandalous story out of nothing. Yesterday she'd spotted a car parked outside and had suspected the driver was watching out for her. Fortunately, the man had driven away after a little while, but he might be back, and she didn't want to show up in *Hollywood Connection* arguing with Jay at the entrance of the house. She was afraid she'd break into tears and would rather not have it memorialized with a photo lens.

"You can come in for five minutes, but I'm timing it," she said, turning the key and opening the door.

They went to the living room. She placed her purse and the keys on a coffee table. He tried offering her the roses again, and she tossed them on a couch and stood behind the table, keeping a distance of a good six feet between them.

Vera had wondered if she'd ever see him again, and she had rehearsed lines in case that scene came to pass, but it was difficult to remember them when Jay was there.

"How are things at work?" he asked. "You were worried about the dance."

"The dance went fine," she said, brushing a strand of hair behind her ear.

"That's wonderful."

He seemed genuinely pleased by her answer, and normally she would have launched into an extended explanation of what it had been like, the numerous takes, the lights and sounds, the feel of the costume against her skin. But she didn't wish to share anything with him now.

"I wanted to apologize," he said.

"It's fine."

"I mean it."

"Apology accepted, now you can leave," she said coolly, even though her chest felt like it was on fire.

"I'm not kidding."

"Neither am I."

"Vera," he said and went around the coffee table, trying to stand closer to her.

She pushed him aside, hugged her arms, and shook her head. "What's the point of this? It's not going to do any good. You made your choice."

"I was confused."

She glared at him. Confused was not knowing whether to have chicken or fish. That hadn't been confusion. It had been a betrayal.

"You were willing to walk away with a snap of the fingers once, you'll walk away again. You don't really want me. It would cost you too much. You want to obey your family, you want to be safe, and that's fine. Why drag it out?"

"I can't make a mistake?" he asked.

She clutched her hands together, and her voice came out almost as a snarl, something primal and rough. "No! Not that kind of mistake. You should have been sure. You should have picked *me*. I would have picked *you* over everything else."

I knew from the moment I saw you, she thought, which was such a stupid, childish thought. That someone could be fulminated by love with one glance, like in the movies. As if she really was Salome gazing at Jokanaan in the bazaar. Yet she'd wanted to believe it was possible. Having never loved like that, she'd wanted the fanciful desires a screenwriter had typed for her.

It wasn't like in the movies, though. It was a folly. Whatever she'd felt, it was a mirage at best, or else the beginning of madness. Thank God she'd been cured from it. Thank God he was gone. And yet.

"I'm sorry," he told her, his voice low.

He seemed rather lost and sorrowful, as if he earnestly understood the wounds he'd inflicted. Vera sighed, miserable, too, her fingers restless, wanting to touch him, and she clutched her hands harder.

He drew his brows together, opened his mouth, and stammered. He cleared his throat.

"I am picking you. Right here and now," he said at last.

She gave him a shake of the head and moved toward the upright piano tucked in a corner of the room, resting a heavy hand against the closed fallboard. "Wait until tomorrow. Tomorrow you'll regret it. You'll go running back to your family. You'll secure a job at your dad's company and marry a proper girl and live a proper life. It's the way these stories go."

"What if I don't want it to go like that, huh?" he asked, striding toward her. "What if I'd rather do something different?"

"Like what?"

"Like . . . like everything. I want to play the piano, I really do. Not the way my family thinks I should, for a year, until I get it out of my system. I want to travel. Drive around without rhyme or reason, up and down the coast.

"I want the other stuff we talked about before. To rehearse lines with you when you're working on a film. When you're not busy acting, I'll read the music you scribble in tiny notebooks and that you're always afraid of showing me."

She felt like scratching the lacquer of the piano's fallboard when he said that; it hurt so much, and she bit her lip, wishing he'd stop talking and muddling her thoughts.

"I want to have a place of our own. An apartment where we pick the draperies and the sheets and the dishes. The décor might clash, because what do we know about tasteful decoration? Plus, we probably won't have that much dough if I'm a piano player and you're a contract player. But it'll be ours. I want to play different songs, find a new sound, explore everything. Together. With you."

That's exactly what they'd fantasized about, drawing silly plans in the evenings and daydreaming about their future, but it all sounded rather far-fetched now. Childish, even.

"And we'll do all of this in secret. So your parents don't find out. How fun, Jay."

"No, out in the open."

"That's not what you said last time. Last time you wanted to lie. Last time you wanted to keep it all hidden away," she said, her voice sharp. "You were ashamed of me."

"I'm a coward and I'm stupid, okay? I should have stood my ground. But I'm in love with you."

She felt like slapping him and somehow managed to reply to him instead. "Don't say that. Don't say love."

"Yes, love," he insisted, standing one step before her, which only made her step back, shaking her head.

"Remember when you told me you broke your engagement?" he asked.

"What about it?" Vera replied, her voice tight.

"You did it because you didn't feel anything at all when you were with your boyfriend. Whether he kissed you or shook your hand, it all felt the same. Well, that's the way it was for me, with everyone else. I've never felt anything. It was like clockwork. But I do feel something now, and I never want to stop feeling it." He smiled. "It feels like my heart is about to come apart right now; it's not a pleasant feeling, but I want it and I want to be forever with you."

Vera looked at him, and her lips trembled as he reached for her waist, but she brushed his hands away, weary.

"Forever is impossible," she said.

"No, it's not," he said softly, his fingers nudging her chin upward as he leaned into her. "There are no limits. Who wants to set them? Imagine a song that said, 'I'll love you for twelve weeks'?"

"We're not the people in a song."

"Says who?" Jay replied stubbornly. "Don't you love me anymore? Have things changed that quickly?"

Vera didn't want to trust him, she wanted to clutch her anger and her sorrow, but she could already feel them being torn away, like a useless veil. It was the way he spoke, both heedless and open, that tugged at her romantic heart. She wanted to love him, forever, as he said.

"Jay," she whispered, pressing a hand against his chest.

He was quiet, his eyes steady on her. How she liked his eyes, their color and their eagerness. How she admired the mischievous curl of his smile or the sight of his furrowed brow when, lost in deep concentration, he labored over a musical piece. She wished to kiss him and was afraid to do so.

"I've never truly known what I wanted, Jay. But I know it now. I want to be free to make choices. Good ones and lousy ones. Yes, I want music and movies and traveling, but I'm not sure *you* would ever be free to do any of that. I'm not sure you can make any choices at all, not the way things stand."

"Because of my parents? Vera, I've never known what I truly wanted, either, but I'm sure about you. Let's get married tomorrow," he said, with a swiftness and a zeal that made her smile despite her reservations.

"Tomorrow?"

"Yes. As soon as they open the doors."

"Where?" she asked, a laugh bubbling from her lips. Vera couldn't help it. It was like trying to fight a riptide.

"Wherever we can find a minister, priest, or Buddhist monk who will officiate. I'm not going to be picky."

"That would be silly. Reckless. You'll probably regret it in a month, and if not, your family will regret it for you," she said, already picturing the stern lawyer the Rutlands would send to deal with her. Surely, they could annul any marriage that might take place. And surely, Jay would buckle under pressure.

"My family is insufferable, so what? They can go to hell."

"It's easy to say that when you're with me."

"I mean it," he said, and knelt down.

"What are you doing?" she asked.

"Begging."

"Truly," she said, pulling back, attempting to pull her hand away. He caught it.

"I'm not going to love in fractions," Jay said, repeating her words. He stood up. "You get the whole of me, Vera. Stupid and flawed as I am, but I'm yours. Let's choose each other, even if it's reckless, even if it's silly. Let's do it because we're young and we are free, and young people should be reckless and silly. Vera, let's choose to live in a song, to live in a dream."

He stared at her and she at him. She drew her hand away from his own, but lifted it to touch his cheek. His eyes were brimming with the sweetest of promises.

Vera kissed him lightly, as if he were made of glass and might shatter, and the press of his lips was equally soft. He pulled away, inspecting her face, before kissing her back.

Vera sighed shakily, taking him by the hand and guiding him to the bedroom. They were quiet, both afraid of breaking the delicate truce they'd achieved.

They kissed for a long time, made love slowly, until she was flushed and smiling. He smiled, too; her damp brow pressed against the slope of his shoulder. Vera's fingers danced against his skin, tracing a melody, while he toyed with her hair.

The sun set, shadows spreading across the room. She understood forever, the minutes ticking by at a sluggish pace, stretching beyond the boundaries of the possible. Forever was Jay and Vera that afternoon.

Son Clave

THE NOISE of the sistrum, of the drums and the flute ceases. The banqueting hall grows silent. Slowly, Salome bows, and the attendants break into applause. Her body burns with the exertion of the dance, and her lungs feel near to bursting, as if she's finished the climb up a treacherous mountain.

Everyone at court is spellbound, infected with delirium. There are whispers, sighs, acclamations. All eyes are fixed on her. Only Jokanaan does not look at Salome; his obdurate gaze remains hidden from the young woman.

"Excellent." Herodias claps her hands. "Excellent, my child. This deserves a prize. What will you give her?" she asks her husband.

Others clap, too, and some even yell suggestions at the tetrarch. Give her a chest of sandalwood filled with black pearls. Give her a ring of yellow topaz and another one of pink tourmaline. Give her a garment made of the feathers of ten exotic birds from ten distant lands. Give her a horse as white as bone that she may ride it decked in purple silks.

Herod Antipas raises his cup, a wide smile on his lips. "You have danced well and now you may claim your prize," he says. "Ask for anything that you desire."

The tetrarch sits in his chair, grinning at her. Salome knows she could be meek and pliant with him. She could let him use her and satiate his lust. He might gift her trinkets, palaces, a menagerie of exotic animals. He'll drink from her as avidly as he downs a cup of wine, but she'd be his favorite pet.

If she is careful, Salome could show her claws. Salome might even whisper in his ear and rid herself of her troublesome mother.

Marcellus also sits at the feast, the promise of marriage and his distant villa fresh on his lips. She could become the wife of an important Roman politician, as Herodias has long intended. Dressed in a stola, head covered, looking demure, eyes downcast.

Salome could learn the virtues of modesty and motherhood, which any good Roman woman must exemplify.

But there are other doorways she might slip through, different avenues that might be crossed.

At this banquet Jokanaan sits, still and quiet and most attractive. Although he may never want her, she could still lead the preacher out of the palace by the hand, guiding him through a wilderness thick with thorns and a plain of salt. She might kneel at his feet rather than Herod's throne; she might wash the abrasions left from the chains that restrain him with her tears.

There, there he also sits. Marcus Julius Agrippa, cousin to Salome. He who speaks Latin as well as the proconsul, but also knows the language of her kin. Unlike Marcellus, this man wields no armor and no sword. Yet how dangerous is his tongue, how sharp his mind. This man has promised she'll own a kingdom.

Salome desires the power augured by her cousin Agrippa. She hungers for the revenge that haunts her every waking hour.

Salome desires the young preacher in chains. She dreams of kissing his lips and burying her face in his neck.

She glimpses a green field strewn with flowers, and a throne of gold.

Salome does not know how to choose.

*

NANCY WAITS in the company of the radio, smoking and drinking in her lonesome room. Benny has left, intent on carrying out her wishes. Or perhaps he has lied and will not harm the girl. After all, Nancy has yet to see that gun he claims he owns. After all, men have betrayed her before.

Her father was the first betrayer, back when he lost his faith in Nancy. When he said she couldn't be a star. All those wasted years of tap lessons and auditions, vanished with one sweeping, scornful word from him.

She dresses in a crimson dress that is tightly cinched at the waist and admires her reflection in the mirror, posing before the glass. She knows that if the public could gaze at her, they'd love her more than any other actress. She feels the possibilities that lay beyond her outstretched fingers, hidden in the dark.

*

VERA LAUGHS, pressing kisses against Jay's neck. The world tastes green and sweet. He wants to take her for dinner, for a drive. Perhaps the drive can last until sunrise. She humors him and tells him maybe it can.

But for now, they lie together in bed, and Jay raises himself to look at her face, resting his head on one hand and carefully tracing a line down her belly with the other hand. He smiles, makes a joke, and she rolls on her side to look back at him.

There is pleasure in the mutual, easy silence that they share as much as their long conversations. There is languor and intimacy, and most of all, there is that love that neither of them has ever sampled before. They are intoxicated with youth and promises.

*

SALOME WISHES she had not danced. She wishes there were no choices to make. She wishes she was not a participant in this story, but merely an observer.

Yet she must speak, she must choose. Many tangled paths stretch before her eyes. Will she be a whore to the tetrarch, as her cousin warned her? Will she be the dutiful daughter who does her mother's bidding? Will she shout before all the honored guests and rail against the injustice that has been committed? Will she demand that the preacher be set free? Will she plunge a knife into her heart and chase oblivion?

She looks at Jokanaan, quiet, with his head lowered, pious and untouchable. He is a man with no blood in his veins, made of ice. If she presses a palm against his cheek he will melt and disappear.

He is a ghost, the beautiful preacher. He has condemned himself to the gallows with his bold words and accusations.

He is a fool, Jokanaan. But his foolishness is also a thing of beauty and innocence.

She looks at Agrippa, her wily cousin who has learned the art of cunning and deception. Oddly enough, he is also made of ice, but he is not bloodless. Through his veins courses the rich, decadent strength of the Herodians. In his body is the essence of a king, as much as the strength of a queen nestles in Salome's bones and marrow.

Perhaps he'll be much too bold one day. Perhaps his ambition will become his own noose, carefully braided over the years with duplicity and hunger.

Perhaps it does not matter what path Salome chooses because all paths are painted with blood.

"I ask that they bring me in a silver charger . . ." she says and she pauses, her breath burning her mouth, her hands clenching into fists. "I ask that they bring me the head of Jokanaan."

*

FINALLY, THEY rise from bed and ready themselves. Jay buttons his shirt, and Vera brushes her hair. She reapplies her makeup as he watches, entranced at the way she presses the crimson lipstick against her mouth.

She blushes when she notices his attention, catching his eyes looking at her in the mirror. She chides him, tells him she'll do it all wrong if he keeps looking at her like that, and he says he adores her. It's true, too. He'll love her forever.

*

NANCY FLOPS upon the bed, staring at the ceiling and wondering if Benny can be trusted or if this will be another heartbreak, another broken vow.

She thinks about the girl and the sound the gun will make when it goes off, and for a moment she is afraid. Not of the consequences, or of the enormity of such a crime, not of what tomorrow will bring.

It's the fear that somehow it won't be enough. That there's a hollowed space inside her chest that cannot be filled, neither with fury nor with vengeance. She fears she's damned, one way or another.

She sits up, thinking of Benny as he drives the car, gun tucked in his jacket pocket, and she wants him to stop but she also wants him to get on with it. To bring this all to its necessary, fated conclusion.

She lies back on the bed and lights a cigarette.

*

THE BANQUETING hall is quiet as the tetrarch calls for the executioner. Salome holds her breath, but she does not close her eyes. Salome must see.

*

NANCY PUSHES the curtain aside, staring out the window. She looks for Benny's car downstairs, looks for him to return. But the night has swallowed Benny. Benny is not there.

*

THE RING of the bell surprises them as they are about to leave. Jay is closer to the door, he's already halfway there, and she's behind him as she adjusts a bracelet around her wrist. He opens the door wide.

*

THE AX falls in one firm swoop.

*

THE SOUND of a bullet pierces the night.

She thinks, as the noise reverberates in her ears, that it is thunder. Such is her disbelief, for a second, that she expects the clouds to weep a storm. Yet the sky is clear.

Vera stands in front of the open door and watches Jay grasp the doorframe. He stumbles and falls. She drops to her knees and looks up at a strange man who stares back at her, startled, the gun pointed at her face.

She does not raise a hand to shield herself, nor does she attempt to run away. She stares at him with eyes that are twin black flames. Whether her sorrow touches his heart, or fear takes hold of his brain, she does not know. But he retreats, as if scalded.

The man steps back and rushes away.

*

A FEW courtiers scream, horrified by the spectacle, while others cheer, the scent of blood only inflaming their senses. Violence is a fine perfume.

Herodias says she is well pleased and compliments her daughter. Josephus utters a prayer. Agrippa smiles triumphantly at Salome.

*

HELP, SHE YELLS. Help me.

She is cradling Jay in her arms as he shivers and blood pours from his mouth. It flows like a river, this blood, dampening his shirt. He cannot speak, can hardly make a sound, and people are coming but it's too late.

Stay, she tells him. Stay with me.

She clutches him, presses her lips against his forehead and his mouth, which is coated in blood, and tries to will life into his body. His eyes are closed now, and she brushes her hands through his hair. A tear sears her cheek, his blood coats her tongue.

She closes her eyes. If someone looks into her eyes in that moment they will be turned to stone. If she gazes at the stars they will smolder and vanish from the sky.

She closes her eyes, to shield the world from her grief, and weeps.

*

THEY PLACE the head on a silver charger.

Guests whisper, debating whether she is foolhardy or wise. She does not listen to them.

A slave brings forth the grisly prize, offering her the head with a timid motion.

She looks down at it. She sees the slash of the ax that cut off the head with one quick stroke. She looks at the mouth and the beard, speckled with blood. She thought maybe in death the preacher might be changed, but his face remains remote and perfect.

Carefully, Salome clutches the grisly bounty between her hands and holds it up, staring into the dead man's eyes.

Joe Kantor

FORTY YEARS in the business. That's the total figure before I tossed out the typewriter and retired. Forty and who knows how many pictures. My first job I wrangled, I was nineteen. I talked my way into it. Told them I could write an outline in three days. I'd never written one, I didn't know how to begin. The chutzpah!

Anyhow, no, I never met Nancy Hartley, although I saw plenty of her in the newspapers when she testified against her ex-boyfriend, Benjamin Alden, in his trial for the murder of Jay Rutland. The lady got quite some press, back then. After the sentencing, she tried to spin her newfound notoriety into an acting career. She was cast in a couple of small parts in B movies, but nothing panned out for her. I heard she cycled through several Las Vegas nightclubs, and in the eighties, she attempted to write and publish her biography. When that didn't work out, she wanted to see if someone would write a script, make it into a movie. A friend of mine, he was working at a production company that she'd been pestering about the project, which is how I learned about it.

Vera suffered through those weeks of the trial. The press

hounded her, and there wasn't much the studio could do, or was willing to do, to protect her. There were a million stories about the case, dozens of people talking about her, but I never chatted to any reporter, not then and not later, when interest in the story first revived sometime in the nineties. Not until now.

Vera left Los Angeles two years after *The Seventh Veil of Salome*. It would have been hard for a seasoned professional to survive a scandal like that, but she was brand-new. Her acting career was toast. She kept in touch with the gang here in Hollywood, but eventually drifted apart from us. Distances and schedules and all that. When Marla died in 1998, she came for the funeral. It's the last time I saw her in person.

Have you heard Vera's music? I have several of her records. That's what she's remembered mostly for: her music work. It's lovely, all kinds of styles and forms, from songs to large-scale orchestral works. She blended jazz, Latin American dance rhythms ... it was a kaleidoscope. She carved a path for herself, carved it with music. Quite the thing, quite the thing. "Salome's Dream." That's her most famous composition. A piano duet. Haunting little tune.

I had the funniest dream last night. Probably because of all this talking I've been doing about the past. Anyhow, I dreamed I was back in the studio when we were shooting *The Seventh Veil of Salome*. We were lounging around the sound stage. Marla and Simon were there, but so were a bunch of other folks we used to hang out with. Orlando. Danny Q. Isadora. Max was there, in his director's chair. The whole lot.

We were shooting the final scene of the movie. I don't mean the scene that they filmed, that was an awful ending! I mean, my ending. The ending I originally wrote. All my best bits, they were trimmed away. My original draft was a skeleton of itself by the time they shot the damn thing. There was a lovely scene where Agrippa goes to Salome's room at night and they're talking on her bed. But you couldn't get that past the censors! Or the jail scene, when she speaks to the preacher and tells him about a faraway land.

Anyway, in the dream, we were shooting the final scene I wrote. Salome on the throne. Close up, the camera pulls back, and it's a medium shot and then it's a long shot and you get a sense of the scope of this massive throne room. And et cetera and et cetera.

I was nervous. I didn't even know why I was nervous, because I was just an onlooker, but I was. I was twisting a script between my hands, muttering to Marla.

Then she walked in. Vera, dressed in her costume. In the dream she was twenty-one years old and she was a princess, full of light and life. It was a delight to watch her, with the diadem in her black hair and the dress embroidered with a thousand crystals. Stars in the night sky couldn't shine as bright as that young woman.

I was a wreck. But then, she smiled at me. She smiled like she smiled one fine morning when I first saw her. Smiled with an earnestness and openness that made my heart sing, so that I ended up writing dozens of scenes for her that were never filmed. She smiled at me. I was twenty-eight. I thought I was going to write a masterpiece. I was a little in love with the gal, or maybe a whole lot, but let's face it, who wouldn't be? In love with the character, in love with the actress. A bit of both.

In the dream, we were young, and we were ready for the shoot. She was smiling and I was smiling, too. The world had no limits, my back didn't ache, the studio was crammed with fools and naysayers, but I had faith in tomorrow.

When I woke up, I swear, for five minutes I was still twenty-eight and the arthritis didn't matter. I could have jumped out of bed and danced a number with the same gusto as Fred Astaire. Five minutes it lasted, that feeling.

I miss them, all of them. I miss the stupid studio, too. You get older and people disappear from your life, like a crowd streaming out of a movie theater. You're the only person watching the screen until the end of the credits, waiting for it to go black. I'm ninety-six years old and everyone else has bowed out of the performance. It was, at times, a humiliating, dispiriting spot, our old Hollywood

Land. But it could also be resplendent. A time of legends and mythmaking.

Anyhow, this morning I dressed, combed my hair, and got ready for this interview. Then I found that old record, the one that has "Salome's Dream" on side A.

I lifted the needle and played the melody. For remembrance. Once I told Vera about the transmigration of souls. Existence is a wheel and upon itself it turns, like a record turns. And she's a melody now, and she's a flash of color on the screen.

If there is anything after the credits end, I hope we'll meet again.

The Last Scene, or Salome's Dream

SALOME SITS still, clad in scarlet and yellow. One of her hands rests lightly on the arm of the chair, while the other supports her chin as she gazes ahead.

She does not dance anymore, not since that day long ago in Herod's banqueting hall.

Storytellers weave contradictory narratives about her, ensuring she will be enshrined in myth.

She wore a robe encrusted with pearls. She wore a robe made of the wings of blue-green scarabs. She wore seven veils.

Upon her head there is a crown dripping with jewels; behind her stand her trusted guards. For she sits on the golden throne of a vast palace where the lilies grow so pale they look like they are made of silver.

Yet sometimes she dreams of another abode, of a land of green hills with yellow flowers where her hair is braided with primroses and a sweet melody drifts from afar. And once in a while, in her sleep, she whispers a name.

That name was the name for love.

Author's Note

WE DON'T really know the name of the infamous Salome. She appears briefly in only two Gospels of the New Testament, where we are told Herodias's daughter dances during a birthday party. The name Salome comes from Flavius Josephus's *Antiquities of the Jews,* in which he identifies a daughter of Herodias by that moniker, but there is no mention of her famous dance or an execution.

The bulk of Salome's story was therefore constructed long after her death, in paintings, literature, and music. Two of her most famous and important appearances happened in the nineteenth century. In Flaubert's "Herodias," she is a side character, and an innocent pawn. In Oscar Wilde's one-act play *Salome,* she becomes the central character and a femme fatale. It is Wilde who identifies her dance as the Dance of the Seven Veils. When Sarah Bernhardt was set to appear on stage as Salome, she was supposed to wear a yellow dress, the color of degeneracy. The play, however, was banned and never performed.

Wilde's version of *Salome* was turned into an opera in 1905 and then adapted as a film by Alla Nazimova in 1923. In the 1950s, Rita Hayworth played another version of the temptress.

It was my thought that, because much of what we recognize as Salome was constructed through successive layers of visual media, a story about Salome should take place in Hollywood during the pinnacle of the studio system, when sword-and-sandal movies were all the rage. It seemed appropriate, when looking at a mythical woman, to think about the place where women were made into myths.

There is therefore myth in this tale, but also fact. Yet, like any Technicolor flick, the facts bend to the whim of the writer. For example, the Herodian family is modified in my telling. In real life, Herodias married Herod II, who was her half-uncle, before marrying Herod Antipas, who was the half-brother of her previous husband. Yes, it's an intricate family tree.

The Herodian dynasty was a family of Idumean descent that ruled as a vassal state of the Roman empire over the Jewish population of Judaea. They converted to Judaism and integrated with the local Jewish community. Wilde and Flaubert identify Salome as a non-Jew, so I followed their cue in this respect.

Many of the details about 1950s Los Angeles are true. For example, Mexicans who wanted to buy property in certain sections of the city had to hide their ethnicity, often by calling themselves the more palatable "Spanish."

I found trivia about numerous movie stars, read the biographies of many Hollywood personalities, looked at menus of restaurants of the era, and pored over tabloids of the 1950s (such as *Confidential*). There really was an actress named Rossana Podesta who was hired to star in a flick called *Helen of Troy* even though she didn't speak English. Meanwhile, Audrey Hepburn was cast as the lead in *Gigi* without having ever had a major theater role, then quickly climbed her way into major Hollywood films such as *Roman Holiday* and *Sabrina*. Sometimes success was swift in Hollywood, other times performers could languish for years in the shadows.

The lives of well-documented stars such as Lana Turner or Elizabeth Taylor allowed me to delve into the dynamics of studio systems, but more obscure actors such as George Reeves provided me with a different sense of the era, one that was less glamorous and more painful. The scandal-prone Barbara Payton, who is now a footnote in history, was one of the inspirations behind Nancy, and actresses such as Rita Moreno, Lupe Vélez, and Dorothy Dandridge provided me a glimpse into a Hollywood that was often hostile toward actors of color.

I read the Bible often when I was growing up and was delighted by the vivid illustrations found within its pages. I sought classical paintings with Biblical motifs that had gory or dramatic scenes.

Judith was a favorite heroine of mine, and I also delighted in the depictions of Salome, especially Gustave Moreau's paintings of her. "Salome Dancing," known as "Salome Tattooed," remains my favorite painting of her.

Sword-and-sandal movies, taking their cue from the Orientalist fantasies of a previous era and adapting them for the screen, were a staple of my childhood, especially during Semana Santa, when the TV was besieged with Biblical tales. Enrique Rambal's peculiar accent in *El Mártir del Calvario*, as well as Hedy Lamarr's fabulous peacock dress in *Samson and Delilah*, assured that one day I'd try my hand at a Biblical story.

Author's Playlist for The Seventh Veil of Salome

LISTEN ON SPOTIFY AT

www.theseventhveilofsalomeplaylist.com/

1. "Avalon" by Roxy Music
2. "I Fall in Love Too Easily" by Karen Souza
3. "Sway (Quién Será)" by Pérez Prado and Rosemary Clooney
4. "Usted" by Luis Miguel
5. "My Funny Valentine" by Chet Baker
6. "When I Fall in Love" by Nat King Cole
7. "A Hard Day's Night" by Quincy Jones and His Orchestra
8. "I'm Not in Love" by Olivia Keast
9. "It Had to Be You" by Billie Holiday
10. "St. Thomas" by Sonny Rollins, Tommy Flanagan, Doug Watkins, and Max Roach
11. "Isn't It Romantic" by Diana Krall
12. "Bette Davis Eyes" by Karen Souza and Jazzystics
13. "No Me Platiques" by Pedro Infante
14. "You Belong to Me" by Jo Stafford
15. "These Foolish Things" by Bryan Ferry
16. "Fever" by Peggy Lee
17. "Like Someone in Love (Vocal Version)" by Chet Baker
18. "Mucho Corazón" by Martirio
19. "You and the Night and the Music" by Lauren Henderson
20. "Better Git It in Your Soul" by Charles Mingus
21. "Nice Work If You Can Get It" by Tony Bennett and Diana Krall
22. "Paloma Negra" by Flora Martínez
23. "Générique (Bande originale du film 'Ascenseur pour l'échafaud')" by Miles Davis
24. "Don't You Want Me" by Alice Lamb
25. "Volver a los 17" by Magos Herrera and Brooklyn Rider

26. "Ev'ry Time We Say Goodbye" by Ella Fitzgerald

27. "Eventually" by Ornette Coleman

28. "Dream a Little Dream of Me" by Shannon & Keast

29. "Come Rain or Come Shine" by Sarah Vaughan

30. "Fiesta in Blue" by Dave Lambert, Jon Hendricks, and Annie Ross

31. "Solaménte los Dos (Bolero)" by Vicentico Valdés with Noro Morales Y Su Orquesta

32. "Un Poco Loco" by Arturo O'Farrill

33. "No Sé Tú" by Luis Miguel

34. "The Captain of Her Heart" by Flora Martínez

35. "Solamente una Vez" by Agustín Lara

36. "Prelude to a Kiss" by Ella Fitzgerald

37. "I Wanna Dance with Somebody (Who Loves Me)" by Talisha Karrer

38. "Ambar" by Camila Meza

39. "Waltzing" by The Dave Brubeck Quartet

40. "Slave to Love" by Jazzystics

41. "Too Young" by Nat King Cole

42. "Blue Train" by Poncho Sanchez

43. "Creep" by Karen Souza

44. "Desfinado" by Stan Getz and João Gilberto

45. "Niña" by Magos Herrera and Brooklyn Rider

46. "Airegin" by Miles Davis

47. "Sing It Back" by The Cooltrane Quartet

48. "True Colors" by Flora Martínez

49. "Someplace Called 'Where' (Live)" by Wayne Shorter, Terri Lyne Carrington, Esperanza Spalding, and Leo Genovese

50. "Misty" by Bob Brookmeyer

51. "Cómo" by Luis Miguel

52. "Chasing Cars" by Meg Birch

53. "I'm a Fool to Want You" by Dexter Gordon

54. "Will You Love Me Tomorrow" by Bryan Ferry

55. "Besame Mucho (Bonus Track—Great Expectations OST)" by Cesária Évora

Acknowledgments

AS USUAL, I send a hearty thank-you to my publishing team for their support in the making of this book. Tricia, Jordan, Ashleigh, Keith, Scott, Alex, and everyone else at PRH, thanks for working with me. I also must thank my agent, Eddie, and the other folks at the JABberwocky Literary Agency. Thanks to Lavie Tidhar, who helped me with several phrases in Yiddish and who said this book sounded like a good idea, and to Crawford Kilian, who has always been kind to me.

About the Author

SILVIA MORENO-GARCIA is the author of the novels *Silver Nitrate, The Daughter of Doctor Moreau, Velvet Was the Night, Mexican Gothic,* and many other books. She has edited several anthologies, including the World Fantasy Award–winning *She Walks in Shadows* (aka *Cthulhu's Daughters*). She has won the British Fantasy Award and the Locus Award for her work as a novelist.

SILVIAMORENO-GARCIA.COM

INSTAGRAM: @SILVIAMG.AUTHOR

About the Type

This book was set in Walbaum, a typeface designed in 1810 by German punch cutter J. E. (Justus Erich) Walbaum (1768–1839). Walbaum's type is more French than German in appearance. Like Bodoni, it is a classical typeface, yet its openness and slight irregularities give it a human, romantic quality.